ELEMENTALS:

The Seven Spheres

Jared Files

StarGen Press

Elementals: The Seven Spheres

Copyright © Jared Files 2014.

Files, Jared.

Elementals: The Seven Spheres / by Jared Files. — 1st ed.

Summary: In the near future, where the nations of the world war with the alien
virtaiyu, seventeen-year-old Kaiba Cassidy discovers one of seven mechanical spheres
that enables him to control the elements of nature, and ties his fate, and six others like
him, to that of the war.

ISBN: 0991032101

ISBN 13: 9780991032105

Printed in the U.S.A.

First Edition, April 2014

The text type was set in Adobe Garamond Pro.

Dedicated to my parents, Jeff and Lisa,
And of course for 'The Seven' that started it all;
Lauren, Neema, Kyle, Evan, Cole, Lehman and Ryker.

DELIVERY

Tempest Island, Middle of the Indian Ocean

The deep rumble echoed through the dimly lit docking chamber of the Tempest research base. Matthew Bennett felt the vibrations in his bones. Looking down the twelve stories, he leaned over the thin observatory railing and grew slightly queasy. He did his best not to think of heights and instead watched the football-field-sized chasm across the room fill with water. On either side of the metal gap were roughly twenty men who waited eagerly in forklifts.

Two operators stood on a platform just below Matt. They looked out over the room behind a station of control panels. The water stopped rising. The screens below displayed the submarine in greater detail. Lists of cargo and shipment details began to appear on the monitors.

Someone shouted, "Lights!"

Matt didn't have to turn around to know it was Commander John Unden. His hoarse bark of a voice had no equal.

Four spotlights boomed to life in the corners of the room, illuminating the water. A large, whale-shaped shadow sat immobile in the dark blue abyss. It was the first time a supply sub had come in the past two months and Matt had grown tired of the freeze-dried meals and protein gels.

Commander Unden walked forward, his boots thudding against the steel walkway. He gripped the rail right beside Matt, but paid him no attention. Instead, he looked down at the water. His expression was stern, hardened by years of conflict and warfare.

"Everything checks out, Commander," one of the operators said.

"Bring her up then!" he shouted. His voice echoed several times.

The metal walls shuddered as the water and the sub rose once more. One of the spotlights shook so violently it seemed as though it were about to fall from its perch.

"You're not supposed to be here, Bennett."

Matt kept his eyes forward, locked on the rising submarine. "I get tired of being their experiment."

"Doesn't matter, you know what you signed on for," Unden said matter-of-factly. "You should go back to the training facility."

"I like a change of scenery."

The water had nearly risen to the edge of the chasm. The submarine now towered above the twenty men. It was much bigger than Matt would have guessed.

"You've got a meeting with the UNM council tonight, twenty-one hundred."

He turned to face the commander for the first time at that remark. "What? They didn't get enough of a show last time?"

"They want to know that you can do it repeatedly and just as well every time."

"I've shown them four days in a row now!"

Unden itched his fingers over his bald head. "They can't take chances with you on the front lines."

"Chances win wars, they need to get that."

"You need to understand that we can't waste this chance at gaining an advantage," Unden said.

"Heard that before. I'm gonna help 'em unload down there."
Matt walked away. He reached the elevator when he heard a crash
that sounded as though someone had dropped a crate.

Surprised, he looked back to the submarine chamber.

"*Bennett!*" Commander Unden roared.

Matt's heart jolted. His skin tingled as the soldier in him came
to life. He sprinted back down the hallway as the emergency sirens
started to blare over the *pop pop* of gunfire. Unden ran from the
observatory point and nearly smacked into him.

Unden's expression was stern, and his eyes were wild. He
grabbed Matt and continued running. "Come on!"

Matt matched the commander's pace. "What happened?"

"Virtaiyu were on that sub!"

Matt's stomach churned at the mention of the creatures.

The two sprinted back to the elevator. Unden threw the door to
the stairwell open and Matt hurled himself down the steps. Unden
stayed right on his heels. They descended the first level within a
second, practically leaping the entire set of stairs.

"What floor is the chamber on?" Unden screamed over the wail
of the sirens.

"It's on the middle of six!"

They were on the outermost point of Tempest, where the
docking chamber sprawled away from everything else, about as far
as you could get.

An explosion rippled through the bottom of the stairwell. Matt
gazed over the side as he ran, and saw wisps of smoke and fire. Several
figures walked through the flames and began to ascend the steps.

Unden tapped his neckpiece. "Austin, execute Protocol 209-E!"

Matt thrust the sixth floor door open and grabbed two assault
rifles from the emergency holder on the wall. He heard Austin's
voice in his ear. "Are you mad?"

"*Blow the damn chamber and scatter the devices!*" Unden
thundered. With his bare fist, he broke the pane of glass that

shielded a nearby fire extinguisher and rolled the red can to the sixth floor stairwell. He kneeled, aiming his gun at the extinguisher. "Go, Bennett! They need you and the sphere, not me!"

Matt hesitated, and glanced from the door to Unden. The footsteps grew louder on the staircase.

"Leave me! That's an order!"

Matt knew Unden was even more stubborn than he was. There was no point in arguing.

Matt nodded. Without saying a word, he bolted down the grey hallway. Several seconds later, he felt the blast explode behind him and he heard the furious shots of the rifle. He didn't stop, he just kept his arms pumping as the damp, warm air whipped across his face. He tried to keep calm and decipher the chatter that buzzed on the intercom. "They're in the armory!"

He neared the end of the first hall and turned right. A group of soldiers rushed past him. He skidded along the slickened concrete and turned the corner.

"Dock station detonated. Casualties—" Then static as the hallway shook again. Matt guessed another explosion.

"Corporal, repeat that."

He came to the end of another hall and this time turned left.

"Surface walls breached! Hostiles neutralizing defenses!"

A computerized voice said, "Heavy boarding parties detected on levels one, four, and twelve. Evacuation planes being raised to flight deck."

Matt tried to ignore the panicked voices, but he couldn't face the fact that he too was panicking. He reached the white-walled sixth floor lobby and paused to catch his breath.

He switched his radio frequency. "Austin Palarc, do you copy?"

Someone screamed for a medic.

Matt gulped in air. He glanced at a wall panel that showed a map of the sixth level and then took off for the research chamber.

Dr. Palarc answered finally, "Bennett? You're alive!"

Matt ignored the obvious statement and asked, "How close are we to launching the six?"

"Five minutes!"

Matt opened a door. "I'm on my—"

The wall to Matt's left exploded into a shower of drywall and dust. A chunk hit him in the head, knocking his earpiece out. He coughed and saw a trio of seven-foot, human-like shadows hidden in the powder, but Matt didn't wait. He clicked the safety of his weapon and fired the whole clip through the hole. The bullets glinted against black armor. Some penetrated, but others bounced off like shiny beetles. Two of the things collapsed.

He sprinted away, ignoring the alien screeches of outrage and the heavy footsteps behind him. Bursts of red fire streaked past his head. He glanced over his shoulder to see a group of eight virtaiyu. Several soldiers charged forward from the perpendicular corridors. He didn't wait to see the fighting, but his ears rang from the virtaiyu's sonic weapons.

He reached the hulking armored door that led to the research chamber. There were only four men defending it.

Matt pointed in the direction of the virtaiyu. "You do not let them through this door. Whatever happens you keep them out."

All the men looked terrified. One man managed to say, "We'll give you as much time as we're able, Bennett."

Matt nodded as they marched away. He scanned his eye on a small pad. The boxy entry slid apart like the doors to an elevator. He jogged into the blinking research chamber as the metal double doors locked shut behind him. Austin, a short man with square glasses, scrambled back and forth, pressing buttons and turning dials.

The ceiling of the room must have been twenty feet tall. At the center of the room was the Terraformer, a sparking metal hunk the size of two men. Endless wires were hooked up to the device. Next to it was a large pipe that ran all the way to a silver ring in the ceiling. The ring was a complex mechanism about the size of a swimming pool. The pipe that led to it was completely enclosed, except for an opening near the floor, which was about four feet off the ground. In the opening were six melon-sized spheres, each a different color.

Matt pointed to the spheres. "Is it ready, Austin?"

The scientist jumped. "Dear God, Matt, you scared the—"

"*Is it ready?*"

Austin gulped, his hands were trembling. "I need your authorization first."

"Fine." The main doorway thudded as though someone was trying to knock it down. Matt eyed it nervously.

Austin's whole body shuddered and he walked over to a white table. He tapped its surface and a holographic map of the world appeared. "I targeted the six largest bases in the States."

Matt quickly glanced at the glowing circles scattered across the map of the United States: Colorado, California, Washington, Florida, New York, and Virginia. "Is there gonna be collateral damage for these places?"

There was another pound at the door. This one sounded like a cannon shot.

Austin bit his cheek and looked over at the spheres. "There's a chance they cause natural disasters upon impact, but we didn't get to those tests yet."

Something in Matt's gut told him it was a bad idea, but he pulled out his authorization card anyway.

"And what about the Terraformer?" Matt asked.

Austin shook his head, "We never planned on evacuating it."

Matt sighed and inserted the card into a small slot on the side of the table as a robotic voice beeped. "Authorization accepted." Still hesitant, Matt glanced back at the targets when a loud screech broke his concentration. He rounded the reinforced doors just as the lights went out.

The machines around him clicked off. Somewhere, a generator started to buzz. The room gave a collective hum and most of the mechanisms of the facility started to turn back on. The only light in the room now came from the shimmering glare of the monitors.

Matt took a step toward the doorway. "Austin?" His voice sounded more nervous than he'd intended. He slung the rifle onto his back, rubbed the metal on his right shoulder, and whispered, "Come on baby." He took a deep breath and clenched his fists. His fingers started to heat up. As he'd been taught, he flung his palms open just when they were hottest. Red-orange flames ignited across his hands and shadows danced around him in the firelight.

"They must've hit the power. Working on it!" Austin frantically waved his fingers across the touch screen table as glaring red warning symbols flared up all across the holographic globe. "We can't lock targets! They just keep switching!"

Matt swore under his breath. He thought about how horrible launching the spheres to random locations would be, but they didn't have a choice. "As long as they don't go to Virt territories, launch them all." His voice was just above a whisper.

"*Randomly* fire them?"

"Do it, Austin!" Matt shouted. The reinforced doors in front of him started to hiss as the silver metal began to glow crimson. The air around the entrance shimmered like a desert mirage. He could feel the temperature in the room rising. His clothes were already drenched in sweat.

Austin looked as though he was about to protest, but he did as he was told. He tapped a few buttons and the opening on the pipe with the spheres started closing.

Matt couldn't see it, but he knew that the pipe would lift the spheres to the emergency railcannon, which would then launch the spheres around the world.

The doors in front of Bennett fell away into a puddle of molten metal. He stretched out his arms, gritted his teeth, and launched a stream of furious fire into the opening. He heard the first thunderous explosion far above him. The room shook when the cannon fired. One sphere was gone. His feet jolted side to side as the railcannon went off for a second time. He struggled to keep his balance as the blazing tongues of red and yellow flames flew from his hands in a raging inferno. As sweat dripped down his brow, he counted silently with each shake of the room: three, four, five spheres were safe. Safe was too generous a word, though, and he knew it. Matt started panting from exhaustion. His arms quivered and his shoulder started to throb. He'd never controlled intense fire for this long and he wondered when his own sphere would shut off his abilities.

The room shook again as the railcannon fired the last sphere. He smiled, but his happiness faded when he heard Austin scream. Matt quenched the fire and turned just in time to see Austin hit the ground. He gazed at the hole in the back of the chamber. Ten virtaiyu armed with sonic rifles strutted from the hole and fanned out into the room. They were all clad in black armor that was coated in spikes, especially from the shoulders, chest and knee caps. Intricate mechanical helmets covered their faces. He felt a breath on the back of his neck; it sent a chill through his spine. He turned to face his assailant.

Matt could see part of its blue-grey face beneath the reflective visor of its helmet. What should have been the whites of its eyes were instead a dark green and its irises were yellow, dotted with a large black pupil. It blinked with its horizontal eyelids.

He wasn't scared. Matt knew the creature would take his sphere, but the world had the other six. He smiled and the virtaiyu flared its narrow nostrils. "You're too late," Matt said.

It seemed to understand by the way its eyes narrowed and that created a small sense of satisfaction within him. He laughed, and swung a punch laced with fire at the creature, but something hit him in the back of the head. He stumbled into a table. His vision swam and the world fell away. Darkness took him.

2

K A I B A

Cassidy Residence,
Pinecrest, California, United States

A trickle of hot water drummed continuously against Kaiba's skin. He stretched in the burning liquid, attempting to ease his aching muscles from the day's combat exercises. He ran his hand over several bruises that continued to throb.

He still hadn't come to terms with the fact that he would be leaving. Kaiba knew he would miss his home and his family. But he hadn't really considered missing combat training, the factory and weightlifting; the routine of things. He had the week and then it would all change. The peace of home would be replaced with the chaos of war. They could show all the videos and simulations that they wanted to, but Kaiba knew he would be unprepared. It was like trying to describe the flavor of chocolate to someone who had never had it, something you just had to experience for yourself.

He grabbed a light green bar of soap, pausing to take in the scent of dampened mint. He wondered whether or not they would ration him soap on the battlefront. But then he didn't even know if there would be any water. He started to massage his left shoulder, doing his best to avoid the worst of his dark purple bruises.

Kaiba forced a smile, almost wishing the mark would remain on his body, tattooed and permanent. He would need all the reminders of home he could get. He rocked from side to side in the shower wondering how he would spend his last days before Shipment. He heard the beep from the small timer on the bathroom counter, signaling that his time in the shower needed to end unless he wanted a fine from the government.

He sighed. He didn't want to go tonight, but they needed the money. The rusty shower handle squeaked softly as he turned it off. He stepped out onto the cold marble of the bathroom floor, dried himself with a towel, and dressed in dark jeans and a black hoodie.

Kaiba paused to stare in the mirror. He pulled one eyelid down, looked one way and then the other. Definitely more bloodshot than they were yesterday. The blood vessels made his green eyes seem brighter than usual, as if a spotlight was shining on his pupils.

He ran his fingers through his bushy brown hair. He needed a haircut. He tilted his head back and forth. He kinda liked a little length, but he was sure the military would shave his head. He was seventeen. Maybe it was time for a little change. What would it hurt? Who knows how long he'd last out there anyway.

As quietly as he could, Kaiba exited the bathroom and crept down the hallway to the stairs. His feet ruffled the cream carpet, and he hoped that wouldn't wake anyone. He descended the steps, managing to fall prey to the one stair that always creaked. He stopped to listen. Nothing. Assuming no one had awakened, he headed to the sliding glass doors at the back of the house and stepped outside.

The aggregate patio felt rough and jagged against the worn sole of his torn shoes. He'd been meaning to get a new pair, but he spent the money on the week's groceries instead.

A fence surrounded the small backyard, except for a small opening that led to the woods. Kaiba had lived in the same two-story, grey stucco house for the past ten years, and he still didn't know quite how far back the forest went. Strong gusts tore through the foliage, howling as though angry. The evergreen and deciduous trees swayed slightly, buffering from the constant winds.

A crescent moon hung in the dark sky encircled by a flurry of ferociously dark clouds that threatened to downpour. *Probably stupid to have showered,* Kaiba thought. He wondered how long the rain would last. It was just drizzly, but the rain made everything seem gloomy. Spring nights should be warm, nothing like this.

He sighed. Nothing was the same anymore.

Another breeze surged through air. Kaiba shivered slightly as the coolness wrapped itself around his body. His dark eyebrows furrowed as he heard the door slide open. He leaned against the side of the house.

"What are you doing out here Kaiba?"

The soft pitter patter of water started to fall.

"Go back inside, Mom."

The door slid open again and Kaiba turned to see his six-year-old brother, Cade, step outside. He yawned and rubbed his right eye. "Hi Kaiba! What're you doin'?"

The light in the house kept his mother's face in shadow, but Kaiba knew she had that look of disappointment. She seemed to have that look no matter what he did or didn't do these days. Kaiba knelt down next to Cade, ignoring his mother. "I'm just going for a late walk. But what are you doing up?" Kaiba asked, gently poking Cade's stomach.

He giggled. "Um, Mom's, um, readin' to me! But I could come to a walk wit you instead!"

"I wish you could," he said, then he scooped Cade up in his arms and lifted him up in the air. "But you have to get to bed."

Cade kept laughing until Kaiba set him down. "Can you do me a favor?"

Cade's big blue eyes lit up. "Wat?"

"Go to sleep and don't cause any trouble for mom. If you can do that, we can shoot cans in the woods tomorrow morning."

Cade's mouth opened and he scampered back into the house without another word.

Kaiba stood up and smiled.

"You know I don't like it when you expose him to weapons. He's too young."

Kaiba's smile faded quickly. "He'll be exposed to them soon, with or without me. Better me than some soldier. Go back inside. I'll be back later tonight."

"I thought you stopped working for them," his mother said with crossed arms.

"You know I can't just *stop* working for them."

"And why not? Every time you go out you put yourself at risk. If the United Nations Military ever found out what you do, Cade and I would also be at risk!"

Kaiba tried to keep his voice down when he replied, "You don't think I know that? But how are you gonna make the money or get the food that we do now? Those UNM ration tickets are a cruel joke. We barely make it as is."

"I'll figure it out, don't worry about that." She stepped forward and put her hand on Kaiba's shoulder.

He took a step back. "You and Cade will need this. I won't let you guys starve while I'm gone. So while I'm here I'll do what I can."

"And you think tonight's raid will keep us from starving?" She said it as though she were speaking to Cade.

"Oh, don't treat me like a boy. I know it won't do much, but at least you'll have just a bit more. You think I like dealing with these people? Let alone having to work with them? They're hard and they take pride that they're rebellious and violent. Every time I'm with them I have to pretend I'm like that too. But in the end, none of their families go hungry. They provide for themselves and they do it well."

She stepped even closer. "Promise me this is the last time."

"Were you even listening? I can't do that either, there's two other raids this—"

"Promise me," she cut him off.

He stood for a moment staring at his mother's saddened grey eyes. "I'll try."

"You will."

Kaiba stared at her for a moment, but said nothing. He started to leave and she hugged him. Kaiba did not return the embrace.

The rain started to fall even harder.

"Go inside, Mom, I'll see you in a few hours."

She coughed a wet cough and then went back into the house. Kaiba stared at the door until the porch light faded. He walked to the side of the house where the ivy had grown nearly to the shingled roof. He swept a patch of the green away and grabbed his semiautomatic shotgun. Then he made his way out front. An old red pickup truck sat a few blocks away at the bottom of the neighborhood. He walked to the truck.

Jordan rolled down the window and called, "Took ya long enough. You get all your make-up on okay?"

"I always have trouble with the eyeliner. You know that."

Jordan laughed and said, "Just get in the car, princess."

Kaiba smiled and hopped up into the passenger side. They peeled out onto the street and the truck belched a cloud of grey from its tail pipe. The houses and scenery seemed to slip away like watercolors down a drain.

"Which spot we headed to?"

"Gates," Jordan answered plainly. "Supposedly we got some new equipment stored there. And speaking of new equipment, you'll have to see the house. My uncle just finished up yesterday."

Jordan's uncle was a brilliant engineer, involved with the coastal defense projects around the nation. Engineers and certain construction workers were the only men exempted from the draft. Jordan had tried to get hired for some time, but he was just too inexperienced, even with his uncle's influence.

"I'm surprised your uncle finished so soon," Kaiba said. He watched a woman in rags prowling through a trash can near a restaurant they passed. "How much more protected is the place?"

"He left the upper levels the same except for some reinforcing of the windows. It's the basement that's most protected. At least now we can feel okay about leaving our families here. Did your mom say when she and Cade are moving in?"

"I think on Saturday, that way they can take us to port on Sunday."

"Hmm," was Jordan's only reply.

Kaiba watched a young girl lock up the local bakery. He felt sympathy for the kid having to work so late on her own. The government chose thirteen as the new age to start legally working. It wasn't fair for them, but when most of the adult population left, something had to be done to cater to the people left in America. Even then it wasn't enough, businesses were still going under.

They passed seven closed shops on just two streets. Foreclosed buildings were always easy to spot because the UNM put big screens on the front to broadcast war news. Kaiba pointed to one on the corner, "Shame that Haley's didn't make it. Member when we'd get root beer floats there after ball?"

Jordan smiled. "Man those were the days. Sucks that now it's just a big useless broadcaster. I mean, really, who actually watches war news, outside, at night?"

Kaiba laughed, "Our government thought it was a good idea."

"And they're always chalk full of those, aren't they?"

They stopped at a light behind a beat up slug bug. It was the first other car they'd seen all night. It had a bumper sticker with an eagle flying over the outline of China. A nuke rested in its talons. Underneath the picture Kaiba could barely make out the words. "Virts. Let's give 'em a welcome."

"UNM bright idea number one." Jordan shook his head, "That worked so well the first time." The light flashed green.

Those initial attacks had been so horrible. The world went in blind. Kaiba could still picture the endless list of names on the news reports. That's when the majority of people were killed, in the war's first few days.

Jordan pulled off on a side street. It took them several minutes to reach the Gates—aptly named for the huge black iron fence that surrounded the property. Two women with rifles sat at the entrance. One of them motioned to another guard after recognizing Jordan. The gated entrance creaked open.

Kaiba tapped his hand nervously against his seat as they rolled up the driveway.

"You all right?" Jordan asked.

Kaiba hadn't even realized he'd been tapping. "Yup. Yeah, I'm good man."

"Bull. I've known you ten years, don't give me that."

Kaiba bit his cheek. "I'm just … tired of raiding, that's all. I'm gonna tell Taniel I'm out for the rest of the week."

Jordan's eyes narrowed. "I feel you trying to take this last week off and everything, but good luck with that. He probably wouldn't even give you a cut for tonight if you ditched out on the rest."

Kaiba hadn't thought about that.

They parked in front of the third garage stall next to a big black pickup. A 2015 from the looks of it, one of the last cars Ford manufactured before the war. Kaiba followed Jordan up the concrete steps to the red door of the house. Jordan was taller than Kaiba was, thicker too. He wasn't fat, just big and muscular. Short blonde hair, almost buzzed, sat on his rather large head. His broad shoulders seemed to bounce as he moved.

Kaiba walked in and shut the door behind him. There were no lights on, except for the glowing chandelier that hung above the door and a dim light that came from the back of the house. They walked under a massive staircase and down a narrow hallway that led to the living room. The back wall of the room was entirely made of glass. A deck looked out over the tree line of a forest. In front of the glass were several brown leather couches and recliners. A group of thirty people or so sat in the furniture whispering to each other. It was a mixture of faces, but most looked to be around fifteen. There was one guy with a graying beard, probably a drifter who hadn't been caught by the UNM yet. There were only two girls, who Kaiba hadn't seen before. They stood talking flirtatiously with Taniel on a black armchair.

Taniel looked up when he saw Jordan and Kaiba walk in. "'Bout time," Taniel said. He had a rat's face: beady eyes, small pink nose, and long teeth. He shook his long black hair as he stood up. "We're hittin' a UNM storage base on the west side of Sacramento." He seemed to speak to no one yet everyone at the same time. "Word is they've thinned the guards recently. And well, I've got plenty of demolitions courtesy of Fifth Era. Now we got some business." He snapped his fingers. A small boy with red hair and freckles came scurrying into the room. He handed Taniel what looked like a curled up rug. The scroll was bigger than the kid.

Taniel unfurled the bundle and laid it flat on the carpet. He tapped it and it glowed blue. Kaiba had only seen roll-screens at the military academy, never in someone's house before.

"This," Taniel said as a holographic projection of a building appeared, "is the compound."

It was surrounded by shimmering blue barbed wire and several watch towers. On the eastern outskirts were woods, mostly thinly spaced trees and shrubs. On every other side were what looked like ruined buildings crisscrossed by narrow streets.

Taniel tapped a glowing office building that lay five blocks from the barb wire fencing. "We'll meet here. I'll be using an EMP to knock out the power when the guards change at three a.m. After that we roll through the fencing taking out whoever we encounter." Several people snickered excitedly at the prospect of firing their guns at live targets. Taniel pointed to the north side of the compound. "This is the easiest access to the cash, weapons, and supplies. Rumor is the brick isn't reinforced. Lay a charge and we're in. Any questions?"

He paused to look around the room. He held a look that dared anyone dumb enough to speak. "Good. Tank," Taniel pointed to Jordan. "You roll with a third of these boys. Elise and I'll take the rest."

The girl to Taniel's left smiled.

"Got it," Jordan said quietly. Kaiba knew he wasn't thrilled about driving. For one the government could scrap any vehicle for metal if it was caught too close to a UNM supply base. But then of course, gas wasn't the cheapest either.

"Let's load up then."

The group was a flurry of motion as Taniel yelled out names for his car. Jordan started to lead the others and Kaiba strode up to Taniel.

He kept his voice low so only Taniel could hear. "After tonight I'm done."

A glint flashed in Taniel's dark eyes. "What?"

"You heard me. I leave in a week. I'm done stealing from the government."

He pulled Kaiba to the side. "Look, you and I both know *they* won't let you bail on them. That's not how the Fifth Era does business. You joined us and you're bound to complete your tasks."

"I don't need them anymore."

Taniel laughed. "So what, you'll embrace being a pawn for what's left of the US system?"

"It's better than being a pawn for the Fifth Era, who's already a pawn for the virtaiyu."

"Wake up!" Taniel yelled. The group stopped moving. "The world's gonna lose! You know how fast the Virts destroyed Asia. Why not choose the winning side and get decently paid instead of having to live off rations? Instead of having to gamble with your life, why not just skip out on Shipment? I did, and look how well I'm doing."

"I would put my entire family at risk."

Taniel gave him a maniacal smile. "Oh, I think you've already done that."

Heat flushed to Kaiba's face. He curled his fists.

Taniel's eyes darted to Kaiba's hands. He made a clicking noise with his tongue. "Probably not the smartest thing you could do." He lifted the flap of his jacket to reveal a black pistol. "Let me make this very clear for all of you. No one walks away. No one. You can do whatever you want after these raids. Go get killed for a lost cause, I don't care. But you're mine for these next few days. You do not walk away before then."

The anger Kaiba felt had started as a seed. But it grew to the point where his body started to shake. He thought of Cade and his mother being cornered by Taniel. The thought made him sick. He felt like a cannon ready to explode.

Taniel dropped the jacket back over the firearm. "I need you and your buddy Tank so let's just get tonight over with."

"Fine," Kaiba growled.

"Crisis averted then," Taniel said to Kaiba. Then he yelled, "All right guys, let's go."

"Calm down, Kaiba," Jordan whispered.

Kaiba hadn't even realized that Jordan had come near him. But he nodded, his mind still clouded with a mix of fear and fury. Jordan continued talking, but Kaiba wasn't listening. He could practically hear the anger whooshing in his head. He stood looking outside at the trees. They hardly moved, but the whooshing sound kept getting louder.

"Don't you think, Kaiba?"

Kaiba held up his right hand as if it would silence Jordan. Something in the clouds glinted green like a falling star. Then he said, "Listen."

Jordan looked annoyed at first, but then he heard the sound too. As the round object fell closer, the noise grew to a whistle and kept getting louder. With the sound of an exploding building, the object collided into the center of the forest.

Kaiba watched in horror as the trees of the forest were toppled over by fissures that spread in all directions. Twenty-five foot pines and oaks were snapped in half as if mere match sticks. The bark and wood fragments shot outward like the pieces of a broken mirror.

A moment later the oak floor beneath his feet thrust upward as though a bomb had gone off. The shaking threw Kaiba down as the entire house started to quake. Cracks thundered through the glass windows and Kaiba felt the sting of glass at his back. He cried out in pain, but his voice was lost amidst the blender-like grinding sound of the breaking house.

"Earthquake!" Taniel shouted.

Kaiba felt his thunderous heartbeat through his entire body. Pieces of the ceiling started to fall. He shielded his head and scrambled back to his feet.

"Let's go, Jordan!" Kaiba didn't recognize his own voice. It was shrill and high, filled with a fear he hadn't felt in a long time. They tried to sprint for the door, but stumbled every few steps as the floor shifted in random directions. Kaiba fell backward as the surface moved right. Jordan extended a hand but was also knocked off balance.

A crack split up the wall near Kaiba. It looked like some creature was tearing a path to the ceiling. The floorboards creaked and then they too began to break apart. Kaiba bounded to his feet, stepping from the cracking boards and onto whatever solid ones he could find. There was a loud bang as the ceiling fell. A mangled bed frame came crashing down next to a support beam. They fell together in a massive pile to block the way to the front door. Kaiba fought the urge to vomit when one boy was crushed under the rubble. People were screaming. Their yells sent a horrid feeling into Kaiba that seemed to pry at his very soul.

Jordan looked around frantically. *"Out the back!"*

They jumped to the quaking deck. Several other people had already made it outside. It was a two story leap to the ground. Beads of sweat fell from Kaiba's forehead. He looked at Jordan, whose face was similarly filled with terror.

"On three!" Kaiba bellowed.

The redheaded boy called out. He was crawling out onto the deck through the shattered glass doors. He had a gash across his freckled cheek. Kaiba bolted for the boy and scooped him up in one swift motion. He flung the small boy over his shoulder and Jordan jumped. Kaiba was about to leap after him when the boards of the deck fell away. They plummeted to the ground with shattered wood and household objects. Kaiba's stomach lurched during the seconds of freefall.

He landed roughly in the arms of a gnarled pine tree. The boy fell from his grasp and tumbled away. The boughs of pine needles softened Kaiba's fall but he still felt the crushing pain throughout his back. He moaned in agony as he bounced to the ground. He lay on the moving surface, bobbing up and down. He felt like a tiny boat caught on rough seas. After several minutes Kaiba realized the earthquake had stopped, but it was his body that couldn't stop shuddering.

Kaiba shifted onto his side, relieved to see that the young boy had gotten up. He looked shaken but generally unharmed.

"Jordan?" Kaiba coughed.

There was no answer. He waited and looked from the trees to the shattered remains of the house. He started to push himself up as pain shot through his shoulder. He reached and felt the inch-long piece of glass that had burrowed its way into his skin. He wobbled to his feet, using the body of a tree for support. The glass was tinted red. He clenched his teeth and stomped his foot on the ground as he pulled the shard out. Blood slowly tricked down his skin, dampening his t-shirt. He pressed firmly down on the wound and grew more concerned about Jordan. He yelled again.

No answer. He looked back at the boy thinking of Cade and his mother. He dragged himself to the boy and said, "It's okay. Stay here and help will come soon."

The boy nodded silently, tears running down his cheeks. Kaiba walked around the rubble of the outside. The night had turned dead quiet, unnervingly quiet. The once-proud forest was the eeriest part of the night scene. It looked as though a herd of bulldozers had trampled through the trees.

He continued to move through the broken foliage, stepping over the massive cracks that had swallowed tree trunks. He continued shouting Jordan's name every few moments, then paused. There was no way Jordan had fallen this far. He looked out again into the broken forest and noticed a crater. The cracks jutted outward from the hole in all directions.

He turned back to the house, which had split in two, and yelled for Jordan again. Only the whisper of the wind mixed with pained moans responded. Kaiba approached the pit. He gazed into the deep hole; it must have been twice his height. Jordan was at the bottom.

Kaiba swore and slid down into the dirt. He flipped Jordan over and shook him wildly. He was limp like a fish.

"Come on buddy, come on," Kaiba panted. He checked Jordan's pulse. It was weak but still there. Relieved, Kaiba sat Jordan back on the dirt. He tried to think what he could do. He hadn't brought his phone; the government tracking systems were too good. The hospital was a quick drive but Kaiba didn't even know whether or not Jordan's truck had survived the earthquake. He looked around the pit, searching for anything that could help him carry Jordan out.

Instead he saw a grapefruit-sized sphere resting next to Jordan's leg. It was pure white, with glowing lines of brighter white that seemed to ebb. It looked like a spider had etched the surface of the object with patterns of its own webbing.

Mesmerized, Kaiba set Jordan gently back down in the dirt. He pushed his body to the sphere and grabbed it with both hands. He held the cold ball above his head for a moment. It started to glimmer like sunbeams along the surface of a lake.

A burst of light flashed, blinding him. The object started to heat up. He jumped in surprise and tried to drop the sphere. His hands wouldn't obey; it was as if they were bound to the circle. He blinked rapidly, trying to clear the stars from his vision. He roared in frustration and thrashed wildly, trying to free his hands from the sphere. The more he struggled the more he lost control of his limbs. His legs started to prickle and he fell forward into the earth. The sensation quickly moved up his body as if he were slowly being submerged in water. He tried to yell for help, to somehow be heard as he was swallowed by this unknown force. He tried to move his head against the dirt, to move his arms, to move anything, but everything had abandoned him.

3

ROLLING
THUNDER

Amazon Rainforest
305 km Outside Rio de Janeiro, Brazil

Nassira had started to get annoyed wandering aimlessly through the dense jungle. She wasn't one to enjoy the feeling of not knowing the way and it bothered her like an itch she couldn't scratch. She pressed forward behind her brother, Bruno, thinking only of the lifeblood flowers. They were used as medicine, antibacterial and anti-inflammatory, something they all desperately needed, or would need at one point or another. But the true value in the flower was the rumors. The refugees never stopped talking about the flower and its potential. Supposedly, when boiled, the flower's thick nectar helped to stimulate cell regeneration. Nassira didn't quite believe such claims, but if it helped to keep the others positive then she wouldn't try to disprove them.

It took about half an hour to reach the clearing in the forested area and even longer to find the neon flag that Thiago had mentioned. It stuck up from the ground next to orange and pink splotched blossoms that were buried under a foot of thorny green bristle. After the flowers seeded, their roots grew both into and above the ground to defend against predators, but that didn't stop people. The thicket had clearly been hacked away at, yet there was still a lot of brush left untouched.

"Glad we found it," Nassira said, setting down her basket.

Bruno unsheathed two machetes from his back and tossed one to Nassira. "I'll say."

They each began hacking away at the thick gnarled roots, Nassira on the left and Bruno four feet to her right. She swung back and forth, slicing through the brush like thick meat. The roots snapped and crunched away fairly easily, but every couple of swings her knife would stick into the thicket and she would have to pry the metal free. It reminded her of all the axes that stuck into tree trunks when the area for the village was cleared. She kept her eyes on the shiny flowers while she worked. It wasn't the easiest of tasks, but those plants made it all worthwhile.

"Do you think I'm a coward?" Bruno asked suddenly as he sunk his blade into more of the plants.

Nassira looked up, confused at the odd question, and wiped a coat of sweat from her brow. "Of course not. Why would you ask that?"

"I dunno, just thinking of the past I guess. Sometimes I regret my choice."

"To what, stay alive?"

"To not fight. To not protect you and Lia."

Nassira wondered where he was going with this, but she tried to offer encouragement, something she needed much more practice with. "You do protect us."

"Yeah, but for how long? How long can we last out here?"

"Our life out here will last as long as it has to."

Bruno put the blade over his shoulder. "The Fifth Era found us once, they'll find us again."

"And we will kill them again," she said with a mixture of confidence and annoyance. She hacked away at more thorns.

"Not indefinitely, we don't even know how many there are or how many more the virtaiyu recruited since we left the city."

Nassira thrust her blade into the dirt. It sank in and wobbled slightly back and forth. "We built this camp plenty far from Rio and we haven't had an encounter for three weeks now. So frankly I don't care how many there are. Why are you being so negative?"

"I just can't help but feel like I could have done more out there. Done something actually meaningful."

"On the front lines?" She laughed. "You're kidding."

"I'm not."

Nassira rolled her eyes. "Oh please."

"I'm serious. I picture that day at Shipment, all of us forced to go and the half that refused. They were shot at as they tried to run away. Yet I was one of the few to actually get away. I see the looks on the faces of the men and the boys who stood in front of those military planes—pity and sadness, both for themselves and for us. I sat there under those bodies and watched like a coward."

"You did what you had to do to survive. All the women had a choice to fight. The men didn't. They called it a draft, but no one was exempted. I'd say it's fair you got to make a choice."

"So I'm no better than a woman?"

Nassira glared at him angrily. "What exactly is wrong with that?"

"I didn't mean anything by it, Nass. All I'm saying is that I do all these meaningless tasks here—fish, hunt, gather—and all the while I ask why? Why did I live that day when so many others died? Why was I spared and allowed not to fight? The only answer I keep getting when I look at my reflection is that I'm a coward, a lucky coward."

Nassira was growing restless with Bruno's pity party, but she kept her cool, trying to be sympathetic. "You survived to protect these people with me. The elderly, the children, they wouldn't have made it in the new Rio. They would have been fresh meat for the dogs out there. We are meant to protect those that cannot defend themselves, and we do that every day. Don't you see that? I know you didn't flee the military for personal gain, that's not you; you did it to help others. Every other person that got on those planes was destined for death. They abandoned their families, maybe not intentionally, but it's what happened. Kids without fathers, mothers without husbands, and sisters without brothers. You stayed and now we give these people hope in this unruly world."

Bruno leaned back against a tree and sighed. "I could have provided better on the front lines, protection for all and not just the sixty of us hunkering here in the jungle."

"Why are you talking like this?" Nassira snapped.

"Well I—"

"Well you nothing. I'm sick of you moping. It's too late to go. Don't you get that? You had your chance to leave, to be a war hero."

"Hero? That's not what I want."

She advanced on Bruno and stuck her finger in his face. "That is what you want! You missed the chance, and you wanna know what else? There's no point in talking about what could have been. This is our life now so better start acting like a man instead of that boy of a brother I've always known you to be."

Bruno sank slightly against the bark of the tree. His eyes were wide with the look of a broken toy or a puppy that had just been swatted.

Nassira lowered her hand away from his face. Her other hand was clenched tightly in a fist, but the look in Bruno's brown eyes made her regret her words.

They stood in silence for a moment and Nassira spoke first. "I'm sorry. That was wrong."

Bruno shook his head. "No, I appreciate the honesty." He stepped past her to gather a large armful of lifeblood flowers. He funneled them into his basket and strode off without another word.

Nassira watched him, knowing it was pointless to try to apologize again. The damage had been done. She shouldn't have said that. It was too much, but he was being dramatic, debating the past when it should have been left alone. She could have made her point without having to crush him, though. What was she thinking? Her mouth always spoke before she had a chance to think. She had her mother's mind, that's what her uncle had always said. It was great for winning arguments and proving points, but not so great for sparing feelings.

She picked up several patches of lifeblood flowers as though gathering the remnants of Bruno's pride. She placed them into her tightly woven basket, careful not to squish the fragile buds. That would spill the precious juices within. There were still so many lifeblood flowers in the patch that she didn't want to leave behind. She debated whether or not she should run after Bruno or just give him time to think. She was never good at apologizing, especially when she didn't feel wrong. He'd acted childishly. Then again, maybe she had as well.

She looked from the small plants to Bruno.

"Wait up!"

Bruno wasn't the quickest of people, but it seemed as though he were sprinting back. Nassira had to run at top speed to catch up. For every step he took Nassira had to take three to match him.

"Come on B, I'm sorry. I didn't mean it."

He kept on striding, not even glancing at her.

"I can't even pretend to know what it was like for you. I wasn't drafted so that gives me no excuse to judge."

Bruno ducked under some low-hanging vines.

Nassira followed him under the foliage and down the hill. "Please just stop for two seconds!"

A boom of thunder quickly answered her as it rumbled through the mountain hills. The noise made her jump, but to Bruno it was as if nothing had happened.

Great, she thought. *Just what I need to brighten my mood.*

The sky had turned to a rainless black mass. It was going to be a dry thunderstorm, no mistake about that by the look of the clouds. They looked ashy, not moist like the blue-grey clouds during a monsoon. Rain would have helped Nassira's mood, rain would have been good for everyone. She stopped walking and looked up, hoping for just a drop or two to fall from the heavens.

Instead the clouds delivered another clap of thunder and a burst of yellow light jetted outward. The lightning bolt crackled down and collided with a boarub tree to Nassira's right. The electricity sizzled through the wood as the tree snapped in half. The upper portion dropped to the ground like a fallen giant.

Nassira scrambled backward, releasing her basket of flowers as she fell into the dirt. The wood crashed to the undergrowth, echoing throughout the forest with a mighty boom.

The fallen tree obscured her view of Bruno.

Nassira watched in dismay as the clouds belched forth one, two, and then three bolts of lightning. The thunder roared in tune with each of the bolts like a symphony of chaos.

Nassira hopped to her feet, fearfully aware of the danger that had become the forest. She calmed down, brushing the dirt from her pants and tried to reassure herself that she wasn't in any true danger. It was just one tree.

She hollered for Bruno again. His deep voice called back somewhere beyond the fallen tree, but she couldn't make out the words. The mess of limbs and bark blocked her path. So she made her way around and darted for him, heart pounding faster with each crash of thunder. Without warning a bolt of lightning, bigger than the others, cascaded down in front of her. She stopped in her tacks as the yellow arc fell upon the ground, zapping the earth no more than two feet in front of her. She felt its white heat like the roiling embrace of a volcano fire. Goosebumps sprang up along her whole body.

She could have died. Right then, in a split second. If she'd been running a little faster... She shuddered, picturing her blistered body left alone on the jungle floor to rot with the fallen logs. What would Bruno have done?

The gigantic bolt had left a blackened spot, three feet in diameter. It resembled a bug splat, fragmenting in every direction. At the center of the electric splatter was a sphere, smaller than a mango but bigger than an apple. Nassira approached the circle, entranced by its vibrant radiance. It may have been small, but its shine rivaled that of the sun. She took her eyes from the object as speckles of black started to appear before her eyes. She blinked furiously and was relieved when the spots had faded. She was further comforted that the forest had grown quiet. The clouds were still storm dark, but no light glistened about their bodies. Nassira shielded her eyes until the ball started to dim. It almost looked as though it were cooling down, like the dying embers of a campfire.

Bruno called again, but Nassira didn't answer. She walked forward, slowly drawn to the ball like a gnat to city lights. She knelt beside the object and cupped it in her hands.

4

Unstable
Alliances

Taniel Avaro threw himself into the nearest shrubs. Branches scraped against his face. His back ached from falling in the earthquake but he didn't dare adjust himself. He had sprinted too far to get caught now. He waited silently as the voices of two UNM police neared.

"I thought we had him by the river," one of them said.

Taniel bit his lips as the flashlight beam waved over his hiding place. He inched his fingers toward the pistol at his hip.

"Are you sure he came this way?"

"I think so."

Taniel wrapped his hand around the gun. He was lucky he'd remember to put a silencer on it. He waited until he could just make out the faces of the cops.

The larger of the two police kicked the ground. "Captain won't be happy if we don't bring someone back."

Taniel held his breath as he raised the pistol and aimed for the first cop's chest. Moonlight streamed through the trees, giving him the perfect shot. He tickled the trigger just as branches cracked to his left. Heavy footsteps pounded.

"There he goes! Get 'em!" the cops yelled and together they sprinted off into the forest.

The night became quiet again. Taniel waited until he was sure they were gone. He smiled to himself and swept the dirt from his clothes. He was lucky they'd taken off in the wrong direction.

"Proud of yourself, T?" asked a voice from behind.

Taniel reeled around with his gun drawn. "Oh," he said lowering the weapon. "It's you."

Kyle Graves was an ugly man: bald, fury eyebrows and a large nose. He frowned. "You led them straight to us."

Taniel pointed the pistol in the cop's direction. "I would've taken care of them before we got too close."

Graves lunged forward and grabbed the pistol. "And then you would have led more police straight to us! Did you suddenly forget all UNM fuzz have trackers in their arms?"

Taniel didn't answer and glared. Graves might have been the Fifth Era leader on the West Coast but Taniel hated how he treated everyone as inferior.

"I should execute you for this." Graves said shaking the firearm.

Taniel shuddered. Graves had killed others for much less than leading UNM straight to their hideout, and unless he lied, Graves might actually do it. "I know who took the spheres."

Graves stood silent for a moment. "You're certain?"

"Positive." In truth Taniel only had a hunch, but it didn't matter. If he didn't gamble with this, he was dead anyway.

"Then he'll wanna talk to you."

"Who?"

Graves smiled, "Eskylious."

Taniel's breath caught in his throat. He had heard stories of the virtaiyu but never dreamed of meeting him. "He's here?"

"Come on." Graves said. He turned and started walking.

Taniel ran his hands through his hair nervously. He gulped and followed Graves deeper into the forest. They slipped through the trees and walked for another mile until they reached a clearing.

An abandoned logging mill sat in front of marsh land. Fifth Era guards were scattered amongst wood piles and they raised their weapons as Graves and Taniel neared.

Graves put his hand out to stop Taniel from coming any further. He whistled a quick three note tune and the guards lowered their weapons. "Now, don't speak until spoken too. Sky's not too fond of meeting young Fifth Era. Just follow me and do as I do."

"Got it." Taniel followed Graves around to the back of the mill. His boots sloshed on the wet grass as they reached the edge of the marsh. Taniel shivered when he saw five towering, human-like shadows. He could tell they were virtaiyu by their massive seven-foot forms and their black armor that rippled like liquid moonlight. Graves bent down on one knee and Taniel did the same.

"Eskylious, I have brought information regarding the spheres."

The largest of the virtaiyu turned around and slowly paced forward. The creature wore a hood that obscured most of its face but Taniel could just make out the blue-gray tint of its skin.

Eskylious towered over Graves and finally said, "But not the spheres themselves?"

The hairs on Taniel's arms stood up at the voice. It sounded as though seven people spoke at once.

"I never saw the spheres, but Taniel did."

Eskylious looked down on Taniel. "This boy?"

Taniel was too much in awe to look up at the creature and instead stared at Eskylious's pale, blue-grey feet. They were shaped like a hawk's, three toes in front with one at the back. Each toe had a curving black talon that looked like a deadly weapon.

"Yes." Graves said.

Eskylious reached down with a scaly, six fingered hand. "Do you fear me Taniel?" Eskylious asked, as he put his longest middle finger under Taniel's chin.

Taniel looked up into the creature's eyes. They were eerily beautiful, bright grey with red-rimmed irises. "Yes but I'm also in awe. I've never seen a virtaiyu in person."

Eskylious smiled, revealing two rows of needle-like teeth. "Smart boy. Tell me why you joined the Fifth Era. What made you want to work with we virtaiyu instead of against us?"

Taniel gulped, hoping he'd say the right things. "I don't think humanity can beat Virtaiyan kind. I saw an opportunity to provide for myself better than I ever could have under the selfish government that rules. At the same time, I want to be a part of the winning side."

"And that is the reason I have hope." Eskylious said slowly. "There is no need for a losing side. Humans need to see that we can live together, but your species must also be shown the error of their ways. Do you know why I and my kind are here?"

Taniel wasn't sure what he meant. "Sorry?"

Eskylious's hands glowed red as if heating up. He slashed two long nails against Taniel's cheek.

Taniel winced as his cheek started to burn.

"Never apologize for not understanding a question human. That's what has wrecked your world in the first place." Eskylious spat. "Answer me again."

"No, I don't know why you're here."

Eskylious inhaled deeply as though angry. He exhaled slowly and backhanded Graves.

Graves fell on his side with a muffled groan.

Eskylious shook his head. "You keep forgetting to tell this to those that work under you and virtaiyu might be painted as villains. We don't want that, now do we?"

"It won't happen again." Graves said as he wobbled upright onto one knee.

"I was younger than you when my world died, Taniel. My elders used to say at that age, the memories don't stick but ah, I still remember it. I can still picture my planet turn from that orb of bluish-green to a flame of apocalyptic red. I swear I felt the heat of the explosion even in space. But I survived. I forced myself to help my kind, and together we drifted the void of space, all the while hoping there might be a world that would give us a place to call home. And do you know what we found?"

"Earth." Taniel whispered frightened.

"Yesss." Eskylious hissed as though savoring the word. "Your Earth. Believe me, I've never been happier than that day and more so when we discovered life here. I assumed humans were an enlightened race. One of peace and prosperity, but we were wrong, so wrong. We observed as you fought against one another." Eskylious held his hands up and grasped at the air, "Poisoned the very skies and destroyed all things natural. How could my kind not strike? Humanity forced us. Wouldn't you agree?"

Taniel nodded.

"Not all humans understand as you and the Fifth Era do Taniel. And the simple keys to making other humans understand are the elemental spheres. It is not just a dream for virtaiyu to inhabit the earth but for humans as well. I want us to live in peace, truly. Don't you two?"

"Yes Eskylious." Graves and Taniel echoed together.

"Yet, I've fought, bled and killed for my race and no *human* ignorance will prevent me from survival." Eskylious shook his head back and forth slowly. "I don't like to murder, I don't enjoy squeezing the breath out of sentient life." His hands started to glow red again. "But I've lost thousands of my kind and I'd crush the souls of a billion more humans to prevent the loss of even a single virtaiyu!" He paused and grabbed the sides of Taniel's face. "But you won't have to worry about that, will you?"

Taniel couldn't respond. He quivered in fear, realizing his lie had gotten him in far more trouble than he'd bargained for.

Eskylious let go and grunted in what appeared to be laughter. "Of course not. Because you know the future holds peace and all we have to do is make humanity's leaders see it. We can do that together, and I promise you it will happen. But it starts with you, boy, where did you see the spheres?"

Taniel moved his tongue around in his mouth trying to get rid of the dryness. He looked back up at Eskylious and said, "With Kaiba Cassidy."

5

The Awakening

Pinecrest, California, US

Kaiba blinked away the darkness. He felt strange waking up in a room and not knowing how he'd got there. It was as though a mere moment had passed since he'd been in the forest and now he was here, wherever here was. He blinked several times and the room came into focus. The bed was white, his pillows were white, even the picture frames that hung on the mahogany walls were white. He stared at a photo of a child standing in the middle of a field, contemplating where he'd seen the picture before. It was one of many framed images.

Around the room were snapshots of sunsets and beach villas, rain forests and mountain ranges. He recognized the exotic photos in the perfectly square room as Jordan's guest room. The only thing that had changed about the room was that several small cracks had formed along each wall. He blinked away several spots of light that had appeared to reveal the smiling faces of his mother and Mrs. Hightower. He spied Jordan standing in the far corner of the room.

Kaiba wondered if they had brought the sphere back with them. He still didn't know if he'd imagined the whole thing. Then he wondered what everyone was so happy about. Kaiba understood when he noticed the jungle of tubes that came weaving from his right arm. His head felt as though it were being squeezed and pulled apart at the same time. It pounded heavier as he thought of the night. He remembered the quake and the broken forest, but after he grabbed the sphere, nothing. He tried to scrape something, anything, from the darkness of his memories, but there was only emptiness.

He rubbed his forehead, somewhat surprised at how cold he felt. There were a mountain of blankets surrounding him, but he shivered anyway. He started to sit up, but stopped as his chest erupted in pain, bringing tears to his eyes. The pain wasn't just in one spot, but over his entire chest. He gasped and grabbed at his abdomen to find his stomach was no longer soft, but rock hard, steel hard. He threw back the covers and lifted up his shirt. To his dismay a half-inch thick plate of silvery white metal coated his body from the top of his chest down to his belly button. He could feel the iron with his fingers, but his stomach couldn't feel his own touch. He felt only cold against the odd plate. Kaiba moved his stomach from side to side. The armor-like layer contorted perfectly with his own body. He would have thought the thing would have remained rigid like steel, not flexible like clothing.

Jordan's mother, a plump woman with curly black hair, scowled and leaned over him, a little too close for his comfort. As she came near, Kaiba could smell the candied cinnamon on her breath. She said something he couldn't hear. He tried to speak but his own words sounded as though he spoke into water. He looked up helplessly and shook his head.

Mrs. Hightower took a pen-shaped object from her coat pocket. She took the blue cap off the stick to reveal a three inch needle. Kaiba wanted to protest but she jabbed the injection into his left forearm.

Kaiba glared at her hotly.

She slowly mouthed the words, "Hang on." Kaiba sat for a moment rubbing his vein. A small drop of blood swelled on his skin like the tear of a rose. Kaiba watched his mother argue with Jordan's mother. It reminded him of the time his family had gone to see a mime show. There were probably ten of the white-faced people, each just as creepy as the next. They had silently argued using over exaggerated hand waving and body movements. This seemed like déjà vu except no one around Kaiba wore a mask of white paint on their faces.

He watched his mother speaking. Her lips were moving so fast Kaiba wondered how she was able to breathe. Then he heard a breath rise from his lungs, a beep and "Will he recover?" all at the same moment.

Kaiba quickly looked to his right at the machine connected to the wires. It beeped every second or so.

"I can hear!" Kaiba exclaimed.

Mrs. Hightower looked away from Kaiba's mother, beaming. "I should say so, hon. I would've injected you earlier but we didn't know when you'd wake. The meds I gave you can screw with your hearing."

Kaiba was about to thank her, but his mother rushed forward and threw herself onto the bed. She wrapped Kaiba into her arms; it felt as though she was squeezing him with the strength of a python. "We were so worried. So, so worried."

"I'm fine Mom," he wheezed "What happened? Is Cade okay?"

"Cade's just fine, sleeping actually—for Christ's sake let him breathe, Maddie. He's only just come to."

She got up looking slightly embarrassed. "Sorry."

Kaiba smiled, mainly because he could breathe easier. "You're fine, Mom."

"As I was saying," Mrs. Hightower said, "after the earthquake hit I picked your mother and Cade up from your house. Sorry to say but it's pretty wrecked."

Kaiba had assumed as much. "But Cade, he's doing okay? Any injuries?"

Mrs. Hightower shook her head, making her black curls bob like mini springs. "He had a few cuts, one worse than the others. Nothing we couldn't handle."

It was the first time Kaiba actually appreciated Jordan's mother's expertise as a nurse. He was even more grateful that she hid her medical experience from the government. Most nurses and doctors were shipped off to the front lines.

"He was rather proud of his stitches," she continued, "said they made him look tough like you. But *you* are the one we should really be talking about here."

Kaiba pointed to his chest. "Any ideas about this?"

Mrs. Hightower scratched her head. "Not. One. Clue. I pried at it with everything but a crowbar." She pointed to Jordan. "He can testify. Won't budge. I was worried it was some kind of parasite. You're lucky though, hon, 'cause your blood pressure and vitals seem to be unaffected by it. All your cuts and glass shards are more of a worry than your new fashion statement. Really it's just an eyesore. I was going to call the police or the UNM about it but we decided against it. What with you boys'... *activities.*" She shot Jordan a threatening glance. Jordan merely gazed at his feet sheepishly. Jordan didn't cower before anyone and yet here he was hiding his tail in front of his mother.

Mrs. Hightower continued, "Luckily, Jordan was able to get you back here in one piece. Although he claims it took several hours. Do you remember the last time you saw each other?"

"Well," he glanced back at Jordan. His arms were crossed. He barely moved his head from left to right. Kaiba almost didn't catch it. "I, I remember leaping from the house as the deck collapsed and then everything just gets kinda fuzzy from there. One minute Jordan was right at my side and the next thing I know I'm here in this bed."

"Hmmm." She turned to Jordan. "I'm sorry I didn't believe you."

Jordan waved her off. "It's fine."

Kaiba watched him suspiciously.

"Other than your minor blood loss from the glass shards you'll be perfectly fine in the next day or so."

"We can take you to the hospital tomorrow if you want," Kaiba's mother said. It sounded more like a demand than an option.

"It's okay. I'd rather not waste a day of my week."

Everyone in the room exchanged glances.

Jordan stepped forward. "Buddy, you only got five days left now."

Kaiba squinted. "What do you mean?"

"You were out for about sixteen hours," Mrs. Hightower answered.

"Nearly a day?" Kaiba exclaimed. One day totally erased. Gone. He would never get those hours back. He'd been cheated; his deck had been rigged.

"It's okay," his mother said, "We still get to enjoy the next few days together. You're safe, that's all that matters."

"Yeah, safe for now at least." Kaiba sat up and grimaced through the throbbing pain in his chest. He started to remove the IV tubes from his wrist.

"Ah ah ah," Mrs. Hightower said. "Leave those in for the night. We'll see how you are in the morning."

"I've slept enough."

"Nurse's orders." And with that Mrs. Hightower opened the door to leave.

Kaiba's mother came forward first. She kissed his forehead. "Sleep well. We'll talk in the morning."

The mothers stood in the door waiting for Jordan.

Jordan stood still as a statue. "I'm gonna stay with Kaiba for a little while. Guy stuff."

Kaiba's mother gave a worried glance.

Mrs. Hightower looked suspicious. "Make it quick. It's late."

Jordan waited until the door had closed. They listened to their mothers' footsteps walking away.

Kaiba spoke first. "Why'd you make me lie?"

Jordan started to roll his pants up to reveal what should have been the skin of his thigh. Instead most of Jordan's upper leg was coated in the same metal as Kaiba's chest. The whole plate was the same thickness but its coloring was different. The material was a dark emerald with indentations of brighter green strewn throughout it.

"What are they?" Kaiba asked, feeling his own stomach.

"Hell if I know. Nothing like I've ever seen."

Kaiba ran his fingers against the soft metal. It was crafted to the familiar outline of his body and yet felt so alien to him. "Nothing like they showed us in school, that's for sure. Why didn't you show your mom yours?"

"You think I wanted my mom knowing about this? I barely escaped her medical check. And that's only because she was so worried about you. She's not the one I'm worried most about though. Taniel and the others were furious."

"To be honest I hadn't even thought about them," Kaiba said.

"Well, more Fifth Era came to that house after the quake, trucks of them. These others weren't drifters or teenagers either. They were older, too old to be here legally and certainly too old to be recruits, my guess is higher-ups in the group. It took me an hour to sneak us out of there."

"I appreciate it."

Jordan held up his hand. "Man you would have done the same for me. But that's not why I mentioned the others. I mentioned them because things just got hot."

"What do you mean?" Kaiba asked.

"The local UNM stations located the epicenter of the quake. They stumbled on the Fifth Era, arresting all they could find."

"Did they take Taniel?"

Jordan shook his head. "He's too crafty to get taken by some idiot UNM police. I'm sure he escaped with others. All I know is that they're after the spheres. And they want them bad."

"But we don't have them. Why are you worried about us?"

"You picked up the white sphere."

"How'd you know that? You were unconscious when I found you," Kaiba said.

"When I fell down into that hole I saw the white ball but picked up the green one. I didn't think anything would happen. I thought I might be able to sell it or something. But it put me under for about four hours. When I woke up you were on your back and the other sphere was gone."

"Gone as in taken?"

Jordan sat on the edge of Kaiba's bed. "Gone as in on your chest."

Kaiba gave a questioning stare. "I don't understand."

"The ball and the plate are the *same thing*. That sphere slowly unfurled itself into this armor. I watched it as it rearranged, transformed, changed—whatever you wanna call it—onto your chest. I know it sounds crazy but we have what the Fifth Era wants."

Kaiba knew Jordan rarely lied. He thought about it for a moment. There were so many wild rumors circulating on the war front and yet nothing this crazy. He stroked his chest, unsure if he could believe what his friend was telling him. "So you think these caused the quake too?"

"I know so. I found out what they do."

"What they *do*?" Kaiba repeated. He gestured for Jordan to demonstrate.

Jordan smiled. "Not inside."

They waited two hours to get out of the house, just to make sure everyone was asleep. They emerged from the guest room and onto the first floor. Kaiba was amazed at how well everything had held up. The improved foundation clearly helped protect the overall infrastructure, lucky for Jordan.

Kaiba really didn't want to see the state of his own house. Mrs. Hightower had said it was bad. She generally kept things in a positive light so if she said it was bad, it was worse. He wasn't even sure if he'd go back. Maybe it was better he remember his childhood home the way it was before the war, the draft, and now the quake. But he thought of his brother's dog tag that sat in the small black box filled with photos. The tag was all they'd shipped back. He'd have to go back for it.

They silently crept outside and into Jordan's backyard, a thirty by thirty-five foot area with dying grass split by cracks, surrounded by a worn-down wood fence. A small pond sat in the left-most corner of the yard. It was surrounded by small tiles of speckled granite that fit together to form a border around the water's edge. Most of the tile had split into pieces. The little pond was once a perfectly constructed work of masonry. It looked more like a semicircle of rubble now. At the back of the pool nearest to the fence corner were seven shattered pillars of black limestone. They looked like the targets of a demolition crew.

"The quake hit this pretty hard, huh?" Kaiba asked.

Jordan smiled. "You could say that." He bent over a two-inch square of the black tile, one of the few that were still intact. Jordan held his hand just above the rock. His fingers fluttered as if they moved along a keyboard. They moved in sync, once to the right and then once to the left.

Kaiba felt two deep pangs at the same time, just as Jordan moved his fingers. One was in his thigh, the same spot as Jordan's sphere. The other was in his chest. It was a sensation not of pain or of pleasure but a completely new feeling in between the two. Kaiba neither enjoyed the presence, nor did he resent it.

He couldn't explain why but he could immediately feel the ground around him. Not just the ground at his feet but the ground in front, behind, and beside him. He could feel the rocks beneath the earth as though he were holding them in his own hands. He stood frozen but he'd never felt more alive.

Jordan's entire body had started to shake. He held his right hand over the stone. His face started to grow red as though he were holding his breath. Slowly, he closed his fist. He clamped his fingers tightly as though he were trapping a fly within his palm. He flung his hands open.

With the sound of a breaking pot, the tile at his feet exploded into pieces as a foot-long crack split it in two. Jordan moved his hand farther away from his body.

The crack followed his motion, controlled by his own will. It jetted forward, breaking more tiles, and sprang into the yard, creating a deep gash in the dirt and grass. At his feet the broken tile pieces started to float with other chunks of rock. They rotated slowly around Jordan's ankles.

6

THE FIRST ELEMENT

Pinecrest, California, US

Jordan gulped for air as he lowered his hand. The crack stopped growing and the levitating rocks fell, clinking against the remaining pieces of tile.

"Well?" he asked casually.

Kaiba couldn't speak. His jaw just hung open like a door on a broken hinge. The sensation within him started to pulse like the quickening of his heart. He was dumbfounded. Kaiba had heard many times that virtaiyu were able to shape, move, and even wield rock, fire, and other elements as weapons. But the military only covered virtaiyu sonic weapons, armor, tactics, and vehicles in school. Frankly, Kaiba got the impression that the military was scared of the sphere's ability. And why shouldn't they be?

Kaiba moved his mouth slowly. "How?"

Jordan looked ecstatic. His face was still glowing red as though he'd just run a mile. "Cool, huh?"

"How did you do that?"

"I honestly don't know. I just … feel it. It's like this adrenaline feeling like when you get really excited or worked up. I feel it through my entire body. Then I can see the stone crumbling beneath my own hands and it happens."

Kaiba thought of one student, Robby, who had mentioned something about how his dad died. He had said the word "geo-kinetics," the ability to move earth. At the time it meant little, but Jordan had just done it as plainly as a weightlifter flexing his muscles. "How many times have you done that?"

"Three," Jordan said. "When I was carrying you home from the woods I tripped and we fell onto concrete. As I hit the ground the rock beneath me just shattered. That's the first time it happened. After I got you back here, I did it again while everyone was taking care of you. But that time I didn't break the rock, I changed it."

"What do you mean changed it?"

"Easier if I show ya." He strode over to the black pillar with the fewest of cracks in it. With a heavy sigh Jordan laid his palm against the stone.

Kaiba felt the return of the presence again in his chest as Jordan moved.

Jordan stood for a moment looking slightly unsure of what to do. He slid his hand up and down the rock as if petting some black dog. With three steady breaths he drew his hand back to his body. A piece of the rock, about the width of a soda can, followed his hand as though it were magnetized. When he dropped his hand to his side the rock didn't fall but instead extended from the pillar like a branch from a tree.

"Whatcha think?"

The question baffled Kaiba. Jordan had asked so casually. Jordan loved asking "Whatcha think." Only normally it was "Whatcha think about this car … this girl … my jacket?" Was he hallucinating?

Kaiba looked at his hands and then down at his feet. He grabbed his shoulders. Everything felt real. "I don't believe it. I just cannot believe it."

"I was pretty spooked when I did it the first time."

"I'm not spooked, just—surprised."

Jordan rolled up his pant leg. The indentations on the metal plate pulsated with bright green that cast a glow around them in the dark, like firelight. "This is what spooks me a little bit. When I move the rock this thing lights up. I feel this pounding all around my thigh. It doesn't hurt, it just feels weird. And the other thing—"

"We should go to the UNM," Kaiba interrupted.

Jordan gawked. "And do what?"

"Let them advise us on what these are, what to do about them."

"Take it easy. We don't need to involve anyone just yet."

Kaiba scowled. "You just manipulated earth! Do you realize that? Like one of those … things. Like a virtaiyu."

"This isn't their business."

"Isn't it? So many people have tried and no one has been able to do what the Virts supposedly can. You've heard the rumors with me and you're the very first person to ever show that manipulating elements is even possible for a human!"

"So why would I go to the UNM? They'd probably try and take it from me."

"Exactly! They could help us remove them." Kaiba reasoned.

"Who says I want it removed?"

"No one, but it's the smart thing to do. Us having this power is dangerous. We could be being tracked right now and have no idea. If the Fifth Era leadership was offering so much for them then who else wants them? I'm certainly willing to bet the virtaiyu. And if the Virts want these then so does our government."

"The UNM wants a lot of things." Jordan said. "That doesn't mean I'll just fork this over. More importantly, how are we—or the government—supposed to get them off? You heard my mom. We tried everything to get yours off your chest, but it doesn't move. It's bound to you. Speaking of which, we don't even know what you can do and you already wanna give it away?"

"How do we know *it* does anything?"

"We don't." Jordan pointed to the rock at his feet. "Here, try."

Kaiba hesitated. "I don't know."

"Oh, come on."

Part of Kaiba didn't want to know if he could do anything, but the other half was far too curious. "How? Just picture it breaking?"

"Don't just picture it. *Feel it*. Feel it breaking as though you were grinding it with your own hands. That's how I do it."

Kaiba put his right hand in front of him as Jordan had done. He tried to picture the stone tile exploding, but no matter how hard he tried the feeling wasn't there. That warm presence was gone and the stone seemed lifeless, unlike the rock around him did when Jordan broke the rock. It just seemed like an ordinary tile. He shook his hand and nothing. He concentrated harder, but still nothing happened.

"Just smash it."

Kaiba looked up angrily. "What do you think I'm doing?"

"I think you're staring at a rock."

"That's what you did!"

"Yes, but I had practice. I fell my first time and the stone shattered. Maybe you should just try to crush it with your bare hands too before you do it without even touching the stone."

"Sounds good to me." Kaiba found a tile with a small crack through its middle. It was mostly grey with tiny speckles of white. He took a deep breath and slammed his fist against the ground.

His knuckles exploded with pain. They seemed to swell outward as if being inflated. Kaiba grabbed his hand tightly, trying to squash the fiery ache.

Jordan burst into laughter.

Kaiba picked up a shard of rock with his good hand and chucked it. The rock hit Jordan in the side but he only laughed harder.

"I think your hand might have caught in your skirt. Try to use a little more muscle."

Kaiba glared angrily at Jordan and then the armored plate thudded. Suddenly the feeling returned and he felt both fear and excitement. It was the sensation during a chase but powerful, more alive. It surged through his body from his chest down to his feet, extending to the tips of his fingers. The sensation spilled out onto the ground beneath him. The yard seemed to beat in sync with his veins and he felt strangely connected to the earth, as if it were an extension of his own body.

He looked at Jordan, who watched him with an interested stare, but Kaiba looked back down at the same tile. He lowered his hand and he felt a rushing, like all the blood was pooling in his palms. He pushed the feeling from his fingers and into the space beneath the tile. The area between Kaiba's feet shook as four tile pieces exploded with a pop, the dirt beneath the tile jutting upward.

Jordan took a step backward.

Kaiba was mesmerized. He continued to let the energy flow from his body and into the earth. As he did so, the ground rose higher until a column two feet wide and five feet high had formed. He lowered his hands but he could still feel the adrenaline-like feeling within the tower of dirt and rock. Not just in the column of soil but in the marble pillars around the pool as well. He wondered what would happen if he drew the energy back into his own body. He pulled back, only slightly, by curling his fingers inward. The entire mound shifted itself to Kaiba as if it was connected by a rope. Enthralled, Kaiba decided to push the energy away. He stepped forward, thrusting his hands. The ground exploded in the opposite direction, scattering rocks and dirt in a wide arc. At the same instant, the seven pillars of marble were tilted back, fleeing like roaches before a light.

The movement caused the feeling to fade from Kaiba's body and it made his chest burn. He gripped at his stomach, feeling both sick and slightly dizzy. He plopped down in the yard.

Jordan rushed to his side. His eyes were wide with shock. "Jesus, you all right?"

"Just need to rest a minute." Though Kaiba wasn't really sure if he was okay. What was happening to him? This was something out of his wildest dreams—a gift, but it could also be a nightmare.

Jordan stood over him looking at the shifted marble stones. "You didn't need to hustle me with that 'I can't do it' act."

Kaiba smiled. "Wasn't an act."

"Yeah, right," Jordan said, walking to the pillars. He touched one tilted back at a forty-five degree angle. "Care to show me that trick?"

They practiced in the backyard until the night turned to morning. Kaiba explained the presence within his body and Jordan tried repeatedly to create a tower from dirt. He quickly grew discouraged with each failed attempt. Kaiba explained as best he could, but then he suggested that Jordan attempt to move one of the marble pillars.

To both of their surprises, Jordan managed to hurl one of the columns into the wooden fence, which shattered under the weight of the rock. He was excited and urged Kaiba to try to create a crack in the lawn. But Kaiba still felt dizzy, exhausted. They resorted to just sitting and talking until the early morning. They talked about the war, about leaving home, and about the future. They tried to avoid talking about Shipment, but couldn't when Jordan asked, "How are we gonna get passed the mandatory physicals before we board the ships next week?"

Kaiba threw a tiny pebble into the yard. He thought for a moment and admitted, "There's no way we will. The UNM will know the plates are Virt tech. You think we should just tell 'em ourselves?"

Jordan sighed. "We talked about this, I just don't like going to the military. They'll think we stole them."

"Maybe we don't say anything unless we're directly asked?"

"I guess that's a little better." Jordan said softly. His voice quivered slightly like a strand of hair brushing against the strings of a violin. His eyes were locked on his feet and his right hand shook.

Kaiba had rarely seen fear in Jordan and for the first time in their friendship he noticed it. He was about to ask about it when the light in the patio came on. For the first time he understood what a deer in the middle of the road felt like as headlights barreled forward. He didn't move as Mrs. Hightower's robed figure stepped from the house and into the still-dark backyard.

"Who's out there?"

"Just us, Mom," Jordan hollered.

She strode to them. "I hope 'us' is referring to you and Cade."

Jordan looked at Kaiba.

"Sorry Mrs. Hightower. I needed some air and I made Jordan help me outside," Kaiba said.

"Unbelievable. I told you you needed your rest."

"I know. I'm sorry."

Mrs. Hightower looked down at them. "Well, hon, let's just get you back into the house. And what in the world happened to the yard? These cracks weren't here earlier. And the fence?"

"It was like this when we got out here," Jordan said.

"I'm sure it was," she said suspiciously. "Well, you'll have to help me this week then. Come now, the news is about to come on. We'll make breakfast."

As they walked to the house Kaiba silently hoped that none of Jordan's siblings would be broadcasted on the Killed in Action list.

7

Too Early

Kaiba had offered to help with breakfast, but Mrs. Hightower insisted that he rest on the living room couch. She made Jordan help with cooking, which would turn out horrible. Kaiba could already smell the burning bacon.

The living room was filled with cream and brown leather couches arranged in a semicircle around a sixty-inch plasma screen TV. It hung on the mantle beside family photos, mostly of Jordan and his two sisters' sporting events.

Kaiba flicked the news on and a reporter appeared.

She brushed her hair back. "And yet, the number of jobs just keeps increasing."

An image of several Pennsylvania weapon and steel factories flashed on screen. "With China's factories now gone," the reporter continued, "the grand re-openings of many US manufacturing plants like these continue to call for more workers. Our government and our troops need your help. If you can spare the time please sign up for factory work. Your efforts will save lives."

Kaiba laughed to himself. Sign-ups. The government forced people to work in their factories; mostly they were upcoming soldiers like himself, women, and even some elderly. But as his mother entered the room he stopped laughing as panic started to creep in. "Mom, you remembered to claim a disability permit, right?"

"I didn't think I'd need to."

Kaiba threw himself upright, *Didn't need to?* Who'll take care of Cade if you're working?"

"I thought we talked about this? Mrs. Hightower is taking the morning shifts and I'll work at night."

Kaiba slumped back into the couch, slightly relieved that his mother had already thought of Cade first. "Can you handle the night shift's work load?"

"You can't worry so much." She patted Kaiba's leg. "Now let's just try and get through this casualty report."

Kaiba looked at the frog clock that hung just beside the TV. The newest updates on the war came every morning at six. It was almost time. Kaiba hated the news; they strung everything out almost like they wanted to make everyone anticipate the KIA list.

Cade scampered to where Kaiba sat and curled up in his lap. He had a couple of Band-Aids across his face and small arms. He yawned loudly. "I'm happy you're otay, Kaiba."

Kaiba smiled. "Are you okay?"

Cade yawned again. "Yeah. Scratches and bumps. Nuffin like you had."

Mrs. Hightower brought the plates into the living room. She gave Cade and Kaiba's mother the first two. Jordan brought Kaiba a plate piled high with eggs, pancakes, and thick slices of blackened bacon.

He handed Kaiba the plate.

Kaiba took a slice of the meat and crunched down on it loudly. It tasted like ash. "Bacon's a little crispy. You thinkin' about becoming a military cook?"

"You cook it next time and I'll watch TV," Jordan said, throwing himself into an armchair.

As everyone nestled into the living room the TV screen crackled and stopped. Black and white lines danced across the surface. The daily 'war highlights', as he and Jordan called them, always played first. The news stations liked to show UNM forces blowing up a Virt ship, rescuing civilians or capturing various positions that showed only the most impressive acts of heroism.

A reporter appeared on screen who started to talk about McCarther Forward Operating Base.

Kaiba rolled his eyes at Jordan. Any information she was about to give was a lie, designed to make people feel confident that humanity was winning the war. He pulled out his phone, clicked on the UNM app and scanned his finger in. When his ID was accepted he typed in McCarther FOB.

A map of India appeared and an arrow zoomed in on the Northern border. He clicked the 'update' button. To his surprise, Virt forces had reached the base. It was a vital stronghold to ensuring virtaiyu didn't stretch farther into India. He zoomed out so he could see the Asian continent as a whole.

When the virtaiyu came they wiped out China and parts of the surrounding countries. They inhabited the new land rapidly—like a plague. Various flags indicated which countries fought in which areas. The US, French, and Australians fought in the areas south of China. Most of the European countries fought on what used to be China's western border, while Russia attacked from the north. Japan, and the United States again, fought from the east.

Kaiba was unsettled that the virtaiyu were pressing farther out instead of falling back. All the world's forces still couldn't hold them at bay.

A familiar voice sounded and Kaiba looked up from his phone.

An old man with a wrinkly face appeared on screen. "Strength be with them indeed. I'm Dan Treal and this is Live War News. The war still rages but we hold hope for your fathers and families who fight in this terrible time. Before we broadcast the KIA list, I must comment on several natural disasters that occurred simultaneously within the last twenty four hours. At five o'clock Australian time, a massive tsunami crushed Australia's northeastern coast. Casualties were numerous and millions are left without power. All UNM forces that could be spared were sent for search and rescue. When we come back we'll comment more on the tsunami, the earthquake in California, and the lightning storms that rattled Coari Brazil. For now, here is the KIA list. I express my deepest condolences from all of us here."

A blue background appeared as the white letters trickled onto the screen. They were alphabetical, starting with the last name. The familiar solemn version of the national anthem was played in the background. The living room was silent with a thick cloud of tension in the air. Kaiba scanned the names as the Cs quickly showed up. Relief washed over him when his father's name didn't show up. He knew that Missing in Action for some was just as bad as death, but he still clung to the hope that his father was still alive.

Two loud knocks rapped on the door just as the H names were being scrolled through. Mrs. Hightower had one daughter in the war and another stationed in San Diego. Kaiba knew this was torture for Jordan too as he awaited his sister's name. No one moved until the first of the 'I' last names appeared.

Mrs. Hightower and Jordan each breathed sighs of relief.

Someone pounded on the door again, this time louder. Mrs. Hightower stood up and went to the door.

"Expecting anyone?" Kaiba asked. If the Fifth Era had found them, Cade and his mother were in danger. He patted his chest, hoping Jordan would catch his drift.

"Not that I know of," Jordan said. He got up and followed.

Kaiba leaned out of his seat, trying to crane his neck to get a better view of the front door. He heard a man's voice and heavy footsteps that sounded like boots. As Jordan and Mrs. Hightower entered the room a military lieutenant followed. Kaiba knew his rank from the two white stripes on his shoulder.

He was dressed in combat uniform. Both his shirt and pants were the universal camouflage pattern of digitally blended greens, greys, and browns. He had a large neck that bulged with veins and a powerful-looking expression. His eyes were slightly narrow, shadowed by the cap on his head. His chin had the squareness of a table.

"My name is Lieutenant Aaron," he said. He stood while everyone else sat. Aaron cleared his throat. "I apologize for disturbing you all so early in the morning, but the UNM is quite insistent in this."

"Insistent on what exactly?" Kaiba asked sharply. He scratched his chest as casually as possible, but he felt as though the soldier saw right through his clothes and into the plate.

"Insistent on their orders, and as your officer I'd change that tone of yours—" he looked down at a card in his hand "—Jordan."

Kaiba rose from the couch, not at all intimidated. He was used to the military BS and rather than let formality bug him he let it fuel him. He stuck out his hand. "It's Kaiba Cassidy, actually."

The lieutenant stared at his hand and then looked at Jordan. "You must be Jordan then."

"Yes sir," Jordan said.

Kaiba hated his steadfastness. Jordan always respected his officers and they loved him for it.

Aaron nodded. "You should follow your friend's example of respect, Kaiba. Clearly your school didn't discipline you enough. We'll fix that."

Kaiba didn't like the way he said it.

Aaron continued, "I regret to inform you both that Shipment has come early. The fleet has come in from Japan sooner than we expected and as such we will be departing from port tomorrow."

The simple statement sent a shockwave of anger into Kaiba.

"Tomorrow?" Kaiba's mother shrieked.

The soldier's tone changed to sympathy. "Yes ma'am. I do apologize for the short notice, but we have a schedule to keep. Your sons are vital to protecting not only this country, but the world as a whole."

"How's this fair?" Kaiba exclaimed.

The soldier's expression didn't change. "War is never fair, boy. The longer time we waste the more of an advantage our enemy gains. You will collect yourself and come outside in five minutes. You need only the clothes on your back."

Mrs. Hightower sounded shocked. "Can't we drive them ourselves?"

"I'm sorry, but we have strict orders on taking all men directly to Coronado. Having family in the mix only complicates things," Aaron said. "I can allow you ten minutes with your sons, but not a moment more."

Kaiba pictured the black box with his brother's dog tag again. "Hell with that, I have to grab things from home."

Aaron took a step forward so that his face was even with Kaiba's. "Impossible. You have all you need with you now. The rest will be provided for you. I suggest you get your head on straight before you enter back into a military setting, Mr. Cassidy. I will be tolerant of your tone for now but do not think I will excuse such insubordination in the future. I'll be waiting outside." He marched from the room, then stopped and turned. "You have a lovely home, Mrs. Hightower."

Kaiba glared angrily at the man as he left.

"How can they do this?" Kaiba's mother said. She had tears in her eyes.

"It's not fair, but it's the way it is," Jordan said.

Cade had wrapped himself around Kaiba's leg.

"Clearly things are worse out there than they seem," Mrs. Hightower said. "I don't care what he says, though, I'll throw

ELEMENTALS: THE SEVEN SPHERES

together a few things for the two of you." She walked from the room with Jordan under her arm.

Kaiba felt furious but Jordan was right. He looked down at Cade and said, "Nothing we can do about it now."

It was the longest ten minutes of Kaiba's life. They sat on the couch huddled together. Kaiba looked into his mother's face. Her cheeks were blotchy as tears rolled down them. Kaiba felt like crying but he couldn't break down in front of Cade. He had to be strong. But as Cade whimpered in his arms he felt a single tear fall. He wiped the droplet away from his eye and his mother embraced him tightly. Then she let go and reached into her pocket. She pulled out the silver dog tag.

She looked at it sadly. "I snagged it for you."

Kaiba reached for the jewelry and held it tight. "Thank you." They hugged again. The seconds ticked by and the time was gone.

They walked solemnly from the house behind Jordan and Mrs. Hightower. Green Humvees were parked in front of several other houses. Mothers cried beside their younger children. Some mothers wouldn't even be able to say goodbye to their sons. They would come home from a night's work to find a note, or nothing at all.

Lieutenant Aaron waited in the driver's seat of the boxy green-brown camo vehicle. Kaiba knelt beside Cade. He felt like crying but he had to stay tough. He clutched his brother's small hands. "You take care of Mom, okay? Be strong for her."

Cade sniffled and wiped his eyes. "I will. Come back otay?"

Kaiba smiled at Cade's innocence. He wiped a tear from Cade's cheek and put a hand on his shoulder. Kaiba kept his voice steady. "I promise I'll see you again buddy."

Cade wrapped his arms around Kaiba's belly. Kaiba squeezed, and then stood in front of his mother. They hugged until Lieutenant Aaron stepped from his vehicle.

"I love you," she whispered

"Love you, Mom," Kaiba said.

She held him at arm's length. "You survive out there and you make it back home."

"I will. Take care of yourself."

Aaron pounded on the side of the vehicle. "Time's up!"

Kaiba wanted to beat the man to a pulp but he did as he was told. He ducked into the Hummer and slammed the door. With a grumbling roar the truck boomed to life.

"All ready back there?" Aaron asked, strapping himself in.

Neither Kaiba nor Jordan said anything.

"Good. Off to Coronado then."

Through the window Kaiba watched as his family and his hometown slipped away. He kept the view in his mind, wondering whether he would ever see it again.

8

STIRRING

Amazon Rainforest, Brazil

It was too late for the bats to be hunting and yet too early for the birds to be chirping. Even the tropical frogs were somewhat quiet in the early dawn hour. A slow breeze whirled through the forest, rustling the trees and attempting to rouse the still-sleeping animals of the Amazon. The emerald forest began to stir like a parent beginning to prepare for a busy day.

Nassira stirred with the forest. Her mind lay in the place between sleep and consciousness. Her head pulsed. The headache surprised her; it was beating harder than the time she'd fallen and split her head on the kitchen table. That morning had been terrible but this one felt worse. She crackled the leaves and dirt beneath her, feeling slightly sick. She grappled with the choice of waking or just fading back into sleep. It seemed such a simple decision and yet so difficult. Then the thought came, why was she sleeping on the ground?

She rolled onto her back and blinked several times, attempting to get rid of her weariness. Her eyelids seemed to have their own will to close again, but she managed to keep them open. Through the trees she gazed at a half-lit moon blanketed by a hazy yellow-black sky. The trees seemed eerily tall. She sat up, recognizing this part of the jungle and then quickly remembered the storm. She rubbed her aching head, and watched a red beetle scuttle along in the fine, cocoa-colored dirt. She stifled a small yawn and reached to cover her mouth. Her eyes caught the glint of metal.

"What the?" she whispered to no one but herself. Her entire forearm was coated by a plate of dull yellow-grey metal that stretched from her wrist to just below her elbow. It seemed about two inches thick. There were many indented lines across the plate that reminded her of cracks in a canyon wall. The lines weaved around several pebble-sized circles. She counted nineteen of the dull mustard bearings embedded in the metal. They reminded her of the sphere she'd found last night. That thing had the yellow brilliance of lightning itself. She looked around her but couldn't seem to find the object. Had she dreamed of touching the thing? It seemed so real … it sure felt real. But a dream still didn't explain the item on her arm. Had the sphere somehow become this? She shook her head at such a crazy thought.

She held her arm up and examined it as a biologist might examine a new creature. What did it do? She traced her finger along one of the indentations that weaved like a tiny river. The yellow-silver was speckled with tiny shimmers like stars in the night sky.

She shook the whole right side of her body but the device just moved with her arm as though it fit perfectly to her. She looked for a button or some kind of release but there was nothing. She grabbed the thing with her left hand and tried to slide it off. It didn't budge. Slightly worried but more determined, Nassira dug her fingers into her skin at the edge of the plate and lifted. Still it didn't move. She gritted her teeth and pulled until her nails cut into her skin. Frustrated, she stopped, but she instantly grew mesmerized by one of the pebble-like circles that had started to glow. She brought her face closer.

She touched the shining pebble and her body went rigid.

Nassira tried to move but it felt like hundred-pound weights were attached to every part of her. The air left her lungs as though she'd been squeezed. She struggled to breathe as a single spark appeared on the metal of her forearm. The feeling of crushing weight disappeared and was replaced by a stinging sensation. Slow at first, then fast. It crept into her as though she'd been nipped by millions of bees. But the stinging didn't just prick the surface of her skin, it struck down deep into her bones. Nassira shook violently as the sharp pricks began to intensify. She flailed in the dirt and screamed, both with agony and with fright. Her whole body convulsed as though she were being electrocuted.

Someone called her name but Nassira ignored it. She cried out louder as three pangs of burning pain erupted. They bit into her arms, her legs, and then in her back, as if someone had thrust spikes of heated iron into her. She squirmed as though she could somehow avoid the pain. She flailed her arms into the ground and kicked wildly. She yelled louder and louder as more stings attacked her from all directions. Her tears mixed with dirt as she rolled from side to side.

"Nassira!" Lia called.

Nassira tried to look at her sister but screamed as another sharp jolt twisted through a muscle in her neck, forcing her face into the dirt. Lia thrust a flat stick into Nassira's mouth and tried to hold Nassira still. Nassira's yelp was muffled. She clamped her teeth down on the wood, hardly noticing the splinters in her mouth. Several more pricks jostled her body. She bit down harder into the wood and slowly the pain faded. She sobbed like a wounded animal, even after the last sting. She let the twig fall from her mouth.

"Shhh, shhh. Nass, you're okay," Lia said as she knelt down.

Nassira's cries were gurgled and muddled. Her breaths came in short, fast bursts. Each gulp for air was wheezy and sounded like the wind trying to squeeze its way through a tight pipe. Several tears rolled down her cheeks. They felt cold against her blistering hot skin. She brushed her tears away hurriedly. She couldn't remember the last time she'd cried. It didn't feel right, especially in front of Lia. But she couldn't help it. She'd never experienced such pain. It was the shock of an outlet multiplied by a million.

Lia put a hand against Nassira's head. It felt reassuring.

Still, Nassira sat until her breath started to return to normal. She slowly rolled over onto her back, even more terrified that she would suddenly explode into pain. She shivered ever so slightly from head to toe and looked into her sister's concerned hazel eyes.

Nassira started to sit up and Lia quickly helped her.

Bruno appeared. "Damn it Lia, I told you to keep her quiet."

Lia ignored him. "You want water?"

The river water wasn't going to be clean. It hadn't rained for a month. The dry season was coming, but Nassira didn't care. She nodded.

Lia disappeared behind some brush.

Nassira lay motionless, still in shock at the torment. Her skin throbbed but she managed to stretch her right arm as far away from her body as her shoulder would allow. She stared at the glimmering plate as though she was staring down a rabid dog. The circles had started to dim again. She wasn't sure if that was a good or a bad thing. Within several moments, Lia returned with a plastic water bottle. She held it out.

Nassira's throat was as dry as sand. She grabbed the container and drank slowly. It was slightly grimy but she couldn't have been happier to have it. She drained the bottle in several gulps and then held out her arm. "What is this?" Her voice was weak, as though it had just been strangled.

Lia's eyes swam with worry and fear. She glanced at Bruno. "Go on."

Bruno scratched his head. "I don't know, sis. You had it when I found you." He strode over and extended his hand. "Someone could have heard you though. We gotta get out of here. Now."

Nassira raised her eyebrows, not taking his hand. "What do you mean someone could have heard me?"

Lia looked out past the forest, in the direction of the village. "We don't have time for this."

"You better make time," Nassira demanded.

Lia kept glancing around, fidgeting.

Bruno, talking fast and keeping his voice just above a whisper, answered, "Fifth Era men were headed for the village when I tried to find you in the storm. I almost didn't find you, but when I did you were unconscious."

Fifth Era rarely came this far from Rio. They preferred their factories in that rotting city. Nassira had worked at the elegant Hotel de Janeiro back when the city wasn't clogged with metal shops and weapons depots. She felt hesitant about what would come. She didn't like having to kill other people. It went against her soul. She instantly saw the three faces in her mind. But this was a new time. Kill the evil Fifth Era or be killed by them. "Why would they come this far?"

"We overheard a few of them," Lia said. "They were looking for something in the storm."

Nassira held up her forearm and shook it. "For this?"

Lia shrugged. "How should I know? Let's just get out of here."

Nassira wanted better answers than she was getting. "But when did I get this?"

"I don't know," Bruno hissed. "Get up. We're leaving."

Nassira cringed. She could tell Bruno was still hurt. She regretted yelling at him. Now he seemed to move as if to impress her, or to prove a point.

A twig fell from a nearby tree, silencing the three of them. Their eyes darted toward the noise. But they all relaxed, realizing it was just a fallen twig.

"What of the others?" Nassira asked.

"No idea," Bruno said.

"So they're still at the village?"

"When I went back to grab Lia and bring her here, yes, they were at the village."

Nassira scowled and looked furiously at Bruno. "So you're just going to abandon them? You didn't even warn them?"

"Be quiet! I didn't want to create panic. They would have tried to come with us and I don't even know if Fifth Era forces reached the village yet."

Nassira's head started to pound again. Her heartbeat quickened as the realization sank in. They had been safe, isolated from the outside world. The men didn't have to fight and the women weren't slaves. She was foolish to think that the peace could last forever. Her ears were ringing as blood rushed to her head. She couldn't believe how selfish they were being.

"Yet!" Nassira said viciously. "They will reach that village."

Bruno towered over her. "And we will be long gone before then."

"I won't be," Nassira spat.

"You can't go back."

Nassira wobbled upright as best she could. Her joints felt as though they had been hammered. She brought her face as close to Bruno as she could, like a wolf might challenge an alpha, but she looked so weak. The color had drained from her tan skin and her eyes were still red from the tears. "What do you mean I can't?"

"I won't allow you to."

"So you'll let them *die*?"

"Please," Lia begged, "keep your voices down."

"If you and Lia are safe," Bruno said, "then yes, their deaths mean little to me."

"What?" she said in disbelief. "Did you suddenly forget who's back there? The *sixty* hunkering in the village? Twelve of those people are younger than ten! The twins, little Caroline, Luan, Jake, Sam, Caitlin ... they're innocent! And don't forget Thiago, Katrina, Brillo, Matheus, and all the elderly back there."

Neither Bruno nor Lia said anything.

Nassira bit her cheek. "If you don't go back with me you truly are cowards."

"And you are a fool!" he growled. "You're too weak to take them on."

"And yet I'm trying harder than you are. I'll stop them on my own if I have to."

She said it confidently, but deep down she wasn't sure if she believed it.

9

THE LIGHTNING BOLT

Nassira grabbed the log and pulled her body up. Her arms shook as she brought herself over the top. Normally she could climb, sprint, and swim through the forest without much difficulty. But her body still trembled and twitched from the electrocution. She moved sluggishly, like the sloth that climbed above her.

Lia and Bruno stood over her. They heaved Nassira the rest of the way over the log. As the sun rose higher, the forest grew more lively. They walked through the sea of green to the flutter of wings, the shrieks of monkeys, and the buzz of insects. Low-hanging vines dangled like chains from the tall trees. Nassira brushed one of them aside. "How far out here were we anyway?"

"I wanted to make sure no one could see or hear you," Bruno said.

Lia whispered into Nassira's ear. "He was so worried for you."

That sent a bottomless feeling of guilt into her. She'd been cruel again to prove her point to Bruno. Nassira wanted to keep talking to keep her mind occupied. "Was that the first time I'd been shocked, or whatever?"

Nassira could feel the ground starting to slope steeper downward, though she couldn't see through the dense undergrowth.

Bruno pushed a bushel of large fern leaves out of their path. "'Bout six hours ago you had another one of those episodes." He grabbed a large, clay-colored tree limb and pushed it forward. He waited.

Nassira realized Bruno was clearing the way for Lia and her. She ducked under the leaves. "Thanks."

Bruno let go of the limb as soon as Nassira was out of the way. The tree made a *phwack* sound as it hit the plants behind them. Bruno said nothing and retook the lead.

They walked on without words, the million voices of the forest doing the talking for them.

Nassira quickly grew soaked in sweat as they descended. She wiped a few droplets from her face with the red tank top she wore. The air was moist and sticky. She glanced at her arm every few seconds to make sure that one of the pebbles didn't start glowing. That fear dwelled within her like an animal inside a cave. Nassira had kept the metal as far away from her body as possible. But as the brush grew more dense, she was worried a plant might scrape against the thing and set it off again. So she decided to cradle her arm as though it were a child.

Bruno looked off into the distance. "We're probably only about a mile from the village."

One mile was nothing on a normal day. In her state it would be much more difficult. The image of the children's innocent, skinny faces swelled into her mind. The thought of them shackled to some wall or herded into a van kept her moving. A plant snagged on Nassira's pants and she stumbled. She was about to tumble down the hill when Lia grabbed her shirt. Nassira leaned back and quickly gained her balance. She breathed a sigh of relief.

"More careful, Nass," Bruno said.

Lia grabbed Nassira's left arm and put it over her shoulder. "I got you."

Nassira was reluctant to put too much of her weight on Lia but she needed the support. "Thanks."

Through the trees, outlines of poorly-constructed wood huts started to appear in the distance. They weren't much but it was the best they could do, especially in these times. Nassira still struggled with living without electricity or running water. It was poverty compared to the one room apartment she'd grown up in. But at least she wasn't taking orders or being beaten like the people of Rio who had elected to stay.

Behind the huts stretched one of the many outlets of the Amazon River. Though Nassira couldn't see them yet she'd hoped that the fishermen would be at work by now, just like any normal day. The group would be carefully laying their traps and bait, praying they didn't encounter a school of piranha. Maybe the Fifth Era hadn't found the little oasis.

As they got closer Nassira couldn't see smoke rising from any of the huts. She couldn't decide if that was good or bad. She'd heard stories. Sometimes villages were torched immediately. That was the "humane" way. But she'd also heard crueler rumors. Sometimes they burned each house one by one, throwing people in and making others watch. She shuddered at the thought, but in her heart she knew that she would fight—and like her father, die trying—if it came to that.

It happened six years ago, when Nassira was only ten. She could still see the people in the streets, the flames, the smoke, and the rubble. She remembered holding her sister and shouting at the man with the evil look on his face—the look of a dictator. There were flashes of the moment when her father was killed. Screams and bellows. A knife. Blood. A gunshot. More blood and her father face down on the concrete and then running. So much running.

Lia's whisper brought her back to the forest. "Nassira, come on."

They had reached the edge of the small village, where the lookout buildings were. Next to the little wood shacks was the river. It looked inviting.

Bruno knelt next to some brush that looked like barbed wire. "You two go to the river and stay there till I come back. If things get bad, leave me. I'll find you again."

"Are you sure?" Lia said.

"Positive." Bruno started to get up.

"Thank you, Bruno," Nassira said.

"Yuh." He slinked to the first set of houses.

Nassira crept with Lia to the muddy river bank. Their bare feet sank in the muck.

They trucked through the sludge and slid down the bank into the lily-pad-covered shoreline. The sun had just started to peak; its rays kissed the murky brown water. There were hardly any boats out on the river. Nassira saw just one, a little white dinghy barely big enough for five people.

Something wasn't right. It was too quiet.

Nassira waded farther into the cold water so that it reached just above her belly. The rubbery green lily pads were easy to move through. Once the water had reached her chest she took a moment to take in her surroundings. To the north were the Alto Mountains. Nassira had never ventured up their dense vegetated peaks. It was rumored that there were vast quantities of lifeblood flowers there. Maybe that's where they would go to escape. Nassira tried to enjoy the view of the immense mountains against the brightening sky and the embracive tickle of the water as she waded deeper.

She held her breath, trying to relax, and she submerged. She ran her hands over her face and long hair. She brushed the back of her shoulders and then her arms. As she felt the metal, her mouth opened and water filled her lungs. She popped out of the river and coughed. Nassira clamped her mouth shut to dull the sound.

Lia looked over at her, worried.

Nassira shimmied through the water and shook her right arm in answer. She swept the water away from her eyes and looked down at the metal plate. Droplets rolled across its gleaming surface. Her heartbeat pounded twice each second. "I don't even know if this can get wet!" she whispered.

Lia's eyes grew wide.

Nassira stood as still as possible as she waited for the torture device to start glowing. Seconds seemed like days. Her eyes were attached to the metal, bound to it. She followed each of the indentations and glanced at every pebble.

No pain.

I have to be more careful, she thought. Relieved, she flipped her wet hair back. It stuck to her neck.

Crack!

A gunshot rang out from the center of the village.

Crack! Crack!

Two more.

Nassira stood on her tiptoes in the water and gazed, horrified, in the direction of the shots. Fear clouded her mind like a thick mist. The adrenaline pumped in her veins. Time seemed to freeze. Nothing moved, not the water, not the forest, not even Lia.

At an invisible signal the sisters sprang into motion. Lia took off first. She heaved herself onto the bank and disappeared behind one of the brown huts as she raced for the village center. Nassira scrambled up the muddy wall of the river bank after her sister. She clawed at the mud and part of the bank gave way. She slipped down back into the water.

"Lia, wait!" she yelled.

But Lia didn't answer. Instead a chorus of voices answered. The scared cries of outrage rose up like an eerie symphony.

Nassira tried to grab and pull her way back up the riverbank. She dug one hand into the soft mush and fell back once again. She snarled in frustration and swam farther down until the bank was easier to get up. Still furious, she scraped her way onto shore and rolled onto the grassy ground.

She popped to her feet, trying to make out some of the shouted words. *"Stop!"* seemed to be a crowd favorite.

What pain Nassira felt earlier had now disappeared. She still felt the aches and throbbing, but she let fear overpower her body. She pumped her arms, matching each step with her breath. She pictured Bruno facedown beside her father. It couldn't happen. He wouldn't be dead. She would reach the center and he'd be alive. He'd be smiling.

She leapt past the piles of wood next to Cici's house. Where was Lia? She could only be a few minutes ahead of her. A crowd of people blocked her view of the town center: a clearing with a small stage and a fire pit. The people shouted obscenities until another burst of gunfire went off. Everyone grew silent.

The shot came from a man Nassira recognized as Jaisen, Rio's self-proclaimed "governor". He was dressed in an all-black suit and stood beside eight gruff-looking men in battle gear. They stood atop a wooden stage that rose six feet above the ground. Each of the Fifth Era members carried machine guns. Jaisen had a golden tie that matched his glinting gold earrings. He stood above the rest on a raised box on the platform. His face was contorted into the smile of a madman and his grey eyes were bright with a vengeful fury. He held a large silver pistol in one hand and something else in the other. Nassira couldn't quite tell what.

Nassira pushed her way through the crowd, ignoring the murmurs and whispers.

Jaisen's voice boomed, "This is what happens when you flee! When you try to fend for yourselves!" He pointed to something at his feet with the pistol.

Nassira couldn't quite see yet as she jostled her way forward. The people started to part before her. Someone whispered, "I'm so sorry Nass."

"I don't ask for much," Jaisen continued. "I supply Rio, a whole damn city, with food, clothes, and housing. And yet, you think yourselves better! You think you're special?" He shook his free hand and someone roared in pain. A fear crept into Nassira. She recognized the scream.

Nassira finally emerged from the crowd and Jaisen's venomous eyes fell on her. Everyone's eyes fell on her. But Nassira could only stare in horror at the stage. Jaisen held Bruno's brown hair in his fist.

Lia yelled at him to stop while Bruno grimaced in pain. Three bodies lay on the stage. There was a man face down in the right corner. A woman lay on her back near the third dead man. Their bodies made Nassira sick. Each of their lifeless forms lay at Jaisen's feet. Their skin was coated with blood, gash marks strewn about their backs as though they'd been whipped. One of the men had a ghostly white face, which lay at an unnatural angle, twisted back to the sky. She just couldn't wrap her brain around the idea that these innocent lives had been stamped out.

"Ah, the final Arujo family member emerges. We had posters up for you in Rio, you know. You were quite the hot topic around town for how you smuggled those children out of the city. I'm surprised you managed to last this long out here. No matter, you're just in time to see the death of your brother." Jaisen smiled, revealing pearly white teeth.

"*No!*" she screamed. She moved closer to the stage.

"Ah, you don't want to join the others, now do you?" he taunted. Two guards aimed their rifles down at Nassira.

Nassira stared up into the barrels and said, "I'll do anything!"

Jaisen smiled. "I know you will." The calm in his voice was frightening. He clicked the safety off of the pistol. Bruno closed his eyes and Lia cried out in fear.

"Please … *no!*" Nassira yelled.

He looked down at her as though she were a bug. She was pitiful and he could crush her at any moment. He then looked out at the crowd. "Let this be a lesson," he said.

Lia continued to cry.

Nassira's heart sank. She looked desperately to the sky. She wanted to scream, to do something, but she couldn't. She would watch as this man put a bullet into her brother's head.

Jaisen continued, "Each of you will understand who's in charge here." He gestured to the man on the far right of the stage. "I can take your fathers."

The words bit into her soul. Maybe if she leapt forward fast enough she could knock the guard on stage off balance.

Jaisen wagged the pistol at the dead women. "I can take your mothers."

Once the man was knocked off balance she'd still have to wrestle the gun from him. But how would she climb the stage? It wouldn't work.

"I can take your uncles."

Nassira wished Jaisen would feel the pain she felt earlier. The force of a billion volts pulsing through his veins. Anger filled her up and she noticed that the pebbles around her forearm plate had started to glow again. Nassira ignored the thing and stared back into Jaisen's menacing eyes. Their gazes were locked.

"And…" he laughed cruelly.

Nassira's whole right side started to prickle.

"I can take your brothers." He started to lower the gun against Bruno's temple.

"No!" Nassira thundered. She thrust her right hand forward. The stinging immediately intensified and a bolt of lightning exploded from her palm. Nassira watched the yellow-white jet crackle forward and collide with Jaisen. The electricity engulfed him and tossed his form from the stage. He hit the ground on the other side of the platform with a muffled thud.

The world had become silent again. It was the feeling of a storm about to break, that moment when sky seemed to hold its breath before unleashing its fury. Nassira stared at her still-outstretched hand unable to comprehend what she'd just done. She let her eyes drift across the slack-jawed Fifth Era guards.

Bruno stood up on the stage. He mouthed the word, "*Run.*"

10

CONNECTIONS OF POWER

Interstate 5
San Diego, California, United States

The Hummer reached the crest of the hill and the glittering Pacific Ocean appeared again on the horizon. Its beaches were crowded, bogged down by the dozen or so army bases, and the three Naval shipyards. Kaiba saw San Diego Bay in the distance. There were ships in the water ranging from aircraft carriers littered with jets and helicopters to the plump transportation vessels that he would probably board tomorrow. Battleships large and small bobbed in the harbors, being restocked and reloaded. Behind the bustling UNM forces stood the city of San Diego. Mighty skyscrapers rose to the heavens as though trying to pierce the few clouds that hung in the polluted sky. Thick black smoke rose up from weapon, tank, and armor manufacturing plants scattered throughout the city.

As the hill flattened out, they were driving practically right by the beach. They passed the first base, Star of Diego, which appeared forged from steel. Multitudes of Hummers peeled in through the barbed wire gating. They ferried the fresh seventeen-year-olds from the vehicles like sheep. Each of the bases were spaced four or five miles apart all the way down the coastline. Between each base stood the towering railcannon defense turrets. They looked like monstrous tripod cameras with long, flat gun barrels attached to them.

"Pretty impressive, huh?" Aaron asked.

Kaiba didn't say anything so Aaron answered himself.

"One of the biggest joint Naval-Army forces in the western hemisphere. Those railcannons are capable of launching steel and explosive projectiles at Mach ten. If the virtaiyu ever come knocking on our door they'll be biting off more than they can chew." Aaron chuckled to himself and continued, "Yeah, it took a year of around-the-clock work, but I'd say it was worth it. These babies cost more money than the US could spare, but in the first year of the war all people wanted was security. These gun batteries helped to provide that. The railcannons were initially concentrated in areas with high populations, but now they practically stretch from the edge of California to just below the Washington-Canada border."

Kaiba already knew that. Battle schools loved to talk about the railcannon technology and apparently, so did their officers.

As they drove closer to the first railcannon, Kaiba realized it was even larger than he'd expected. The shiny pewter metal must have been thirty feet high and each of the three support legs twice that thick. He wondered how the coast would have looked untouched by these metal giants.

It had taken eight hours and forty-five minutes to get from Pinecrest to San Diego. Kaiba had fallen asleep twice and they had only stopped once to go to the bathroom. He watched the road in front of them peel away as they passed base after base. A pair of seagulls scavenged in the middle of their path.

"Stupid gulls," Lieutenant Aaron growled. He sped forward, forcing the sea birds to take flight. "No better than rats. Let me tell you guys something—" and he started off on another rant. Little did he realize that Jordan was still sleeping.

Kaiba looked out the window, ignoring him, nervously trying to preoccupy his mind from what was to come. Would he become a government test soldier? Or would he be killed and stripped of the device? The way he saw it, no good could come of the plate on his chest. Kaiba watched the clouds above drift like ghosts in the sky. He regretted ever touching the sphere.

They drove for several minutes following the traffic. The towering buildings of San Diego threatened to block out the sunlight. They passed boarded-up windows of long-abandoned shops, but for every failed business there were two more thriving ones. The Hummers rolled through the streets and reached the San Diego-Coronado Bridge. Some called it the Ocean's Walkway. The two mile, 200 foot tall, pre-stressed bridge rose above the ocean like a giant. It sloped out over the bay at eighty degrees to North Island and the Coronado base. A tank rolled on the opposite side of the bridge back to San Diego. It was the only vehicle Kaiba had seen that wasn't a Humvee. They turned left after crossing the bridge when their Hummer screeched to a stop, throwing Kaiba against the seat in front of him and jostling Jordan from his slumber.

"Didn't realize there would be a line," Aaron said. "Welcome to the Hammer of Coronado."

It was the biggest base they'd come across, dwarfing the others. A long stretch of Hummers trickled forward through the barbed steel gate like ants returning to the hive. The base was composed of four story barracks aligned in three rows of fourteen. Armories, training facilities, vehicle depots, gun ranges, and helipads were scattered amongst the barracks. Naval docks lined the glittering water of the bay.

Kaiba watched the armed guards overseeing the convoys and ushering them forward.

It took some time, but they finally made it through and Aaron soon pulled up to one of the barracks. It had a big red star above the main doorway.

"Well," he said. "This is where we'll get situated."

Several other vehicles had parked outside the barracks and other grim-faced boys stepped out.

Kaiba was quick to hold Jordan back before they entered the building.

He kept his voice low. "What do we do about our ... armor?"

"Play it cool. They won't know if we don't show," Jordan said.

They walked through the door of the barracks and Kaiba's heart sank. As though they'd entered an airport, a line of people marched through a metal detector.

Kaiba shot Jordan a nervous glance.

Jordan's eyes bounced back and forth as he watched the other boys filing through the detectors.

A soldier with a buzz cut kept the line moving. Aaron was the first to go through. The soldier looked at him and asked, "You packin', Aaron?"

Aaron withdrew a curved knife and a black pistol. He handed them to the man.

The soldier nodded and Aaron stepped through. A green light blipped and his weapons were returned to him.

Kaiba's mind raced. They would be discovered right here, in the middle of all these people. Punished by death for having Virt technology.

"Step forward," the soldier said.

Kaiba stared at him but did nothing. His breath felt heavy and his legs wouldn't work right.

"I won't ask again. Step forward!"

Kaiba looked back at Jordan, who appeared just as frightened. He had no other option. He took a baby step forward then hurried through the gate.

The green light blipped.

Kaiba couldn't believe it.

"Next!" the soldier shouted. Jordan also walked through safely and patted Kaiba lightly on the back. He had a big smile on his face, like a child at Christmas.

Kaiba couldn't understand how the machine hadn't detected the plate on his chest... unless it wasn't made of metal. Either way, he didn't care. They were both safe, at least for now.

They met their eight squad mates. Kaiba was horrible with names and didn't even bother trying to memorize them. The group marched with Aaron and they received their uniforms: identical camouflage and brown boots, and a vest under their combat uniforms that Aaron called Liquid Armor—black cloth with small pockets of fluid woven into the upper chest and stomach. Kaiba was careful to change facing the lockers so no one would see his chest. When he slipped the vest on he couldn't feel the fluid through the sphere-plate already embedded into his chest. After changing, Aaron led them to a room the size of a basketball gym. Two hundred other men stood at ready position, hands behind their backs, looking attentively forward. A middle aged man stood waiting at the front of the room. He wore sharp angled glasses that rested on the tip of his skinny nose, and he stopped adjusting the collar of his pink shirt as Aaron and the others lined up at the back of the room. They were the last group to show up.

"G'day, men!" the man said in a heavy Australian accent. He certainly wasn't a soldier, Kaiba knew that for sure. "I am Mr. Sursten."

His voice echoed around the room through the speakers. "I suspect you are interested in the fluid material you are all wearing. Case ya care, I invented 'em." He smiled. "Let's test 'em out. Pair up!"

The crowd of soldiers moved and Kaiba partnered with Jordan. They were told to spar with one another, punches only. Kaiba quickly regretted choosing Jordan, until he learned that the fluid of the cloth hardened to match the strength of the impact. When Jordan hit Kaiba's shoulder the liquid went rigid and Jordan's hand stung.

Sursten let them practice several minutes before ordering everyone to stop. He told them the liquid in the vest was composed of a nano-superfluid that would stop any sniper shot, but it was ineffective against rapidly repeated impacts. He warned them not to rely on the armor and to remain careful out on the battlefield. When Sursten left, they were taught several formations, drilled on military formality, marching, and were questioned about any specific talents. Kaiba was surprised at the amount of people who had experience with ships and planes. They were most likely to be thrust into the Air Force and Navy. Ever since the draft started no one volunteered for the Navy or Air Force, they were chosen during Shipment.

After the mini training session Kaiba and Jordan were told they had the rest of the night off. They were to report the next morning at 05:00. They decided to grab dinner from an elderly woman selling hot dogs, Cade's favorite food. They spent what little money they had and found a bench that overlooked the ocean. It sat on the outskirts of the base and from what Kaiba saw no one came this far out. The sun had started to set and clouds of pink and orange spilled into the sea-blue sky.

Kaiba wrestled with the anger inside of him as he ate the hot dog, thinking of his younger brother. He couldn't hold back the anger that swept over him. He looked at the scattered rocks at his feet as the feeling of adrenaline began to flow through his veins. He held out his hand and focused on a large, egg-shaped rock. He visualized it between his fists and squeezed. The rock started to crumble and crack as Kaiba pressed his fingers tighter. The rock popped with the sound of a firecracker.

Jordan set his hand on Kaiba's shoulder.

Kaiba released his grip and panted. He caught his breath and said, "I'll never get to see Cade grow up."

"That's not true."

"It isn't right that they can strip us from our families. The UNM doesn't own people, even though they act like it."

"I think you're mad at the wrong thing," Jordan said. "It's the virtaiyu's fault that we're even in this position."

Kaiba knew he was right, but it didn't make him any less angry.

"I know you're pissed off. I am too. But some day I want to go back to our hometown and have it still be there. Families back with their fathers, husbands back with their wives. I want a world that's safe so that my mother doesn't have to live in constant fear."

"I want that for Cade," Kaiba said, looking at Jordan for the first time.

"Then you fight like hell out there for him. Neither of us knows what the future will hold, and these spheres only complicate things. But whenever your back is against the wall you do whatever you have to so he has a chance to live in the world you and I grew up in. I see Shipment as our chance to make a difference. I'll have your back out there. That has to count for something."

Kaiba nodded and said, "Thanks, Jordan."

"Don't mention it. When I saw you manipulating rock in public it made me think you could use a little pep talk."

Kaiba scratched his head. "Can't argue with that."

They sat as the sun lowered itself against the sky, taking in a beautiful thing in a world full of violence.

Kaiba stretched out and let his mind wander. "I still think it's strange that we were never told much about elemental manipulation. Maybe they didn't even know about the spheres."

"If Taniel knew about them, then so did the UNM. They just don't want us to know."

"How can you be so sure?"

"I can't be."

An idea started to form in Kaiba's head. "Then let's find out on our own. Doesn't your sister work for part of the intelligence sector here?"

"Not much of a sister, but yes she does."

"Let's use her to get to the archives. They have to have classified information that isn't shared in schools."

"You're willing to risk walking straight into an intelligence sector? What if she finds out about our spheres?"

"I don't see any other options. This is our best bet to see if the UNM left anything out regarding the spheres."

Jordan didn't look pleased. "I'll come with, but I wouldn't expect much out of her. She's never been reliable in the past."

They asked upper officers about the intelligence and surveillance building and found it without too much trouble. They were questioned immediately upon walking into the multistory complex. Kaiba lied about wanting to review military tactics and weapons and somehow his bluff worked. They were directed to the fourth floor.

It was awkward to see her sitting all alone, like a CEO waiting for a nervous intern. She'd made advances on Kaiba when they were younger and he'd rejected her each time. It wasn't that she wasn't pretty, with her long blonde hair, big brown eyes, and athletic body. Lots of guys were interested. But the fact that she was Jordan's older sister made her advances both weird and uncomfortable.

Kaiba walked to the desk. "Kate."

She returned the nod and the short greeting. "Kaiba."

"You know why we're here?"

"The front desk inquired, but I'd like to hear it from you. Best keep this short, I have plenty of other things I'd rather be doing."

"We need access to the EVE."

Kate pursed her lips. "The Electronic Virtaiyu Exo-database isn't for grunts."

"I realize that, but we'd really like to review some things before tomorrow."

"That's no concern of mine," she said, swiveling back and forth in her chair. "You should have paid closer attention in battle school."

"Just let us see it," Jordan said sternly.

She looked him up and down as though they had never met. If the two didn't share similar facial features there would have been no real reason to believe they were siblings.

She scowled. "I'm not at liberty to give you access."

"For once in your stuck up life help me out for no other reason than I'm asking you to."

Kate leaned forward and rested her chin on her clasped hands. "We are related only by name."

Jordan slammed his hands on the front desk, causing a pencil holder to topple over. Kate jumped.

"Let us in or I'll just take your AxS card."

She let out a cackle of a laugh. "You've never hit me in your life."

"Not while our parents were around I didn't," Jordan said. His entire chest leaned on the front desk so that he towered over her.

Part of Kaiba actually wanted to see Jordan deck her, but he didn't get the chance.

Kate's eye twitched and when she realized Jordan was serious she said, "I can give you thirty minutes. That's all my card grants anyway." She took the necklace around her neck and released the AxS card.

Jordan ripped it away without saying a word.

Kate stood up and came out from behind her desk. "Follow me and act like you belong here."

They walked down the narrow passageway, passing only two men in black business suits. The men eyed them suspiciously, but said nothing. Kaiba's footsteps echoed against the granite, making the space seem larger than it actually was. Kate led them to an all-black door without a handle at the far end of another hall. She placed her palm on the door and the black surface of the door turned a frosty blue. Beside her manicured nails appeared a small white outline in the shape of a rectangle.

"Card, Jordan," Kate said.

Jordan placed the card in the space.

The door beeped and rose into the ceiling like a garage door, to reveal nothing but darkness.

Kate stepped in first and the white tiles at her feet glowed with bright fluorescent light. Each step caused another tile to glow until a chain reaction occurred. Like fire spreading from tree to tree the tiles burst to light in a circular pattern around the room, stretching up the walls and onto the ceiling. When all the panels were illuminated it was evident that the room was a perfect circle made up of nothing but white tile. The space was empty except for a single stand in the center of the room, which Kate strode up to. It had a touch pad that Kate tapped with her middle finger. The white tiles on the wall in front of them turned black, then glowed with hundreds of shaking blue lines.

"Welcome Katherine and guests. I am EVE." It was a mechanical female voice that sent a shiver through Kaiba. The lines on the wall fluctuated to match EVE's voice, "How may I be of assistance?"

"My guests have questions for you."

"And I have answers."

"I didn't know you would be here with us," Kaiba said to Kate.

"Protocol," she said flatly.

Kaiba looked nervously at EVE's voice pattern on the wall, which was a flat line at the moment. He thought about how he could phrase his question without raising Kate's suspicion.

"Can you display Virtaiyan weaponry?"

"Certainly." The panels on the walls of the room dimmed. "Here are all known sonics." The space to the left of EVE's voice glowed again as twenty-five rifles and pistols appeared. They shimmered in 3D blue light, seemingly extruding from the walls. Kaiba walked closer, recognizing most variants of the sonic rifles and echo repeaters. He'd only seen one sonic rifle fired in person and the destructive sound waves it produced managed to destroy the concrete wall of a building. He spotted several single shot burst pistols, and even a vortex cannon that must have been twice his height. He'd seen the standard-issue weapons many times, but they were not what he was looking for.

"Anything you wish to review in particular? I can bring up specific schematics if you so wish."

Kaiba acted like he was about to ask something and then stood silent for a moment. It was strange for him to see the weapons bathed in varying shades of blue light. "You know I was thinking more along the lines of virtaiyu *non*-standard issue weapons."

"Of course, my mistake," EVE said. The wall of sonic weapons faded and were immediately replaced with different shimmering blue guns. "These are the known fire-based weapons." There were far fewer guns, which Kaiba hadn't seen before. "Flameshots and lumoburst-based arms are rarer amongst virtaiyu and are normally utilized by unit leaders, specifically kinesis prone individuals."

Kaiba was unsure of where to look so he kept his eyes locked on the vocal movements. "And what is a kinesis prone individual?"

"Katherine, do they have adequate clearance for all information?"

Jordan shot his sister a dirty look.

"They are fresh Shipment recruits," Kate said.

"Then they will learn soon enough," EVE said.

"Can't you spare just a simple definition?" Jordan asked.

"I cannot."

"I'd like them to know," Kate said.

"Very well Miss Katherine. A kinesis prone virtaiyu has the ability to manipulate the elements."

More panels flickered and the shadowed form of a virtaiyu stood by a river. It moved its hands, and water from the river rose.

Kaiba was excited and fearful at the same time. So it wasn't just earth; water could be manipulated also. The UNM had known after all.

"And how does one become kinesis prone?" Jordan asked.

"Current knowledge suggests it is a genetic trait."

"There is no other way to gain the trait?" Kaiba asked. He waited, but EVE didn't answer. "Can armor or any sphere-shaped equipment confer this ability?"

The lines on the wall were still for too long. "Unknown."

Kaiba was unconvinced. It was a computer after all, but her voice sounded like she was lying. He looked back at the wall with the flame weapons. A small rounded object caught his eye. He touched the light of the ball and asked, "What is this sphere?"

Another series of panels flashed and pulled the ball up. It was magnified so that it was larger than Kaiba. Various notes were typed all around it. Its surface was jagged and Kaiba was disappointed.

"These are molton grenades," EVE said. "They contain enough heat to melt through four feet of titanium."

"Do the virtaiyu use any other sphere-shaped equipment? Perhaps that can be molded or changed into armor?"

Again EVE was slow to respond. "You are referring to the Terraform Keys." A single red orb appeared where the molton grenade had been. It looked exactly like the sphere Kaiba had found only colored a deep red instead of white.

"Yes," Kaiba said, gazing with hope at the ball.

Kate stepped closer to the perfect sphere. "What is that?"

"The seven Terraform Keys were recovered in—"

The lights clapped off and then back on but EVE's vocal lines and the picture of the object were gone.

The clack clack of high heels came from the doorway.

"Who are these men?" asked a woman with large round glasses and short, choppy red hair.

"Jami..." Kate said as she watched her walk into the room. "My brother and his friend. They were just leaving."

"As they should, it's getting late. Learn anything of interest?" she said, glancing from Jordan to Kaiba.

Kaiba was sweating. He couldn't help it. "Just needed a quick review before tomorrow."

"A wise thing to do."

"Thanks for ... um ... letting us use the facility," Jordan stammered.

Kaiba grabbed him and they hurried out of the room. They didn't stop even when Jami called to them. Rather than wait for an elevator they ran down the stairwell.

"I knew the UNM was hiding something!" Kaiba exclaimed as they burst back outside.

"Water is another element, and if we can control earth what else can be controlled?" Jordan asked.

Kaiba hustled to pound on the crosswalk button at the street intersection that led back to the barracks. "If they have fire-based weaponry I think it's a safe bet that can be controlled as well."

"We'll have to find out. And why are they called Terraform Keys?"

The walk symbol flashed. Kaiba could hear the rumbling of a car engine. He looked up to see a yellow convertible speeding forward and they hustled across the street. His skin prickled as they reached the halfway point of the intersection. The car was coming too fast and not slowing down.

Kaiba looked at the car and his head spun. He felt dizzy and for a moment the world around him changed. He was in a forest, with people all around him. There were men with weapons on a stage.

He blinked rapidly, worried he was hallucinating. The forest disappeared as though he'd imagined it and he was back on the crosswalk. He shouted at the driver. But it didn't matter, the car kept coming.

Kaiba's body felt as though it was being punctured by hundreds of needles.

It happened as a reflex.

He threw his hand up at the car when it was only a few feet away. As he threw his hand forward a thunderous cracking sound split the air and a stream of electricity burst from his palm.

The driver looked up just as the bolt of lightning struck the convertible. The yellow voltage sparked about the exterior, then jumped to the driver. He held the steering wheel and swerved off the road, colliding with a lamp post.

Kaiba could only stare in horror at the power that had just lurched from his hand.

Kaiba rushed back across the street to discover that the driver was Mr. Sursten. The man's face was cut and his legs looked crumpled. Two ambulances rolled up. Medics descended on the crushed convertible shouting to one another about how to save the man's life. They immediately grabbed the Jaws of Life, a massive pair of metal cutters, to remove Mr. Sursten from the car. Kaiba had to steady himself as he walked up to the first paramedic he saw.

"Will he live?" Kaiba breathed.

The woman wore a blue medical uniform. "Stand back."

"Please, I have to know. Will he live?"

Two other paramedics had just laid Sursten onto a stretcher. His legs were mangled, twisted in unnatural angles.

"We don't know yet. We will do everything we can, but we can't do our job unless you let us. But please stand ba—"

"Courtney, I need a defibrillator!"

The woman turned to help the others. They ripped Mr. Sursten's shirt from his skinny body and checked for a heartbeat. Courtney brought forward a pack with two handles. The man who looked in charge rubbed the paddles together and slammed them against Mr. Sursten's chest. His body heaved, but still he lay limp.

The paramedics repeated the shocking twice more until the lead paramedic appeared satisfied.

Jordan walked up. "He'll be fine, Kaiba."

Kaiba watched as the paramedics wheeled Mr. Sursten to the first ambulance. The gurney came right past Kaiba, forcing him to look at the body of the man he'd nearly killed. His clothes were shredded and his body riddled with cuts. His legs were hard to look at, bloodied and broken. But it was his face, tinged black with burn marks, that Kaiba had the most difficulty looking at.

Kaiba looked down at his own hands as though they were a monster's claws. He couldn't understand how the bolt had been unleashed and he was battling with the voice in his head over the idea that maybe he had meant to kill the man. Surely he didn't mean to do it, but this body seemed to sway Kaiba's mind. This man was innocent, cut down at the hands of a horrible accident, cut down by his own hands.

"That's them!" someone shouted.

He turned to see Jami, the woman from the EVE room, on the street corner yelling at a Humvee that had just pulled up.

Four soldiers stepped out and aimed their rifles on Kaiba and Jordan. "Freeze!" one of them shouted.

Jordan stepped back, alarmed.

"Hands on your head or we will fire!" another one of the soldiers ordered.

Jordan looked as if he was about to attack, but he raised his hands above his head. Kaiba did likewise, too much in shock not to obey. He couldn't get over the fact that he might have murdered a man.

The soldiers crept forward. "On the ground!"

The boys dropped to their knees, slowly interlocking their hands behind their heads. The soldiers handcuffed them and threw them into the Humvee.

The whole bumpy ride Kaiba couldn't take his eyes off his hands. He kept picturing the man's face, and his limp body. *How can I live with myself?* Kaiba thought.

11

The Ides Of Australia

Newport Bay, Australia
(32 km from Sydney)

The glass door slid shut behind Emily and the bright light of the afternoon blinded her for a moment as she stepped outside. She raised her hand to shield her eyes from the intense glow.

Through the specks of light the Australian coast materialized before her. She let the warmth of the sun diffuse into her for a moment, testing the temperature. It was much hotter than she'd originally anticipated. She scowled at the heat and walked around the outside of the Olympic-sized pool. She paused, glancing back at the head of the water where the ornate statue of Neptune stood atop a raised platform. It was elegant, of well-crafted marble and of course expensive. Normally she would have heard the rush of water as it fell from the Greek god's outstretched trident and against the rocks that fed into the pool.

A beefy woman balanced at the top of the statue, a wrench in her hand. She glistened in the baking sun like a freshly cooked ham.

Emily saw the strain of concentration on her face as she tried to fix whatever was wrong with the thing.

Emily descended the marble steps and grabbed her surfboard from the shed at the side of the house. "House" was a bit of an understatement. In fact her family's dwelling resembled more a palace. Five stories tall, the Sursten family mansion was the biggest in Newport and certainly one of the largest in all of Australia. It was also one of the most beautiful—white frame supported on Corinthian style pillars and black tiled roofing. Not to mention that no two of the walls were the same. Each had been handcrafted works of art from the finest French and Greek artists. Architects often came to gawk at the horrendously lavish estate, but that was before the war. In the 'Grouse days', as her father called them.

Emily still wasn't quite sure what her father had invented to create this life of luxury. Multiple pieces of advanced military technology, that much she knew. A locator? Maybe armor? Or a tracking device? She tried to remember, unable to find the right object in her memory. The more she thought, the more troubled she grew. The thought of her dad made her sick with worry. Sure, he wasn't on the frontlines in India or the Middle East, but the world was different now, more dangerous nearly everywhere. She had begged him not to go to the military base in California, but he said they insisted. Once he was called he never said no.

Now she was stuck at home, which wasn't bad. She took care of scheduling immigration flights to the Americas, utilizing the three family-owned jets. People were easy enough to get along with over the phone. In person it was a different story. It was trivial having to deal with so many people and Emily often yearned to do more. The war raged, yet she just sat in the luxury of her home, not having to work too often or do much of anything for that matter. Certainly very few nineteen-year-olds received that privilege nowadays.

Her white phone bleeped. Devon's tan face appeared on the flat, transparent screen, with his text message: Where r u?

Emily slid her finger across the smooth surface. A digital keyboard flashed open. She tapped the keys, O, M, W and the words *On my way* appeared.

She pocketed the device back in her swim shorts and flung the board over her shoulder. The grass tickled her bare feet as she strode through the backyard, a sweeping meadowed hill that led to the flat beach, and she saw the ocean stretch for miles before her. She reached the silver gate and opened it.

Sammy barked behind her. The Labrador's golden tail wagged happily. Her tongue drooped from her mouth like a slimy pink slug.

Emily walked through the gate. "All right girl. C'mon."

Sammy trotted forward and the two stepped onto the great white sands of Newport Beach. Emily remembered when surfies, people who surfed more than they worked, practically lived on the beach. It was nearly impossible to get a spot on the sand, let alone catch a wave in the ocean.

She walked a ways toward the suburbs, closer to town. She heard a child cry out from the streets. Emily watched as the little boy attempted to lead his mother through the tight bars of the steel fence and to the ocean. She saw the frustration on the mother's face as she scolded her child. Emily hadn't gotten used to the idea that her family owned the beach now. When the town proposed the buy to Emily's father last year, he thought it was a joke. Clearly they desperately needed some cash.

Sammy rolled in the sand, kicking up a cloud of yellow. Emily bent down to rub the dog's belly and then looked out at the glittering waves of the Australian Ocean. She could hear the grumbling voice of the sea. Emily stood mesmerized and tried to match her breath with the breathing of the waves. She breathed in as the waves receded and out as they crashed upon the white sands. The sea had a nurturing effect on her, and had ever since she was a little girl.

A gull squawked, breaking her sense of tranquility. She followed the bird as it glided on a warm updraft toward the sea. Then she spotted Devon near the water's edge. He sat on a large piece of driftwood, a surfboard on his lap. He waved. His bare muscular body rippled like gold in the sunlight.

She waved back and quickened her pace. Then she slowed back down, self-conscious that he might have noticed her walking faster. The last thing she wanted was Devon to suspect that she was excited to see him. After all, it was just another day of surfing in the daylight. But even those wouldn't continue. It pained her to know that Devon would leave to fight soon, just like every other male. He was lucky to have dodged the draft the first time around, but no eighteen-year-old had ever managed to get past two rounds of draft numbers. The sad thing was they both knew it and neither could bear to admit it.

Devon looked up from waxing his red, eight-foot board. "Glad you could make it."

She smiled. "Had to fight Mama Sursten off."

Emily stuck her own board into the sand and tied her long blonde hair up. It felt grimy to the touch. She made a mental note to wash it later.

"More problems?" Devon asked. He stood and clapped the chunks of wax from his hands.

"Nah, she just wanted to go boating today is all."

"Hmm." Devon picked up a small piece of driftwood and hurled it off in the distance. Sammy sprang into action and leapt after the stick as though it were a live cat.

Emily dared to skim her eyes over Devon's thick chest and defined abs. She was reminded of the Neptune statue in her pool. He looked as if chiseled from the same stone.

He patted the dog, and threw the stick again. "Why'd you say no?"

Emily shrugged. "Didn't feel like going on the yacht I guess."

He laughed. "Right, I forgot how difficult an adventure on that ship must be."

There was no such thing as an "adventure" with her family, especially her mother. Emily threw her phone and shirt into the sand. She adjusted her bikini top and grabbed her board. "It's not the ship that's the problem, it's the mother."

Devon grabbed his board and the two walked to the surf. "Your oldy isn't that bad, Em. 'Sides, your mom's pretty cute." He winked.

"Gross!" She hit him on the shoulder with her surfboard. "If you lived with her you wouldn't think so. But if you think you can stand her, maybe we will go on the boat later."

"Is that a formal invite, Miss Emily?"

She smirked. "I never ask twice."

They stepped into the foaming waters. In the heat, the ocean felt like ice against Emily's skin. She shuddered as the water rose to her waist. Goosebumps sprang up on her arms and neck like tiny icebergs. It felt like a breath of fresh air for her whole body.

What looked to be a good-sized wave started to form in the distance.

"Dibs!" Emily exclaimed. She pushed her stomach onto the board.

"I would have insisted that you go first anyway, Richie." Devon smiled again.

Emily scowled as she paddled into the upsurge. She hated that nickname. She'd always been embarrassed as a kid that her family was one of the richest on the planet. She'd accepted her wealth, but the name still bothered her.

She dug her arms into the water and propelled forward like a torpedo. Her board bounced up and over each rift in the water. The whole while she kept her eyes locked on her wave. The crest of the water started to rise. Emily turned her board so it was parallel to the surf. Just as it surged forward, she hopped up on both legs.

Every time she caught a wave, it felt like flying. She was weightless for that instant the water carried her.

Emily tilted the board right by adjusting her weight. She tasted the salt of the sea, and felt the kiss of the wind on her skin. Beads of water flew as she glided her hand along the roiling ocean.

The blue started to curl over the top of her. She ducked slightly, putting most of her weight to the front. She sped up, the wave crashing behind her. The rushing water caused her to drift almost all the way back to shore.

Not bad for the first wave of the day.

She checked to make sure Sammy was still on the coast. The dog sat halfway down the beach pawing at a dead crab. Worry alleviated, she jumped off the board. A forest of bubbles surrounded her. She watched the spheres of air rise and ascended with them, helping herself to a fresh breath of the sky.

Emily pulled herself back atop her wave carver.

"Not bad, Richie," Devon yelled from the distance.

She threw up her hands, daring Devon to show her up.

Surprisingly, he did. He caught a ten foot swell, gliding across the water like an ice skater. He twisted his body and launched off the crest of the wave. In midair he grabbed the tip of his board and fell perfectly back onto the surf, a rare good showing for Devon.

Emily knew he would never admit it, but she was a better surfer than he was. Even so she'd always been jealous of his graceful power, which just seemed to come naturally. The ocean controlled most people. It controlled Emily through fear for a while, but Devon moved as though he alone controlled the waves. She wished she possessed the same natural trait instead of having to practice and work to hone her skills.

Devon dived into the water, and came up pretty close to Emily. His mouth was full of sea water.

Emily raised her hands in front of her face. "Don't even."

Devon's eyebrows bounced up and down. He spit a stream of water at her.

Emily gasped as the water hit her face. She cupped her hands and splashed him several times. He splashed back and they laughed together, Emily feeling like a kid again. He had that effect on her. Droplets dripped from his thick brown hair and onto his shoulders. Her eyes met his glimmering green ones for an instant.

She looked away.

The pair paddled back into the Australian Ocean. She tried to concentrate on the next wave but her mind wandered to Devon. She often wondered what it would be like if they took their friendship one step further. A lot of people just got married before the guys were shipped off. She thought of the bonfire that Kristen held two summers ago. The game they played and the feeling of Devon's lips on hers. It would be pretty much the same if they were married, she was sure of it. But it just felt too soon. The war created a sense of rushing things and she couldn't fight the feeling that gnawed at her soul. If he didn't feel the same way, their closeness would be risked. Almost every day the two surfed on the ocean. Laughing and talking, oblivious to the world around them. His presence soothed her. Other than when Devon talked about other girls, leaving her too afraid to initiate anything. Still, she couldn't help thinking his words seemed somewhat empty when he spoke of the others. She clung to that hope tighter than anything she ever had. But the hands of time were growing shorter.

Emily cut across another wave and laughed when Devon fell on his next surf. They rode the water for a couple of hours until Emily felt the twinges of hunger in her belly. "Lunch?"

"You know I'm down. Will Maid Marian be cooking?"

Marian had once been Emily's nanny.

Emily shook the water from her hair as they paddled in. "I'll have to ask."

"Sammy!" Emily yelled as she picked up her phone and dialed. The dog came running from down the beach.

Marian answered, "Yes, Miss Emily."

"Is it okay if Devon swings in for lunch?"

"I'm preparing as we speak. Any requests?"

Emily tilted her head to Devon, but he said nothing. "No thanks Mare."

"Loves, dear." The phone clicked as she hung up.

When they arrived back at the house Emily could smell the alluring wisps of barbequed meat and fish. Marian had set up a huge buffet on the second floor balcony. The old woman waved as they approached. Emily smiled and waved back, thinking of how amazing Marian was.

They put their boards in the shed and came into the house on the first floor. The smell of freshly marinated beef met her at the door. It was a nice change from the overpowering vanilla scent that had attached itself to every room. She took off her sandals and led Devon through the white tiles to the staircase.

Emily stopped at the second floor. "Pick me somethin' good, I gotta talk to my mom."

Devon gave a little bow. "Will that be all, Miss Emily?"

She rolled her eyes and walked up the stairs to the third floor. She paused when she heard her mother laugh. She heard the voice of a man. Rather confused she went to her mother's bedroom.

They were mid kiss when Emily walked in. Blood pulsed to her face. "Mom?"

The man with thick graying hair looked at Emily with a panicked look in his blue eyes.

Emily's mother's sandy brown hair was nearly as messy as her orange sundress. Her black eye shadow was even messier, smeared everywhere like paint. They stared at one another for a moment.

Emily rushed from the room, her head full of fury.

Her mother called, "Emily, wait!"

But she was already on the second floor. She could hear footsteps behind her, but she walked out onto the deck anyway. Devon looked up from the buffet as the glass door slammed shut. "Are you okay?"

Emily ignored him; she couldn't find any words. Even if she could they would have emerged from her lips as yells and cries. She looked at the endless quantities of food arranged in front of her. Succulent shrimps as big as her palms sat nestled between bright red crab legs. There were sizzling platters of brown battered fish, bowls of clams and scallops that steamed in butter. All this food and she didn't care about eating. She felt sick. She started grabbing one of everything just to seem occupied when her mother walked out.

Devon held up a plate. "I already got you—" He was cut off.

"Emily." Her mother grabbed Emily's shoulder.

Emily rounded on her and threw her plate on the ground. The glass shattered and sprayed food across the wooden planks of the deck. "Don't touch me."

"Emily, I can explain."

Emily saw the unknown man slinking out of the house behind her mother. She pushed her mother's cheek in the man's direction. Her hand made a slapping noise like an oar against water. Devon jumped to his feet. The color had drained from his face so that he resembled a ghost.

The motion was harder than she'd intended, but she didn't care. She held her mother's face to the house and pointed. "*How?*" she spat. "How in the world can you *explain?*"

Her mother stepped back, her eyes ablaze. "How dare you!"

"How dare *you!* If only dad knew."

"I don't know what you're talking about. I was merely discussing designs with Mr. Harrison."

Emily uttered a helpless laugh. "I can't handle this right now." She pushed past her mother and walked back into the house.

Devon jogged after her. "Emily..." he started to say.

Emily stopped walking. "Devon, I appreciate whatever you were going to say, but I need to get out of here. Just follow or don't, either way don't say a word."

He gave a sad, understanding nod and patted Emily's back.

The helicopter ride to Sugarloaf bluff was a quiet one, other than the pounding of the rotating blades. Emily always went to her second home on Sugarloaf when she wanted to think. After slapping her mother, she really wasn't sure she'd be able to leave the mansion. Emily didn't ask, so she merely assumed it was okay to go. She was somewhat glad that Marian made Jones pilot. Emily had wanted to fly alone, but she still couldn't think straight. It was probably a good thing she wasn't in control of the aircraft. Within ten minutes they reached the helicopter pad just beside the towering creamy-orange painted lighthouse.

Emily's headset crackled as she unbuckled herself.

"When shall I pick you two up?" Jones asked.

It was the first words any of them had spoken the whole time.

"Just give me the night," Emily said weakly. "I'll call you."

He nodded. "I am sorry, Miss Emily."

The comment was a stone of kindness that had penetrated the waters of hatred in her mind. Not hatred at Jones in particular, but at the world. Emily saw the sincerity in his eyes. She stared at his old wrinkled face, contemplating whether to hug him; Jones had always been like a grandfather to her.

But she merely mouthed the words *thank you*.

Old Jones smiled.

She could feel the wind behind her surge as the helicopter took off. Devon had been silent, exactly as she'd asked, but she truly did just want to walk alone for a moment.

"Can you wait inside the house for me, please?" Emily asked.

"Sure thing," Devon said.

They made their way off the helipad and around the grey two-story house. Devon went inside and she crossed the dirt road that led to the front of the lighthouse. She stopped at the garden just beside the building.

There were flowers of butter yellow, crisp violet, and vibrant red. Emily remembered how she and her father had picked flowers in this exact same spot. They always brought back a bouquet for her mother. She picked one of the few blue flowers, her father's favorites, and rolled the smooth stem through her fingertips as she made her way to the rocky edge of the bluff. The red rocks were surprisingly dusty, more so than the last time she had come. Every step she took created a small cloud of dirt. She hopped from each of the flat rocks she could find, careful to avoid the jagged shards. She finally reached the edge, a flat rock of spotty grey-brown. Emily felt on top of the world as she stared out at the twinkling ocean. The sun had just touched the edge of the sea, causing orange clouds to spill over the horizon and into the darkening blue skies. Several boats drifted to the white shores of the bay.

Emily looked down at her feet and over the edge. A blast of salty sea air caused her eyes to water. Mighty ocean waves crashed against the cliff making her think of her dad once again. He used to be a surfing legend. To him those waves would have been nothing.

She sat down and laid the phone at her feet. Should she call him? He deserved to know. Yet, it would only upset him and probably make him lose focus. She decided on just sending a simple text message asking how he was.

Though she knew he was certainly miserable enough in the United States, breaking his body with hard work and dealing with soldiers. Little did he know his wife, her mother, cheated behind his back. The image was burned into her brain. It was a scene from her worst nightmare, like a picture that illustrated the breaking of her family. She stared at the phone, wanting to cry, scream, and hit something all at the same time. She slowly massaged her face and then her phone buzzed. She expected Devon, maybe her dad's response text, but she looked at her dad's face on the screen, startled that he would call. He never called when he was away on business. Emily let the phone scuttle around on the rock and then she reluctantly picked it up.

"Emily?" an unfamiliar, raspy female voice asked.

"This is she. Who is this?"

"Emily, we dialed this contact assuming you are the daughter of Mr. James Altree Sursten. You are?"

"Yes, who is this?" she asked nervously.

"I apologize. This is the Coronado General Hospital. That's Coronado California, in the United States of America."

"I'm well aware of where Coronado is. Is my dad okay?"

"I apologize that this conversation isn't in person, but there is truly no easy way for me to say this. As such, I must just come out with it. Your father has been in an accident."

Panic shot through her. "Accident? What kind of accident? Is he okay?"

"He is in critical condition. Stable for now, but the car crash left severe internal bleeding, numerous broken bones, and organ damage."

Emily's mind raced. "Car crash?"

"Yes. The accident wasn't his fault. The UNM arrested a man who is a suspected terrorist. The means of the crash are still being investigated. I can connect you to the UNM if you so wish, but first we need permission to operate on your father."

Now Emily was really worried. She turned from her view of the ocean and started sprinting back for the house. "Operate on what?"

"He has a collapsed lung that needs immediate attention. The lung may stabilize on its own, but the procedure is very expensive and we cannot operate without the permission of a family member."

"Money is of literally no issue. If it will save him, you do it."

"Yes, Miss Sursten, but it will cost—"

"As I said, *money* is not an issue!" Emily shrilled. "And I expect the very best care that hospital of yours has to offer. I want a private wing and your top surgeons and doctors. No nurses … they don't know anything."

"Oh, well, that isn't exactly something I can arrange."

"Do it and I'll pay five million in cash plus whatever the actual cost is."

"My goodness!" the woman on the line said. "I'll see right to it."

"As you should. I'll be in Coronado as soon as I can."

"Shall we expect you in the next week?" she asked.

"The next twenty-four hours. And while you're at it, give me the number of the UNM men who arrested this man. I'd like to have a word with them."

Emily hung up, quickly recording the number, then dialed Old Jones's helicopter. The list of things she needed to do grew with every passing second.

She reached the house and told Devon what had happened. He looked at her sadly, telling her everything would work out fine. Emily didn't need his comfort, but it felt nice to have nonetheless. They hugged one another before getting back on the helicopter.

She knew that this was probably the last time she would see Devon. But neither could say goodbye.

12

PAY OFF

The Hammer of Coronado
Coronado, California, United States

Taniel was more nervous than ever. They had planned on nabbing Kaiba from his home, only to discover that Shipment took place earlier than anticipated. Graves kept his head though and made contact with a Fifth Era member still working for the UNM.

It hadn't been easy. They met Jewel Julio just outside of Pinecrest to arrange a fake drop off for Taniel and two other boys. They forged ID tags, which was probably unnecessary, and forced Taniel to cut his hair. None of that worried him though, as much as the fact that their entire plan rested on his hunch that Kaiba had the sphere. If he was wrong, he was dead.

Taniel held his seat as the Hummer bounced again. He replayed the earthquake in his mind. He remembered watching two people climb out of the pit in the forest, and Taniel did his best to convince himself it was Kaiba and Jordan. The more he thought the more troubled he became.

He stared out the windshield at the line of Hummers. They had been diligently following the trickle of vehicles all the way to San Diego. He didn't know which one Kaiba and Jordan rode in, but he would find out. They neared the gated entrance where ten guards stood with black rifles.

Jewel, Taniel's driver, said, "Keep calm. Just act nervous. They expect that from all fresh recruits."

Taniel laughed. "Easy enough."

A guard with a beret walked up to Taniel's side of the truck. He rapped on the window with his gun.

Taniel rolled it down and the guard smiled when he saw Jewel. "Glad to be back, lieutenant?"

"Yes sir." Jewel said with a smile. "Didn't know we checked IDs now?"

"Captain wanted us to check every fifteenth rig." The guard shrugged and looked at Taniel. "Who do we have here?"

"Nathan Gladden, sir." Taniel said in as military a fashion as he could muster. He passed his false ID forward.

The two other boys did the same but Taniel was too nervous to hear them.

The guard looked over the IDs suspiciously. "Where ya'll from?"

Taniel answered, "Pine…Pinecrest. It's outside of Sacramento."

The guard peered at the list he held in his other hand. He looked up and smiled, "Don't be nervous now, Nathan." He handed the ID back. "You'll do just fine. Just remember your training and the rest will take care of itself."

Taniel smiled, knowing he'd got the best of the man. "Thank you sir."

He nodded. "Alright Jewel, they put the Pinecresters and everyone else from North Cali in Hammer, the biggest base."

Jewel saluted. "Thank you sir."

Jewel rolled up the window and said, "We got lucky there. Good acting with the stutter, Taniel."

Taniel nodded and kept his eyes forward. The Hammer of Coronado truly was bigger than the other bases. The idea that his organization would have to take down forces like this intimidated Taniel. But Eskylious intimidated him even more. They wouldn't be alone; the virtaiyu would help and that meant victory.

Jewel drove them near an armory. "Alright Taniel, spread out over the compound like we planned. I'll take the other two and let you know if we spot them. Otherwise it's up to you. Now get going."

Taniel jumped from the vehicle. He slipped into the shadows of the buildings and wandered aimlessly down back alleys. Then fatefully he spied Jordan's oversized head. Kaiba walked beside him.

Taniel tailed the two as they made their way to a small hot dog stand. Taniel stopped in an alley just adjacent to the stand. He found the ladder to the roof of a brick structure and climbed up. He sat near a small air duct with his eyes locked on his prey.

Kaiba and Jordan made their way to a bench that overlooked the ocean about two blocks away. Taniel could just see them from the rooftop and he watched curiously. Kaiba sat with his arms stretched in front of his body and he shook slightly as though he were cold. Then he heard a loud pop like the burst of a firework.

Taniel couldn't figure out what the popping noise was, but he remembered Graves explaining that the abilities would be weak at first. It took time for the device to fully bond with the user and it took even more time for the user to fully figure out how to work the device. He couldn't decide if he should alert the others. The popping hardly seemed substantial evidence to order a raid on this base. Taniel wasn't even sure if Kaiba or Jordan had a sphere. He needed hard proof. He watched them rise from the bench and walk back toward the center of the base. Taniel leapt from building to building, but he lost sight of them when they went into a multistory complex. He waited for a little longer than half an hour. Finally the two emerged from a stairwell exit. They looked panicked. He followed them as they crossed the street and then saw a moron in a convertible as he barreled forward. The driver had dropped his cell phone.

He hated himself knowing he would say nothing, but he couldn't take his eyes away. He heard a shout as a bolt of lightning exploded from Kaiba's hand.

Taniel smiled deviously and dialed Graves's number.

"What is it, Taniel?" Graves said.

"Tell the virtaiyu I found a sphere."

"You're sure?" he yelled.

"Track my phone, order the attack. Better double my pay while you're at it. I think the other one has a sphere too."

13

INTERROGATION

Abbey Street, Hammer of Coronado
Coronado, California, United States

Kaiba and Jordan were shoved from the truck and hurled into an interrogation room. It was small, no bigger than eight feet by eight feet. Kaiba was shaking and he couldn't help it. He kept staring at the mirrored wall, unsure of who watched on the other side. He sat straight up as though a pole were strapped to his back and he left his hands cupped together on the small square table. Jordan sat across from him looking much less tense. He leaned back in the cheap black wire frame chair and rocked back and forth ever so slightly.

"I almost killed him," Kaiba said finally.

"If you hadn't, we'd be the ones in the ambulance instead of him."

"That doesn't change the fact that I almost killed him. This wasn't some firefight, this was a man driving in traffic. And I crushed him."

Jordan leaned forward in his chair. "You protected yourself. And how did you do that anyway?"

"It just happened. I didn't hurt him on purpose and now he's probably dead!"

"Probably, but I'd stop saying that. You'll only make yourself feel worse."

"What do you think they'll do to us? Do to me? I deserve all the punishment they can give." Kaiba was talking nervously fast.

"Don't know. They're probably debating that right now."

Kaiba looked around the room again. "I want them to take it from me."

Jordan put his chin on the table sluggishly. "I'd be careful what you say."

"They already know we have them! After what I just did how can they not know?"

"Until they come out and say it, I'm going to assume they don't know. You would do both of us better if you did the same."

Kaiba tapped his chest. "I don't care. I … don't … want … this."

"It just saved your life."

Kaiba tried to stand, but his ankles were bound to the chair. "At the cost of another man! Besides what does it matter what we say?"

"They'll cling to every word, and you nearly already spilled the secret. We have something they want. We have leverage. Now be quiet."

Kaiba leaned to Jordan. The legs of the chair scraped the floor. "I'm willing to give it to them. After what I did to that man, I don't deserve what I have. I wasn't meant for this power and I'll be glad to be rid of it!"

Jordan shook his head. "You were pretty thrilled when we were in my backyard. And they don't know how to get it from you anymore than you know how to get rid of it."

"Then they'll be glad to have my help searching for a way."

"You're painting them in too positive a light," Jordan warned.

"Meaning?"

"Meaning we are not the Republic we once were," Lieutenant Aaron said, walking into the room. He was dressed in a tank-top to reveal a large, veiny snake tattoo on his bicep. He slapped a thick folder down on the table. "An individual's rights are secondary to preserve the greater good. What you have will be taken from you. We do not value your life." He plopped himself into the third chair.

"Then what do you need us here for, steroids?" Kaiba said angrily.

Aaron smiled smugly, sarcastically, "Ah, you like jokes. That's good. I didn't like you the minute we met."

"Glad the feeling was mutual," Kaiba said.

Aaron opened his arms wide, as if welcoming guests. "It's a privilege for me to interrogate you. I'll be straight with the two of you, this doesn't end well any way you cut it. When the war started we used to take murderers out back and shoot them. So how 'bout you answer my questions and we can get you into your cage faster."

"If you took murderers out back and shot them, what do we need a cage for?" Kaiba asked.

Aaron glared and opened the folder to reveal a roll-screen the size of a sheet of paper. He uncurled the object and the traffic camera footage revealed Kaiba electrocuting the car as it slammed into a light post.

"Can you explain this to me?" the lieutenant asked.

"Nope," Kaiba said calmly.

Aaron looked from Jordan to Kaiba and smirked as he drew a large, curved blade from his belt. He put down the blade and spun it slowly on the table top. "Don't think I'm above torture here. I'll do what it takes to get it out of you."

Kaiba noticed Jordan squirm in his chair. He didn't do well with being threatened.

"Uncuff me. Maybe I can demonstrate what happened, maybe I can't," Kaiba said.

Lieutenant Aaron drummed his fingers on the table and looked at his knife as it swirled. He smiled. In one motion he grabbed the blade and lunged at Kaiba. Kaiba's heartbeat skyrocketed. Aaron placed the blade against his neck and Kaiba could feel the cool teeth of the knife against the hairs of his throat. Kaiba struggled against the chains on his wrists when another man burst into the room.

He yelled, *"Stop!"*

Aaron looked at the man with wide eyes. "Colonel."

The colonel strode forward and shoved Aaron back. "Get out."

Kaiba released his breath, utterly relieved. The lieutenant stood with a straightened back, saluted, and scurried from the room. The colonel went over to the roll-screen. "My apologies," he said. "He's a soldier, not an interrogator. Besides, this is way above his clearance. I'm Colonel Barnes. Not your enemy, just a friend." He took out a key and unlocked both Kaiba and Jordan's handcuffs. "I will trust that you'll hear me out, otherwise the soldiers outside this room will tear you to shreds before you can take five steps out of here."

It was clear by Jordan's face that he didn't trust the colonel. "Friend, huh?"

Kaiba massaged his hands and set them on the table.

"I never said I couldn't be your enemy," Barnes said.

They leaned back obediently.

Barnes took out a phone, slid his fingers across the device, and a picture appeared on the roll-screen. It was of an Air Force pilot standing in an open room.

Kaiba noticed the gray shimmering plate that contrasted with the man's dark skin. It was wrapped around the man's bulging left bicep.

"Did either of you hear what happened in Colorado?" Colonel Barnes asked.

"Afraid not," Kaiba said.

"Yesterday a massive maelstrom consisting of three class five tornadoes ripped through the Colorado Air Force Base. If you didn't know, the Rocky Mountain state isn't exactly famous for its tornadoes. All but seven of the 2,400 pilots and soldiers died." He pointed to the man on the view screen. "One of the survivors was Evan Howard, and he can ... do things."

Jordan asked, "Such as?"

"Abilities about as strange as unleashing a bolt of lightning from thin air. Can you each show me the plates?"

Jordan and Kaiba looked at each other.

"I know two spheres landed in the Pinecrest vicinity. Just show me."

They each stood and showed their plating. The colonel glanced back and forth from the two boys. He smiled. "Amazing."

Kaiba hated the way he seemed so impressed.

Colonel Barnes grabbed his phone. "Confirmed. I've got two. Green and whitish-silver. Yes. Hang on for a second." He knocked twice on the mirrored wall nearest to him.

Aaron entered the room again. He had a long rod in his hand that looked slightly like a metal detector. The colonel snatched it from him and shut the door once again. He moved the phone and approached Jordan first. "I just need to put this over your thigh."

Jordan looked at him suspiciously, but didn't do anything.

The colonel pressed the rod against the plate. It blipped loudly. He spoke into the phone again. "Got it? Good. Here's the second."

"May I?" Barnes asked.

As if Kaiba had a choice. "Go ahead."

The colonel prodded Kaiba's chest, but he didn't feel the jab.

"Send the files to the Pentagon." There was a pause. "I see. Let me do this first and we can talk after." He hung up, set the phone back on the table, and the picture of the pilot disappeared. It was replaced with the image of the sphere that Kaiba had encountered in the forest.

"Colonel, we just want to be rid of these things," Kaiba said.

Jordan shot Kaiba an angry glare, but he kept his mouth shut.

"If you haven't already tried, it's impossible. Although I would love to help you get these off, take them back for the military, I have no idea how to get them off you. That being said, we need to get you into better hands, people who know these devices better than I do, and know how to deal with them."

"You're saying you don't even know what they are?" Kaiba asked.

"I know they're pieces of virtaiyu technology."

"Known as Terraformer Keys?" Jordan said.

"Yes. The nation—all nations for that matter—were put on high alert after a research base off the coast of India was compromised. I was contacted by the UNM Council and the Pentagon after what happened in Colorado."

Kaiba still wanted to know more. "What are the keys to?"

"They sent us basic logistics regarding the spheres and their capabilities. Beyond that, nothing more was given."

"You mentioned the pilot's sphere, how many others are there?" Jordan asked.

"I was told there are seven, which is why finding two is such an accomplishment. The other four are yet to be accounted for. At this rate I'm sure they'll turn up soon enough. For now, come with me. We'll get you two out of here."

Kaiba glared at the man. "And what if we say no?"

"You would be foolish."

Before Kaiba could say anything else a faint wail came from outside the room.

The colonel grew tense, like wood freezing in the winter. When he flung the interrogation room door open the sound doubled in volume and the air flashed a bright red.

There was a group of soldiers in the hallway who looked just as confused as Barnes was.

"Form up on me," the colonel ordered. "Stay close."

The sound was deafening and Kaiba had to cover his ears as they emerged from the building. To their dismay, the sirens screamed from every building and post in the base as though a hurricane were about to hit. Street lights flashed and tracer rounds from tanks and turrets illuminated the dark skies. The booms in the distance could only have come from the railcannons. Kaiba's stomach sank as he looked at the virtaiyu ships that flew in over the ocean.

14

WHEN THE SKY FALLS

Hammer of Coronado Base
Coronado, California, United States

*K*aiba James Cassidy,

I hereby congratulate you on your admittance into the Pinecrest Academy. What trials we shall prepare you for will be useful not only to yourself, but also to this nation as a whole. The battlefield will be a place that we cannot accurately simulate for you. It will be a place of ear splitting sounds and images the brain cannot take in without first trying to reject. We will prepare you for bringing order to this field of war. Always remember, for every ounce of chaos that lives on the fields of war there will always be a soldier that will bring order against whatever foes stand before them. You are now one of those soldiers. Although I don't know what you will face, I know you will stand proud, not only for the United States of America but for the world. I look forward to preparing you, soldier.

—Captain B.L. Larten

Kaiba had believed in this man's words wholeheartedly when he'd first read the letter. He didn't think to question; he was an empty mind that would take whatever information was presented to it. As a captain this man had surely seen the field of battle, plenty of war zones, maybe special operations missions, and as such Kaiba valued his insightful words. He listened to them day in and day out at school and he regarded this man with admiration.

But as he watched the exploding skies above Coronado, Kaiba realized that Captain Larten could not have been more wrong. There was no order on the battlefield. And no soldier could bring anything but more chaos.

Kaiba felt helpless standing outside the interrogation building. Others had started to emerge from barracks across the base with the same bewildered face that he had.

A hundred planes whistled above like banshees in the sky. The alien ships looked like mechanical manta rays, U-shaped front, with large wings at the middle, and a long narrow tail at the back. They weaved toward the base in a coordinated flock that moved together in perfect harmony. Some fell prey to the railcannon defenses, but most weaved through the gunshots like graceful acrobats.

One plane flew directly above Kaiba. Its wings folded upward, slowing it from its hypersonic speed above the roof of a barracks. There were no doors on the plane. Instead the underbelly of the craft had three rows of glowing lilac circles: teleportation chambers. The ship hovered for a moment and virtaiyu soldiers started to emerge from the holes.

They dropped down and thudded against the rooftop. The first thing Kaiba stared at was their faces. Each virtaiyu had long slender faces, two round, wild looking eyes and narrow noses with four slits. Two skinny slits stretched near the tear ducts of their eyes to the mid nose, and two wider ones rested just below and above their thin lips.

ELEMENTALS: THE SEVEN SPHERES

As they yelped to each other, their mouths opened to reveal two rows of pin-shaped teeth. They moved quickly and their bluish-grey skin seemed to absorb sunlight rather than reflect it. Each had various light blue markings tattooed over their faces. Their necks were slightly longer than a human's and their shoulders stuck back at an angle. Like elves, they had two pointed ears, which fanned back on the sides of their white-haired heads.

They wore pitch-black armor with metallic thorns that twisted in every direction. Some wore matching helmets and each one held a sonic rifle in its six, talon-like fingers. Kaiba had seen their terrifying forms in his training many times. He knew they were reckless, often unpredictable, and their soft spots included the head, groin, and lower back. He knew their tactics—small numbers and brute force. But he could never have known the fear he would feel at being forced to fight against a living, breathing virtaiyu. Not just one, either, but hundreds of them. He stared at the creatures, unable to bring himself to make a move.

Colonel Barnes forced him into action. "Come on!" he shouted. He pushed Kaiba to a row of Humvees lined up against a chain link fence.

"How's this happening?" Jordan shouted.

"They must have known you had the spheres!" The colonel flung the driver's side door open. Jordan hopped in shotgun. The vehicle roared to life.

"Kaiba, can you operate a turret?"

Kaiba nodded, but flinched at an ear-splitting hum that reverberated in the air. The next moment an ambulance in front of the barracks exploded. The shot came from the largest virtaiyu on the roof. His sonic vortex cannon was the size of a child and the barrel smoked with grey wisps.

"Then get on back!" Barnes ordered. He addressed the soldiers, "Stay on our ass. We need to reach those helipads!"

Kaiba climbed through the back seat and stood up through the shoulder-width hole at the back of the truck. The machine gun turret had boxes of ammunition on either side. The round barrel was heavy but Kaiba hefted it to the sky. He aimed at the rooftop, homed in on the largest virtaiyu, and squeezed the trigger.

A stream of bullets blasted from the gun, spraying hunks of rock and debris from the rooftop, up and into the air. He saw the other eight virtaiyu dive into cover, but he knew he'd killed the largest one as it crumpled to the ground.

Kaiba took his thumb off the trigger to let the dust settle. He immediately regretted the decision as the other virtaiyu stood up and fired their silver rifles at the Humvee. The shots made the air shimmer like the heat above blazing hot pavement. The energy barreled forward in an ear-splitting wail.

The colonel stomped on the gas and took off out of the parking lot. Kaiba ducked as the energy barely soared over his head. He popped back up as the energy collided with a truck that followed them. It flipped up into the air and crashed before getting more than a few feet out of the parking lot. Kaiba slammed his thumb down on the trigger again. This time he didn't release it and the turret coughed bullet after bullet onto the rooftop until the building was too far behind them.

The wind whipped through Kaiba's hair. He turned the mounted gun back to the front. He got a much bigger view of the growing devastation across the base. They were on the main street, which stretched into the distance to the ocean. The battleships and aircraft carriers bobbed roughly on the sea. Several fighter jets attempted to take off from the ships, but were blown to pieces as the virtaiyu Mantas attacked with sonic energy from above. Cannons and machine guns belched gunfire into the sky, trying to aid the railcannon batteries that couldn't seem to do enough damage.

Soldiers poured from every building in a panic. They ran to street corners to help the other men locked in firefights. Most ducked behind cars for cover as the virtaiyu weapons rained down on them. From one building came three tanks, their barrels alive with burning fury. Kaiba flinched as they sped by one tank that fired at an Exo; the virtaiyu's single-pilot, walking tank. The machine was shaped to resemble a virtaiyu, but was the size of a building. The Exo shrugged off the explosive round and tore through the tank with its gauntlet-like hands. A Manta descended next to the machine and deposited more troops onto the streets. Other Mantas started to touch down across various rooftops, spewing more virtaiyu from their hulls. As every new enemy alien landed they fired seemingly at random into whatever groups of people they saw. Several virtaiyu even launched lightning from their hands.

Kaiba felt strangely alive, but more frightened than he ever had. Combat was a rush, exhilarating and deadly. He fired the turret at all the enemies he could see and it provided him with a reassuring sense of power.

They reached an intersection and two cars collided just in front of them, forcing them to swerve. Kaiba felt himself start to fly sideways. He grabbed the handle of the gun and accidentally sprayed the sidewalk with bullets. Several soldiers were luckily shielded by debris, otherwise they would have been cut down.

Kaiba felt foolish, but his attention was immediately drawn to his left. An open field of concrete was filled with rows of vehicles, most notably six CV-22 Ospreys. The planes were like helicopters except that their wings had two propellers that were able to adjust both horizontally and vertically. Several of the aircraft had already started to lift off, which left only two Ospreys remaining on the ground.

Kaiba barely heard Colonel Barnes yell, "You get on one of those planes!"

They turned left on a narrow road that swerved for the airfield. The colonel slammed on the brakes just in front of an Osprey. The loading ramp was down to reveal that the interior was filled with people—a dozen at least. The rotors had just started turning.

Kaiba leapt off the top of the Humvee and tucked himself into a roll. Jordan helped him to his feet and the two followed the colonel up to the plane.

Then the air sounded like the strumming of an electric guitar's strings.

Kaiba turned to see the shot come from the forward cannons of a landing Manta. The shimmering projectile collided with the Osprey and it was ripped in two, spewing fire and metal in a devastating explosion. Seven virtaiyu dropped from the plane just before it took off into the skies once again to avoid an incoming fighter jet. The only remaining Osprey was about a football field's length away.

The virtaiyu strode at them. All were adorned in black helmets except for the one at the head of the group. Its face was narrower than a human's. It had silvery hair that fell down behind his shoulders and cascaded down his back. A suit of black metal with a fiery red trim clad the creature's form. It held no weapons, unlike the virtaiyu that stood directly at its back.

Jordan took a powerful step forward and raised his arms at the same time. Kaiba didn't know how Jordan did it, but the concrete at his feet rose to the sky in a thick wall of rock. The barrier shook like paper in a windstorm as the virtaiyu fired their sonic weapons.

The colonel drew his pistol from behind the rock. "Get to the Osprey! Tell the pilot to take you to the USS *Archfrost*!"

Kaiba and Jordan started to move for the Osprey. As more shots pounded into it, the wall of stone crumbled. Kaiba watched as the virtaiyu ran forward faster than anything their size should have been able to.

Barnes strode in front of the boys. He aimed at the lead virtaiyu and fired three shots. With inhuman speed the virtaiyu raised its hand. The bullets struck just in front of it, against a wall of shimmering purple. The shield faded as quickly as it had appeared. Kaiba turned as the tingling in his hands started to grow. He unleashed a jet of lightning into the group. With a loud bang, the bolt collided with the lead virtaiyu, forcing it to its knees.

Jordan charged forward, realizing that they would be unable to outrun the virtaiyu. He thrust his hands into the ground and a column of earth shot out just in front of another virtaiyu. The rock slammed into the alien, throwing it several feet into the air.

In a flash of bright violet, the virtaiyu without the helmet teleported. The stone at its feet shook, causing pebbles to scatter at the sudden dispersal of power—and he appeared right in front of Kaiba. The virtaiyu smiled menacingly and it drew a sword-like blade.

It swung at Kaiba, who barely dodged. Kaiba's hands continued to crackle. He shot another bolt at the same instant that Jordan thrust another pillar from the earth. But the creature was too fast; it teleported away and reappeared just behind Kaiba. The creature wrapped its powerful arms around Kaiba's neck. Kaiba could smell the creature's fishy breath as his own breath was being squeezed away. Another gunshot rang out. This one hit home and the virtaiyu dropped dead.

Kaiba pushed the carcass away from him.

The shot had come from another Humvee that had just rolled over the top of the other virtaiyu.

"Go!" Colonel Barnes raged. He grabbed Jordan and pushed him to the plane.

The rotors of the final Osprey were starting to power up. Kaiba ran after Jordan and the colonel, forcing himself not to look back. Before he could get more than a few steps he was tackled from behind.

Kaiba hit the ground hard. His chin skidded on the rough concrete. He struggled against what felt like a large man. Kaiba kept his hands crackling and grabbed the man's arm.

The attacker released his grip, howling in pain.

Jordan had reached the plane. He stepped to Kaiba, but the colonel grabbed him. The men from the Humvee started to get out. But they were not soldiers. The driver was a bald man in a thick black cloak. Three other armed men in similar large fitting jackets stepped from the vehicle behind him.

"Get on the plane, Jordan!" Kaiba yelled as he stood up.

Jordan struggled against the colonel's grip. He had a fury in his eyes that only happened when you were about to lose a family member.

"Go!" Kaiba roared angrily. Jordan got on the plane. Kaiba turned to see the men pointing their guns.

The bald man looked at him. "Come now, boy. We're gonna go for a little ride."

The man who'd been shocked stood up, laughed, and thrust a bag over Kaiba's head.

15

B O U N D

En route to Crest Airport, Australia

The helicopter only had enough fuel to return to Newport
to drop off Devon. Their goodbye was short and part of Emily
wished she could have told him how she felt. There would be other,
more appropriate times. Or so she hoped. She had to settle for the
limousine, and left without even saying a word to her mother. Emily
studied the boy's face as though it were an assassin's target. He was
younger than she was by just two years. They had sent her every
document that contained Kaiba Cassidy's name in it. She had his
birthday, knew his family members, his medical history, and even
his closest contacts. She read the information from her phone in the
palm of her hand. She would find the boy and demand he pay for
what he'd done; not with money, but with everything he held dear.

Emily thought the accident had happened in a remote area, but
she was more frightened when they told her it had actually occurred
within a military base. The fact that her father wasn't even safe in
what was arguably the most secure of areas unnerved her greatly.

She looked up from the phone and steadied herself as the limousine approached the airport. Normally they would have avoided the airport altogether and just gone to the private hanger. That wasn't an option this time, since Emily's father had flown their private jet to California and Emily was forced to call in another.

She could already see the angry crowd scavenging around the outside like some pack of abused wolves. It struck her as odd that so many wanted to leave Australia and get to a land they had never even been to before. Of course New Zealand was dealing with invasive forces, but Australia hadn't seen any conflict yet. In her opinion most were being overly cautious, fueled by paranoia and fear. Perhaps it was the American railcannon tech that so many wanted to be protected by.

They were fools to think that complaining about the lack of air transportation would make any difference. The moment the car approached, the mob started screaming. Emily rarely made appearances at the airport other than when there was a problem. The crowd clearly recognized her vehicle. Some ran after her with their massive signs in hand. When the car came to a stop the mob swarmed around the car and started to beat on the metal with the frenzy of a mighty storm.

"Hope this won't end like the last time," Emily said.

Her driver, Mo, gripped the steering wheel tightly. "That makes two of us, Em. Just let them clear some of these people away and then I'll escort you to the terminal. The port's expecting you and will supply extra guards for your safety."

"Thanks. I called earlier asking them to clear the entrance, but that obviously didn't happen. Lucky that you have such a way with people."

"I don't, but my fists and my Taser sure do," Mo said as he eyed a gangly, bearded man knocking the front windshield with a sign.

Emily smiled. "Use the Taser sparingly?"

"No promises." He thrust his door open into a man, quickly slamming it back shut. He immediately shoved another guy to the ground. His strength never ceased to amaze her. He was tall as a tree and built like a mountain. He made his way to Emily's door with relative ease. The bodyguards from the other vehicle had just started to move protestors away. There were six men that stood together making a small opening for Emily in the sea of people. She fumbled with her own Taser, hoping that she wouldn't have to use it.

She opened the door and the mob descended on her. She kept moving despite the jerks on her shirt, hands on her jeans, and the occasional lunge for her hair. She stomped the urge to fight back—that would only enrage the group. Instead she continued to move within the circle of men who shoved back the others. They waded through the bodies, and Emily did her best to ignore the insults and outcries. It wasn't her fault that she couldn't just give everyone plane tickets. She was rich, not-all powerful.

An elderly woman stood between two broad-chested men at the airport entrance. In front of them was an electric fence. The gate swung open and Emily walked through, her bodyguards filing in behind her.

The crowd grew restless and Mo tased a man in the neck.

He shrugged when Emily scowled at him. "You said use it sparingly."

Emily couldn't help but smile.

"I'm sorry to hear about your father's accident, Miss Sursten," the elderly woman yelled. "I am Selena Tileres and I'm willing to help in any way that I can."

"Thank you," Emily called. They were in close proximity, but the roar of the crowd forced them to keep their voices at a volume close to a shout. Selena entered the airport building and Emily followed her, leaving the sounds of the mob behind.

Emily ignored the stares from people in the airport and made her way to the security checkpoint. She didn't have to say anything to know the others were following her. "Is my pilot ready?"

"He is preparing the airplane as we speak," Selena said.

Emily bypassed the lines of people waiting in the security checkpoint and opened the employee-only door. She strutted through it.

They walked down the staircase and emerged on the runway. A 76-foot jet sat immobile, gleaming in the sunlight. Emily neared the towering giant and paused to take in the letters that spanned the tail of the aircraft. They read, "Red Wing Airlines."

The entry door to the plane was open, forming a staircase with red carpet that touched the black pavement. On either side of the stairs stood men Emily assumed were the pilot and copilot. She guessed the man on the right was the pilot; he was dressed in an all-black suit with a large wing-shaped gold pin attached just above his breast whereas the other man wore just a white shirt and tie.

As she got closer both men bowed slightly.

The nicer dressed man said, "Welcome! I'm Captain Sefred and this is my copilot, Mr. Hillens."

She smiled back courteously though she didn't feel in the least bit happy. She felt annoyed. "Pleased to meet you both. I take it we're ready for takeoff."

"On your command," Sefred said.

"Then let's get to it," Emily said.

Sefred gestured for Emily to go first. "Please, after you."

"I appreciate that, but I insist. I'd rather the two of you start this beast all the faster."

"Ha! Eager to fly! I like that." Sefred strode up the steps with Hillens at his tail. Emily was about to follow them when a man's voice called her name. She didn't recognize the voice, but turned warily to the sound, expecting a protestor with something to throw.

Instead, a man in tattered clothes and a bundle at his back hurried to the plane. He was ghastly skinny, so that the arms extending from his t-shirt were little more than bones and pasty white skin. His eyes were strangely bright blue, like two hearts of the ocean. A flat mop of hair plopped down his head and the bundle at the man's back turned out to be a young child who grabbed at the hair as if it were a toy.

Mo and Emily's other bodyguards instinctively formed a barrier around her. She watched Mo's hand go to his pistol. She wouldn't give the order unless she felt threatened, which wasn't likely since he was carrying a child. But the man could have easily snatched the young girl as a ploy to gain sympathy.

"Do I know you?" Emily asked.

"No, Miss Emily, but I must ask you out of the kindness of your heart that I be allowed—"

Emily didn't like the way he said her name. They were strangers not old friends. "Let me stop you right there. I've heard all the sob stories and I'm sorry, but I can't allow you onto this plane. Just save up money for a ticket and buy one like everyone else."

"Please, you don't understand."

"No, I don't and even if I did it wouldn't change my mind." She tapped Mo's shoulder. "Would you please escort this man away from my plane?"

Mo grabbed the man and Emily took her first step up the stairs.

"We were victims of the tsunami!" the man yelled.

Emily reeled back to him as if she'd been yanked back by a leash. She scowled at him, unwilling to believe that he'd been devastated by the massive rogue wave that occurred just three days ago on the outer, Northeastern Australian shores. "Why weren't you evacuated on the day following the tsunami like all the other victims?"

Mo held the man tightly, but he didn't let it bother him. "I lost my daughter. She was swept from my very arms. I'm lucky to have found her in the safety of others."

Emily looked at the deep folds under the man's eyes. She studied his grizzled face. She glanced at the child and felt sympathy but she couldn't trust the man.

"If I'm the problem just take my daughter and leave me behind! I only want better for her." Emily glanced at Mo, trying to read him. She couldn't tell what his eye flicker meant.

"Please," the man begged. "Do you have any idea what it's like to lose everything in a single instant? Everyone you've known, everything you've ever earned, washed away by the power of the sea."

Emily saw the desperation in his eyes. She stared at the man, flipping the choice back and forth in her mind. But it wasn't the man that changed her mind. It was the young girl who continued to giggle on her father's back. She took no notice of anything except the long black hair of her father.

"Do you even know where I'm going?" Emily asked, giving in at last.

The man's face lit up as he smiled. "The airport had said California. That's where my ex-wife lives."

Emily noticed for the first time that the man was gripping his side tightly with one hand. He'd been holding it the whole time but she hadn't noticed until this moment.

"It's a long flight. Are you injured?"

"Only aftereffects of the tsunami. Nothing I can't manage."

"All right then," Emily said. "Get on before I change my mind."

"Oh thank you! I knew that all the rich weren't as bad as people say."

Emily tilted her head. "Thanks, I think. What's your name?"

"I apologize! I'm Adam. Adam Xiong and this is my daughter Nicole."

Emily started up the stairs. "Well, come on then. I'm in a hurry."

Before Adam could go up a single step, Mo stopped him.

"Emily, I need to search him."

How could she be so stupid? "Of course. Nothing to hide, Adam?"

"Of course not." Adam set his daughter down.

Mo patted Adam's legs, chest, and groin area. When he patted his sides Emily noticed Adam shudder in pain. When Mo felt Adam's back he turned instantly concerned. Mo shoved Adam away and drew his gun. "He's got something strapped to him!"

Adam's eyes grew wide. "It's okay!" He flung his shirt up to reveal a half-inch plate of metal on his back.

It was unlike any metal Emily had ever seen. It didn't look like a bomb. There was no vest that held it in place. It almost looked as though it was a part of his back rather than something he wore. The strangest thing was that the metal was tinged blue, with interlacing indentations of darker blue. But whatever the thing was, she didn't like that Adam had kept it secret.

"To think I felt sorry for you," Emily said angrily. She spat on the ground and Mo cocked his pistol.

"Please!" Adam protested. He held his arms above his head. "It's no bomb. I can prove it!"

Emily looked at him suspiciously. "Why should I believe you?"

"Bring me a cup or glass of water. You won't regret it!"

Adam's daughter sat on the ground crying.

"He's stalling, Em. I'd feel better if he had a bullet in his skull," Mo said confidently.

"I'm telling you," Adam said. "This will speak for itself."

Emily couldn't see what harm a bottle of water could do. She tilted her head to Mo, who tossed the man a bottle of water.

Adam unscrewed the cap and set the water at his feet. He closed his eyes, which Emily thought seemed odd. She watched his chest rise and fall several times as he breathed deeply. He lowered his hands by his side and stretched them out in front of his body. The water within the bottle rose upward, suspended in midair just in front of Adam's outstretched hands. He opened his eyes and moved his hands to the sky and back to the ground. The water rose and fell with his exact movement. He curled his hands together as though gripping a ball.

The levitating stream of water came together, forming a perfect circle. The water swirled around like liquid being sloshed around in a bowl as Adam's hands moved in a circular motion. He stopped moving suddenly and clenched his fingers into two tight fists. The water froze into a jagged ball of ice and hung in the air. It hovered for a moment and then fell to the pavement, spewing chunks of ice fragments just in front of Emily's feet.

Emily stood motionless, afraid and also in awe. Her bodyguards shifted nervously. Selena had backed up in terror.

Adam lifted his hands slowly to his head and turned so that his back was facing Emily. He breathed deeply as he lifted his shirt to reveal the metal once again. It shined brightly blue and flickered like a light switch being turned on and off.

"As I said, it's no bomb."

16

The Path Less Traveled

Four Miles Outside Vladimir, Moscow

The sun hung in the grey skies, watching as snowflakes fell lazily down. Ian Orokov glared at the snow as he trudged through it. Every inch of his body was covered in clothing, apart from his eyes and it didn't matter; he could feel the skin-cracking cold. The temperature was negative eight degrees Fahrenheit when he had escaped from Vladimir and now it felt colder. It would be worth it to be home again and to get his son back.

He stopped for a moment and dug at the foot of snow beneath him. Solid ice appeared instead of roadway. He cursed and turned around to make sure his footprint path was straight. When Ian was convinced he hadn't strayed from the highway he swore again.

The other inmates said he was a fool and Ian was starting to believe them. The prison guards didn't expect anyone to try and escape. Some said this path was worse than being shipped to the war front. He could still hear the dogs as he slipped into the snowy woods. But that had been one day earlier and he knew that Vladimir

Prison didn't have the resources to pursue him. He was home free, so long as he could survive.

Calm, he moved to the left and dug into the snow again. No roadway. He dug in three more spots and each time came up with ice. Ian slammed his boot down in frustration. He ripped off his left glove, unzipped the front pocket of his jacket and pulled out a small map he'd been given.

Just as he'd thought, the hundred mile trek from Vladimir to Moscow was a straight shot. No turns, just roadway. Yet, now he couldn't find the road. He pocketed the map, convinced that he was still headed in the right direction. He was about to keep going when he saw a glint of purple in the snowpack.

He paused and stared. Off to the right, the snow surface gleamed violet as though someone shined a flashlight from underneath. Curious, he approached the light. He fell to his knees beside it and swept away some of the snow. The light remained the same. Something was buried beneath the ice.

Ian dug down until his glove struck something hard and purple. He uncovered further to reveal a mango-sized sphere that glimmered with light. Its surface seemed to move back and forth as though alive.

He stared at the object and removed one glove. He held it in his palm and the ball turned dark purple. Cautiously, he set it back into the snow.

"Weird little thing." Ian said as he stood up. He turned from the object when the air flashed with lilac light. Ian felt something in his fingers. He looked down and the sphere had appeared in his palm.

He jumped in surprise and tried to set it back in the snow. It remained locked in his fingers. The ball flashed again and Ian collapsed. He tried to move but his limbs were paralyzed. He struggled with all his might, but he could do nothing.

The sphere kept flashing and Ian lay thinking only of his son and the wooden steps of his house. He could still see the ugly green door. He'd hated the thing and now it was all he could picture. Ian closed his eyes as the ball flashed violet again.

He felt his stomach lurch. When he opened his eyes, his face lay mere inches from a green doorframe.

17

THE COST OF POWER

Amazon Refugee Camp, Coari, Brazil

"**K**ill them!" one of the Fifth Era guards snarled. "Kill all of them!"

The world exploded into motion. One of the guards fired right at Nassira's head. Instinctively Nassira threw her armored forearm up to protect her face. The bullets clinked against the metal and fell to the ground like silver rocks.

In the same instant Bruno leapt off the stage and barreled forward into the crowd. He grabbed both Nassira and Lia and threw them away from the guards.

The crowd panicked as the guns unleashed their projectiles. A few of the villagers, the older boys, surged forward, attempting to swarm the small stage, but more to act as targets to protect the small children and elderly as they scurried away. Nassira wished she could have helped them, but she had her family. That was all that mattered now.

They rushed for the first hut they saw. Bruno kicked in the makeshift door. Lia cowered into the building and Nassira trailed her. Bruno thrust the door shut and Nassira hugged him. "I'm so sorry, Bruno, so sorry for everything."

"It's okay. Don't worry about that now."

"What do we do?" Lia asked, terrified. Her upper lip quivered ever so slightly.

Bruno paced back and forth as sprays of gunfire echoed outside.

Nassira cracked the door open and watched in terror as the guns made quick work of the crowd. The teenage boys would get a few steps and collapse. The mob tried to protect each other, but it was no use. From what she could tell only three people actually made it onto the stage. Nassira looked around desperately as more people hit the ground in showers of red. She tried to shut out the horrible sounds so she could think. She looked at the fleeing people knowing that to chase them meant death. She looked off in the opposite direction of the fleeing crowd. "The river!"

Bruno looked. "It's too far."

"It's our only shot." Nassira looked into Lia's fearful eyes and squeezed her hand. "Whatever you do don't look back."

"I won't," she panted.

"I'll lead then," Bruno said.

"Lia, you stay on his heels," Nassira said.

"Okay. Okay," she repeated. She looked like she was in shock.

Bruno bolted out the door.

Nassira pushed Lia forward and they sprinted as voices and gunshots chased after them. She was careful to run right behind Lia so that if a bullet did come it would strike her and her alone. They rushed past several huts, leaping over wood piles and ducking behind barrels. Gunfire peppered their trail, causing the wood of the objects to crack apart.

The bank of the river came into view. Bruno jumped first. Nassira sprinted, with Lia nearly losing her grip. She managed to hold on to her hand as she pushed off the ground. The girls plunged into the dirty water as bullets whizzed over their heads.

The water engulfed the pair and Nassira kicked off the mucky bottom.

Lia coughed at the surface. "Where do we go, Nass?"

Nassira looked down one end of the river and then the other. "The boat!" she cried. It was the same one she'd noticed before. It sat in the middle of the river between two outlets. One part of the river bent around the village grounds and the other wound deeper into the forest. Nassira had never been down that outlet before, but it was their only option.

Bruno was only a few yards ahead, already darting for the boat.

They swam to the small craft as two Fifth Era thugs appeared on the river bank. The larger of the two, an Asian man with long greasy hair, yelled, "There!"

Nassira raised her arm out of the water, focusing on the smaller of the two, but she felt no tingling in her arms.

They aimed their rifles.

"Get down, Lia!"

They submerged as bullets spiked through the water. Nassira gripped Lia's hand tightly as they swam for the boat. She could barely see through the flakes of dirt in the water but the dark shadow of the dinghy was unmistakable. It was still a hundred yards away. She felt Lia tug on her hand and they rose to the surface gasping for air.

"We have her here!" the Asian man shouted.

The two men ran forward again and Nassira quickly ducked back in the water. More bullets chased them as they submerged deeper. Nassira propelled herself forward, growing less and less optimistic about the situation. She held her breath for as long as possible and rose to the surface again. The boat was still too far off. The popping of gunfire met their rise to the surface. Nassira held her forearm up again to protect her face just long enough to take another breath. Nassira swam desperately, but she felt Lia slowing down. They rose once more and Lia panted for air.

Nassira yelled "Stay!" just before they went back in. Nassira let go of Lia's hand and quickly swam for shore. She rose from the water so that only her head could be seen, much like an alligator before it strikes. She gripped the edge of the river bank and leapt onto shore. The men were caught off guard in the middle of reloading. Nassira landed an elbow on the bigger man's weapon and then jumped on the smaller one. They toppled to the ground.

"Nassira!" Bruno yelled from the river.

"Go!" She gouged at the man's eyes, her nails scraping against his pale skin. He yelped and rolled to the side. He cocked his legs and thrust them into her stomach. Nassira flew backward onto the grassy bank. Her ribs seemed to vibrate and fire swam in her belly. She clutched her skin and looked back. The world was upside down, trees and river were on top and the sky was on the bottom. Nassira watched as Bruno hefted Lia into the boat. They looked so scared and yet they were both free. They were safe.

The men grabbed Nassira's arms and ripped her to her feet. Nassira could hear the growl of the tiny motor boat. She looked into the blue skies and smiled. What could they take from her now? Lia and Bruno would be safe and that made all the difference. She watched them for a moment, when she saw the object just out of the corner of her eye. It moved fast, too fast. Before Nassira realized what it was it collided with the boat in an explosion of fire. She wailed and wriggled her arms free from her captors. She rushed to the river and fell to her knees. Pieces of the boat had flown in all directions after the rocket had detonated. A large speedboat rushed at the explosion, checking for survivors. Nassira couldn't breathe. She sobbed into the earth, her spirit broken like the pieces of the boat.

18

Now Boarding

Crest Airport Runway, Australia

Emily stared at the blue metal on Adam's back and yelled, "I want all bodyguards to stay behind, besides Mo!" Selena and the others looked shocked. Emily extended a hand. "Adam, come with me."

"Are you mad?" Mo growled.

Adam picked up his daughter and approached the staircase smiling.

Mo ran to Emily's side, "You're letting him board and sending all other guards away? What are you thinking?"

Emily pulled Mo's head down to her level. "I won't risk other men, who I don't trust, trying to take that thing from Adam. This is too valuable. Now come on."

Emily walked up the stairs thinking about the artifact. She knew having too many people involved in this would result in violence, something she wouldn't stand for unless she was the one to orchestrate it. Besides, Adam had a young girl and that meant he could be manipulated.

What Adam had done had fascinated her and she needed to know more. She just hoped her decision to keep him in close quarters would prove smart and not foolish.

Emily walked through the cabin door. The inside of the plane resembled a hotel suite rather than the actual cabin of an airplane. The carpet was black with sharp rectangles of grey nestled with intermingled triangles. The white plush sofa that sat next to the white leather seats was designed with the identical geometric pattern. Comfortable pillows of black and white were neatly arranged on the couch seats. Beside the couch was a narrow glass table supported by a curving black base. Crystal glasses sat around an expensive bottle of red wine and a tray of fresh cakes, tarts, and other treats.

Emily sat on the couch, arms tightly folded, and waited for Adam to take the seat just in front of her.

The moment he sat down, Emily said, "Tell me how you did that with the water."

"Of course, but can we get airborne first? Nicole has trouble with flying and I'd rather get her settled before I explain."

Emily sighed and yelled for an immediate departure. "Let's go, Captain!"

Adam's daughter cried loudly as they climbed into the sky. Emily found it nearly impossible to talk over the wail of his daughter so they waited until the girl was finally asleep. Emily hated the sound of children crying; it was quite probably the most annoying sound. Adam took Nicole farther to the front of the plane, then returned, so he could talk without disturbing the child. Emily grew more impatient with each passing moment. When Adam sat back down across from Emily, he pointed to the tray of sweets, which rattled slightly from minor turbulence.

"May I? I'm starving."

Emily grabbed the whole tray and thrust it into Adam's arms. "Talk."

He grabbed a small raspberry cake with white frosting. He ate the desert in one bite. Then he smiled. "What would you like to know?"

Mo stood silently at Emily's side, watching the man with the utmost distrust.

"How'd you control the water?" Emily asked.

"It's because of the plate."

She leaned forward. "How did you get it?"

"The tsunami obliterated my home. Before it did I was sitting on my porch gazing out at the ocean."

Emily rested her hands on her chin, trying not to get angry. "I didn't ask about the tsunami."

"You have to know the beginning in order to understand the end."

Emily didn't like having to wait for things, but she held her tongue.

"I gazed out at the water when something glinted in the sky. It looked like the reflection of the sun against a plane. As the glint disappeared beyond the horizon, a wave formed. I was forced to cling to a lamp post as the waters tried to sweep me and my daughter away. My daughter was ripped from my arms. When the water finally did start to recede the wreckage was horrendous." He coughed loudly and then gripped his side. "Piles of rubble and people were scattered everywhere. As soon as I was able I started to search for my daughter. I stumbled upon rock pile after rock pile until I came to one that had a sphere that glinted amongst the stone."

"What kind of sphere?" Emily interrupted.

"It was a ball that looked mechanical. Advanced and nothing like I've ever seen before. My hand brushed against it and the last thing I remember is falling flat on my face." Adam coughed again.

Emily noticed that the side of his shirt was slightly wet and stained a dark red. "But how did you learn to manipulate the water?"

"I would say it just came naturally. It's like I can sense the water, I feel its presence like a living thing." He coughed again, this time more loudly. "I don't know if that makes any sense to you?"

Emily looked at the red on his shirt again. "No, I can't say it does. If I offered you money for the plate would you sell it?"

"I would gladly give it to you for taking me and my daughter with you, but you cannot have it."

Emily poured herself a glass of wine and swirled the rose-colored drink in her glass. She raised it to her lips and took a small sip. It was dry and slightly bitter. "I have a lot of money, Mr. Xiong. By the looks of you and your daughter, you could use some."

Adam shrugged. "We could, but no matter how much I do or don't want to, I cannot remove the plate."

"Why's that?"

Adam stood up and pulled his shirt up. "It won't budge from my skin."

Emily smirked. "If Mo can remove it, may I keep it?"

"Of course," Adam said.

Mo stood up and grabbed the plate. He tugged, but the plate didn't move an inch. He pulled up and down, back and forth, but no matter his strength, the plate remained. He soon gave up.

Adam sat back in his chair. "Believe me, I have tried just as hard."

Emily took another sip of wine, not at all satisfied. Suddenly she felt very insecure sitting across from Adam. "Tell me, why did you choose my plane? How did you know my name?"

Adam shifted in his seat. "Don't take this the wrong way, but I read up on you."

Emily eyed him suspiciously. "You read up on me?"

He nodded. "Only because I heard your family controlled a good section of the remaining airlines that were still in service."

Emily relaxed. "So this trip to see your ex-wife was planned before the tsunami?"

"Yes, except I wasn't supposed to come with."

"I should think not. You know I hear a lot of rumors concerning the virtaiyu. Most of them are false, but I have heard things about their knack for controlling natural aspects, some call them elements. They say some can spit fire, and change the winds. Some are said to be able to create lightning, teleport, and even change the ground at their feet. And then, of course, I've heard of others who can shape water as you did earlier."

"I've heard some of those things as well."

"And yet I've never heard of a *human* who could do any of those things."

He shrugged. "But I can. I hope that once my daughter is safe this will be a bargaining chip for me to go to war."

Emily set her glass down and wagged her finger at Adam. "See, that's the other thing I don't understand. Why aren't you out fighting in the war? You have to be what thirty-four, thirty-five?"

"Thirty-one."

"Exactly. All men your age are off on the front. Why aren't you?"

"I wanted to, but I'm Chinese."

Emily felt deeply embarrassed. Her face flushed red. How stupid could she be? She hadn't even realized it.

"When the virtaiyu wiped out most of Asia, the rest of the world rallied together, as I'm sure you're well aware," Adam said. "What most don't know is that they left us out. You have no idea how bad I wanted to avenge the destruction of my homeland. Do you know what that's like? Not only have I lost my home here in Australia, but my cultural home was also destroyed. They say that seventy-eight percent of those with Chinese bloodlines were wiped out in that instant the weapon hit. The Great Wall obliterated beside the Emperor's palace. All great cities, centuries of knowledge and wisdom, gone, along with all the people who created and descended from them. All of this in the span of two minutes." He looked up, then slid his hands down his face slowly.

Emily saw the pain. She couldn't even imagine losing everything she held dear, let alone the feeling of having your heritage destroyed. She believed he meant her no harm.

Adam coughed again as he tried to laugh. "Two minutes. That's all it took. And then the United Nations wouldn't let any of us fight. They said our race had to be preserved and refused our call for vengeance. That's why I was forced to move to America, only when my wife divorced me I wanted to start over again. I moved to Australia, only to have all this happen." He coughed again, this time louder. He spit something into his hands. It was red.

He smiled sadly. "Already lost 1.5 billion people and now another member of my race is going to die."

Emily rose to her feet. "Are you all right?"

Adam wiped his hands on his jeans. "A car was swept along the street by the tsunami. It collided with me." He broke into another fit of coughs that sounded like a dog's bark.

Emily tried to get closer.

Adam waved her off. "Just fine, don't worry." Though he sank in the chair as his side seeped with more blood.

"Mo, grab the first aid kit," Emily ordered as she grabbed a blanket from the couch. She rushed to Adam's side and pressed down firmly on his wound.

Adam winced, then jerked side to side as he coughed harder.

She tried to steady him and looked at Mo for help. Mo set the tiny first aid kit down and removed some bandages.

Adam's coughing stopped for a moment. "Don't bother, this will get the best of me. Docs say the bleeding is from the inside, went on for too long." He pointed to the front of the plane. "She is all that matters."

Adam's breathing had changed to a wheeze. It wasn't quite a choking kind of breath, but more as if an airway had been clogged. He grabbed Emily's arm.

She was terrified, but she didn't shy away.

"Her mother…" He had tears in his eyes. "Georgia Xiong."

Emily didn't know this man, but she wanted to be there for him. She took one of his hands.

"You must find her," he wheezed.

His fingers grew less tight on Emily and he entered another fit of vicious coughs. He managed to utter the words "San Diego." And then Emily watched helplessly as his eyes rolled back in his head. His breathing slowed and his hand slipped and dangled toward the ground.

Emily shook him and said softly, "Adam?"

But she knew. He'd passed.

19

THE GATEWAY TO ICE

Location Unknown

The bag had been forced onto Kaiba's head, though he struggled to the best of his ability. He was prevented from seeing all but the brightest flashes of light through the black mesh of the bag. The sound of the sirens and gunfire grew steadily softer as he was dragged across what felt like gravel. With the gooey earplugs slammed into his head, he was surprised he could hear anything at all. He kept his head aloft in order to try to get a glimpse of something, but someone kept forcing his chin to his chest. He barely heard the dull honk of a car horn, which was his second indication that he was being led away from the base. He was pushed against the cool leather interior, pleasantly aware that they hadn't shoved him into the trunk. He felt the car swerve and then nothing but the drone of the wheels against what he assumed was open road.

They drove for what seemed like hours. His only way to keep track of time was to count, which grew both tedious and difficult. He felt like a man forced to count the grains of sand as they trickled through an hourglass. When he had counted 703 seconds he gave up and tried to listen to the voices of the others that rode with him in the car. He wriggled his ears, but the muffle of sounds was just too faint. He abandoned trying to scrape words from the darkness and instead fumbled with the cuffs around his wrists. They were firmly fastened about his skinny bones, almost too tight, like a belt around a fat man's waist. With his left hand Kaiba attempted to squirm his other wrist through the metal hoop. The harder he pushed, the more pain that cut into his skin. He fell forward slightly as the car came to a stop, which ended the short-lived attempt at removing his hands from the chains.

Again he felt two men's firm hands gripping his shoulders. They dragged him from the car, and though he couldn't see it, he felt frigid water at his ankles.

They're going to drown me, Kaiba thought. He didn't see any way to get out of this one. No hands to use and no way to see; two basic requirements for someone who needed to swim.

He breathed steadily through his nose, anticipating the embrace of the deep ocean, small pond, or gaping river about to take him down. He would be able to kick at least, maybe that would be enough to save him. He felt the push at his back, and he toppled forward, preparing himself for a desperate and pathetic attempt at swimming. But when he hit the water it didn't feel like water at all. It was much too cold and far too fluffy to be water. He felt the substance through the bag and shuddered in what felt like a half foot of snow. He could feel the wind laced with ice pellets against his body. His legs started to shake, but he was more curious as to how he'd suddenly reached snow. There were no mountain ranges within a day's drive of San Diego. Even those ranges would be hard-pressed to have snow on them this time of year. There was no possible way they had been driving for a whole day, either. Unless, of course, they had slipped Kaiba a sleeping pill or something of the sort, but he felt fine, neither groggy nor disoriented.

He was lifted to his feet and the bag was finally removed. The sudden transition from a world of black to a world of whirling white forced Kaiba to shut his eyes. He slowly opened them, but squinted to give his eyes time to adjust. He blinked rapidly as the bald man stuck his gnarled fingers into Kaiba's ears, removing the plugs.

"We won't drag you through this storm, boy. You follow me and don't try anything funny. If you do, they won't hesitate to gun you down. Got it?"

Kaiba just nodded, unable to speak through the duct tape around his lips. He found it curious that these men had taken him captive and not just killed him outright. They knew of the sphere bonded to his chest; what was the point in keeping him alive?

"Come on then." The man led the way. He was dressed in a thick black cloak and a knitted brown hat. Kaiba appeared to be the only one dressed improperly for this particular ice-land, because the men at his back were garbed in similar furry jackets.

Kaiba spared a glance behind him. A V-shaped structure, slightly taller than himself, stood erect in the snow. The space between the V was glowing with a hint of lilac. It was as out of place as a tree in the middle of a business office.

"Eyes ahead," one of the men behind him ordered.

Kaiba obeyed, though he couldn't shake the feeling that he'd seen that V-shaped structure somewhere before. It looked all too familiar. He pondered as they trotted through the rapidly deepening snow. Each time Kaiba took a step, he sank to his ankles, which he could no longer feel. His pant legs had frozen over. With each step he tried to stomp his foot harder into the snow to try to get circulation back into his toes, but he felt only minor tingles. The loss of feeling in his feet made it quite difficult to maintain his balance in the ice.

The bald man moved well for his age. He left giant holes in the snow and Kaiba soon found that hopping from each of the freshly-concocted tracks made keeping his balance much easier. This way he didn't have to make his own path and could conserve more of his energy. The three men behind him started to follow the pattern of footsteps too.

Kaiba tried to pinpoint any buildings or tents among the landscape, which should have been easy. The world was just a flat plane of endless white that stretched in every direction. It conveyed the sense of being in the middle of the ocean, so much so that Kaiba bet that if he turned around he could still make out the metal V.

The bald man kept fumbling with his GPS. Kaiba started to wonder whether or not he truly knew where he was going. The thought made him feel insecure. Not only did Kaiba not know where he was or where he was headed, but his captor didn't seem to know either.

"How much farther, Graves?" a man behind Kaiba asked.

The bald man replied, "Just a little bit."

"They were supposed to pick us up at the entry point."

Graves turned to Kaiba and the men behind him. Had Kaiba's face not started to tingle from the sheer cold of the wind, he was certain he would have been able to feel the heat of anger rising from Graves.

"You don't think I know that? Would you care to lead us there, Knoll?" Graves said.

"No, but they should have been here by now."

"But they ain't here, are they?

Knoll said, "No. I just think—"

"Here's a thought: leave the thinkin' to me." Graves took a flare gun from his belt. He pointed the black firearm above his head and a bright crimson ball blossomed into the grey skies. "That'll get 'em here faster, so quit your whining."

They started to walk again and Graves turned out to be right. Kaiba heard a grumble off to his left. From out of the white emerged three black snowmobiles, each with a single rider, though the seats were clearly big enough for two, maybe three, people. The snow trails billowed behind them like thick clouds of silver dust. Kaiba nervously followed the haze of ice trails, wondering where they were going to take him. So long as it was out of the storm he didn't quite care much.

The snowmobiles slowed to a stop just in front of Graves.

A fat man sat atop the lead vehicle. He removed his face warmer to reveal a thick red beard. He spoke first. "Got caught up with the soldier again."

"Spare me the details for now," Graves said. He told the men who stood behind Kaiba. "Load him on with Esvir."

The men at Kaiba's back thrust him onto the snowmobile with the red-bearded man. They tied his legs to the passenger rails with thick ropes, as if he were going to try to fall off.

"He's young. Shame he had to find one," Esvir said.

"You probably would have ended up fighting him at some point in the war anyway. We'll just spare him a prolonged, torturous life." Graves looked at one of the snowmobile drivers. "Get off and ride on the other one." The person driving did as he was told and hopped onto the back of the third snowmobile. "Taniel, hop on with me."

Kaiba felt anger stir within him like a great beast at Taniel's name. He glared, searching the men as Taniel stepped out from behind the others. He wore a hefty black mink coat that shined like his dark hair. He smiled tauntingly as their eyes met, then jumped on the machine behind Graves.

The men that had escorted Kaiba stood with confused looks on their faces. Knoll moved to Graves's machine and Graves took out his pistol. "You three get to stay and keep watch over the Interligate."

Kaiba assumed he was referring to the V.

"It's inactive!"

"But it can be reactivated from the other side, now can't it?"

"We'll freeze out here!" Knoll exclaimed.

"Just think about the sun. That supposedly makes you feel warmer," Graves said.

"You have an extra spot with you and we only need two people to watch the teleporter."

That explains how I traveled so far, Kaiba thought.

Graves tilted his head. "I said three people, but you're right, we do only need two people to watch the gate." He shot Knoll.

Kaiba's eyes widened.

"Now you two can watch the gate together without having to listen to him. I expect to find you right where I left you."

The other two men exchanged glances.

"Objections? No? Splendid. Esvir, will you lead the way?"

"Not like you know the way through this blizzard," Esvir said, replacing his face warmer.

"Don't make me kill you now," Graves said, joking as though he'd not just committed murder.

"Can't let you get too mighty," Esvir replied. He set the pair of ski goggles back onto his skinny nose and revved the throttle. Kaiba felt the machine shudder beneath him as it lurched forward. They barreled through the forceful winds. Kaiba could hardly see. The chunks of hail kept hitting him in the face. He was glad to have the tape covering a good portion of his lower mouth. It protected his bare skin from the force of the elements. He steadied himself as they neared a hump of snow. The Yamaha launched over the glacial dune, causing Kaiba's hands to shake and the chains on them to jingle. He was comfortable on almost all machines, but he felt uneasy having to rely on nothing but rope to hold him in place. They landed in a plume of ice and Kaiba was jostled to and fro. He could hear the twang of the rope and hoped it would hold his weight.

They continued to cut through the white wastes when a small grey structure appeared in the distance. It had a thick layer of snow around its flat roof and many barred windows, giving it the appearance of a prison compound. The front was only three stories tall but a large, sweeping dome stretched behind the entrance. The front gate was blocked by a large metal panel. As the snowmobiles approached the entry, the panel split in two and opened inward like the mighty doors of a castle. Rather than stopping, Esvir pulled back even harder on the throttle and they started to plummet downward on a snow covered slope. Heavy fluorescent lights were hung above the hill, and as they drove on the lights turned on to illuminate the path. Kaiba was surprised that ice still remained at the floor of the building. The slope started to level off to a large parking garage filled with tracked vehicles and snowmobiles. There were skis and snowboards racked against the walls of the garage as well.

Esvir removed his hat and stepped off the machine. He withdrew a pocket knife and cut the ropes that secured Kaiba to the snowmobile. "Welcome to Taras."

Kaiba stepped down from the engine and waited beside Esvir.

"Before we left you mentioned a problem with the soldier?" Graves said. He descended from his snowmobile as if it were a king's fine horse.

"I did. We think he's been able to resist what we've been giving him," Esvir said.

Graves started to walk to a single door at the far end of the garage. "So up his dose."

"We've already done it."

"Well do it again, problem solved. Is the girl the same?"

Esvir shook his head. "Still won't talk, but so far hasn't put up any resistance. We gave her a smaller dose, slightly worried that it might be affecting her more negatively than we'd originally thought."

Graves opened the door and they walked into a narrow hallway. "Fair enough. Speaking of dosages, it's time for yours." He looked right at Kaiba.

Esvir reached into his pocket and pulled out a tiny orange bottle. He pulled a red, pea-sized pill from the vial.

Taniel stepped forward and ripped the duct tape from Kaiba's mouth. Kaiba forced his jaw shut as Esvir tried to pry his lips apart.

"Oh, come on," Esvir said. He punched Kaiba in the stomach and Kaiba leaned forward, gasping for air.

Esvir seized his advantage and forced the pill down Kaiba's throat. Kaiba coughed, trying to spit the tiny capsule back up and to breathe, but it was no use.

Graves smiled. "Not so bad, now was it?"

"What was that?" Kaiba asked crossly. He opened and closed his mouth trying to shake the frozen rawness from his cheeks.

"The same thing I gave you earlier today," Graves said.

Taniel snickered.

Kaiba lunged at him. "Why don't you kill me, coward? Or take these bindings off and let's hash it out!"

Taniel backed up, alarmed.

"*He* wouldn't like that, boy," Graves said. "Esvir, would you please?"

Kaiba growled. "I'll—"

But Esvir had slammed the strip of duct tape back over his mouth. Kaiba glared at Graves wondering who "he" was. If Graves wasn't pulling the strings then there was someone else working as the puppeteer of this play. He doubted the virtaiyu were involved, or they would have nabbed Kaiba from the battlefield when they had the chance. Perhaps the Fifth Era weren't working with the virtaiyu after all.

"Did you hear from him before you left?" Graves asked.

"No. Supposedly he was busy pulling out forces from Coronado. I'm not exactly sure when he'll be here, but we should prepare to have him arrive at any time."

"Did they know about the soldiers we killed?"

Kaiba wondered if he was referring to the virtaiyu that they had run over, or other UNM forces.

"No. He'll assume they were just casualties of battle. We'll get complete credit for bringing in another Elemental."

They led Kaiba through a series of hallways. The first room Kaiba caught a glimpse of was filled with large monitors and TVs.

There were newscasts playing from around the globe. Kaiba even spotted part of the aftermath of what had occurred in Coronado. Beneath the screens were all sorts of makeshift desks and tables. Men and women sat at the stations with their heads buried in their keyboards, pounding furiously as if the world depended on them.

They reached a set of double doors.

"I'll take Taniel to the living quarters," Graves said. He spit at Kaiba. "You got him?"

Esvir nodded. Graves and Taniel disappeared down the adjacent corridor.

Esvir pushed through the doors to reveal a cafeteria of sorts. Kaiba could only guess that the cook must have been horrible, judging by the rancid smell and the lack of people in the dining hall. They exited this room and Kaiba was led down a staircase. The air grew thicker, warmer too, and the lights were not kept as bright as they were in the other rooms. A single steel door gleamed in the dark walls, with a single guard standing at the front.

"Got another one huh?" he said. He rapped on the metal twice. "Nice work."

The door slid open.

"All part of the job," Esvir said. Behind the door was an armory with weapons of all shapes and sizes.

Kaiba wondered who would keep an armory so close to a prison. They exited the armory into a dark room. There was a small drip falling from the ceiling that created the sensation of being trapped in a cave. Esvir pushed Kaiba forward and leaned down to open a tiny trap door. Kaiba peered down the hole. He saw the outline of a ladder that led into darkness. Before he could step onto the first rung, he was pushed from behind.

His stomach rose for a moment and he fell to the bottom, crashing hard on his knees and chest. Pain burst in his legs, but he was glad to have landed face down so that the chest piece took most of the impact. Esvir slid down the ladder and scooped Kaiba up. Kaiba wobbled to his feet and was led down the dark hallway to another staircase.

Kaiba gazed into the dimly-lit room realizing that it was actually composed of several prison cells. Esvir walked up to the first cell at the bottom of the staircase and opened the rusty metal door with a small key. The bars creaked as they swung open.

Esvir undid Kaiba's handcuffs and shoved him into the cell. He fell into a small pile of hay that was to be his makeshift bed.

"Enjoy your stay, boy," Esvir called as he walked back up the rickety staircase.

UNDERSEA

Over the Pacific Ocean

Emily was forced to remain seated, staring at the body of a man she'd only just met. She couldn't strip her eyes from his lifeless gaze. She'd never seen death up close and it scared her. This was nothing like the movies or television. This was a living, breathing man who had just died. She grabbed one of the blankets from the couch and draped it over him.

Her hand brushed against his cold skin. She shuddered.

Mo had gone to the rear of the plane to look after Nicole, who had just awakened from her nap. The poor little girl was alone in the world now.

Emily slumped into one of the big, cream-colored chairs. Then she heard a grinding that sounded like two forks being rubbed together. She looked at Adam's covered body, which seemed to be the source of the sound. The plane banked left slightly, just enough for Emily to see an object roll from beneath the blanket. The ball rolled right to Emily's feet. It was of the purest blue she'd ever seen. Speckles of icy dots were strewn about the sphere like the speckles on a robin's egg. She pivoted into the aisle, looking at the object with the utmost curiosity.

This ball must have been what Adam had been talking about. Did death somehow play a role in its removal from his body? She decided to pick it up. She cradled it with both hands as though it were a precious diamond. It was twice the size of an orange and heavier than she would have guessed possible for its size. She put it in her lap, feeling suddenly tired. She fought the urge to fall asleep, but she couldn't resist it. She yawned once, rubbed her eyes and then stretched out comfortably. When she was about to fall asleep she heard the sound of the grinding metal again and could have sworn she felt a tickling sensation in her back.

✳ ✳ ✳

Sharp jostling roused Emily from her sleep. The cabin rocked violently. She sat upright. Mo sat across from her with a concerned look on his face.

"You all right, Em?"

She felt dazed, but her senses began to sharpen. "Fine, just took a nap."

The cabin rocked again, throwing the tray of cookies from the table with a loud clank. The cookies scattered onto the floor beside several broken glasses. Emily had to steady herself as she rose to her feet.

"We're nearly to Cali. Are your 'naps' always eleven hours long?"

Emily's back pounded. "Eleven hours? You didn't try to wake me?"

Mo shrugged. "I was busy trying to keep Nicole calm and moving her father's body to the back of the plane."

As he spoke she skirted her fingers along her spine. Her stomach rose into her chest. There was metal there. "Oh god." She breathed.

Mo's eyes held an accusing stare. "Why'd you take it from him? It could have been the thing that killed him."

Emily craned her neck to see the bluish plate that now stretched from just above her hips to the middle of her shoulder blades. She'd seen the device on Adam and felt desire. Now that it was bound with her, she wasn't sure if she actually wanted it. She twisted her back, unsettled with this new piece of her body. "I didn't take it from him on purpose!"

She told Mo about the ball, but he didn't seem to believe her.

Mo crossed his arms. "Curious or not, you shouldn't have touched it."

Emily scowled. "I don't pay you for your advice, Morgan."

She'd expected Mo to get angry, but he took the comment and merely said, "Of course. If that will be all, Miss Emily, I will tend to the girl."

Emily hated it when Mo was so formal. "Fine."

Mo gave a courteous bow, which only infuriated her more. She buried her face into her hands, unsure if she'd done the right thing. Maybe it would just take some getting used to. The plane thundered again, causing Emily to stumble. She grabbed the chair nearest to her to keep her balance.

The pilot's voice came over the intercom: "Emily, report to cockpit."

"Now what." Emily grumbled. She stumbled her way through the aisle like a drunken beggar. She had to duck into the cramped cockpit of the plane. It glowed in the darkness from the multitude of gleaming buttons and dials.

Captain Sefred turned once she entered. "Won't be able to land in San Diego, I'm afraid."

"And why not?" Emily demanded, in crueler a voice than she'd intended. She knew her interaction with Mo was spilling over into her words.

"We received a distress signal being relayed from the radio towers at both Coronado and San Diego. I'll spare you the aviation details, but the base fell under attack from virtaiyu forces. Evacuations have been ongoing for the past two hours."

The statement came as a hammer blow. If the base had been overrun then her father was more than likely dead. The thought brought Adam's eyes into her head once again. But they were in her father's face. Her skin crawled and she shook away the grim image of her father beneath a sheet. "Did the message say where the base was being evacuated to?"

"Few miles up the coast."

The cabin shook violently again as lightning split across the skies. The rain pounded furiously against the windshield. Emily hated flying into storms.

"Then head there," Emily said matter-of-factly.

"Not that simple. We got a big stretch of ocean left to cross. We can alter course to get to the new base, but we aren't even sure if this bird's fuel tanks will get us there."

Emily looked at the fuel gauge whose tiny orange hand hovered just above a large E that glowed in red. "We can glide from this altitude though, right?"

"I'll hope it won't come to that. What with all this turbulence I'm not sure we'd make it. But that's not our only concern. Check out the radar." He pointed to the largest circular panel near the center of the cockpit dashboard. The radar was split into four equally divided quadrants. A blue circle lay at the center of the divisions, which marked their plane. In the top right quadrant were five or so large green circles that blipped in and out.

Emily stared at the blips. Dread sank into her body like water sinking into a sponge. She had a hunch, but she asked, "What are they?"

"We can't know for sure. They might just be planes evacuating from Coronado." He sounded doubtful.

Emily called him on it. "But more likely?"

The pilot scratched his head. "More than likely they're virtaiyu planes."

Emily's worst suspicion was realized. The storm wasn't even close to the worst of their worries. She never would have imagined facing the virtaiyu. She wasn't a fighter. Tenacious maybe, but apt for battle? Certainly not. Of course they'd probably be torn to shreds in the air anyway. "Can we avoid them?"

"On our current course, no. Not unless they suddenly begin dispersing or moving back for the coast, which isn't likely since more signals keep appearing. I can attempt to fly to Coronado anyway and hope that the virtaiyu have already had their blood lust satisfied."

"That's suicide," Emily scoffed. "We don't know if the Virts occupy the base now or not." She stared at the radar as another signal appeared.

"It may not matter what we do. The virtaiyu may have already detected us, just as we've detected them."

The pilot didn't sound like he'd chosen an option. He seemed to be rattling off all the possibilities.

Emily noticed him sweating. "Are you asking for my decision?"

"Miss Emily, this is your plane and none of these options are very good. I do not see one alternative better than the others. So yes, I am asking for your choice."

Emily could feel the weight on her shoulders, but she needed another opinion. "Give me a moment."

She stuck her head from the cockpit. Mo was still angry at her, but he would have to ignore his feelings. She yelled Mo's name. He came immediately and they stood in an awkward silence for a moment.

"I need your opinion."

"I'm sorry, but I am not paid for giving advice," he said with no emotion. "I'd be happy to renegotiate our contract, though, after we land. Is there anything else?"

Emily stared in disbelief. She'd never seen him like this. She clenched her jaw tightly. "No, that's it."

He bowed again and Emily stepped back into the cockpit. She'd lost his respect and she wasn't sure there was anything she could do to gain it back. Was he acting like this because she'd used his full first name? Or was he truly mad that she'd touched the sphere? Why did he care what happened to her anyway?

"Well?" Sefred said as she entered.

She looked at the now eight dots that glowed green on the radar. She sighed. "We head for the evacuation point and pray we miss the virtaiyu."

The pilot straightened his hat. "As you wish."

She wasn't sure what would happen or if she'd made the right decision. She felt exhausted even though she'd just slept for an apparent eleven hours. Her back felt stiff and Emily needed something to take her mind off of the world. She pictured Adam as he manipulated the water and so she desired to attempt the same. She wondered why Adam seemed to keep popping into her head. Witnessing death may have been haunting her more than she thought.

Emily saw Mo and Nicole sitting at the very back of the plane. The girl was asleep; did she know about her father? Emily hoped not. She felt horrible for the toddler and she would see to it that Mo got her to San Diego. She stared at the girl, but rather than comfort her, she grabbed the silver ice bucket from the table. It was one of the few items that hadn't fallen from the turbulence. All the ice within it had melted so that the water filled it halfway full.

She sat in a seat as far from Mo as possible, just outside of the cockpit. The tray table was small, but it was just big enough for the ice bucket.

She grabbed a bottle of water that sat in the cup holder of her seat. The cap twisted off with a crack.

She took a sip of the clear liquid and then emptied the rest into the bowl. She pulled out her phone to gaze at Kaiba again. She hoped that he hadn't been killed in the war. Emily only wanted him to answer fairly for what he'd done. And he would answer to her and her alone.

She dipped her finger into the bowl and swirled the water back and forth. She lowered her whole hand into the cold liquid. The plane shuddered again, causing some of the water to slosh from the bowl, but Emily kept her hand in. Her back felt as if someone were pressing firmly down on her. The pressure continued to grow and Emily slowly withdrew her hand from the ice bucket. As if by magic, a thin stream of water followed her hand. She raised her palm six inches above the rim and stopped. The water hovered in midair. The space between her skin and the liquid felt connected as if by a string.

Emily moved her hand from side to side and the water mimicked her motion. The pressure in her back extended into her hand. She smiled, realizing that she was shaking with excitement.

Money had given her so many possessions, but the thing on her back could not be bought. For the first time Emily had an object that no other person possessed. She felt privileged and powerful. She looked at the water and saw the blurred reflection of herself. Her eyes were sparkling as blue as the moving water was.

The plane bucked much harder than before. The bucket and the floating water crashed to the deck, startling Emily.

Oxygen masks fell from the overhead compartments. Emily's heart doubled in speed. She snatched the nearest mask and thrust it onto her face. The air smelled old and tinged with chemicals. The cabin shook again, tossing Emily like a rag doll. She gripped the armrests tightly wishing she'd tightened her seat belt.

From the corner of her eye, Emily saw fire on the left wing and a fast-moving object.

"We've been hit!" the pilot yelled.

The plane pitched forward into a dive and Emily hit her head on the wall in front of her. Pain exploded in her forehead. Luggage compartments popped open all along the cabin as the air started screaming.

They dived faster in a downward spiral.

Emily gripped the space in front of her tightly, careful to cover her head. This was it; everything in her life would end in this moment.

Copilot Hillens screamed from the cockpit, *"Brace for impact!"*

Emily realized that the front of the plane was the worst spot to be in a crash. But there was nothing she could do about that now. She placed her hands over her face and ducked as low as she could.

A moment later the plane crashed into the water with a deafening roar. The aircraft buckled and cracked. Windows burst open, spraying glass as ocean water poured in. The plane tilted at a steep angle, causing a waterfall to flow in from the gaping hole in the back of the aircraft. Emily could barely see in the torrent that filled the cabin.

She spotted Mo as he started to come nearer and shouted to him, "Get Nicole out!"

Mo obeyed. He kicked the exit door open and jumped with Nicole in his arms.

Emily scrambled to lift herself from the chair, but her leg was pinned against an armrest. The water rose around her.

She tried to rip her leg away. It barely budged. Cabin lights flickered and sparked before failing. The water had reached her chin. She saw the body of the copilot float past her. She stripped off the nonfunctioning oxygen mask, took a deep breath of wet air, and plunged into the frigid Pacific Ocean. She wriggled back and forth, pulling at her trapped leg. Panic started to set in like a deadly poison. Ten seconds. Her pants ripped as she tore at them with her long nails.

Thirty seconds. Her ears popped as the plane dived deeper into the ocean.

A minute. Her lungs grew weak as she wriggled back and forth. In a desperate attempt she twisted to the left and then to the right.

Her leg popped free.

She opened her mouth in surprise releasing just a little bit of precious oxygen.

Emily thrust her arms forward and streamlined along the sunken cabin. The salt stung her eyes, but the tightening in her chest was the greatest pain. She forced her mouth shut even though her body screamed for air. She swam to the exit door and emerged from the torn metal of the plane and into the dark Pacific Ocean.

She scooped at the water. The rippling surface was still so far away. She struggled to get much farther when her body started to shudder. She tried with all her might to resist, but it was no use.

This is the end, she thought. At that moment her mouth burst open and she inhaled a massive gulp of saltwater. She screamed a bubbling cry, flailing around as the water filled her lungs. The salty liquid tickled the back of her throat as she inhaled more of it. Her neck felt as if she were being strangled.

She hung in the ocean with the water at the back of her mouth, but she didn't pass out. There was no light at the end of a tunnel, no endless abyss. In fact she felt strangely refreshed. It was as if she'd just taken a breath of air. Emily inhaled and exhaled again. The water moved in front of her mouth as she took several slow breaths.

I'm dead, Emily thought, and yet she still felt alive. The sea was loud with gurgles and sounds she didn't recognize. She looked back down as the front of the plane plunged deeper. The space around her glowed with a light blue aura that shined through her shirt. She lifted the wet cloth and brushed her fingers against the blue metal.

She took another breath, and as she did the plate grew even brighter. She exhaled and then the blue grew dark like the ocean.

It wasn't possible. She breathed again and the plate did the same thing. She didn't know how the little plate conferred the trait onto her and it didn't matter. She didn't care. She twirled in the water, watching the bubbles rise to the surface. She laughed, thrilled with the sensation of breathing under water.

She swam to the tumbling surface of the ocean and the moment she breached, a wave crashed into her. She rolled with the tide as if caught in a washing machine.

Emily broke to the surface once more. The seas howled with storming gales. Waves crashed all around and there was no land for as far as the eye could see. A terrible rain sprayed from the black skies, pounding the Pacific with the pressure of a shower head. Pieces of the plane's tail and wings floated like tiny rafts. Several Virt ships flew overhead. She heard a high-pitched wail getting closer. In the distance she saw the glowing outline of a plane as it skimmed over the waves. She ducked back under the water, worried the aliens might somehow be able to sense her. She stayed under until the glowing underbelly of a manta-ray-shaped fighter passed by.

When she swam back up she spotted a floating seat cushion. She grabbed the item and looked out at the scattered bits of the airplane, suddenly remembering Mo and Nicole. When she was certain there were no more virtaiyu ships she yelled, *"Mo!"*

Although she was loud, her voice was lost amid the raging ocean. She didn't know if they had sunk, or worse, been picked up by Virts.

The water in front of her started to rise. She paddled with the pillow away from the forming wave. Emily thought of the bowl of water on the plane. She focused on the surging ocean. Before it could crash upon her she held her hand up. She felt pressure in her back and hands again. The wave stood immobile. She flicked her hand in the opposite direction and the wave crashed away from her.

She felt so powerful, almost godlike.

The water continued to churn violently and she realized for the first time that she had no clue where she was. The pilot had said they were off the coast, but which way was the coast?

Another wave started to form and she had an idea. She kicked hard with her legs and pushed the space around her. The water shot backward and propelled her forward up into the wave. Just as it was about to crash, she rose to its crest. She looked out for a brief moment, but there was no sign of land or Mo and Nicole. She crashed back into the water as the rain started to fall harder, blurring her vision. The sea seemed to stretch for miles in all directions. If she chose to swim in the wrong direction she could be too far out to sea and then die without ever seeing a glimpse of land.

I can control water and I'm still helpless out here, she thought. Maybe she couldn't die of drowning, but she was still vulnerable to exhaustion. If she stayed put, however, there was no way anyone would find her. The captain had surely put out a distress signal, but with the base gone it was unlikely that anyone would come to her rescue. She debated on which way to start swimming and eventually just picked at random. She swam for a grueling hour, switching between hard swimming and floating on her back, when she saw the black outline of a massive boat. It was a military vessel with heavy turrets on the port and starboard sides. Its bow was long and pointed like the beak of a hawk that enabled it to split through the waves. UNM was painted on the side in great golden letters next to the name *Archfrost*.

"*Here!*" Emily shouted at the top of her lungs. She tried to stay calm as the boat got closer.

A man leaned over the side of the craft.

"Over here!" Emily cried, waving her hands.

The man looked in her direction and pointed once when he'd seen her. He shouted down, but his words were muffled. He disappeared for a moment and returned with something in his hands. He threw a circular orange buoy, which landed just in front of her. Emily snatched the floatation device and hung on tightly as the surf crashed into her again. The water rolled her over and she held her breath tightly. Then she smiled, realizing she didn't have to anymore.

She was dragged up the side of the boat and spared a glance back out at the ocean. It was Mo's duty to die for her if required, but she realized that she actually cared for the man. And now he was lost at sea with a young girl. The worst part was the fact that she didn't know whether they had made it or not.

21

C O N F L I C T I N G
I N T E R E S T S

Aboard the USS Archfrost

Emily shivered in the pounding rain, clinging tightly to the rope as she was lifted up the side of the *Archfrost*. As she neared the deck she could tell that her rescuer was about her age. Drops of water glistened atop his slightly oversized head and down along his muscles. Several other people, some military, others in everyday dress, stood behind him struggling to tug.

"Easy does it now," he said.

He extended a large hand, which Emily took gratefully. He started to lift her over the shaking guardrail and grabbed her side with the other hand. She didn't like how far down his hand was on her hip.

"I'm good now," Emily said, releasing his hand and lifting herself.

"Just tryin' to help." He took a step backward.

Emily looked at him. He was surprisingly handsome in a rugged kind of way. "You have, thank you. What's your name?"

"I'm Jordan."

"Emily."

He smiled. "Well you're lucky to be alive. We heard the distress signal as the plane went down." Then he noticed the torn pant leg. "Your leg all right?"

"It's fine," Emily said, though it throbbed painfully.

"How many were aboard the plane?" Jordan asked.

Emily shifted the strands of her torn pants then looked up. "Five, including myself."

Jordan asked with interest, "So few?"

"Private flight. Both pilots are dead, but I was hoping you might have seen a man and a small girl."

Jordan motioned to those behind him. There were people huddled all across the deck. Most of them were soldiers. Others were ordinary people dressed in business suits or rags who sat in tight circles holding one another and weeping. Some stood amongst crates and others under un-assembled tank parts. There was also an abundance of what looked like spent shell casings.

"I'm sorry, but no. We've been on the lookout since we saw the crash, though."

Emily knew he would say that. She reached up and tied her hair into a ponytail. She squeezed the water from it. "Seems like there's a lot of you."

"Came from Coronado," Jordan said. "Virts hit without warning."

"How many survivors?"

"As far as I'm concerned you're looking at 'em," Jordan said sadly. "We took off with as many as we could, but so many were left behind. Word is that some other boats and planes made it out to Sand Point, but I don't know how many."

Emily wondered if her father had made it. "Is Sand Point an evacuation site?"

"One of them, yes. You're not from the States, are you?"

"Australia," Emily said.

"Ah. I thought your accent sounded Australian."

You're the one with the accent, Emily thought. "Do you know if the hospitals were evacuated?"

"I don't know for sure, but we have wounded below. Why do you ask?"

"My father was in critical condition in Coronado," Emily said.

"I'm sorry to hear that. I hope he made it out ok. Was he injured in the war?"

"No, car crash," she said. Her mind was already set on checking below. Something told her that her father wouldn't be there. Saving an already-dying man wasn't exactly a military priority for an evacuating base. "Would you mind leading me down to the injured?"

Jordan looked at her funny.

"Did your dad cause the accident?" Jordan asked.

"Why are you so interested in my father?"

Jordan shrugged. "Curious."

"No, he didn't," Emily said shortly. "Someone named Kaiba did. Speaking of which, I have to find him as well. I have a picture, if you've seen him." She reached into her pocket and pulled out a drenched cell phone. "Damn it." She turned it and water rolled off its surface. She threw the phone on the deck. It cracked into several pieces. "Well, I could have shown—"

Jordan interrupted, "What will you do to this guy when you find him?"

"Help the police bring him in, if he isn't already in prison. If they can't then I'll deal with him myself. He'll pay for what he did to my father."

"You sound pretty determined," Jordan said. "How do you know he's not dangerous?"

Emily smiled thinking of the blue plate on her back. "Just a hunch."

Jordan looked Emily up and down. He had a strange glint in his eyes. Then he shouted, "We got a Fifth Era terrorist here!"

Soldiers around the deck whipped their heads in her direction. They drew their weapons instinctively.

"What the hell are you talking about?" Emily demanded.

"I won't stand for you trying to hunt down Kaiba."

"You know him?" Emily shrilled.

"For most of my life."

Emily watched as the soldiers neared.

"Sorry," he said plainly.

She scowled. "As am I." She turned to the sea as the pressure returned to her back and hands. She threw her arms up and a massive wave rose to the deck. In one motion she twisted and slammed her hands on the ground. The wave curled over the top of her and crashed into Jordan and the other soldiers.

The ocean hurled them back, washing over the deck with wild ferocity. Another soldier rushed from her right. Emily curled the water on the deck, pushing it forward so that the soldiers were carried away from her. She let the water fall when one man was forced off deck into the ocean.

The rest of the soldiers on deck ran to her. There was no way she could take them all on. She glanced back at the sea, debating whether to leap into it when another soldier came at her. She couldn't explain how—she did it without thinking. She balled her fist and the puddle at the man's feet turned to ice. Before he could fire his weapon he slipped across the white frost. Emily jumped over the man and ducked behind a cargo crate. Bullets peppered the metal container.

"I am not a Fifth Era rebel!" she yelled.

"Hold your fire!" Jordan shouted. "You have a sphere?"

The bullets stopped flying, but Emily stayed crouched behind the crate, unwilling to abandon cover. She didn't trust him. And if he knew Kaiba then he was no friend of hers. What was worse, he knew her secret. "How do you know about the sphere?" she called from her hiding place.

The rain rolled down across her body and was pounding so hard that her skin was starting to ache. He didn't answer right away, which made Emily distrust him even more.

"You manipulated water, not too common a thing."

"No way could you know that a sphere caused this unless you've seen it first-hand," Emily said. "You played your cards wrong."

"Come out and we can talk."

Emily laughed. "Put the guns down and I'll consider it!"

She heard the crackle of weapons being set on the deck.

"It's done," Jordan called.

Emily was alone. She didn't see a way out unless she worked with these people. She cautiously stood up and was surprised to see that all the soldiers beside Jordan were unarmed just as she'd asked.

A man stood in front of Jordan in a military jacket with several medals adorning it. "We don't want any trouble, Emily. We want to help you with your gifts."

Emily glared. "Why should I believe you? Jordan already lied trying to frame me."

"That was before I saw that you had a sphere," Jordan said.

The rain continued to roll down across Emily's face. It dripped along her nose. "I want to know about your friend Kaiba."

She saw Jordan's face twitch.

The man with the medals stepped closer. "We will tell you everything you want to know, granted you give us information in return."

"You don't look like you're in a talking mood, Jordan."

Jordan stood silent.

"He will give you what you want," the officer said.

"You can't guarantee me that." Emily said.

"I can. I'm his ranking officer, Colonel Barnes. All we want is to talk to you."

"Then let's talk."

"Let's get you dried off first. Come below. We can even search for your father." Colonel Barnes said.

Emily looked at the discarded guns at each of the soldiers' feet. She felt like a criminal making demands. "No weapons."

The Colonel nodded in agreement. "No weapons."

Emily was still hesitant, but she wanted to know about Kaiba and how these people knew of the spheres. "What do you want to know?"

"As much as I can," Barnes said. "Come with me."

"You're just going to let her live?" one of the soldiers demanded. "She swept Simmons off the deck!"

"Better fish him out then," Barnes said. He pushed past the man, leading the way for Jordan and Emily.

The civilians on the deck gave her nervous looks and whispered among each other as she passed. She tried to ignore them but she was disturbed when someone murmured, "What is she?"

Emily followed Jordan and Colonel Barnes below the deck of the aircraft carrier. The halls of the ship were filled with an array of pipes that wound around every corridor. She felt slightly claustrophobic in the tight passages. She tried not to think about it. She could soon hear the coughs and cries of pain coming from nearby.

"I assume you will look for your father alone," Barnes said.

"I'd prefer it," Emily said.

Barnes led them to several winding corridors lined with injured people. They lay on the floor tightly beside one another like packaged sausage links. Makeshift beds were fashioned from extra clothing and mats. Three nurses bustled among the crying and moaning people.

"Go on then," Barnes said, waving her forward.

Emily stepped in between the injured, doing her best to avoid disturbing them. Some reached for her ankles, calling for her help, for food and for water. Every face was in pain, but none belonged to her father. She approached a nurse bandaging a man's abdomen.

"Have you treated an Australian man with white hair? Car crash victim?" Emily asked.

"I'm far too busy," the nurse said angrily. She looked out of breath and gestured to the number of injured. "Grab some bandages and help out."

"Looks like you're handling this just fine," Emily said sarcastically. She quickly sidestepped the woman, ignoring her curses, and continued to look for her father. She went down another corridor similarly packed with bloodied people, but her father was nowhere to be seen. She couldn't act surprised. She'd expected that he wouldn't be aboard the ship. She carried only a sliver of hope, and now it was gone. Now she just hoped he'd made it on another boat or maybe a helicopter. Either way, she wouldn't give up finding him.

She crept carefully back to Barnes and Jordan.

"No luck then?" Barnes asked.

"Clearly," Emily said.

"Come on then." Barnes took them to a spacious coffee room with several cabinets along one wall. He removed a blue towel and tossed it to her.

Emily caught it gratefully and wiped herself off before taking a seat opposite from Jordan. He didn't look too fond of being around her. As far as Emily was concerned that was his problem. His friend was the one that caused her father's accident. She'd done nothing wrong other than want justice and compensation for her father's suffering.

"Let's start with you, Jordan," she said. "How do you know Kaiba?"

Colonel Barnes took the seat to Jordan's left.

Jordan scowled. "You could say he's like a brother to me."

"Explains why you lied to me."

"Threaten my friends and I'll do what I have to to protect them."

Emily crossed her legs and wiped them off with the towel. "Worked out well for you on deck."

"Would have gone better if we were on land," Jordan said.

"Doubtful," Emily said, shaking the remaining water from her head. "How'd Kaiba nearly kill my pap?"

"You ask one question and get one answer," Barnes said. "We will do the same."

Emily glanced between the men. "I don't play your games. Answer me first. How'd he nearly kill my father?"

Jordan's foot tapped the floor. "Your dad was electrocuted and then he crashed into a lamp post."

"Electrocuted?" Emily said, suspicious. "How?"

"I don't know how!" Jordan yelled. "Your father would have killed us if Kaiba hadn't stopped him. It's his fault; the moron was too busy texting."

Emily lunged at him. "Don't you dare insult my father! I'll crush you!"

Jordan stood to meet her. He towered above her. "What water will you use this time?"

Barnes stepped between them. "Sit down!" He slammed Jordan back into his chair. "Explain to her without the insults, Mr. Hightower!"

Emily's blood burned, but she was thankful Barnes had intervened. She didn't know what Jordan was capable of and he did have a point, there was no water she could use. She stared at Jordan, her chest rising and falling. She trembled slightly, but sat down awaiting an explanation.

Jordan licked his lips. "When your dad *barreled* down on us while on his cell phone, Kaiba released a bolt of lightning. I don't know how. I don't think he knows how either. It just happened."

"Does he have a sphere then? Is that how you knew about mine?" Emily asked as calmly as she could manage. Her eyes were locked with Jordan's. Had she not been so furious she would have appreciated how beautiful they were. She wanted to attack him and she saw the feeling was mutual by the way his irises seemed to beat.

"He does," Barnes answered for Jordan.

"So there are others?" Emily reasoned.

Barnes struck Jordan's leg.

Jordan looked reluctant, but rolled his pant leg up to reveal a metal plate that looked identical to Emily's. There were the same intricate curving patterns woven across the metal, but it was tinted with greens instead of blues.

Emily's eyes widened. "What can you do?"

"Shift rock and stone," he answered without blinking.

"Not much use there when you're on a boat."

Jordan shrugged. "You won't be very effective on land."

"Cut it out," Barnes warned.

Emily took her eyes off Jordan. "Are the spheres a UNM science project?"

"They are virtaiyu technology," Barnes said, "recovered from early on in the war. The base that housed them was compromised and the spheres were scattered around the globe. We are trying to locate them."

"What is their purpose?" Emily asked.

"All we know is that all nations were put on alert to find them. Commander Unden was flying into Coronado to analyze both Kaiba and Jordan. Hopefully he'll land at Sand Point and be able to shed more light on the situation."

"Will I get to keep it or will the military try to take it from me?"

Barnes scratched his head. "I don't know of a way to remove it from you. To my knowledge you will get to keep it, but I can't say for sure. I suspect they will try to help you train."

Emily wondered if he was telling the truth. If he knew that death released the sphere, he didn't indicate it. But then again why would he?

Emily shifted in her seat. "Train for what exactly?"

"You can control water," Barnes said. "That's something the military can utilize in a million different ways."

"I'm not a soldier," Emily said.

"Knew you were all talk," Jordan mumbled.

Barnes glared at him, then continued to speak. "You may not have a choice."

"They can't make a woman fight," Emily said, toying with her hair. "The UNM draft laws say so. Only women who *volunteer* must fight. Since I have done no such thing, they have no power over me, especially in a different country."

"This is a rare circumstance. I'd say that's exception enough."

"Then let's go to court," Emily said. "There's no exception for that in the law."

"Good try," Jordan said.

"Please, they'd deny you the chance," Barnes said. "Besides, it's not for certain that they'll make you fight, but I would consider it a near certain possibility."

Emily should have known that this power would come at a cost. "And if I refuse?"

"I don't think that's an option."

"They can't force me into battle."

"They must do things differently in Australia then," Jordan scoffed. "Because when the first draft dodgers said that, they were either captured or murdered. In the end everyone fights."

She knew he was right. Did she really believe that she would be left alone with such an ability? Part of her wished she hadn't grabbed the sphere. The other part wondered if she could prove herself on the field of war.

"Just wait and see what the commander says. No sense for needless worrying," Barnes said.

22

PRISON CELLS AND UNEXPECTED COMPANY

Taras Prison, Location Unknown

Kaiba gritted his teeth as he ripped the duct tape from his mouth. He opened and closed his jaw slowly and massaged the raw skin. He picked the straw off his body and shifted on the dark mulch that coated the cell floor. It was a stuffy warm cellar, but Kaiba still felt the shiver of the ice that clung to his pants. He brushed his legs and rubbed them back and forth trying to generate as much heat as he could. The more he rubbed, the more his legs tingled, which he hoped meant that the numbness was fading. He checked his skin. It looked normal, no purple or black, which were sure signs of frostbite. That much was a relief.

He stood up, having to duck under the low ceilings. He squinted in the dim lighting that came from a string of dusty LED light bulbs just outside the cage. They didn't throw much light, just barely enough to see in. There was nothing else in Kaiba's cell except for a bucket in the corner next to him. He wondered what the rusty pail was for. As the putrid smell wafted his way, he was repulsed more than he could stand. He moved as far away from the bucket as he could. He was surprised that there were no loose rocks, no crumbs, and no sign that anyone had been there before him other than the strong-smelling bucket. As he made his way to the back wall of the cell he found jagged tally marks that appeared scratched as if by fingernails. As he ran his hand along them he realized for the first time that everything in the room was made of solid stone. The fact was so simple and yet so liberating. He stepped across the dirt-coated rock floor with a joyous feeling in his belly. He stuck his hand out, focusing on the largest block of stone just in front of the gate to his cell. He tried to feel the earth as if it were a living thing. Doing so seemed to work before, but this time he couldn't sense the ground around him. His chest didn't tweak nor did he feel any overpowering sensation.

He didn't let these things bother him and instead imagined the rock rising by his own willpower. He stared, holding his focus, but no matter how hard he concentrated the stone wouldn't budge. He walked to the pewter rock, lowering himself so that he rested on one knee just above it. His hand hovered an inch from the floor and his body shook as he tried to move the earth. He held his breath, focusing his entire being on the rock, but it was of no use.

As he tried to produce the adrenaline-like sensation, his arms and back started to burn and sting. The more he tried the worse the pain got until finally he gave up. He breathed heavily, discouraged and frustrated.

"Odd way to get your bearings," said a voice.

Kaiba almost jumped in surprise. He hadn't known that anyone was in the prison with him, let alone watching him. He looked questioningly at the cell opposite his own. The man was squatting. His chin was round, and coated with thick stubble like every other inch of his face. The light brown facial hair seemed to create a mask that revealed only his beady hazel eyes. They glinted back at Kaiba like some winter animal in the night. Even bent over he looked like a body builder.

"Just looking for any hint at a way out," Kaiba said innocently.

"I see," the man said though his voice was edged with curiosity. "You'll be hard pressed to find one."

Kaiba scooted himself as close to his bars as possible to get a better view. The man's large hands were wrapped around the bars of his cell. Even in the dim lighting Kaiba could see the letters UNM inked into his knuckles. "You were a soldier?"

"Am a soldier," he corrected. "Once you become one you never lose it. And you? You're pretty young. You get drafted and yanked out by these thugs? Or are you just a war dodger turned rogue?"

"Captured. I was about to be shipped off when the base at Coronado was attacked."

"California?"

"Yeah, that's the place," Kaiba said.

"Shame they've already started attacking the US. Why'd they snag you? You don't look especially dangerous."

Kaiba thought up a quick lie. "To protect my squad. I went after one of the men here, calls himself Graves. When I jumped on his back they knocked me out and I woke up with a bag around my head and them at my side."

The man smiled. "A clever lie, but they would have shot you unless you were of any worth."

Heat flushed to Kaiba's face as often happened when he was caught fabricating the truth. He'd hoped the man hadn't notice. "And how can you be so sure?"

"Because they should have shot me, but they didn't. I'm under the impression that we're here for the same reason Mister…"

Kaiba hesitated for a moment, but couldn't seem to reason any harm. It wasn't like he was going anywhere soon. "Kaiba."

"Nice to meet a cellmate who actually talks. I'm Captain Bennett." He smiled, revealing teeth abnormally white compared to the filth of his skin. "Tell me Kaiba, do you feel as though there's a burning sensation in your back and arms?"

The question seemed to catch Kaiba off guard. How could the soldier have known what he was feeling? "Only a bit, why?"

"Did you take the meds?"

"They forced a tiny red pill down my throat if that's what you mean."

The tattered shirt Bennett wore indicated that he'd been there for some time. He pulled back one sleeve and leaned against the bars with his right shoulder.

Kaiba was shocked to see the metal on his skin. It was tinged red and stretched all the way from the base of his neck to the edge of his shoulder. "The meds mess with your nerves. Whatever they gave us can suppress our ability to use the spheres."

Again Kaiba had been taken off guard. He hadn't considered that this prisoner could also have a sphere.

Bennett draped his shirt back over the metal as though to protect it. "Where'd you get the bond?"

"The bond?"

"Jesus, kid. Where'd the sphere attach itself to you?"

Kaiba held the man's gaze for a moment. "My chest." He lifted his shirt to reveal his own plate. It felt strange exposing himself to a total stranger, but for the first time, apart from Jordan, Kaiba had met another person who had his same problem.

"Dumb lucky place to have it," Bennett said.

"Why's that?"

"The material that makes up the spheres works like armor. Yours is much better placed than on your shoulder." He patted his metal. "Judging by the white color I'd say you can control air. Am I wrong?"

"I created lightning and can move stone. I don't know anything about the air."

Bennett's face went grim. "I was afraid you'd say that. Have you been able to do anything else?"

"What else is there? It's not enough that I can barely control what I've got?"

"I had hoped your element would have been picked up last."

"Last?" Kaiba asked. "What do you know of the other spheres?"

Bennett was barely visible in the shadows. "There were seven spheres scattered round the globe, three of which the virtaiyu now control thanks to you, me," then Bennett pointed to the cell on Kaiba's right, "and her."

Kaiba hadn't even thought to look, but a girl with ochre skin and long dark hair lay on her back in a cot made of hay. Her face was the most beautiful Kaiba had ever seen. Thin dark eyebrows nestled above her piercing hazel-green eyes that were locked on the ceiling. A peppering of light freckles patterned her upper cheeks and the sides of her nose. She was skinny, with long, muscular runner's legs. She didn't move as though she were asleep. Her breath was so quiet it was hard to tell if she was even conscious.

"Who is she?" Kaiba asked, not looking away. Yellow-tinted metal stretched from her wrist to just before her elbow.

"They called her Nassira. She was dragged in the day after I was. I can't figure out if the meds affect her differently or if they broke her spirit somehow. Either way she's yet to say a word to me or anyone else in this place," Bennett said.

Kaiba tore his gaze from the woman. "If it'll give you any peace of mind, I know another sphere is reasonably safe."

Bennett stroked his chin, scraping dust and dirt away. "And how do you know that?"

"When I was taken from Coronado, my best friend got away with his sphere."

Bennett looked slightly relieved. "And which element does he have?"

"He can move the earth like I can. I don't know what you mean by element."

"The seven spheres correspond to their own force, which we call elements," Bennett said. "Your friend's corresponds to earth." He pointed to the cell next to Kaiba. "And Nassira's corresponds to lightning."

"And what about yours?"

He tapped his shoulder. "I trained with this one day in and day out. Now all I can manage to do is this." Bennett closed both of his fists together and then opened them slowly. At the center of his cupped hands was a tiny fleck of fire no bigger than the flame thrown off a match stick. "Not very impressive, I know, but when I first got here I couldn't even manage to do that. That's why I think my body is fighting through the meds."

Kaiba watched the flame with an insatiable curiosity. "Fire is your element then?"

"You're quicker than you look Kaiba," Bennett said sarcastically. Bennett let the flame die out. "Air, water, and psychic are the other three elements."

"How is 'psychic' an element? You're telling me a sphere will let someone read minds and palms?"

"Don't be stupid, boy. There are two distinct categories of elements. Air, earth, and water make up what we classify as the Natural Elements. They are abundant all around us and are primarily manipulated. In contrast are fire, lightning, and psychic, which are known as the Energy Elements. These must first be created, and can then be manipulated just as the natural ones. Psychic is just the name we gave to the energy."

"That's only six," Kaiba said. "If there are seven spheres, what's the seventh element?"

"Have you used fire at all?"

"No," Kaiba said. "Can you shoot lightning?"

"My sphere doesn't work the way yours does. I only have the ability to create, shift, and control fire in all of its forms. You have that ability too, but clearly it's yet to activate in you."

"Why would I gain the skill to create fire?"

Bennett tapped his breast. "That plate at your chest holds a connection to the other spheres. All the ancient cultures, Greek, Roman, Japanese, Chinese, and Egyptian, believed in the forces of nature. Water, fire, earth, and air were the commonalities between the societies, but there was another force. Despite the various languages, the same word was used by each population. They called it aether."

Kaiba whispered the word as if it were a new taste.

"We don't fully understand it, but aether is the blending of each element and that's why your sphere interacts with the others. Whenever another person bonds with a sphere you will inherit that power as well. You have earth and lightning as you claim, maybe even fire. Under this medication I guess we won't find out."

Kaiba took in the statement slowly. He had difficulty believing that more was to come. The thought was more frightening than he cared to have imagined. "Why are these spheres called the Terraformer Keys?"

Bennett looked like he'd just been slapped across the face, "How do you know about the Terraformer?"

Kaiba coughed from the dirt that hung in the air. "I'm assuming it's a weapon. I don't know. I only know these spheres are the keys."

"Then I'll keep it that way," Bennett said.

"Enlighten me."

"I think it's better you don't know."

"If I have one of these keys I should know what it unlocks."

Bennett shrugged. "You're entitled to your opinion. Doesn't mean you'll get your way."

"How'd you know about the Terraformer then?" Kaiba asked. "Were you a researcher *and* a soldier?"

"Never assume that a warrior cannot be intelligent. Do I look sciencey to you?"

He looked just the opposite. Kaiba shook his head.

"Damn straight. I became a marine in the good old days when all we had to worry about were inside threats and outside terrorists," Bennett said proudly. "I didn't wait for a draft. I dedicated myself to war just as my father did."

"How'd you get your sphere then?"

"My performance. Even before the virtaiyu hit, I was on the government's radar as a hot shot." Bennett made his fingers into the shape of a gun. "Sharpshooter." He smiled and pretended to fire the gun. "Long story short, I was eligible for a program called the Tempest Project. I was pulled off the front and became the first person to ever bind with a sphere. They used me as a test dummy. When our base was attacked by virtaiyu we were forced to scatter the spheres around the globe."

"So how'd you get captured if your abilities were so strong?"

"The virtaiyu attacked the base, they had too many," Bennett said. "Not to mention they can control the elements too. I was surrounded and there was no way I could have escaped. They killed everyone else at the base and took me on their ship."

"I'm sorry," Kaiba said.

"Happens. Wasn't like I was very close to any of them anyway."

It sounded like he was lying but Kaiba didn't press and instead asked, "How'd you end up at this Fifth Era base?"

"I assumed I was being taken to China when Graves and others attacked the Virt ship to claim me for themselves. The Fifth Era says they're allies with the Virts, but all they really care about is sucking up to virtaiyu leadership."

"That explains why Graves ran over virtaiyu soldiers in Cali," Kaiba said.

"The virtaiyu will do and pay anything for the spheres. That's why the Fifth Era will do anything to capture the spheres for themselves."

At that instant the string of bulbs flicked off, leaving the jail in total darkness.

"A note of warning, Kaiba. When they force you up tomorrow, try to vomit the pill."

"You still didn't answer me. What is the Terraformer?" Kaiba asked.

There was no answer.

Kaiba felt his way through the dark and crawled back to the prickly hay. He smoothed a clump of it together as a makeshift pillow and wriggled his way under the grass. His clothes were still damp from the snow, causing strands of the dry hay to stick to him.

He laid on his back. The ground was hard and unforgiving, but it wasn't as bad as he would have thought. He started to distribute handfuls of the straw onto his body for warmth. When he'd spread out enough of the stuff, he closed his eyes and fell instantly asleep.

23

THE FIRST
DREAM

Moscow, Russia

The house had been abandoned for some time. Ian searched
the contents of the residence as though he were searching through a
life he'd lost. Iris had their wedding photos, pictures of cousins and
herself as a child, but the one he cared most about was the single
photo of her and his baby boy. It wasn't on the wall, or in his old
bedroom. It wasn't in the kitchen or in any of the boxes that filled
the single-car garage. He flipped drawers, checked under the bed,
and then finally he saw it in the bathroom. A five-by-seven photo
in a tiny frame made of pure silver. He held the photo as though it
were the rarest gem in the world. The baby's eyes were blue like his
own and the child had the same wispy blonde hair that Ian once had
as a young boy.

He felt sorrow looking at Iris. He'd been told she'd fallen to the
tuberculosis strain several weeks after giving birth to their son. He
often regretted having to spend his prison time while she struggled
in sickness. But it was the code of the Vory, Russia's mafia, to never

let a brother take the fall for you. Ian had honored the code, but after spending his time in a pit for so long, and losing his wife, he spat on the rules. He turned his back on his blood brothers. He knew going in that it would be difficult, but it would have been worse had they discovered that he'd secretly kept a family. Now that he was released no one would tell him how to live anymore. The law was beneath him.

He took the photo and felt the back of his neck. The metal plate still didn't feel natural, but he was getting used to it. Ian still didn't understand how the sphere enabled him to jump and create energy. After a day of experimenting, he didn't really care. The sphere would ensure no one would get in the way of reaching his son. He went back to the ice-ridden streets of Moscow. The orphanage was four blocks from their old house. He reached the rickety wooden building and was surprised to see that the thing hadn't caved in yet. The snow on the roof would surely break through any day. He thought it a cruel twist of fate for history to repeat itself. Ian always hated the fact that he'd never known his parents and if he hadn't been so lucky he surely would have perished.

Ian hoped his son was equally lucky. He knew the boy would no longer be in the orphanage; surely someone would have adopted a baby, and a baby as cute as his son at that. A part of him hoped the child would still be playing with other children in the home. Maybe he would be happy, safe, and most importantly naïve of the dangers that the world was going through. It was a foolish thought made only for a dreamer, if there were any such people left in the world, and Ian felt rather imbecilic for thinking it. It was his first thought of hope since he'd left the prison.

He climbed the broken steps of the boy's home and hollered to see if anyone was there. As he'd suspected, it was completely empty. The smell of the place made his nose crinkle. The wooden floors were sprinkled with rat droppings and animal carcasses. He saw the room he remembered and strode over to the metal filing cabinets. He wasn't sure what Iris had named the child, but he hoped the file would still be in the cabinet. He opened the bottom drawer and thumbed through the wrinkled manila file folders worn down by time.

Within moments he found his last name, Orokov, and opened the file. The same picture of his wife and son were attached to a single sheet of paper. The first name was Drelen. Ian said it aloud, amused at hearing his son's name for the first time. There was no other useful information on the document, until he read a small paragraph at the bottom of the page. The writing in purple ink read: Adopted March 4, 2021 by Yiel Banko. Beside the name was an address that Ian memorized quickly when he heard a creak outside the office door.

A man in a torn green coat and heavy beard stood in the doorway. "What are you doing in my house?"

Ian eyed the bum. "This was a public orphanage, no one's home, beggar."

The man drew a knife. "Well it's my home now."

"You really don't want to do that," Ian said. He smiled, matching the dangerous appearance of the knife.

"Oh, I think I do. Get out."

But Ian stood where he was. The beggar ran from the doorway. Ian waited as if in no danger at all. As the bum's knife started to fall, there was a flash of purple and Ian was gone. A moment later he reappeared behind the beggar. Ian grabbed the man's wrist and twisted it. "No one will stop me from reaching my son."

The man howled in pain as Ian grabbed the knife and thrust it down.

Taras Prison, Location Unknown

Kaiba jolted upright clutching his own chest. He heaved air into his lungs like a whale that had come up from the ocean. He'd felt the sting of the knife, but his chest was still on fire. Though his eyes were open, the world was tinged with weaving lilac lines. He sat up trying to gain his vision, but the world continued to pulse in and out.

Graves stood over Kaiba and kicked him in the ribs.

Kaiba rolled on his side and clutched his chest even tighter. The kick to the ribs felt like a mere pat in comparison to the burning in his chest.

"Grab him," Graves said to his two bodyguards.

Kaiba was seized on either side and thrust to his feet. His head felt as if it were being pounded repeatedly with a hammer. The bright violet light pulsed faster. He tried to focus, but he couldn't. His vision swirled in circles.

Graves reached for Kaiba's shirt and lifted it. "So another has bonded." He looked up at his men. "Wait until this passes, most of these events last only a few minutes."

Graves turned out to be right. The world gradually returned to normal and Kaiba began to focus again. His thoughts were racing and mixing all together. What element had just activated? This Orokov person he saw in his dreams must have had a sphere. Yet, he didn't even know whether Ian was a real person or not. And if he was a real person, Kaiba couldn't understand why he was having dreams about someone he'd never met. He was even more confused about this activation. When lightning activated, he'd projected it, but this element afflicted him in a negative way, hurt him even.

Kaiba blinked as sweat dripped into his eyes. The room was no longer glowing or blinking and everything seemed normal. The first thing he saw was Bennett against the bars of his cage. He looked intrigued and almost amazed. Kaiba caught a glimpse of his own chest to see that the bottom of the plate had a circular indentation that glowed with a purple light.

Graves took a step forward with something in his hand. He thrust the pill down Kaiba's throat before Kaiba could make a move.

Graves patted Kaiba's face. "Good morning, sunshine."

The men at Kaiba's sides thrust a bag onto his head. He heard Bennett fight as they tried to give him a pill. There was rustling and a cry of fury. Then Bennett moaned.

Kaiba was dragged for several minutes and when the bag was finally removed he was in an open room with a giant monitor on one wall. Bennett and Nassira stood at his sides. Graves walked to the monitor and stood with his hands behind his back. The monitor flashed on and a single virtaiyu appeared on screen.

A seven-foot figure in all black armor walked forward. The creature's face was a blue-grey color like all the rest of its kind. Tattoos of bright blue crescent moons were scattered about the alien face, as were several scars that resembled ritual markings. The most notable cut was the one in the shape of a C around the creature's left eye. It was crimson like the color of exposed muscle. Its eyes were a dark grey that reminded Kaiba of storm clouds and the inner rims around its irises were tinged red.

"Eskylious," Graves said, giving a slight bow.

Out of the corner of his eye, Kaiba noticed Bennett's mouth drop open.

The creature tilted its head. "These are the three?"

"Indeed they are," Graves answered.

As he spoke Kaiba was kicked in the back. Pain shot through his body and he was forced onto his knees. Bennett and Nassira suffered similar treatment.

Graves approached Bennett first. He ripped the sleeve from his arm revealing his shoulder. "This whelp has bonded with fire." He approached Nassira, who still had no emotion. He picked her arm up and showed it. "Lightning."

"And the boy?" Eskylious asked.

Graves smiled. "Aether."

The virtaiyu blinked twice, once vertically and once more horizontally. "You humans have proved your worth, more so than I could have ever imagined."

Graves beamed with pride. "Shall we execute the prisoners and have the spheres ready upon your arrival?"

"No," Eskylious said. "I much prefer to execute them myself. They deserve punishment by my hand for bonding with something so sacred. I shall be there personally."

"We are honored," Graves said, smiling. "Now the Fifth Era of the world can finally begin."

Eskylious smiled to reveal two sets of needle-like teeth. Yellow spittle hung from his maw like a spider's web. "And so it begins."

Then the monitor went black.

Graves fumbled with the bag and walked back over to Kaiba. "Looks like you'll be staying with us a little longer."

They were tossed back into the cells with nothing but a wet-moldy bagel each. Kaiba picked as much mold as he could from the bread and took a mouthful of the squishy food. It didn't taste half bad and he was too hungry to care. Then he looked up at Bennett who scarfed his entire bagel, mold and all. Nassira didn't touch her food.

"Who is Eskylious?" Kaiba asked the moment he'd finished eating. "You recognized him on screen. I saw you."

Bennett swallowed his food quickly. He laughed, his voice high and shrill like a maniac. It made Kaiba feel as if everyone was supposed to know who this Virt was. "He's the one in charge—not only of the virtaiyu, but of the Fifth Era forces as well. The UNM has been hunting him down since the first delegation at ground zero. Today was the first time I've ever seen his face in person."

Kaiba was shocked. "He was the one—"

"—who murdered the forty linguistics professors when we tried to negotiate. Yes, that's the one."

The professors were trained in different dialects and languages, both modern and ancient. Only, Eskylious took their knowledge of the languages, used some recording device to learn for himself, and then killed each of the delegates, all on national television.

"Bennett, now is as good a time as any. What is the Terraformer?"

Bennett contemplated his decision. "I will tell you if you agree to try something for me."

"Name it. I'll do it."

"Very well. The UNM thought that these devices could tip the war in our favor." He shifted. "In a way they were right. Your power will continue to grow, and yes, we will be powerful enough to defend ourselves. But that was never the main function of the spheres. Their main purpose, as you know, is to act as keys to the Terraformer. The Terraformer was the weapon the Virts used to destroy China. Its technology is far beyond anything we have. In one instant the Virts destroyed the continent, wiping all living things within the blast radius off the face of the earth. Then they reformed it the very next moment."

"How could they do that?"

Bennett sighed. "From what we understood, the weapon created a kind of black hole that absorbed all living matter around it. After some time the mass detonated with the power of a thousand nuclear warheads in a blazing explosion of light that scorched the surface. The blast wave travelled radially, destroying everything in its path."

Kaiba leaned forward, gripped with fear and fascination. "How did the black hole not consume the world? And how could the virtaiyu settle on the surface so soon afterward?"

"Because the surface was neither barren nor burned. When the explosion finally stopped traveling outward, its wake left behind a lush countryside of plentiful plains and abundant forests. Their weapon erased what existed and replaced it with something new."

"That's impossible."

"Kid," Bennett said, "you can shoot lightning and I can create fire. Impossible isn't really in our vocabulary anymore."

"Can't argue with that. How many keys will it take for the Terraformer to become active again?"

"As far as I know," Bennett said, "all of them."

Kaiba was slightly relieved, but his stomach still felt knotted up. "How do we recover the Terraformer?"

"I don't think we can," Bennett admitted. "But the first step is for us to get out of here. That mark on your chest and what you experienced was the activation of another sphere."

Kaiba nodded. "I heard Graves say that. What do you want me to do about it?"

"The element that activated is what I believe to be psychic."

Kaiba thought of Ian and how he'd somehow teleported. He told Bennett everything he'd seen in his dream. Bennett listened intently until Kaiba had finished.

"That makes this easier then," Bennett said. "I need you to try to teleport like this Orokov person did."

Kaiba still felt a lingering pain in his chest. He scowled at the thought of his body erupting into more pain. "Neither of us know if this man is even real."

"As I said, your sphere has a connection to each of the others."

"And you believe I can do what this man does?"

"I'm saying it's a possibility," Bennett said.

"How am I supposed to use psychic on these suppressant pills?"

"We wait for twenty hours until the effects start to wear off." Bennett stared blankly for a moment. "In the meantime we pray that Eskylious doesn't arrive."

24

A Psychic Void

Taras Prison, Location Unknown

The ceiling dripped a cold clear liquid that smelled of gasoline. Kaiba watched the droplets fall, thinking of the dream he'd just had of Ian teleporting across towns and street corners. Between the dreams of Ian and the pain in his chest, Kaiba wasn't at peace whether sleeping or awake. His stomach still burned with aching fire that came in waves of varying intensity. He'd tried to teleport a few hours earlier, but his body erupted into violent seizures. Even when he regained control of his limbs they still burned. One moment, his skin would prickle and he could scratch away the irritation, but at other moments his skin would contract and he would seize up in writhing agony. And so he lay on the floor hoping that the worst of his torment had passed. He'd survived the night, or was it day? No light shown in the dungeon, except for the ever-buzzing LED lights in the hall outside his cage.

Bennett whistled.

Kaiba glanced over to see the captain's face pressed against the bars of the cage. "How's the pain?"

Kaiba put his hand behind his head. "I'll make it. My body's getting used to never being comfortable."

"Time for you to try again."

Kaiba rolled over to sit up. "Straight to the point, I see."

Bennett cracked his knuckles. "Can't afford not to be."

"You don't know what it's like," Kaiba said.

"That's true," Bennett admitted. "But you're our one shot at getting out of here."

Kaiba stood up and walked to the bars. "I'll break into seizures again."

Bennett rose to his feet in a similar manner. "I'd rather you attempted and got hurt than sat here wondering what if."

Kaiba thought of the shadows, how the world blurred and was replaced with shifting bright lights. "I can't. I don't even know how."

"'I can't' is a phrase used by the weak. You have to. There is no other option."

"You're in no position to tell me what to do."

Bennett hit the metal bars and they wriggled back and forth as he yelled, "Try again! Don't you understand how important it is that we get out of here? If you don't attempt it, you might as well just die!"

Kaiba glared at Bennett, knowing that he was right. If he didn't act he would die. Then he heard a shifting to his right. The girl with the ochre skin was sitting up, watching him.

"You need to do this," Bennett said. "It's been about twenty hours since they last medicated us. From where I'm sitting our abilities will be at their strongest now."

"And if they aren't?" Kaiba asked.

"Then we're no better or worse off."

Nassira was still looking at him and he felt strangely put on the spot.

Kaiba looked away from her. "Do you even remember anything the Tempest researchers said about psychic?"

"I'm not even sure they knew what the psy element did, to be completely honest."

Kaiba uttered a helpless laugh. "That's comforting."

"Why not just imitate how you saw the Russian using it in your dreams?" Bennett offered.

"One moment he's jumping a single foot and the next he's teleporting across fields. Not an ideal person to learn from. Plus, he's inconsistent. His power doesn't seem to be totally under his control."

"Then do a small jump," Bennett said.

"Say I do manage to teleport, what then? You'll still be stuck."

"One step at a time. Just worry about this first part."

Kaiba stood, remembering Ian's first jump in the orphanage.

Ian had made his first leap easily, but what had he done? He didn't seem the least bit fazed by whatever shifting energy seemed to throw the world into motion. He'd remained calm and collected even though he'd never jumped before.

Then Kaiba remembered the knife that the beggar held.

That was it. Ian had concentrated on the object before he jumped. All Kaiba had to do was focus on something and the rest would take care of itself.

He tore a tiny edge off his sleeve, crumpled it up, and threw it on the floor just outside the bars. Then he closed his eyes and put his hands out at his side. With his right hand he tapped his chest and his skin started to tingle. Kaiba pictured the small crumpled piece of tan fabric against the dirt floor. He imagined standing on top of the cloth, his shoe crushing it into the black dirt.

His head started to spin and Kaiba opened his eyes as the tingling grew throughout his body. The world moved back and forth, swaying like seaweed in an ocean current. Everything had turned black with deep, varying hues of purple. Even Bennett looked different. His skin was a moving hive of dots that buzzed and collided in on itself.

Kaiba thought he was going to pass out from the sickening motions of the room, but he remembered the crumpled piece of cloth once again. He looked at it on the floor just beyond the cage and it provided stability. It stayed still, unlike the rest of the jail. He thrust his arms back and sprang forward.

He felt the air burst around him. A bright flash of light and then he was on the other side of his cage. His skin was coated in sweat and he was panting. He lifted his right foot and underneath it was the piece of cloth.

Bennett smiled. "Yes! Now get me out of here."

Kaiba was shaky, but he didn't feel the urge to pass out anymore. "How do you propose I do that?"

"You aren't naked."

Kaiba scowled. "Clearly."

"Hear me out. Your clothes were touching your body when you jumped and they stayed on you. So maybe whatever you touch stays on you also."

Kaiba said, "Gimme your hand."

Bennett had to squeeze his large forearm through the narrowly-spaced bars.

Kaiba extended his hand and Bennett squeezed back tightly. "Be gentle now." He winked. "Never done this before."

Kaiba could feel the space around him starting to slip away. He pictured the tiny piece of cloth again and both he and Bennett appeared right by it.

Bennett grabbed Kaiba's shirt. "That is what I'm talkin' about. Come on, let's get out of here."

Kaiba looked at Nassira. She hadn't the slightest care that they had just escaped. Instead, she was tossing a pebble against the back wall of her cell. The rock clacked loudly as it bounced back to her hand. She seemed to be deep in thought, or perhaps just trying to keep herself busy. Either way, her silence made Kaiba believe something was severely wrong with her.

"We should get her out first."

"She'll drag us down," Bennett said.

"She's also got an element."

"If we get caught because of her, the virtaiyu will have three elements again instead of just one."

"I'd rather they didn't have any," Kaiba said.

"If she won't move you're carrying her."

Kaiba ignored the comment and crouched next to her cell. "Gimme your hand."

She didn't stop tossing the rock.

"Come on," Kaiba urged. "We have to get out of here."

Bennett was on the bottom step of the staircase looking up to the top. "Just leave her. They could be coming any moment now."

"Please, if you can hear me just give me your hand."

Still she didn't respond.

Kaiba closed his eyes and pictured the space right beside Nassira.

"What are you doing?" Bennett hissed.

Kaiba jumped forward and ended up in the cell beside her. "I know we're in a bad situation, but we can get through it. Give me your hand."

Her voice was so quiet he almost didn't hear her say, "There is nothing left for me in this life."

Kaiba took a chance, grabbed her arm, and managed to teleport back outside the cage.

She wriggled free of his grip and yelled, *"Don't touch me!"*

Her voice echoed and Kaiba went numb. Someone must have heard her.

She shoved Kaiba and he stumbled into the staircase.

"You little..." Bennett leapt down the stairs and smashed Nassira in the side of the head. She fell.

Kaiba lunged forward and caught her. She went limp.

"You knocked her out?"

"Of course I did! She was going to get us caught, if she hasn't done that already!"

Then several loud voices came from the top of the staircase.

Bennett swore. "I won't get imprisoned again because of her."

"Then what do you suggest?"

"You get us out of here," Bennett demanded. "Picture a monitor in the computer room, one of the snowmobiles in the hanger bay. I don't care!"

"I jumped two feet, now you want me to teleport between rooms?"

"Let's hear a better idea!"

Kaiba searched the prison cells. There was a small space underneath the stairs. He set Nassira down in the middle of the floor, then pointed to it.

Bennett shrugged. "You better hope."

The space was just large enough for the two of them to squeeze into. They stood shoulder to shoulder, although Kaiba was tightly pressed against the underside of the staircase. One step dug into his shoulder blade. They waited until the voices of two men came closer.

"What the heck was that girl yelling about? If she thinks she can just summon us with a simple call she's got another thing comin'," one of the men said.

Their footsteps clanked, vibrating the stairs above Kaiba. He was nervous, but if they couldn't take out two people how were they supposed to escape from fifty?

The second man answered, "This is the first we've heard of her. Since Eskylious wants her alive I'd consider this a good thing."

Kaiba held his breath as the two men stepped onto the dirt floor of the prison.

"How'd she get out?" A tall man with a thick scar across his right cheek strode over to Nassira.

The other man was short with a thick mustache and a plump belly. He waddled over and shook her.

Bennett slowly pointed at Kaiba and then at the plump man.

Kaiba nodded. His palms were sweaty; he'd never killed anyone before. Not even on the raids with Fifth Era when so many of his acquaintances had murdered for fun. He wasn't sure if he could do it.

Bennett held up three fingers. He lowered one finger, then the other.

Kaiba had learned several ways of taking a person down from behind in school. The thought of breaking someone's neck sent shivers down his spine; he wouldn't be able to take the cracking sound. For some reason he'd always favored choking a person out. He'd hoped practice was just like the real thing. But then he saw the pistol at the fat man's hip. If he could take the gun then maybe he wouldn't have to kill.

When Bennett's final finger went down, Kaiba ran at the fat man. He jumped on his back and wrapped his forearm around the man's neck.

The man squealed in surprise.

With his other hand Kaiba took the gun and drew on the man.

Bennett hit the scarred man in a flurry of three moves and he was out cold on the dirt floor.

"Please don't shoot!" the fat man pleaded.

Bennett looked at him in disgust and strode forward. He put his hands on the man's head and twisted. The cracking sound was horrendous.

"You didn't have to kill him!" Kaiba said.

Bennett put a finger in his face. "This is war. The strong prevail and the weak die."

He leaned down and patted the unconscious man's body. He was unarmed, but Bennett found a map in the front of his jacket. It was a roll-screen in a plastic coating. He tapped the surface and something flashed that Kaiba couldn't quite see.

"What a find." Bennett extended an open palm. "Now gimme that gun."

Kaiba held out the pistol and watched furiously as Bennett took the man's jacket. Then Bennett pocketed the map.

"Don't glare at me like that. In case you forgot, we're in some frozen wasteland. You'll do good to take the fat man's coat. Should provide your skinny bones with some extra warmth."

Kaiba looked down on the man. He hated the thought of robbing from the dead. This was no ordinary circumstance, though, and if it was as cold outside as before he would need the protection. He reluctantly took the furry coat and wrapped it around himself. It was too big, but he had a feeling that was a good thing.

Bennett stared at the girl angrily. "Still wanna take her?"

"I do," Kaiba said shortly.

Bennett shook his head and sighed, "Fine. She'll only make things harder for us. And Kaiba," Bennett said. "Don't try to spare any more lives. These men are not innocent. The next time you hesitate will cost you."

"I won't kill as freely as you do. These are people, not aliens."

Bennett smiled. "You're young. I remember when I was like you, but you'll begin to see that the enemy faces blur together. Human or virtaiyu, they're just the same."

25

BREAKOUT

Taras Prison, Location Unknown

Bennett took the prison keys from the first man and threw him in a cell. He knelt beside the man he'd knocked out and his eyes darted to Nassira. "Make sure she stays like that."

Kaiba nodded as Bennett picked up the scarred man by the scruff of his collar.

"Wake up now," Bennett said, slapping him back and forth across the cheeks. He stirred slightly, which only encouraged Bennett. "That's it, get up."

He forced his palm firmly against the Fifth Era guard's cheek and finally his eyes popped open. Before he could yell Bennett clasped a hand over his mouth and waved his gun back and forth.

"Wrong answer."

The man's eyes were wide.

"Now if you want to keep your life, you tell me where the Interligate access keys are."

Kaiba wanted to know for sure what an Interligate was, but he knew that interrupting would be a bad idea.

The man gave a muffled chuckle.

Bennett laughed along with him and shook his head slowly. He took a piece of cloth from his jacket and wrapped it around the barrel of the pistol. He forced the gun against the man's knee cap and pulled the trigger.

Kaiba flinched at the muffled screams of the man.

"Now," Bennett said when the man stopped crying. "I'm going to remove my hand and when I do, tell me where the keys are." He placed the homemade silencer against the man's temple. "Otherwise my friend has another bullet for you."

Kaiba took a step forward. He wouldn't let that happen; no one deserved that.

The man nodded. Kaiba relaxed and Bennett removed his hand.

"Taniel has the key," the man sobbed, "Please don't kill me!"

"Where is he?"

"He was in the monitor room just before the cafeteria, but they could have moved him. I don't know!"

"Describe him."

Kaiba interrupted, "I know him."

"Well then…" Bennett slammed the butt of the pistol against the man's head, knocking him out again. He slumped to the ground. "You'll be identifying him."

"You'll let him live?" Kaiba asked, surprised.

"I only kill when the situation demands it. Just help me."

They threw the man beside the other and locked the steel gate. Kaiba struggled to imagine waking up beside a dead friend. The thought unsettled him greatly.

Bennett knelt and grabbed the man's fallen rifle. "Now, if we can reach the monitor room and snag that key we might be able to get out before we're noticed. Otherwise we'll have to fight our way out."

"What is the Interligate you talked about?"

"They really didn't teach you anything in battle school, did they? The Interligates have the ability to transport matter through time and space instantaneously. It's how you got from sunny Cali to winter wonderland so quickly and it's how we'll get back."

Kaiba remembered the virtaiyu pouring from the underside of their planes at Coronado. "They have similar devices on their Mantas too, don't they?"

"On pretty much every vehicle. It's their primary mode of transportation and they have gateways scattered all across the world. That's how they can strike and retreat so quickly. Now let's get out of here."

"We only have a pistol and a rifle," Kaiba said. He doubted their chances at escaping. "Our abilities aren't even back yet."

"Oh really?" Bennett said, raising his eyebrows. He clapped his hands together and a small burst of sparks appeared. They grew into two small flames that coated his hands. "You try."

Kaiba focused on the stone floor. He could feel the adrenaline, but it was much weaker than he'd felt it in the past. He flung his hand upward and a small piece of tile broke. He'd meant to make a barrier, but his body wouldn't obey.

"Not a hundred percent, but we'll manage," Bennett said. "Grab her and let's go."

Kaiba hefted Nassira into his arms. She was heavier than he would have thought, more muscular.

He struggled to carry the girl up the stairs. The three of them reached the top, after Bennett offered to help. Kaiba peeked around the dark stone doorway at the top of the stairs. A dirt hallway extended to a dimly- lit ladder at the far end. They cautiously approached the ladder and Kaiba attempted to ascend it. The rungs were slick and every step threatened to send Nassira and him sprawling to the ground. There was a wooden cellar door just above his head, the same one that Esvir had pushed him through when he first arrived. Kaiba pushed up and the door creaked open. He stopped to listen. Hearing nothing, he scuttled through the door.

"Clear, Bennett," Kaiba said.

With Bennett's help all three of them were able to reach the munitions room. To Kaiba's surprise most of the gun racks were empty. Bullets were scattered on the floor as if hastily loaded. Unlike before, there was no security either inside or outside the room.

"Strange," Kaiba said. "Why would they leave an armory unguarded?"

Bennett searched the contents of the area. "Dunno." He found a discarded smoke grenade and pocketed the item. "This'll come in handy. Let's go."

"I'll go," Kaiba said. "I'm the only one who knows Taniel. No sense for the three of us getting caught."

"They'll send more men to check on us when the guards don't come back."

"Then wait here and keep watch. If I can't get the key before they come back we're screwed anyway."

Bennett stroked his beard. "That doesn't eliminate the fact that we'll need a ride out of here. You go for Taniel and I'll find the snowmobile keys."

"No need," Kaiba said. "They left the keys in the snowmobiles. I watched them when I came in. Just stay with Nassira."

"Fine. But if you're not back in ten I ditch the girl and come for you."

"Deal," Kaiba said. He made his way to the cafeteria, creeping in what shadows he could find. He slid with his back along the walls and crouched low as he neared the double doors. He slunk through, careful to check his corners, but there was no one in sight.

Alone, Kaiba stopped to wonder if the UNM had discovered the facility. That would explain why everyone had been called to fight. That also explained the abandoned armory. He felt excited at the thought of rescue. But he also wondered if Eskylious had arrived.

He jogged out into the hall and to the computer monitor room. He approached cautiously, doing his best not to make a sound. He poked his head through the scraggly door cutout, but froze at a man's voice.

"Why were we stuck to monitor?"

Kaiba relaxed, realizing that the men were at the far end of the room. They sat just in front of a giant screen with twenty different images. Kaiba looked at each monitor, but there was nothing except for snow and ice around the compound. No attacks.

"Someone had to check radar for when they get close."

If the UNM were picked up on radar, Kaiba would have to find a way to alert them that their attack was no longer a surprise.

"Why couldn't the Taniel boy stay?"

"He was the reason we caught the Elementals in the first place. Graves keeps him by his side like a puppy now. Look."

Kaiba saw the man point to one monitor. A group of soldiers stood in rows, with Graves, Esvir, and Taniel at the front. They didn't look ready for war, they looked ready for a parade. His worst fear had been realized; the virtaiyu must have been close. He noted the position of the snowmobiles crammed against the side walls. The two men continued to bicker and Kaiba bolted back to the armory.

His goal to take the Interligate keys had just become much more difficult. The entire compound was armed and on the ready for the virtaiyu leader. He found Bennett and Nassira sitting right where he'd left them.

"Got it already?" Bennett said, surprised. He tossed a sniper shell into the air and caught it.

Kaiba explained what he'd seen and Bennett's face grew stern. He took out the holomap of the compound. "Judging by this, there doesn't seem to be any other way out."

"Even if there were we wouldn't have a ride," Kaiba said.

Bennett took the smoke grenade from his pocket. "This should provide us enough time to sneak out." He juggled the bomb in his hands. "No telling how long this will last. It's kinda light so I'd guess only a few minutes."

"That's all we'll need."

"It's a lot of soldiers," Bennett said doubtfully. "I'll distract them with these first." He took three disc-shaped explosives from his pocket. "When the first goes off, you go for Taniel. I'll secure the ride and then toss the smoke when I'm ready."

Kaiba glanced at the girl. She was still unconscious. "And the gate?"

"You'll have to jump us through."

The three of them made their way back to the monitor room. Several times Kaiba nearly dropped Nassira, but he managed to get her to the edge of the garage without too much difficulty. He set her behind a utility closet door and peeked into the assembly, beside Bennett.

The soldiers stood motionless as Graves spoke. "When he arrives look down at your feet. The virtaiyu do not like to be looked in the eyes by more than one person. It's offensive to them and one as powerful as Eskylious must be treated with the utmost respect."

Kaiba's gut twisted as he heard Eskylious's name. He leaned farther around the corner to get a better view.

Bennett grabbed Kaiba and pulled him back. "If Eskylious gets here, we're screwed."

"We'll have to work fast," Kaiba whispered.

Bennett peered into the room, trying to think. He spied the keys in the snowmobiles along the wall just as Kaiba had said. "Make your way down the line of the machines and don't make a sound. When you reach the third snowmobile, watch me for your cue."

"On it," Kaiba said. He waited for Graves's voice to boom over the microphone before darting behind the snow machines. The space between the walls was just large enough for him to squeeze between. He crawled forward, stopping with every pause Graves took. The stops were brief, but each one made Kaiba think he'd been seen. He inched his way to the third blue Yamaha, made sure he hadn't been spotted, then poked his head up. He saw Taniel near the front, standing proudly beside Graves.

Kaiba squinted at his neck, but there didn't seem to be a key. He crawled a bit farther and peered just above the front skates of the snowmobile. From his new view Taniel definitely didn't have the key, but then he noticed the silver twinkle at Esvir's fat neck.

His mind was racing. Taniel would have been much easier to overpower, but Esvir was a different story. Kaiba would just have to improvise. What choice did he have? He turned his attention back to Bennett and gave a thumbs up.

Bennett nodded and crept to the back row of soldiers. His hands were glowing bright red-orange with heat. He disappeared from sight for a moment.

Kaiba squinted trying to follow him when someone yelled, "Put it out!"

Bennett darted back to the doorway as a soldier with a flaming jacket knocked down the men around him. He struggled to rip the burning coat from his back as the fire grew bigger.

"What the hell is going on?" Graves roared, rushing forward. The crowd of soldiers parted before him as the man started to stamp out his coat.

Kaiba spared a glance at the doorway and Bennett ushered him forward. He reached the last snowmobile without having to worry about being discovered, everyone was too distracted. He felt the pistol at his waist, but he didn't want to use it. Instead he stood up and moved to Esvir.

"Well?" Graves demanded.

"It just caught fire!"

"It just caught fire?" Graves repeated, laughing. "Sounds like you misused your lighter. Maybe this'll work."

A shot rang out and Kaiba took his chance. He ran, jumped, and smashed his right elbow against Esvir's temple. The man stumbled, and before he could recover Kaiba ripped the key from his neck.

Taniel fumbled with his machine gun. "Kaiba?"

An explosion rocked the room.

Smoke rose like a thick fog accompanied by the hot flickers of fire. Soldiers bawled in pain and everyone scattered in the chaos. Two more explosions detonated and Kaiba struggled to retain his balance as the shockwaves blasted through the room. Then, in the center of the soldiers Kaiba saw the smoke grenade twirling in the air. It hit the ground spewing grey smoke as if from a factory smokestack.

Kaiba tried to see where Bennett was, but visibility in the room grew worse by the second.

Bennett yelled from somewhere close by, "Up the ramp, Kaiba!"

Kaiba ran for the exit ramp, flinching at every rifle shot. Soldiers started to emerge from the mist. Kaiba drew his weapon with one hand, crouching low and holding out his other hand. He only hoped his abilities were back at their full potential. His fingers tingled as he readied the lightning in his hands. A flash of light burst through the smoke, not from his hand but from the snowmobile. Gunfire echoed from Bennett's weapon as the machine screeched to a halt.

"Get on!" Bennett screamed, firing more rounds into the coughing soldiers.

Kaiba leapt onto the back of the snowmobile, thudding against the stiff padding. He grabbed Nassira's limp sides.

The soldiers called orders to one another, but Bennett revved the throttle. They skidded up the icy exit ramp, leaving a trail of white in their wake.

The drone of the engine dulled all other sounds, but Kaiba could still hear Bennett shout, "Get ready!"

Kaiba braced himself as his world started to turn purple. As they reached the flat ground of the domed building, twenty virtaiyu came into view. They stood in front of the castle-like entrance, which had just started to close.

Eskylious stood at the front. His shiny black armor crackled with lightning and he smiled as Bennett sped forward.

A single rock was visible just outside the gate and Kaiba focused in on it. When they were just five feet away from crashing Kaiba gripped the sides of the machine and kicked with both legs.

They were bathed in purple light for a moment and the next they appeared on the other side of the entrance. A raging blizzard made late afternoon into night. The virtaiyu rushed out of Taras just as another flash of purple went off. Kaiba watched as Eskylious appeared right behind the snowmobile. He fired his sonic rifle but missed. Kaiba had to clamp his hands over his ears as the wailing projectile whirled by him. Eskylious teleported several more times, firing his weapon as he went, but he couldn't keep up. They raced into the storm and even through the screeching winds Kaiba could hear Eskylious's animalistic howl.

26

THE COMMANDER
RESURFACES

Aboard the USS Archfrost

Emily spent the next hour answering Barnes's questions about how she came across the sphere. He asked her everything about Adam, where he came from and about her own personal life. He asked whether she'd encountered Virts along her way, which Emily found peculiar. If he'd asked about them, then the Virts must have been after the sphere. That didn't make much sense though. Virtaiyu could already manipulate water and earth, unless of course the sphere did something else. She explained about her first experience with watching Adam control water, and her own first efforts with the bowl. She knew she'd made a mistake telling Barnes about Adam. He immediately asked how she ended up with the sphere if Adam had it first. She told him how Adam had died and his sphere just fell off. Barnes didn't know that death released a sphere's bond. Jordan sat silently throughout the whole conversation, listening attentively.

When Barnes had his fill of questions, Emily made her way back out onto the deck. It had finally stopped raining and the night was turning into day. Though the sky was still dark several beams of light broke through the clouds. She avoided everyone she could and they just watched her like she was some sort of freak. The bow of the ship was the most deserted, and for good reason. Waves crashed against the bow, spewing clouds of white foam and water. She stood off to the side to avoid getting soaked. The wind whipped across her, and soon the large port of Sand Point came into view.

It was a U-shaped harbor with seven rectangular docking stations. Along the docks were towering red cranes used for loading cargo. There were only two ships. The vessels must have been from Coronado because one was riddled with fires. The other looked as if it was sinking. It had cracks and breaches in the hull and tilted so that the bow pointed up. The ships were unloading passengers as rapidly as they could get off, though Emily couldn't tell just how many people each boat carried. As they got closer she noticed that there were people in the water, more than likely ones who'd jumped for fear of being dragged down with the ship.

The shore was coated with jagged rock formations nestled against creaking wood decks. The harbor was filled with cargo boxes and several worn-down warehouses. City skyscrapers rose up just behind the harbor filling the skyline with city lights.

Emily looked back out at the sea as the *Archfrost* pulled into an open berth. She thought of Mo and Nicole again. She hoped they were all right, but she had bigger problems at the moment, ones she couldn't control. In her heart she knew that Mo would press on. He was a strong man who could survive any situation, especially when tasked with defending another person. As much as she wanted to look for him in a helicopter or other aircraft, her loyalty lay with her father. If she lost him, Emily would never forgive herself. Mo would understand, or at least she hoped he would.

She pushed them from the forefront of her mind, realizing that thinking about them was making her miserable.

Instead she watched metal planks extend from the starboard side of the ship and they clanked against the dock. The men and women flooded off the ship in a mob. Emily watched them rush, wondering whether she too should flee. Perhaps she could escape with the crowd and disappear into the city. She could worry about finding her father instead of being forced into something she didn't think she was capable of.

"Not thinking of running off now, are we?" Barnes asked as though reading her mind.

"Wouldn't dream of it," Emily said, quashing her wish.

"Good choice. I know this is a lot for you to handle, it's a lot for anyone to handle. But I ask that you try to cooperate with us as best as possible."

"Have I not done so already?"

"I'm referring to Jordan," Barnes said.

Emily leaned her back against the railing. "What of him?"

"Like it or not, the two of you hold a closer connection than anyone else."

"I won't abandon trying to find my father," Emily said sternly. "Nor will I just forget that Kaiba was the one to cause his injuries and possibly his death."

"I'm not asking you to. All I'm asking is that you try to work with Jordan for the time being. When you think about it, the UNM will have to find Kaiba as well. If he possesses a sphere then we share a common goal: finding him."

Emily was somewhat surprised. She hadn't considered mutual interests. "We want to find him for very different reasons. I doubt yours is revenge."

"Kaiba's incident could have been an accident. From what you described, your first encounter with water was beneficial, and under your complete control. I would bet that other first encounters aren't as peaceful."

"Accident or not my father's fighting for his life."

"And you think harming Kaiba will change that?"

Emily knew she wanted Kaiba to suffer, but she didn't know how she was going to do it. "I haven't really made up a plan for what I'll do to him yet."

"Ah, I see," Barnes said. "Then I wouldn't worry about that until the situation presents itself. For now I need you and Jordan to put aside your differences. We are on the same team after all."

"I am on no one's team," Emily asserted.

"I think you'll feel differently when you learn about what the UNM does—what we fight for."

Emily watched as Jordan pushed his way past the crowd of people. He stood at Barnes's side with his hands clasped behind his back.

Barnes saw the anger in Jordan's gaze. "I was just explaining to Emily, while you are in a military setting the two of you will act neutral toward one another. Clear?"

"Clear," Jordan answered.

Emily stood in silence until she realized Barnes was talking to her as well. "Yeah."

"Good," Barnes said, taking a step for the off-ramp. "Commander Unden will be waiting for us just past the docks."

They followed him down the metal sheet, their footsteps clattering loudly.

Emily hated the idea of taking orders. She'd never been ordered in her life. She did the commanding in her household, no one else. Even her parents just made suggestions. They never once demanded that she do something and she in turn didn't demand of her parents. They all treated each other equally. But now, in America, her affluence meant nothing. She was regarded with no special interest except for the metal she wore on her back. She was worried she would be treated no better than a pawn, or worse, a science experiment.

"Anything we should know about Unden?" Emily asked.

"I'm told he's stern and likes to get his way. Call him Commander and you won't have a problem."

Jordan looked concerned. "So you haven't met him?"

"Unden keeps to himself. He was involved with these spheres long before any of us knew about them."

Emily felt nervous about meeting a man who would ultimately change her future for better or for worse. Barnes escorted them past medical personnel, soldiers, and ship repairmen who bustled about the dock. There was little space to move around, and several times Emily thought she was going to lose Barnes and Jordan. The farther they walked, the more crowded it got. They weaved through shipping containers and the workers who unloaded them until finally reaching the street.

An all-black limousine was flanked on both sides by military Jeeps that sat waiting by the curb.

A bald man in a dark military sport jacket stepped from the vehicle. The right side of his uniform was pinned with more medals than Emily could count. He had a silver cane in his hand that he steadied himself with. Emily thought the man's face looked a little like Kaiba's. They had the same bulky nose and similar bright green eyes.

Emily watched as both Jordan and Barnes saluted. She stood, feeling slightly out of place.

Unden walked closer. "I was told there would be two boys."

"We were separated," Barnes said.

He snorted. "You each have a sphere?" His eyes drifted from Jordan to Emily.

Both she and Jordan nodded.

"I've been told he has the earth element. What about you?" Unden said, directing the question to Emily.

"Water," Emily said, trying not to be intimidated.

"I see. We have a meeting with the UN Security Council," Unden said. "And we're late." He opened the back door of the limo. "Get in."

They climbed into the dark interior of the car and Emily felt back at home in luxury once again.

"Lucky you found the two of them, Barnes," Unden said. "But what happened to our third?"

"Taken by the virtaiyu, sir."

Unden twirled the handle of his cane. "I was afraid you were going to say that. Well, at this rate we have more spheres than the Virts do."

"How do you plan on getting my friend back?" Jordan asked.

"I don't plan on doing anything just yet," Unden said. "As far as I'm concerned chalk your friend up as a casualty. The President may wish to pursue him, but that's out of my hands."

Jordan was furious. "You'll just give him up that easily?"

"If you happen to know where he was taken, share it. Since we both know that isn't the case I'll stay logical. The virtaiyu now possess two spheres and perhaps others. The Council won't like to hear what that means for the war."

"Two?" Barnes asked.

"I learned another was taken when Tempest fell."

"What's Tempest?" Emily asked.

"It was the base that housed the spheres," Unden stated.

"And the Terraformer," Jordan added.

Unden was clearly caught off guard. "How do you know about the Terraformer?"

"I have my resources," Jordan said.

"Then your resources are knowledgeable."

"They didn't say what it did, though."

Unden leaned forward. "That's of no concern to you."

"I want to know why the virtaiyu are after these spheres in the first place," Emily stated. "They can already manipulate the elements, what's their value?"

"I am not at liberty to disclose that information to either of you unless the Council says otherwise."

"And yet you wanted to meet with both of us," Emily said. "If you aren't here to disclose information, then what am I here for?"

"I can only speculate because the UNM is in process with their decision. You are bearing classified artifacts that belong to the United Nations Military. My guess is that from here on out the two of you will be treated as property of the UNM. You will have no personal agendas, and no outside contacts. Forget the meaning of the words free will; it no longer exists for either of you."

Jordan said, "I doubt you have the power to subdue us."

Emily was glad to have him on her side for once. "You have no right. And with our power you wouldn't stand a chance."

"Let me make something very clear. This is not a democracy. The technology bonded to you can change the face of this war. Not only for us, but if they were in our enemy's hands, kiss the planet goodbye. With those stakes I am granted any and all power so long as it protects the people of the United States, and by extension, the people of the world."

"You couldn't take the spheres even if you tried," Jordan said.

"Is that so? To my knowledge there are two ways a sphere can be removed. The first is to remove the limb that the sphere is bonded to. The second is termination."

Emily's skin crawled. "Mine is attached to my back."

"Then option two would have to suffice for you."

Jordan sat back in his seat. "You can't just kill us."

"I could, and it would be easy. Given the amount of time that's passed, I'd place each of you in the first stage of neural synchronization. Your spheres haven't adjusted to your body and as such you can't manipulate for longer than a few minutes. That being said, the UN Council voted against me using execution to get them."

Emily didn't like that the government was voting on whether or not to take their own citizens' lives. She was especially uncomfortable with the idea of being caged like an animal. "So you'll hold us against our will until … what?"

"I will do nothing without the Council's vote," Unden said. "But you will be detained while the UNM attempts to find the other spheres. During such time you will be monitored and trained in the art of elemental manipulation. We have captured several virtaiyu whose knowledge has been useful, to say the least. If, and I emphasize the *if*, the two of you prove to be skilled in using your elements of water and earth, there is a chance that you'll be permitted to fight in the UNM ranks."

Emily nearly stood up. "You can't imprison me, I have to find my father!"

Unden shrugged. "Forget your past; it'll make things easier for you."

"I will do no such thing!" Emily said, outraged.

"I am not allowed to take the spheres by force. That being said, certain 'accidents' could happen that might just be out of my control."

Emily stared in disbelief. "Is that a threat?"

Unden rested his chin atop his cane. "Only if you would like it to be. If you want to keep your lives, and more importantly the spheres, you'll do as I say."

27

FIRE AND ICE

Somewhere in the Frozen Tundra

The blizzard only got worse the farther they went. Kaiba could hardly see an inch in front of his face. "We need to make camp!" he yelled. His body was growing numb.

Bennett revved the throttle. "She's about outta gas! I'll put as much distance from Taras as I can. Then we'll try to find shelter."

They rode onward and Kaiba found himself hugging Nassira and Bennett tightly despite the fact he no longer felt their warmth. His skin was like ice and his bones were being gnawed. At this rate he was sure to have frostbite.

Night had set in and the headlight of the snowmobile made the snow sparkle like stars in space. Bennett cut the engine as they approached a tree line. The top of the plant barely stuck up from the snow. Bennett rubbed his hands together. Fire returned to his palms, but the strength of the storm and the thick falling snow put out the flames.

"Help me out here, Kaiba!" he cried.

The wind continued to scream and Kaiba hopped off the bike and into the deepening snow. He trudged over to Bennett who was hunched over his hands trying to grow the fire.

"I need you to block as much of this wind as you can! When I'm ready, move out of the way."

Kaiba stood closer, putting his chest close to Bennett's hands.

The fire started small, but slowly grew until it engulfed his fists. The flickers of heat could not have felt better. When the flames started to turn a yellow-white Bennett yelled, "Move!"

Kaiba sidestepped and Bennett thrust his arms at the snow. Like the stream of a flamethrower the fire bit into the ice and steam rose like a geyser. Long shadows were cast along the white snow as Bennett continued to unleash his firestorm. He moved his hands so that the molten energy made an indented circle in the snow. Once the outline was made he focused on the center. The snow melted faster as he tried to burrow. The fire continued for several minutes and Kaiba stood as close as he dared without getting burned.

When Bennett finished there was a deep hole large enough for the three of them to fit in. Bennett leapt down first. Kaiba grabbed Nassira who, although awake, looked lifeless. She shivered uncontrollably. Kaiba wrapped his arms around her and then jumped into the ice cave. They tumbled down and landed in soft snow. The walls of the cave still dripped and steam rose lazily to the sky.

"Good idea," Kaiba said through chattering teeth.

"Not the best, but it'll work." Bennett looked down. "She doesn't look so good."

Nassira's face was tinged blue like frozen meat.

Kaiba took off his jacket and wrapped it around her. She moved her arm and flung the jacket off. "No."

Kaiba frowned.

"Don't ... nee ... need you," she stuttered and closed her eyes.

Bennett stepped forward. He let the fire fade, but he kept his hands glowing red hot. "We should have left her back there. Would have saved us trouble." He shook his head at her. "This is gonna hurt."

Bennett bent down and rolled back the sleeves that covered her arms. She screamed as Bennett ran his glowing hands along her skin. He started with her arms, then her legs and stomach. When he'd finished Nassira rolled onto her side without even acknowledging what Bennett had done.

"Won't do much, but she won't freeze yet," Bennett said. "We gotta get a fire going."

Kaiba looked at his glowing hands. "You have one."

"I mean an actual fire. I can only create one for so long."

Kaiba looked around the cave and spotted a piece of green pine sticking out from one of the walls. "The tree line we stopped by." He pointed. "Burn a path until the branches catch."

"Good thinking," Bennett said, unleashing more fire. The snow melted away and the temperature in the hole began to rise. Then there was a crack and a small flash as the frozen wood began to ignite. The fire burned the green pine needles from the branches and then reached the truck of the tree. It took a minute, but the tree trunk finally caught fire. Bennett burned as much snow around the plant as he could. "The flames should heat the rest of the snow around the trunk and create a path for the smoke."

Kaiba watched the smoke funnel through the top of the hole. "And what makes you think Eskylious or the others won't spot that?"

"I couldn't see my own breath in the blizzard. We shouldn't have to worry until the storm passes."

Kaiba dragged Nassira closer to the fire and ignored her protests. He watched as the flames grew bigger as Bennett inhaled and decreased as he exhaled. It seemed to be at his will and under his total control.

"Can you teach me?" Kaiba asked, watching the glowing flecks of heat.

"I can try," Bennett said. He reached for a burning branch. The fire jumped to his palm, but it didn't appear to burn him. "Fire is the element that you first have to create and then you manipulate."

He grabbed the smallest branch he could find and broke it from the tree. He dipped it into the snow, suffocating the flames.

"Here," he said, tossing it to Kaiba.

Kaiba caught the burnt stick.

"I was taught that fire is a loyal servant. But it is also an aggressive lord." Bennett made a small flame in the center of his hand. It swirled around his wrist in a circle as he said it. "If you think yourself above fire it will consume you with its raging inferno. If you respect it and strive to understand its power and ferocity, then you can tame it. You can never truly control fire, but you can work with it and direct it. From my experience the element is chaotic, unpredictable, and incredibly powerful. That being said, you cannot think of fire as chaotic, it will make casting much harder. I prefer to think of fire as nothing more than heat, just pools of warm light. So first, I want you to create fire on the tip of that stick."

Kaiba reached for the twig, unsure of how to proceed.

"Hold on," Bennett said. "This will help you get warmed up. Close your eyes and breathe slowly."

Bennett waited for him to do so. "Now picture a roiling magma flow cascading down a mountain side." He paused then said slowly, "Imagine standing beside the river of that red lava as it belches molten rock, scorching the surface beneath it bare. Feel the blistering heat waves and the crushing fire that dances across the melting surface."

Kaiba felt his body starting to sweat as he imagined the scene. His entire being felt fevered.

"Now open your eyes. Take both of your hands and rub them together like this." The flame on Bennett's hand disappeared and he moved his palms slowly back and forth.

Kaiba copied and felt the heat start to swell in his palms. He'd used friction to warm his hands before, but this felt different. The warmth multiplied until it was hotter than anything he'd ever felt.

"Feel that burning in your hands. I want you to become that heat. Be one with it as though it were a part of your soul and feel it rush through your veins."

Kaiba tried to think of what it would be like to *be* fire. He imagined himself bathed in its energy.

"Now close your hands together. Hold that warmth as it blisters against you. When you feel the heat at its maximum, release it."

Kaiba clamped his fingers tightly. He could feel something in his bones, something powerful and hot like the sun. Although his hands blazed, the temperature didn't burn his skin. He let the heat grow until it had reached its hottest. Just as Bennett had said, he stared at his hands and then flung them open.

Fire danced around his fingers and Kaiba smiled. He held the fire in front of his face, twisting his palms back and forth.

"Incredible," Kaiba said breathlessly.

"Powerful feeling isn't it?"

Kaiba cupped his fingers and the fire grew larger. "How do you create a stream of fire?"

"Always ready for the next step," Bennett laughed. "Part of training with an element is practicing for yourself. I'll take the first watch and let you practice."

"Come on," Kaiba begged. "Give me another tip, anything."

"Learn to use fire on your own. That's what they told me at Tempest."

Slightly annoyed, Kaiba said, "That's unhelpful."

"That's how I felt, but you'll get the hang of it. You already know how to use earth and lightning. Fire won't be that much different," Bennett said as he climbed up to the hole he'd carved. "I'm gonna go scout, stay put till I get back. Then you can keep watch." Bennett left, leaving Kaiba alone with Nassira.

Kaiba's body shook just as it did with earth. He sat in the snow
and decided just to watch the flame. Its center was red-orange
and its tips were yellow. It flickered side to side in the air like a
kite. Kaiba held it carefully in his left hand, nervous that it might
disappear. He poked the flame with his finger and the fire moved
in the opposite direction. He poked the tip of the flame from above
and it shrunk in size. He smiled to himself and drew his hand
farther away. As he did so the speck of fire reached upward, trying to
follow his movements like a plant reaching for the sun. Kaiba moved
his finger in a rapid circle like a whirlpool. Again the fire imitated
his movement. He cupped the heat, wondering how to increase its
size. He decided to try to push his energy into the flame as he did
with earth. The feeling surged down into his hands and the fire
exploded, growing up his arms and burning the sleeves of his coat.

Kaiba threw his body against the side of the cave wall. Some of
the ice melted, but he succeeded in putting out the fire. He pulled
his arms from the steaming snow, surprised that he had no burns
other than the blackened jacket. Nassira was asleep on the ground.
He sat next to the burning tree and tried to make fire without the
use of wood. It took a while, but he succeeded. Instead of pushing
all the energy into the fire he only pushed a little bit. The flame
grew, but it didn't explode as before. Excited by his discovery he held
his hands away from his body and aimed them at the tree.

He took a deep breath and pictured the inferno scene that
Bennett had described. When he felt himself starting to sweat
he opened his eyes and pushed the adrenaline into the fire. Just
as before, the fire exploded, but this time it flew to the tree in a
directed stream. Kaiba laughed, amazed with this new ability. He'd
been afraid in prison, not because he thought he would die, but
because of the power that lived inside of him. Perhaps these new
abilities were a gift. He just had to ensure that he practiced enough
so that no one got hurt. He wouldn't tolerate hurting someone as

he had Mr. Sursten. He hoped the man was okay as he sat down against one side of the cave.

Kaiba kept one hand ignited, but clenched his fingers over his other hand to extinguish the flame. For the first time, he wondered if he could use two elements at once.

Shining through Kaiba's shirt was a glowing red circle. It was a similar glow to the purple circle that had illuminated on his chest when the psychic element activated. As he stared at the plate longer, he noticed that there were six spherical outlines arranged in a perfect larger circle. In fact, the plate looked much different than it had back in California. Kaiba hadn't seen them before, but there were faint outlines of two triangles in the center of the plate that connected the spheres together. Then he understood: each circle on the plate corresponded to the different elements. Curious, he touched the circle that appeared a dim yellow and it burst with bright yellow light. Kaiba felt a strong tingling in his other hand. He wiggled his fingers and sparks of lightning jumped across his skin. Fire in one hand, lightning in the other, Kaiba stood. He used the tree as a target again.

He yelled. A bolt of lightning and a stream of fire launched from his hands at the same time. They burned and shocked the tree in a dazzle of red and yellow. "I'll be ready for you, Eskylious."

28

TARAS PRISON

Location Unknown

"*You let them escape!*" Eskylious raged. The ground beneath him quaked as he burst into the room with virtaiyu behind him. A cluster of men stood by the ramp. Eskylious's hands glowed yellow and he unleashed lightning upon them. They fell to their knees, crying out to the sky as they were electrocuted.

Taniel stepped from the dwindling fires and looked up at the alien as terror grabbed hold of his heart.

Eskylious descended the ramp, stepping over the bodies. "*Graves!*"

"Yes, Eskylious?" Graves quivered. He walked to the virtaiyu, shaking from head to toe. His head was bowed.

Eskylious's hand turned purple. He clubbed Graves in the chest and he went sprawling back against the wall. Lilac rings of light appeared around Graves's hands and legs, pinning him in place. Eskylious flicked his wrist and another ring of purple appeared around Graves's neck. "How did you let them *leave?*"

The rings tightened. He choked out the words, "They escaped. Guards … incompetent."

Eskylious's eyes flared red and fire appeared in his hands. "Is that so?"

Graves fumbled with the ring of light trying to pry it off his neck. "Yes."

Eskylious faced the men that had just put out the flames from their own bodies. Some stood with burnt clothes and ash on their faces. From Eskylious's hands flew a mighty wave of fire. Taniel threw himself to the ground as the inferno spread and grew larger like the burst of a shotgun. Soldiers were enveloped and Eskylious only smiled at their agonized cries.

"Cyrax!" he yelled.

A female virtaiyu with gruesome war trophies pinned to her armor stepped forward. She had a yellow cut along her cheek that looked like a tattoo.

"Eliminate them, leave none alive."

Taniel gasped and froze, unsure what to do as Eskylious noticed him. "You know Kaiba," Eskylious said. "Spare him."

The female nodded and electricity appeared in her hands. She shouted something in her native language. It was a guttural noise and instantly the soldiers behind her aimed their sonic rifles. She yelled again and Taniel had to cover his ears. The sonic waves tore through the air, cutting a swath into every man. When the virtaiyu stopped firing only Taniel was left alive.

"You follow me," Eskylious demanded. "We have work to do."

The United
Nations
Council

Marriot Hotel, Sand Point, California

Jordan and Emily remained silent for the rest of the limousine
ride while Barnes and Unden talked quietly about the war effort.
Emily spared several glances at Jordan. She wondered if he was
feeling the same sense of hopelessness that she was. Neither of them
had committed a crime and yet their fate was to be decided by the
vote of people they had never met. At gunpoint Emily knew that
trying to escape was useless, especially since there was no water
around. Maybe Jordan would be able to get them out of a bind if
they found themselves in one. She stared out the darkened windows
at the streets of the city. She was surprised by the number of
policemen and security guards. They seemed to be on every corner,
pushing back everyday citizens. She assumed the appearance of the
UN Council was the reason for the upped security.

As they pulled up to the towering hotel Emily saw the news crews and photographers.

"Best to avoid answering the press's questions," Unden said.

He stepped out of the vehicle and his bodyguards ushered Jordan and Emily forward. Emily felt so strange without Mo to protect her. It was different for her to be surrounded by unfamiliar guards. She felt as if she were wearing someone else's clothes. The men looked tough enough, but she felt strangely vulnerable.

Unden limped forward and interviewers gunned him with questions. Even in times of world war the press still thrived with what news they could find.

One woman yelled, "Commander, what is the reason for the appearance of the President and other UN Council members today?"

Emily had always thought that meeting the President from any country would be an honor. Now she resented the opportunity since he would vote to decide her fate.

Another shouted, "What are the UNM's plans to retaliate against virtaiyu forces and how will the military change its tactics to prevent further attacks on American soil?"

"Is Coronado lost? And if so what plans are in place to eradicate the Virt threat?"

Unden ignored all of them and went up the elegant stairs of the hotel. Jordan and Emily followed behind Barnes and they did their best to ignore the reporters' questions. The security guards in front of the hotel stepped aside and they all went through the revolving doors. The floor was a green-grey stone that contrasted against the warm yellow walls. Tubular hanging lights reached down from the high ceilings. They stretched to the far end of the room, where a waterfall trickled into a small pond. Elegant chairs with tiny red rose upholstery were arranged around the waterfall while others were placed around sitting tables.

The most peculiar aspect of the room was that the entire lobby was abandoned except for one woman at the front desk.

Emily looked around cautiously. "Where is everyone?"

"Escorted out," Unden said. "The Council didn't need any distractions and this was the easiest place to hold a meeting. This way."

They walked past the woman at the front desk, who bowed slightly. She looked nervous. Unden led them to two eight-foot mahogany doors just on the other side of the waterfall. Two Secret Service agents stood out front.

"It's secure?" Unden asked.

"Yes sir," one of them said. "Will they be any trouble?"

Emily knew he was referring to Jordan and herself.

Unden laughed. "No, they wouldn't be dumb enough to strike at the leaders of the free world." He opened the doors.

The southern wall had a stage with a long rectangular table resting on top. At the center of the table Emily recognized President Trentis; his short spiky white hair was unmistakable. He, like everyone in the room, was dressed in a fine black business suit. At his sides were several other leaders Emily didn't recognize. One lady looked exceedingly French, and another man Russian. In all there were probably seven individuals. The remainder of the table had holograms that displayed the faces of other country leaders. At first Emily hadn't known they were fake, the people looked so lifelike and were even 3D.

The rest of the spacious room was completely empty apart from two chairs that sat in the middle. Emily felt overly nervous at the sight of these powerful people.

President Trentis stood as they entered. "Please take a seat."

Emily and Jordan did as they were told. Unden made his way to the stage and stood at the right end of the table beside several security officers.

"You know who I am, but I do not know either of you. Please introduce yourselves."

Jordan stood up and waved nervously. "Jordan Hightower, Mr. President."

Emily remained sitting. "Emily Sursten."

Trentis straightened his tie and sat down. "Commander Unden has informed me of your ... predicament and it's no easier for you than it is for us. By your power and ours, the devices you now possess must be protected at all costs."

Emily interrupted him. "Unden claimed that we would be regarded as property of the UNM."

"In a way he is correct. I wish it wasn't so, but these times are unlike any other. The Council and I have voted on how we will deal with you and those we encounter in the future. We have decided that you will be allowed to keep the artifacts. It's better that they be protected by people than sitting as objects of curiosity in a vault. We can move you, protect you, and with the unique abilities they grant, we hope that you'll be able to protect yourselves." He took a sip of water and cleared his throat. "That being said, we cannot allow either of you to operate without supervision. We will do our best to train you with the resources that we have so long as you will obey the chain of military command. Do you feel this is a reasonable request?"

"You act as if we have a choice. If I am to act as a carrier of this device I have a few conditions. First being, I would like to know why they're of such value," Emily said.

"Very reasonable." The President looked around to the other Council members. "Does anyone object to her knowing the truth?"

No one spoke.

President Trentis went on to explain the Terraformer, and the seven Terraform Keys. "We hoped every individual would be able to control fire or water much like the virtaiyu do, but that wasn't their designed purpose. We learned that these spheres granted the wearer elemental control purely as a defensive mechanism. Their true secret is that they act as the keys for activating the Terraformer, which we tried to do, but were unsuccessful."

"Why?" Emily asked. "You had all the keys."

"Yes," the President said. "All of them aside from the one that was bonded to a test subject in Tempest. When the base became compromised they acquired the Terraformer. Lucky for us, it is useless without the keys. Should they recover the spheres before we do they will be able to destroy any country at will just as they did to China."

Emily had to take a deep breath. The weight of what the President said meant that a piece of humanity's safety resided with her. She'd seen the power of controlling water, but she could never have fathomed that her device would act as a key to one of the most powerful weapons known by man- and alienkind. When Unden had talked about having no free will Emily had resented him for it. Now she understood. If she fell into the hands of the virtaiyu it could mean one step closer to losing the war and the death of everyone she held dear.

Jordan was in a similar state of shock. "Do you know where the other Terraform Keys are?"

"We know the relative locations of the spheres, but I fear that the virtaiyu know them as well. The good news is that the Terraformer cannot be fired without having all of the spheres. Missing just one will be enough to stop the weapon."

"Mr. President," Unden said. "I fear that may not be entirely true."

The President looked confused. "Do you have new information?"

"The data lost from Tempest was recently recovered. I fear that although the Terraformer cannot be fired to its full potential without all seven spheres, it can still be fired with only one or two keys," Unden said. "Our researchers were merely unsuccessful in doing so."

Several of the council members whispered to one another.

The President rubbed his right temple. "And what is the Terraformer capable of with only one sphere?"

"I think I speak for all of us when I say that I do not want to find out."

The President sighed, turning his attention back on Emily and Jordan. "I hope this news expresses the true severity of this situation. I realize that it is unfair of me to ask either of you to completely submit to the UNM, but I am afraid I can do nothing else. That being said, what was your other condition, Emily?"

Emily couldn't believe that the President of the United States was being so understanding. She had so many thoughts running through her head she felt as though she was going to pass out. The room was spinning and she had to look down at the floor to keep from feeling sick. "My father," she said breathlessly. "He was injured at Coronado. I have to find him."

"If I can dispense resources to find your father, will you agree to put all of your focus on training with the sphere and keeping it under your protection?"

Emily gazed up in complete shock. "You would do that?"

"My extra resources are slim, but if you swear to protect that sphere and obey the UNM, I will."

She stood up. "For my dad, I swear it."

President Trentis smiled. "And what about you, Jordan?"

"Sir, I vowed to myself when this war started that I would do everything in my power to make sure that the people I love would live to see the world the way it used to be. I am with the United Nations Military, and though I will not agree with all commands I'll be given, I devote myself to the safety of others."

"That's all I wanted to hear," the President said. "Now, we have arranged for the two of you to stay at a makeshift training facility at Sand Point Air Force Base. It's not the biggest of places, but it'll act as a safe house for each of you. As you've already met Commander Unden he will act as your caretaker, due to the experience he has with the Terraform Keys. Barnes will accompany you also. With that I release you to their guidance and I wish the both of you the very best of luck." He rose to his feet and the other Council members stood as he did.

Jordan got out of his seat and Emily copied him.

"We will be in touch," the President said.

30

I N T O   T H E
D E E P   E N D

Sand Point Air Force Base, California

Emily and Jordan walked behind Unden as they approached the Air Force base runway filled with military planes. There were lines of soldiers in front of a massive hanger bay similarly filled with aircraft of all kinds. Men and women stood at attention and saluted. Emily immediately felt intimidated, but she was careful to mask it with a false confidence she hoped no one would detect. Her upright posture and long stride lent her an air of self-assurance.

"At ease," Unden ordered as they got closer.

The soldiers slapped their hands to their sides and stared at Emily and Jordan as though they didn't belong.

"Have the areas been prepped?" Unden asked.

"Sir," a young pilot said, stepping out of rank. He had two stars pinned above his right breast. "There is a courtyard at the back of the hanger, and the aquatics room should be equipped with all you need. Living quarters have also been arranged. If you're tired I can escort you, sir."

Unden laughed. "Sleep will be the last thing we need." He turned and Emily caught the glint in his wild eyes. "Which of you wants to work first?"

Emily looked at Jordan, who seemed intimidated. She volunteered, "I will."

"Very well," Unden said. "Jordan, you don't have to participate, but I do expect you to pay attention. You'll want to know what Emily is capable of."

Why would he need to know what I'm capable of? Emily wondered.

The aquatics center was located to the right of the hanger bay. It was a blue room made of stained glass with two Olympic-sized swimming pools separated by a long narrow strip of tile. The place was moist and humid. Emily's breath grew heavy the moment she walked in and her nostrils flared at the pungent aroma of chlorine. Her footsteps echoed loudly as Unden led them to the pool on the left in which several floating platforms had been scattered about.

"I cannot, nor have I ever controlled water," Unden said as he stood at the pool's edge. "Even so, I know more about water manipulation than you do. I have observed Virt elemental techniques, including water and earth, for the past two years. For both our sakes I hope that you are quick learners. But before you can use water manipulation you should know about the plate as a defense. Jordan, come here."

Jordan obeyed reluctantly and stood at Unden's side.

Unden removed a black pistol from his waist. "The Terraformer plates are made of a unique material both light and durable. They serve as armor and are your best points of defense. Emily, turn around."

Emily eyed the gun nervously. "Why?"

"Don't you trust me?" Unden said.

"I don't know you."

Unden's lips curled, not in a smile, but like a wolf's mouth before it eats. He handed Jordan the gun. "Shoot her."

Emily took a step back. "Are you mad?"

"Nope. Shoot her."

Jordan stared at the weapon. "I won't."

"You made an oath to the President of the United States." He slammed the gun into Jordan's hand.

Emily shuddered, staring into the barrel of the gun.

Jordan's hand quivered.

"I'd turn around, girl," Unden said.

She tried to look for an escape, but realized she had no choice.

"Do it, Jordan!" Unden roared, his voice echoing off the walls.

Emily shook like a leaf in the wind. She couldn't feel her hands and her mouth had turned to ash. The safety clicked off.

Then the gun exploded with a *bang*. She closed her eyes expecting a lance of pain to barrel through her like a spear through a fish. Then she felt it, only a small poke in her spine as though someone had merely flicked her skin. She breathed in and out, almost hyperventilating.

"See," Unden said. "The plates are strong enough to stop bullets, and also blows from close combat weapons."

"You're insane," Emily said, clutching her chest and turning around slowly. She noticed Jordan was equally as frightened when he dropped the gun. He looked as if he'd been the one who had been fired on.

"I'm knowledgeable," Unden countered, leaning over to grab his fallen firearm. "And now you know the most important defense you have."

"I'm done," Emily said, making for the door.

"Not an option."

"What if something had gone wrong? What if my plate wasn't the same as the others? How 'bout I pop a round off at you, see how you like it!"

"I order you to stay. You're a soldier now and you are bound to orders," Unden said. "I told you you'd be fine and you are. Don't overreact."

"Easy for you to say," Emily mumbled. She was starting to regret her agreement to work with the UNM. She'd assumed the leaders of the UNM had more composure and less recklessness. If the entire military was like Unden, she'd gotten into much more than she'd bargained for.

"All I want to do is help you to access your power. You will become one of the strongest people, but you have to work with my methods. I only know how to teach by throwing you into the deep end and you'll have to accept that. Now, how much else do you really know about your water sphere?"

"Why are you asking me?" Emily spat angrily. She didn't come closer, preferring to stand at a distance. "You have the answers, so just tell me what I need to know."

"Each Terraform Key is similar in that they each have a finite amount of time to which a person can use its conferred powers. The longer you're bound to the plate the longer and stronger you will be able to control water. This holds true for all elements. What do you feel when you manipulate?"

"I feel a connection to the water and this pressure that surges in my body," Emily said.

"The connection is what we call 'affinity'. When you're near water the plate automatically senses it and relays the sense or affinity to the rest of your body. You will naturally feel this affinity, but it is your responsibility to act upon it."

She came closer to the edge of the pool again. She approached as a lamb might approach a lion. "How long does the affinity last?"

"Let's find out."

Unden lunged forward and grabbed her. Emily struggled against his grasp, but he tossed her into the pool.

She tipped back on the edge, swinging her arms wildly, but her back slapped hard against the water and she plunged down. Furious, she swam to the surface and came up yelling. "What was that for?" She gripped the edge and started to pull herself up.

Unden placed his heavy boot on her fingertips.

She growled in pain. He leaned down and brought his face close.

"I told you, I teach by throwing you into the deep end. Lesson one, use the water to lift yourself up." He stepped back and Emily pulled herself up anyway.

"What are you talking about?"

Unden kicked her into the water again, which sent a jet of pain into her side. As Emily popped back up, he said, "Rely on your abilities! Water is a fluid element. Just as water fills a cup and conforms to its shape, you can shape the water and make it conform to your will. That includes lifting your own body."

She glared at him, furious. She'd get him back for this. She swept her wet hair from her eyes. "Let me up to practice then."

Unden crossed his arms. "Lift yourself onto the edge using the water. Otherwise, you'll stay in that pool until you figure it out."

"How?" Emily snarled.

"Tell me, how does a wave rise in the ocean?"

She thought for a moment, picturing a foamy wave forming on the beach. "The crest of the wave forces the water around it down. How else would it form?"

Unden nodded and ignored her sarcastic remark. "Then act like the crest of that wave."

Emily frowned, kicking her legs back and forth, still struggling to keep her head up from the weight of her clothes. Then she looked left and right as the pressure started to intensify in her body. This affinity was like a new muscle that she had to learn to work. Unsure of what to do, she splashed, trying to make a wave, but nothing happened. Then she pressed her hands downward, pushing as hard as she could. To her surprise the water around her body rose upward while the water just a little farther out started to lower. She repeated the motion and rose higher until her head was level with Unden's knees. She smiled to herself, but then the water started to lower back down again.

"Focus," Unden barked. "This is only the first step. I want you to hold yourself up, force the water to remain in its upright position as though you were holding an object beneath you."

She held her hands firmly trying to grab the water. Though she tried, the water continued to lower itself. She repeated this technique several times, but it was no use. She sank in again, and then she had an idea. She forced the water around her up in the shape of a tube. Like a fountain, the water carried her up until her head was even with Unden's. As the column of liquid started to fall she swirled her hands in tiny circles. The water similarly started to spin and swirl, but the water pillar remained at the same height. She moved her feet forward as though walking along the pool's bottom. The water followed her body. Cautiously, she approached the pool's edge, lowering the water steadily as she went. Unden started to back up as she approached and finally her right foot felt the solid edge. She stepped with her left foot and then released her grip. The liquid rushed downward with a noise similar to a crashing waterfall.

Emily looked up smiling like she'd just proved to Unden that she wasn't worthless.

Unden gave a slow clap. "Not bad. Now let's try something else. Are you familiar with surface tension?"

She pointed to one of the floating platforms. "It's what allows objects to float on top of the water." She shook her body, trying to rid herself of the endless cold droplets.

Unden stepped forward and placed his boot on the surface. Emily was tempted to push him in and see how he liked it, but she restrained herself.

"I can rest my foot on the top of the water only because my muscles are holding it in place," Unden explained. "But if I were to try to step onto the water I would plunge right in as you did. You, however, can increase the surface tension in two ways. One is by using just the water and the other is by freezing it."

"I only froze the water once, on the deck of the *Archfrost*," Emily explained. "I don't know how I did it."

"Colonel Barnes informed me that you looked natural fighting with the water. He said you didn't hesitate to make that wave or to freeze the puddle at the soldier's feet. Did you picture it happening before you did it?"

Emily groaned, "Yes but I—"

"That's all that you need. You tell the water what to do with your body and your mind. Everything else will take care of itself. Now, just do as you did before and freeze the surface of the water." He pointed to a platform in the middle of the pool. "Walk to that raft there."

Emily took a step closer to the pool water. The surface rippled and bounced. That moment on the boat had happened so fast. She just acted in response, not really questioning, but was satisfied that the result played in her favor. Clenching her fist made the liquid turn to solid ice, but that was only a small puddle, this was a pool. She said, "Screw it," and took a step in. She clenched her fist before her foot hit, but it didn't matter. Water filled her mouth and she came up coughing. The edge of the pool was slippery, but she managed to pull herself back up. She brushed her body off, fuming the whole time. "I don't think I can do as I did before."

Unden grabbed her by the back of her shirt.

"Hey!" she cried, stumbling. "Touch me again and I'll jam that cane of yours up your-"

"Walk all the way down the side of this pool," he demanded, pushing her in the direction of the tiled walkway that separated the two pools.

Emily was starting to get sick of orders. "Why don't you make me?"

"You sure about that?" Unden asked sternly. He patted the holster.

Emily did as she was told. "You sure about that?" she mimicked under her breath. She took her time walking the path. She called Unden every curse word she could think of until she was within earshot. "Need me to roll over now?" she said snobbishly.

Unden's eyes narrowed. "We're not going to get along, are we?"

"Pretty safe to say."

"Makes my job easier," Unden smiled. "What did you feel when you walked down there?"

"Annoyed," Emily said.

"Humor me. What did you feel beneath your feet?"

"Honestly, you Americans," she said, rolling her eyes. "Solid ground, what else would I feel?"

Unden paced back and forth with his hands behind his back. "The ground is just as solid as ice is. Make that pressure in your body emanate through your feet. Just flex your calves and your toes and try to move your affinity outside your body."

She was surprised, but the tip worked. She flexed her legs and the pressure in her back and arms crept downward. It felt like something was crawling beneath her skin. Once most of the affinity had pooled in her toes she took the time to imagine the water freezing. She placed her right foot on the surface of the water. It cracked and froze, forming a pad beneath her foot. The blue turned to white and arcs of frost jetted out like the branches of a tree. Emily struggled to keep her balance on the ice cube and took another step. The moment her foot hit, the ice spread out making a larger solid platform. "Couldn't have told me this first?"

"I wouldn't stand still if I were you," Unden said.

Emily tipped back and forth on her iceberg, it felt like balancing on the top of a ball. She looked down and the ice was starting to crack. She pushed the pressure out from her toes, causing the ice to reform and spread even farther out, but the water of the pool threatened to melt it again. Then she realized that the ice had only frozen the top layer, she needed to freeze the space under her. She let the affinity come out below her and she started to feel more stable.

Unden saw what she was doing. "You'll run out of energy before you freeze to the bottom of the pool. Just run to the platform and freeze as you go."

Emily ran and each footfall sunk only slightly into the water just before another patch of ice was created. She smiled to herself wondering if a certain religious figure had felt the same as she did now. She reached the plastic platform, stumbling only once. She stepped onto the bobbing buoy and turned to face Unden. "Good trick."

"Should come in handy. Now let's see your skill with water. You can manipulate well, no?"

Emily took a deep breath and pretended to grab the water in front of her. She could feel the cool liquid in her fingers even though she wasn't touching it. She lifted her hands up and a shifting wave formed. She held it in place. "I have no trouble with this."

Unden took a remote out of his pocket. Three tiles in the aisle between the pools started separating. From the dark spaces rose cylinders that looked like cannons. Each of the three cannons had three barrels. They lifted themselves out of the ground until they were level with Emily's height.

Emily glanced at the devices nervously. If Unden was willing to shoot bullets at her, what were these? "Care to explain?"

He tapped the remote and the cannons shook. Yellow tennis balls appeared in the barrels of each cannon.

Emily breathed a sigh of relief.

Unden strode to one of the pitching machines. "On breaks, I'm told, the soldiers here like to balance themselves on these platforms and try to shoot each other off. I want you to stand in place and use only water to defend you."

Emily split the wave in half. The water curled itself closer to her body. "Easy enough."

"Glad you think so." He tapped another button and three balls shot at her. She pulled more water from the pool and just before the balls hit she engulfed them with her waves and pulled them under. The second barrage flew and she barely had time to throw up another thin wall of water, but these balls shot right through her barrier. She ducked and they just missed her head. She wondered if she could shoot them out of the air. The third barrage fired with a loud pop and Emily didn't create a wave.

This time she focused in on the lead ball and punched at it. A stream of water shot from the pool and collided with the ball. She smiled and jabbed at the other two balls. They flew away from her and echoed against the pool house windows. She kept her water boxing up for several minutes until she felt the pressure in her body starting to subside. Each pitching machine had begun firing three balls at once. She aimed water at each of the clusters, but nothing happened. She covered her face as the balls thwacked against her, leaving dark red marks.

"Ouch!" she yelled. The pitching machines threw again, but the pressure had totally faded from her body. She leapt from the platform and into the cool waters before she could be hit again.

"An hour and two minutes," Unden said as she pulled herself out.

"I wasn't on the platform that long," Emily said.

"I'm referring to your affinity. It lasted longer than I would have thought," Unden said. He looked over at the pool door. "Jordan, you're up!"

Her First Words

Moscow, Russia

Ian arrived at the address of the man he'd discovered to be Yiel Banko. He knew nothing about the guy and Ian hoped the man would understand about his record. He'd been imprisoned to provide for his family. Surely that would be considered honorable. He paid the cab driver and got out at the lone mail box along the dirt road. Tall brown grass rose along the street, obscuring the view of most of the estate, but Ian could still make out the large mansion at the end of the driveway.

He was happy that his son had grown up in such a nice home. He brushed the snow from his shirt, nervous about coming face to face with his son for the first time. He hoped the house was still occupied. Ian had heard that the war caused many people to move to safer locations, mostly in the Americas. From his perspective, there was no safer place than the middle of isolated Russia.

He made his way down the dirt-snow driveway, stopping to take in the view of a large frozen pond. He'd always wanted to fish with his boy; maybe he'd still get the chance. He continued walking until he reached the front of the mansion. Two stone-faced gargoyles sat atop brick pillars. Beside them were two lamp posts. Neither was illuminated, which wasn't a good sign. Ian approached casually and rapped on a golden door knocker the size of his head. He could hear the knock echo through the house. He waited for a minute, then two, but he heard no movement. He tried again. Still there was no answer. He was about to leave when he caught the red light of a camera in the right corner of the doorway. He stared up into the device.

"Mr. Banko," Ian said politely. "I'm here to see my son, Drelen. I'm his blood father. I would really appreciate the opportunity to meet—"

The double doors swung open.

"—him," Ian finished. He stuck his head into the house. "Hello?"

A man in an all-white suit stood behind the door. He had a thick black beard. "This way," he said.

Ian followed the man up a coiling set of stairs to the third floor. All the carpet in the house was coated in a thick layer of dust and in some places mud.

Ian was unsettled by the griminess of the place. They made their way to the top floor where a single cracked door lay just off its hinges. A dim red glow crept from behind the door. The butler ushered him in.

The walls were bookshelves, filled with texts from what looked like every language. All were coated in cobwebs. The room centered around a roaring fire where a large oak desk sat. Papers, books, and pens were strewn about its surface. Behind the desk a man Ian assumed was Yiel sat in a large red leather chair.

"Mr. Banko?" Ian asked as he crept forward into the room.

The man stood up from his chair. "Yes. That's right. Banko used to own this house. He was a good man that Yiel. Always generous with his money, kind to his family. Even those he adopted."

Ian had a brick in the pit of his stomach. "You are not Banko?"

The man ran his hand over a dusty book and pulled it off the shelf. "Shakespeare's *Macbeth*. Have you read it?"

Ian looked nervously around the room and remembered the play's theme. "Everything is not what it appears."

"Indeed," the man said. "I am not Banko and you are not just a concerned father looking for his son. We both have much more to ourselves."

"Then perhaps you could reveal a little about yourself?"

The man snapped his fingers. The white-suited butler grabbed Ian from behind.

Ian struggled as the man tightened his grip against his throat. The space around Ian started to grow purple. He pushed his legs against the ground and teleported away. A moment later he reappeared back at the entrance to the room.

The man smiled. "So you do have one."

Ian drew his gun and aimed at the man.

"Use that and you'll never see your son."

"Who are you?" Ian asked.

"You may call me Wel. Please show me the device."

Ian held his gun to Wel's head. "Where is my son?"

"Safe. Show me the device and I'll lead you to him. Shoot me and you lose your only link to the boy."

Ian lowered his weapon and turned his back on Wel and the white-suited butler. He dropped his hood to reveal the metal that stretched down the back of his head and to the third vertebrae in his neck. "Satisfied?"

"Extremely," Wel murmured. "Here is the difficult part: we each need something from the other. You want to know where your son is and I want that sphere at your neck. But I cannot get it unless I kill you. You will not sacrifice your life and so I offer you a deal."

"What do you want?"

Wel held up a picture of a young soldier. "This is Matthew Bennett. He's a United Nations Military grunt that was captured a few days ago."

Ian didn't like making a deal with someone he didn't trust. But he didn't have a choice. "And you want him rescued?"

"I want him dead," Wel said plainly. "He's been taken to an underground facility in the Antarctic."

"Why haven't you killed him yourself?" Ian asked.

"My motives are my own. You have the ability to jump across space in a single instant." Wel walked to Ian. "You kill this man, bring his sphere to me, and I'll tell you where your son is."

"How do I know my son is safe?"

Wel smiled and held out the paper with the soldier's face on it. "You don't."

Ian looked him up and down. He grabbed the paper. "Where in the Antarctic?"

Ice cave, Somewhere in the Antarctic

Kaiba woke in a cold sweat. His shirt was damp and he shivered in the cool air. He sat up in the darkness and squinted at Nassira's silhouette. Her breath formed a misty cloud that rose to the entrance of the cave and into the howling arctic plain. The fire had nearly gone out and the fragile embers burned like tiny candles amidst the ashes. Bennett was probably still out on lookout.

Kaiba rubbed his hands faster. He felt his palms increase in temperature and then he closed them. He could feel the burning flames. He opened his fingers when the heat was most intense and smiled at the two glowing red flames in the middle of his hands. He cupped his fingers and the two individual flames became one. Shadows danced along the icy walls and Kaiba started to lower the flames to the tree trunk when a spark shot from the opposite side of the cave. The electricity ignited the wood and it popped and crackled as the embers burst to life.

Nassira was sitting up and staring. She still hadn't said much after their escape from the prison, but Kaiba had a feeling that she was going to say something. He waited, the silence lasting longer than he intended, as he looked at her. She was truly beautiful and he felt embarrassed for staring at her for so long. Her lips moved ever so slightly and Kaiba felt himself get excited.

"Why did you save me?" she said at last. Her voice was soft and yet powerful at the same time. She had a slight accent—Spanish, maybe Portuguese, but Kaiba couldn't be sure.

The question surprised him. "I'm sure you would have done the same for me."

She stared blankly. "I wouldn't if you were in my same position. Why didn't you leave me?"

Same position? Kaiba thought. "I saved you for what you have on your arm."

"It's a curse."

"Maybe so, but with you out of that place we stop those men from getting more powerful. We saved you from death."

Nassira sat up on her knees. "Who are you to stop death?"

Kaiba didn't like the broken look she had. But he was starting to wonder if she was even grateful that he'd risked his own neck for her. "You would rather we left you there?"

"Yes. I would rather I was killed back at the cell."

"You don't want to live?" Kaiba asked, wondering if she was suicidal.

"You have no idea what I've lost. Do not sit there with those judging eyes, American." She said "American" as though it were a viral disease.

"If you'd share instead of shutting out the world I wouldn't have to judge. Maybe I can talk you out of whatever dark thoughts you have."

"I don't want to be talked out of them!" She stood up and was yelling now. "In one instant my family was lost! Their boat blown to pieces by the cruelty of those I didn't even know. I saw those men take my sister and murder my brother for this object around my wrist. They did nothing wrong and I caused them to suffer. So if you saved me for it, you can gladly come take it!"

Kaiba truly felt sorry for her, but immediately knew how to connect with her. "I'm sorry about your siblings. I know what it's like to lose a brother."

Nassira looked down on him, confused.

Kaiba looked around the walls of the cave slowly. "That feeling is all around you, huh? I know because I had it too. It's a sinking that wrenches at your mind day in and day out. You're not at ease in the day because that's when you spent your time with them. Then at night you can't sleep because they live again in your dreams."

Nassira sank into the snowy ground, not even blinking.

Kaiba held himself together as he thought of his brother. This was his chance at connecting with someone who no longer wanted to live. "It's like a torture you can't escape isn't it? You think of them, your memories with them, but that's all they are now, memories." Kaiba took out the dog tag that hung around his neck. He held it in the firelight. The name Drake Cassidy was engraved on the silver in plain block letters. It had been some time since he'd actually looked at it. He felt the moisture in his eyes, but he kept it at bay. If he couldn't do this she would never stop being a risk to getting home.

"No matter how much I want to, I can never bring my brother back. That's a fact that haunted me, still haunts me. I ran away from home after he died. I was ten. We have these woods behind my house. I climbed a tree and sat in it for two days and two nights. Didn't talk, didn't eat, and hardly slept. When I came down I didn't talk much either. Nothing really seemed to matter. I didn't want to be a part of the world, I'm sure that's what you're feeling now."

She nodded.

"But then I realized that my brother had his life stripped away from him. He didn't get to choose and it isn't fair that I no longer wanted to breathe when he never even got a chance to fully live his life. I know it's hard, the most difficult thing you've had to face, but you have to keep going. That's what they would want for you. And if you can't do it for yourself, do it for them and live in their memory."

A single tear fell from Nassira's right eye. She wiped it, but didn't take her eyes off of Kaiba. They stared in silence and when she spoke her voice cracked. "I can't fight this feeling of hopelessness; they were my reason for living."

"Then you have to find a new reason." Kaiba flexed his fingers and sparks rippled across them.

"You can also?" she said amazed.

Kaiba nodded. "I'd say you've been given a pretty good reason for living. Your sister might even still be alive."

"They would have executed her."

"Would you give up on her that easily?"

"No," Nassira admitted.

"No," Kaiba agreed. "You can protect people by using that plate on your wrist."

"But I didn't choose this. I don't want to be a hero."

Kaiba laughed. "I can't tell you how many times I've said that to myself. I didn't choose this either. None of humanity chose anything that's happening, and once again history is repeating itself."

"Aliens attacking hardly seems like a repetition of history." Nassira said.

"My brother used to tell this story after the virtaiyu first hit China. Do you know what happened to the Native Americans and the Aborigines in Australia?"

Nassira shook her head.

"Both Americans and Aborigines were natives to their respective homelands until the British came. The 'White men' were as alien to the natives as the virtaiyu are to us. And when the British succeeded in killing all that opposed them, they took the land, huddled up the natives and set them on reservations. Some native peoples remain, but they are fragments of what they once were. That is exactly what is happening now. Only it's not just in Australia or America, it's on a global scale. It affects the entire human race." Kaiba tapped his chest. "I'm not saying I'm fighting for all of humanity, it's selfish, but I'm only fighting to protect my family and friends. They are what matter to me. Not some BS about owing it to a war effort. But if I fight for my family, if you fight for yours, and everyone else does the same, we might just end up ok."

The wind whistled harder outside, drawing Nassira's attention. She held her hand to the entrance of the cave. Her hand and the veins in her arms started to glow yellow. She lowered her hand watching the sparks that jumped along her fingers. "I don't know if I can control it, but you have my word that I'll try. I'll fight for those that I know."

Kaiba smiled. "That's all anyone can ask."

"Can you promise me something?" Nassira asked.

"I can do my best."

"If we get these spheres and ourselves out of this, can I return home to search for my sister?"

"You can do as you please."

Nassira leaned forward. "But will you, Bennett, and whatever other Elementals there are help me?"

Kaiba was silent for a moment as he realized just how great a promise she was asking him to keep.

"I listened. I know your best friend has one. Earth, fire, lightning, and you with all three? The men who attacked my siblings wouldn't stand a chance."

He knew he couldn't speak for the others; binding them to a promise wasn't his right. He thought of the best words he could without making a formal commitment. "I promise to help in all ways that I can."

Nassira smiled for the first time. "Thank you, Kaiba."

It was foolish, but Kaiba blushed when she said his name.

ESCAPING WINTER

Ice cave
Somewhere in the Antarctic

Bennett returned within the hour. He was slightly blue from scouting in the cold of night. He reported seeing snowmobile teams and two Mantas. Luckily they were traveling in the opposite direction of the Interligates. He rested for two hours and Kaiba kept watch from the small entrance. He kept himself busy watching the snowflakes and creating embers in his hands.

They set out as the first beams of light broke through the cloud cover. The snow fell in thick wet clumps across the icy ground, which caused Kaiba to keep slipping on the frozen snow. He'd become used to the cold that had settled into his bones and even creating fire no longer kept him warm indefinitely.

Bennett led the way with his head down. In one hand he held a small flame as if it were a lantern. With the other he fumbled with the faded map encased in plastic. "Judging by this we should hit the ring of Interligates within the next few miles."

"How many exactly?" Kaiba asked.

"'Bout six. Not impossible to do in a day and I want the hell out of this frozen desert."

Kaiba didn't argue, unwilling to try to teleport again. Nassira looked livelier and less solemn than she had the entire time she'd been with them.

Soon the familiar tingle returned to Kaiba's nose, cheeks, fingers, and toes. He kept his hands lit with fire, but the winds and snow kept fighting to put the flames out. The harder he tried to keep the fire alive the more exhausted he got, until he finally gave up and just walked with his hands in his armpits. He shook his fingers every few seconds, trying to chase away the numbness.

The ice grew thicker as they moved toward the mountains. The horizon was reasonably clear and the monolithic peaks rose up in the eastern sky like the walls of a great city. At the base of the mountain was a vast winter forest. The trees stretched for miles and each of the thick green pines was coated in snowy white ice.

The majestic wood reminded of Kaiba of home. He wondered what Cade would be doing at this very moment. Hopefully he had enough food.

Nassira stumbled behind Kaiba. Her teeth chattered and her face was tinged blue.

"You all right?" Kaiba asked.

"Fi ... fine."

"Hold up, Bennett," Kaiba said. Bennett stopped and waited with his arms crossed.

Kaiba rubbed his hands together as though he was going to create a flame. When they felt hot, but not too hot, he clenched his fingers around Nassira's. She started to jerk backward, but relaxed slightly at the warmth. They stood for a moment.

"I didn't need that," she said.

Not much of a thank you, but as Kaiba stared into her eyes he didn't quite care. "I know."

The clouds moved in, causing the wind and snow to beat down on them. After about a mile the snow had deepened and was no longer fit to walk on top of. Instead Kaiba sank to his knees, with the snow crunching beneath him. He tried to lift his feet, but the snow sucked at his limbs like thick mud. After some time he decided to shuffle rather than heave his body up and down.

Hours seemed to pass as they walked the frozen plains. Kaiba followed the dim glow of the sun as it traveled behind the clouds. The snow thinned as they reached a hill about the height of a three-story house. Bennett slid once climbing it and swore loudly, which amused Kaiba. As they reached the top of the hill twelve Interligates came into view. The V-shaped structures were spaced about a quarter mile apart in a perfectly straight line. The land behind the Interligates was mostly flat except for a few small piles of scattered ice clumps.

"These don't look like the Interligates I came out of," Kaiba said, wondering whether Bennett had led them astray.

"There are two Interligate hubs in the area. This place has the one we need."

Nassira looked out at the teleports. "And which one do we need exactly?"

Bennett pointed to a silver Interligate all the way on the left. Jagged icicles hung from its massive frame. "That one will take us to New Mexico, according to the map at least."

"Why New Mexico?" Kaiba asked.

"The others make sense: Washington D.C., borders around China, Bangladesh, and Moscow, but New Mexico shouldn't be a target for the virtaiyu. My guess is that they're keeping tabs on a base called Karlen City. It's on the outskirts of a desert. I have a friend from the military stationed there that should be able to help us out."

Nassira scowled. "Have you been to Karlen City?"

"Does it matter? Either way we get out of this cold and into the sun."

Kaiba didn't like the idea of trading one wasteland for another. "Do any of the Interligates go somewhere safer in America?"

"You doubting me?"

"I'd like to know our options."

"There's no option," Bennett asserted. "We're going through that Interligate."

Nassira stepped forward. "And what if it spits us out in the middle of the desert?"

Bennett glared at her. "Won't happen. The Fifth Era have these Interligates positioned at locations of importance."

Kaiba stared at Bennett's hand. "Can I see the map?"

"How 'bout you take a guess and see where you end up," Bennett said, motioning to the other Interligates.

"Let him see the map," Nassira said. Her fists were balled.

"Either follow me or wander into a random Interligate. Your choice."

Kaiba felt his body heat up. His eyes caught Bennett's, but he'd made his decision. He reeled back and threw a ball of fire.

Bennett lunged forward and batted the fire from the air with his forearm. It disappeared in a puff of black smoke. Without a second thought, Bennett jabbed Kaiba in the stomach and grabbed his neck before he could move. Kaiba felt his breath become heavy. He swung at Bennett again who grabbed his arm and twisted it so sharply that Kaiba had to drop to his knees.

"You wanna see the map?" Bennett dropped the wrinkled piece of plastic at Kaiba's feet.

Kaiba snarled, still fighting Bennett's grip.

Bennett kneed Kaiba in the back and released his arm to put him in a chokehold. He forced Kaiba's face to just above the roll-screen map. "Go ahead and look at it!"

A bolt of lightning thundered just above Kaiba's head and barely missed Bennett.

Kaiba felt Bennett's pressure lighten for a moment as he looked up at Nassira.

She stood with both arms stretched out in front of her. "Let him go, Bennett."

"New girlfriend, Kaiba?"

"I won't ask again," Nassira said sternly.

Bennett laughed. "You already missed your first shot."

Kaiba saw the fury in her eyes.

"Warning shot," she said. Sparks continued to flicker on her palms. "Something I only offer once."

Bennett held her gaze. "Fine." He tossed Kaiba in the snow. "I'll fold."

Kaiba coughed loudly as his lungs filled with frigid dry air. He clutched his throat, massaging it.

Bennett stood over the top of him and pointed. "Just remember you started that. Go ahead and look at the map. When you realize your mistake catch up to me." He turned and strode down the hill to the Interligates.

Nassira knelt beside him. Her voice was soft. "You okay?"

"Yeah," Kaiba said. "Thanks for the help."

Nassira picked up the map. "Don't mention it." She looked at it blankly as though nothing were written on it.

Kaiba stood up. "What's it say?"

"I can't read," she said, embarrassed.

"Oh," was all Kaiba could manage. He'd never run into any illiterate people before.

"My mother died before I had the chance to learn," Nassira explained, holding out the map. "With all the work I did in the city I didn't really have time. Instead I focused on learning to speak English instead of reading it."

"No need to explain," Kaiba said kindly. "Here, I'll take a look."

The map was divided into two halves. The left half had only six Interligates arranged in a square. The right half showed the twelve Interligates in a straight line. Each Interligate had a small box labeled with the location that it led to. Just as Bennett had said, one went to Washington D.C., four went to borders of China, (central, eastern, western, and northern near Russia), one to Bangladesh, three to Moscow, and then to New Mexico. But then Kaiba noticed the Interligate in the middle of the others, one that Bennett hadn't mentioned. It was labeled Coari, Brazil.

He looked up at Nassira almost worried that she'd somehow seen it.

"What is it?" Nassira asked.

If Nassira knew that an Interligate was linked back to her hometown she would try to go back to find her sister. More than likely she'd try to get revenge on those that had killed her family. Did he have the right to keep this information from her? It wasn't his place. And yet, if she went back and was killed then the Fifth Era would possess another Terraform Key.

"I'm sorry to say it," Kaiba said regretfully. "But Bennett wasn't lying. The only useful Interligate is the one that goes to New Mexico."

Nassira sighed. "I had almost hoped one went back to Brazil."

Kaiba went rigid, but realized she truly had no idea. He hated the idea of lying. He tried to avoid it, but if his family could be put in any danger by his account he had to take care of what was most important. If that meant telling a lie and postponing helping Nassira, then he had no choice. He truly wanted to tell her, but he couldn't just let her go to Brazil and get killed. If she were in his position she would understand. Those that were enraged couldn't think straight. Kaiba knew that first hand. He sounded as apologetic as possible. "I'm sorry Nassira. None of these go to Brazil."

It took another half hour to reach Bennett at the Interligate. He'd melted the snow beneath him so that he rested on a patch of dirt with snow rising all around him.

He looked up once as they came close, but then looked back at the fire in his hands.

"I'm sorry," Kaiba admitted.

Bennett twisted the fire like a child trying to entertain himself. "Realized you're a fool?"

"Just take the apology," Kaiba said. He hated having it rubbed in his face.

Bennett waited for Nassira. "And you?"

"I?" she asked.

"I'll take your apology," he said, extinguishing the flames. He put his hands on his knees, waiting.

She appeared appalled. "For what?"

"For nearly electrocuting me."

The wind whistled as Nassira stood silently.

Bennett grinned. "I can wait here all day."

Kaiba nodded to her, hoping she'd concede.

"Fine. I'm sorry," she grumbled. "Now can we get out of here?"

He stood up and smiled. "Good." He walked to the Interligate.

On the right shaft of the V was a circular indentation coated in ice. Bennett's hand glowed with heat. He held his palm over the keyhole, which caused the ice to melt and roll down the metal like candle wax. He removed the blue key from around his neck and inserted it into the hole. With a quick twist the Interligate started to hum.

There were grey stones embedded in the metal that started to glow a light purple. At the same time the empty space between the V started to flicker with lilac light. Then the light started to fill the empty space, rising from the bottom of the V like water filling a cup. Once it reached the top, the center of the Interligate looked like a mirror rather than a doorway.

Kaiba saw his reflection, but nothing of what lay on the other side.

"I'll go first then," Bennett said. He took a confident step forward and then in a flash he was gone.

Kaiba took a reluctant step toward the towering device.

"I'll follow him," Nassira offered.

"You sure?"

She stepped forward as an answer and disappeared.

Kaiba just stared at the light, which rippled like the surface of a pond. He touched the glowing space and his finger went through. It felt like a thin gel, neither hot nor cold.

He took a deep breath. He didn't know why he was so hesitant to step through. Something was holding him back, and he got the feeling that he was being watched. He spared a glance behind him and on the hill stood a single man. Kaiba was nervous and looked back at the Interligate. He spared another glance at the man, but he'd disappeared. Kaiba wondered if his mind was playing tricks on him. He didn't want to, but he stepped through the light anyway.

33

THE COURTYARD OF STONE

Sand Point Air Force Base, California

They had to go through the main hanger in order to reach the courtyard. Unden led as usual and Emily had to struggle to keep up. She was distracted. It was a massive space that reminded her of her garage, except that these ceilings were at least forty feet high. Pilots in jumpsuits chatted with one another while others tested their flight equipment. Sweaty workmen were present also, ferrying machine parts, weapons, and other fragile equipment between what seemed like an endless number of fighter jets and stealth bombers.

A pair of welders caught her eye. They were working on a plane she'd never seen before. It appeared to have some sort of pod in its underbelly. The torches threw off mountains of sparks as the heat touched the metal of the pod.

Emily nearly ran into Jordan when he stopped to let two men pass. They carried a rectangular crate labeled Highly Explosive. She felt strangely excited, wondering the whole time if this was the kind of environment her father worked in. She kicked herself for not learning more about the military. For her, every missile and gun was the same. As she walked through the hanger she realized just how naïve she'd been.

The three of them went through a metallic doorway in the left corner of the hanger. It squeaked open to a dusty sunlit courtyard of peach-colored stone. Emily coughed in the thick dust, realizing that some workmen were digging pits on the long edges of the rectangular courtyard.

"I thought these would be completed already," Unden said angrily, striding over to the nearest pit.

A man with a hardhat and a jackhammer stuck his head up. "Just working on the piping, sir. It'll be done by tomorrow."

Unden snorted and turned his back on the man. "Looks like the two of you get to sleep tonight after all."

Emily wondered what the pits were for, but the thought of rest sent shivers of excitement down her back. Her thoughts were growing sluggish and her body was exhausted. The last time she'd slept had been on the plane and that felt like ages ago. "What a relief."

"I suppose. Take a seat," Unden said, pointing to several stone blocks in one corner of the courtyard.

Emily gladly plopped down. She would have been totally content in the late afternoon sun had it not been for the hammering of the tools and the clouds of dust.

"Earth is the element of strength," Unden began. "It requires focus, and a calm collectiveness to master. Your every movement must incorporate power and solidity. Unlike water, earth is not fluid, it is solid and your moves should reflect as much. The first thing you should know is how to move stone with your touch."

"Commander," Jordan said. "Might I demonstrate what I already know so that you can teach me more?"

Emily was surprised at this. The whole while Unden had talked Jordan's eyes had been fixated as though watching his childhood hero. She wasn't even sure that he had blinked. Jordan struck her as the kind of person who would jump on a grenade if a superior asked him to.

Unden was silent for a moment and Emily thought he was going to yell. He didn't. "Confidence. I like that." He waved. "Let's see then."

Jordan slammed his right foot against the stone, which shattered into pieces as a result of the impact. The next second he swung his right arm forward as though throwing a baseball. A foot-wide crack shot through the stone and ripped right past where Emily was sitting.

In one motion he twirled and slammed his hands down against the stone. Two feet away, tiles flew into the air along with a column of brown rock. The wall of earth grew to a height of five feet, at which point Jordan stood upright again. Emily watched him take a deep breath and stone tiles started to levitate. She wouldn't have believed it if she hadn't seen it. Controlling water was strange enough, but watching someone else manipulate an element filled her with wonder.

The levitating stones started to spin as Jordan moved his fingers in tiny circles. Emily recognized the motion that she'd done while stabilizing the platform of water. She watched with admiration as Jordan moved, especially the way his powerful arms rippled and the look of concentration in those piercing eyes of his. Then Jordan punched at the air and the rocks flew forward into the wall. Each stone exploded against the barrier until it cracked and fell.

Jordan was panting as he turned to Unden, who looked shocked, as if unsure how to respond.

"That's all I've been able to do," Jordan said. "I'm sure there's much more."

"Yes," Unden said, but Emily could tell even he was surprised. "You still have a long way to go."

Jordan's affinity must have been higher than her own.

What if I really did have to fight him? How could water stop something as solid as earth? He could change the ground at my feet before I even had a chance to get at him, Emily thought. For the second time, Emily was grateful that she could forget such questions. They were on the same team now.

"I showed Emily how to increase her mobility using water and I think you should learn the same," Unden said. "Have you attempted to move the ground at your feet as you did by creating the wall?"

Jordan focused on his feet and pulled at the air as though lifting two dumbbells. He rose atop a platform of stone. "Like that?"

Unden nodded. "Have you used a skateboard before? Maybe snowboarding?"

"When I was boy."

"Good. It should help. The benefit that you have is that the ground can be changed in so many ways. One of the most beneficial is enhanced movement. Virts call it Enhanced Geo-transferration. I prefer the term earth surfing. From what I've read, Virts can earth surf in two ways. The first way is by running and moving the ground in front of you to match your steps," Unden said. "This is more difficult. Instead, I want you to use that platform and propel yourself forward by moving the earth at your back."

Jordan looked unsure, but he didn't protest. The first few attempts ended in failure. He would throw his hands back and create cracks in the ground, causing the stone under him to move only a foot. On another try Jordan pushed so hard that he accidentally launched himself off the platform.

Emily had to try not to laugh. She did have to admire his persistence. He wouldn't give up and it proved to work in his favor. After another three failed attempts, which ended in Jordan falling, he jumped back on his stone. This time Jordan leaned down and gripped the edge of the rock with his left hand. With his other hand he shifted the ground behind him.

The courtyard rumbled and the stone sounded like a car running over gravel. It happened so fast. Jordan and the rock platform jetted forward like a rocket. Stone fragments and dust trailed his movement and then he stopped abruptly ten feet from where he'd started.

"If you can hold that, you'll be able to go the speed of cars without having any assistance," Unden said.

"I can't believe it," Jordan said. He stood still to appreciate the trail of broken rock he'd left in his wake. He looked like an artist taking in his latest masterpiece.

"Try again," Unden ordered.

Jordan continued his movement all across the courtyard. He got to the point where he could jump from one earth platform to another. Then Unden taught Jordan how to create multiple pillars of stone at one time. It took several tries, but soon Jordan had created a maze of jagged stone towers each nearly the height of a person.

"Good," Unden said. "Now surf between them as fast as you can."

Jordan ran forward as a jet of rock sprang out of the ground. He jumped on the rock, hunched back over, and grabbed the edge. He threw his hand back, but nothing happened.

Unden looked at his phone. "An hour and fifteen. Better affinity than Emily."

Emily scowled.

"That's all we can do for now," Unden said. Then he whistled and Colonel Barnes rushed out of the hanger bay. "Show these two to their quarters Colonel. Get them food and have them here by 0700."

Barnes saluted. "Yes, Commander."

"What're we doing tomorrow?" Emily asked.

"The pits will be filled with water," Unden stated. "That will allow you and Jordan to spar. Dismissed."

Emily couldn't help but notice Jordan smile.

They ate the terrible canned food in the mess hall. Emily picked silently at the pink meat, preoccupied about fighting Jordan tomorrow. Barnes asked how the training went, but she didn't answer. Jordan, on the other hand, seemed ecstatic about what had taken place.

When she'd finished she was taken to a room barely large enough for the twin bed. It was a hard mattress with only a thin sheet as bedding. Strangely, Emily didn't care.

She had trouble sleeping that night. She couldn't fight the dread that Jordan could humiliate her tomorrow. He was stronger and had more affinity than she did. Emily played what she knew over and over in her head. She could crash waves into Jordan, but unlike on the *Archfrost* Emily couldn't just drag him into the ocean. She'd have to try to use ice. She drifted to sleep thinking of any way she could gain an advantage. She'd need everything she could throw at him.

34

N E W   L A N D S

White Sands, New Mexico, United States

Kaiba had expected a sense of spinning, falling, and maybe even nausea. But he felt nothing as he walked through the gateway. In an instant he emerged, and towering sand dunes met his eyes. The sun was high, spewing its yellow rays across the white sands. There was a slight wind that kicked up grains of sand in thick clouds. An Interligate rested just behind him, humming and glowing with the same violet aura as the one in the tundra.

Bennett stood several paces from the Interligate. He knelt strangely, with his neck twisted at a weird angle to the sands. If Kaiba had made a sound coming through the gateway, Bennett gave no indication that he'd noticed. Nassira stood in a similar manner at his side.

"What's so interesting?" Kaiba asked taking a step forward.

Bennett reeled on him. *"Don't move!"*

But it was too late. Kaiba's foot hit the ground, crossing the red glint of a laser light.

With a clap of thunder, the first trip mine detonated, spewing a plume of sand and fire into the sky.

Kaiba stumbled away from the gate as another explosion rippled to his right. The heat of the blast singed the hairs off his arms. Bennett ran from the explosion with Nassira in his grasp. He threw her near Kaiba as another mine exploded in a wave of scorching red.

Kaiba wanted to run, but there was no way he was going to escape the force of the blast. The moment the fire was about to engulf them, Bennett threw his hands forward and the explosion suddenly changed direction, parting before Bennett's body like water around a rock. More explosions went off and with each additional blast Bennett twisted his hands and was able to bend the fire into a dome. They were trapped in a bubble of fire. The yellow and orange swirled like the colors of a paint palette, creating a heat that rivaled the heart of a volcano. Kaiba was certain that if he extended even one hand it would be singed right off. He watched with amazement as the fire spun; it was almost hypnotizing.

When the explosions had finally ended Bennett pushed forward and the flames shot outward in all directions. The fire sputtered and disappeared in streams of thick smoke. He lowered his hands and sank to one knee. His clothes were soaked with sweat. He was shaking and Kaiba was worried he was going to pass out.

"Almost cost us our damn lives," Bennett gasped.

"A bit of a warning would've helped," Kaiba said. He was sweating just as heavily. He could hardly believe the change from the freezing cold to this unbearable heat.

The Interligate was in ruins, ripped to pieces by the force of the explosions. The desert had changed too. Cratered pits littered the landscape, tainting the yellow with black burnt ripples.

Nassira put a hand on Kaiba's back. "Should have warned you."

At the same instant, five Jeeps roared over the crest of the nearest sand dune. They had raised suspensions so that the body of the Jeeps sat up higher than normal.

"Just what we need," Bennett said sarcastically. He pulled himself upright, but remained sitting as the Jeeps rolled to a halt.

Nassira tensed up, preparing for a fight. Kaiba did the same, hoping he had enough strength to take on five cars full of potential enemies.

From each vehicle came six or so fully armored soldiers, all adorned in heavy Kevlar vests and armor-plated pants.

Kaiba knew the armor was weak under the arms and around the neck. He wasn't sure how they would hold up against an electric charge. He hoped they'd be vulnerable.

From the lead vehicle emerged a tall man with dark brown eyes. His hair was a curly black that matched the thin scruffy beard on his rough face. He had a large flattened nose and light almond skin that looked tanned by the sun. His voice was deep like the rumble of the mountains. "Best to surrender, Fifth Era."

The men from the other vehicles formed up behind him.

"We are not Fifth Era," Kaiba said. "We escaped from their prison."

"You were lucky enough to survive this mine field. Do not feed us lies lest we decide to shoot. I can assure you my bullets will be much more accurate than these explosions were."

Bennett stood up with crossed arms. "I was unaware they let doctors do the soldiers' job. Is your unit that desperate?"

The man looked Bennett up and down. He broke into a large smile. "They made an exception for me to kill you." He set his gun on his shoulder and addressed his men. "Lower your weapons." He walked forward and embraced Bennett in a tight bear hug. "You look worse than ever!"

Bennett returned the hug. "Time in the slammer tends to do that. You would know all about that though, Mr. Al Qaeda."

"You don't look like you've been tortured like I was. Did they catch you for robbing another med cabinet?"

"I'm much stealthier now," Bennett said. "If you hadn't lived by your doctor's code I wouldn't have been caught."

The man shrugged. "Someone had to keep you in your place."

"Ha!" Bennett clasped the man's shoulder.

"Who is this?" Kaiba asked.

"This," Bennett said, "is my dear friend Dr. Abdu Naheed."

"'Acquaintance' is a better term," Abdu said jokingly.

"I'm Kaiba."

He stepped forward. "Pleased to meet you Kaiba."

They shook hands and Abdu's eyes drifted to Nassira. "And you are?"

She looked both tense and nervous. "Nassira."

"Pleased to meet the both of you." He stared at the destroyed Interligate and asked Bennett, "What was on the other side?"

"You don't know?"

Abdu placed the butt of his rifle in the sand. He leaned on it like a walking stick. "The gate hasn't gone off for months. We didn't even know if it still worked. We kept watch, but it wasn't our job to explore it. We assumed our defenses would be adequate enough."

"Thanks for those, by the way. You're lucky I'm bound to this firestarter or those mines would have ripped us to shreds," Bennett said.

"Can you blame us? We had to be prepared."

"With good reason. The other side's a winter wasteland holding a Fifth Era compound."

Abdu gripped the handle of his weapon. "How many?"

"Didn't get a clear count. Eskylious arrived there moments before we escaped. It has to be a leadership camp."

Abdu looked surprised. "Eskylious was there?"

"The Fifth Era have contact with him. Don't know if they expected a reward or just better treatment for turning us in. Won't matter now, since we escaped."

"But you managed to destroy our only link to the base," Abdu said with a hint of discouragement.

"We might not have access to them through this Interligate, but there are others." Bennett rummaged through his jacket and pulled out the roll-screen.

Abdu took the map, his eyes growing wide as he glanced over it. "There are at least fourteen gates here."

"Might even be fifteen," Kaiba said. "The Coronado, California one wasn't on the map."

Abdu looked worried. "There's an Interligate in Cali?"

"There must have been, otherwise I wouldn't have been at the compound."

"Why would they take a regular soldier like you?"

"They each have one," Bennett said.

"Have one of what?" Abdu asked.

"A transformed sphere."

Abdu turned to Bennett in disbelief. Then he opened his arms wide with excitement. "May I see them?"

Kaiba knew the drill. He grabbed the collar of his shirt, growing tired of revealing his bond, but he pulled it up so the top edge of the silver plate was visible. Nassira rolled up her sleeve to reveal her forearm.

Abdu came closer, his eyes bouncing back and forth between them. "And what are their elements?"

"Nassira has lightning," Bennett answered. "Kaiba is, well, aether."

"The Fifth Era almost got the aether element?" Abdu stated furiously.

"He's safe now."

"I'll consider us lucky then. I can't imagine what would have happened had Eskylious gotten that sphere back."

"Eh, lucky they had me as a hero I guess," Bennett said.

"They'd have done fine without you." Abdu whistled. "All right boys, load up."

The soldiers got back in the trucks. Kaiba climbed into the back seat of the first vehicle beside Nassira. Abdu drove with Bennett at his side. The Jeep bounced wildly as they sped along the desert. Each turn caused the whole truck to vibrate. The air was dry, tinged with the scents of dirt and hot rubber from the tires.

"How many elements have activated?" Abdu asked as he floored the gas pedal to ascend a sand hill.

"So far four: fire, lightning, psychic, and earth."

"Ah," Abdu said as he avoided a large rock. "You can add air to that list as well. A pilot by the name of Evan Howard is supposed to arrive in Karlen City this week."

"The spheres are being recovered much sooner than I'd have thought," Bennett admitted.

"I'd consider us lucky, even if a couple of teens ended up with the spheres. How do you feel with your abilities so far Kaiba?"

"I have the basics, but I'm in no means confident in them," Kaiba said humbly.

"We can work on that. Just takes time," Abdu said. "And how's your aim with lightning, Nassira?"

"Okay," Nassira said. She still seemed uncomfortable.

"I've got something I'd like both of you to try when we get to base camp," Abdu said.

Bennett pivoted in his seat to face the back. "Abdu worked closely with the Tempest operations. No one knows quite as much about the elements as he does. The city of Karlen was originally in the process of being modified to house the elemental spheres, but they were worried about its location."

"After Tempest was chosen to serve as the primary base for the Terraformer project Karlen was turned into the finest weapons development and experimental technologies facility. The smartest from all over the world poured money in. Now the government's furious that Karlen wasn't used," Abdu said. "They could have seen a Virt attack coming for miles around. Sadly, you won't get to see it until at least tomorrow though."

"What do you mean?" Bennett asked.

Abdu slowed the car as a large lake came into view. On the shore closest to the Jeep were twenty-five tents and a camper or two. "We couldn't test these weapons back at Karlen, city ordinance said lightning was too dangerous. So we decided to test 'em here and give the boys a little relaxation."

"Leave it to you to want to head back to the sands," Bennett said.

"Man of habit," Abdu joked with a wink.

"Shouldn't we alert the UNM about the Interligates?" Kaiba asked.

"I'll take care of that," Abdu said. "But by the looks of you guys, you could use a bath."

Kaiba smiled at the thought of being clean. "That would be awesome."

"Good, that will give me time to ready the weapon test," Abdu said as he parked outside of one of the campers. "I'll see if I can't round you up some food as well."

Bennett stepped from the vehicle. "Thanks, Abdu."

"Of course. After you clean off come on back and I'll show you guys the merchandise." He looked between Kaiba and Nassira. "I think you two will be able to make great use of them."

35

U P G R A D E

Weapons Base Camp, New Mexican Desert

The lake glittered like a jewel. It was cool to the touch and Kaiba sank till his knees hit the wet sandy bottom. He scrubbed his arms and back, feeling completely content. When he'd scraped the dirt from his body he sat, not thinking, but merely relaxing. He dived deeper and the water streamlined through his thick hair.

Nassira walked the shoreline barefoot and the water brushed the underside of her calves.

Kaiba watched her for a moment, and then called, "You sure you're not comin' in?"

She shook her plated forearm. "Water and electricity aren't the best of friends."

He stood up, motioning to his metal chest. "No problems for me. Come on, it feels good."

She smiled. "Thanks, but I'm good right here."

Kaiba returned the smile and flipped onto his back. He didn't think that was her reason for staying at a distance. Was she really so shy? She kept so much to herself Kaiba wondered if she liked it that way. They had been on the beach an hour and she hardly said anything, preferring to just walk along the water as if deep in thought.

He was watching the clouds drift lazily across the sky when he felt a pang in his chest. He looked at the plate. On the top left corner, the blue sphere indentation had started to glow.

"Hey Bennett?" Kaiba called.

Bennett was face down in the water with his ears sticking out. He stood up and the water dripped down his tattooed chest. "What's up?"

"This something I should be worried about?"

"Looks like a good sign to me, someone's got the water sphere. Lake must have triggered it."

Kaiba squeezed his arms. "Feels like there's pressure building up inside me. It's different than the usual adrenaline."

Bennett explained the concept of affinity and the limits of the Terraform Keys. "Each element has its own way of creating energy inside you. Water must come with pressure. Try to use it while you have it."

Just like with earth and fire Kaiba could feel the water stretch out around him. Normally water felt like a thicker air, it didn't give too much resistance and his limbs could glide easily through. But now the water felt prickly, as if composed of individual balls instead of a fluid mass. He stuck his hand into the lake, feeling each of the tiny droplets. The pressure had increased and so he pushed it into the lake. He felt as though the water were flowing into and out of his own body. The sensation felt unnatural, like he was urinating out of his skin. He pulled up on the lake and beads of water clung to his fingertips. As he moved his hand farther up, a stream of water began to form, connecting his hand and the surface. The blue hung there like saliva on the lips of a dog. He moved his hand back and forth, watching the water mimic his motion. He swirled it for a minute, fascinated with the fluidity of the movements.

"You're a natural," Bennett said.

"It's not me. It's the plate that's doing this."

"It can't function without you."

"I wanna try something," Kaiba said, letting the water stream fall. "Mind if I splash ya?"

Bennett threw his arms out making his body as wide as possible. "Be my guest."

Kaiba dunked both hands into the water. He imagined gripping a heavy object and the pressure started to build in his hands. He counted down in his head and when he couldn't hold back the pressure any longer he pushed forward, releasing the energy. The surface of the lake exploded into a towering wave. The surf surged forward and collided with Bennett, knocking him off his feet and throwing him onto the sandy beach. He rolled several times until the water started to recede. Kaiba was worried that he'd accidentally hurt him.

Bennett came up coughing and swearing. "You'll pay for that one!" He wiped the sand from his eyes.

Kaiba laughed, realizing he hadn't been hurt. "Guess I don't know my own strength. Besides, I had to get you back for the Interligate thing."

"Get me back? Oh here, let me help ya with that." Bennett ran and tried to tackle Kaiba.

Kaiba laughed and moved out of the way. "You're slowin' down, marine."

Bennett picked himself up, spitting water. He charged again, but stopped when he saw Abdu on shore.

"Done playing around?" Abdu asked.

They both shrugged and Bennett answered, "If there's food."

Kaiba hadn't eaten so well in years. The salted pork was perfect, the burgers were juicy, and the canned pears tasted almost like the real thing. They even drank soda that Kaiba hadn't tasted since he was a boy. Bennett, Nassira, and he scarfed down the food, finishing in minutes. Afterwards, Abdu took them to a targeting range crudely drawn in the sands. Several target boards were positioned at the far end of the gun range at various distances and heights.

Weapon racks lined the head of the range. Abdu approached one rack with six tube-like objects, each the size of a person's arm. They were colored jet black. Silver bolts studded along their lengths led to a melon-sized barrel. A single holographic scope rested on the top beside two high-tech touch pads. At the back of each machine were three red cables connecting to a square backpack that hung just above each tube.

"Lightning is one of nature's most powerful forces. When we started this war," Abdu said, "we thought we could fight fire with fire, or in both of your cases lightning with lightning. Many of the virtaiyu have the knack for electrokinetics. Our armor has its weak points and the virtaiyu were able to exploit this through the power of lightning bolts. We were vulnerable, but we knew they would be just as vulnerable. So we developed these." Abdu grabbed one of the tubes from the rack. "We call them the personal ion cannons or PIC for short."

"What can we use them for?" Kaiba asked.

"They were manufactured to create electricity and direct it with the utmost precision."

Kaiba looked at the dozen or so other PICs. "Why not outfit every soldier with one?"

"A good question." Abdu picked up one of the backpacks. "Electricity naturally wants to take the path of least resistance. To overcome this instability we used a beam of light to ionize the air around it and thus lower resistance. The lightning is naturally attracted to the path of ionized light and thus it will travel perfectly where the light is aimed."

"Sounds like a powerful weapon," Bennett said.

"It is," Abdu emphasized. "The problem is that even with these power packs we don't have enough portable energy to create both lightning and an ion channel. Because of this, the cannons are useless to us, but I hope not to you. Both of you can create lightning. All you have to do is release the energy and the cannon will direct it."

Abdu removed the three cables from one ion cannon and grabbed it with both hands. He offered it to Nassira and then handed another one to Kaiba. "Go on, try them on."

Kaiba turned the PIC to the open end. It was wider than he would have expected, and also lighter. He slid his arm into the hole and it extended down his forearm until just before his elbow. The barrel stretched about three inches longer than his fingertips.

"What's with the bar?" Kaiba asked as he wrapped his fingers around the barrier that prevented him from sliding in any farther.

Abdu tapped on Kaiba's cannon. "Pull it toward you."

He yanked back and the cannon hissed as the air was pumped out. The machine tightened around his skin as if he were having his blood pressure taken. When the PIC was fully fitted, he felt it shudder and two jagged lines of bright yellow glowed on the surface.

Nassira fitted hers at just the same moment.

"How do they feel?" Abdu asked.

"Tight," Kaiba said. He swung his arm back and forth trying to get used to the weight.

Nassira tried to loosen the cannon with her other hand. She grimaced and pulled against it. She looked like a warrior, with the Terraform plating on one forearm and the cannon on the other.

"They're programmed to fit as close to your skin as possible without causing circulation loss," Abdu explained.

"That's comforting," Kaiba said. He could feel each pump of blood squeezing its way down his arm.

Abdu smiled. "I think so too. Now for some fun. See the silver switch right in front of the scope?"

Kaiba located the penny-sized switch on the top side of his PIC. He flipped it and the barrel of the cannon spewed a red beam of light no wider than that of a flashlight. Nassira's cannon glowed in a similar manner.

"All you gotta do now is aim and create the lightning," Abdu said. "Kaiba, aim for the target on the far left. Nassira take the right."

Nassira didn't hesitate. She threw the cannon up and fired a straight shot of arching lightning. The wood target exploded on impact.

Kaiba stepped forward and aimed the light beam at the red ring-targets on the wood board. He took his time making sure the light hovered right over the center. The familiar tingle that had felt like so much pain just seemed normal now as he flexed his fingers in and out. He concentrated on the beam of light and three bolts of electricity exploded from his left hand.

"Not that way!" Abdu yelled.

The lightning shot to the sky and then darted back to the laser, coiling around the red light like a snake wrapping around its prey. The crackling energy loosely followed the path of the ionized light, but completely missed the target and instead hit the sand and a truck in the distance. Sparks danced around the vehicle with dazzling brilliance for several seconds.

Abdu stormed up to Kaiba. "Okay. Ready to listen this time?"

"I did as you said!" he protested.

Abdu grabbed his left hand and jammed it against the barrel of the PIC. "Metal conducts electricity, doesn't it? Seeing as you can't electrocute yourself just stick your fingers into the three cord sockets and then fire the electricity.

"Got it," Kaiba said, embarrassed when he saw Nassira looking at him.

"Show me whatcha got then." He took a step to the side and crossed his arms impatiently.

Kaiba let the electricity dance along his hand. His fingers tingled and he tugged on the bar inside the cannon. The line of ionized light appeared. He rested his cheek on the cannon and moved the beam of light to the center of the target.

In one motion he unleashed all the lighting from his hand as he slipped his three fingers into the socket holes. A thunderous boom echoed as the lightning exploded from the barrel of the cannon. It engulfed the wood in a mighty cloud of sparks.

"Much better!" Abdu said, enthused. "I knew you'd be perfect for this."

"I don't see why they'd need the cannons if they can aim lightning on their own," Bennett said.

"Two reasons, Benny. The first is that rain and heat will mess up their natural abilities. And secondly, the EMP function, which I think is the most useful. An electromagnetic pulse has two ways of being generated, but both are fundamentally the same. The first way involves a nuclear warhead being detonated high in the air which, obviously, I won't be demonstrating. But the second way is to generate a standard pulse, which is quite simple and arguably more effective due to its ability to aim at either a single target or multiple targets."

"Do I even need to create additional lightning to do that?" Kaiba asked.

"That's both the good and the bad part. Notice the five blue bars at the top of the cannon."

He hadn't noticed the equally-spaced gumstick-sized rectangles before.

"When you tap the bars it will convert the power of your cannon to its pulse generator mode."

Nassira and he tapped the touch screen bars and they glowed a bright yellow.

"Each one of the bars represents the natural power levels of the cannon. While in pulse mode you can fire ten EMP bursts, two per bar." Abdu whistled loudly and behind him came a vehicle that looked like a go-cart.

Nassira raised her eyebrows. "A race car?"

"In the middle of the desert you get bored. Shoot it before it hits us." Abdu looked at the driver. "Go for it, Ty!"

"What are you talking about?" Kaiba asked.

The driver revved the go-cart's engine and it burst forward like a rocket.

Kaiba and Nassira aimed instinctively at the front of the cart. They fired and rings of blue-white light emerged from the barrels. The light struck the car, which sparked and immediately started to slow down. Two feet from Nassira it stopped in its tracks.

"Looks like your EMP works fine." Abdu said happily.

"How did it stop the car?" Kaiba asked

He grinned. "EMPs have the ability to disable and even destroy electronic devices, which is exactly what happened to the car."

"Then why doesn't it affect everything around it?" Nassira asked.

"If you hold the charge it will detonate in all directions. I don't want you doing that here because it would disable everything we got running on electrical power. I don't think any of us want that."

Kaiba tapped the yellow bars. "Makes sense."

Nassira held her cannon to support its weight. "How will I recharge the pulse generator?"

"You won't," Abdu said. "You'll need a new PIC, but I'll talk to UNM research to see if they can't make some improved designs. For now, it's best not to waste any shots."

For the rest of the afternoon Kaiba and Nassira practiced aiming their new cannons. Kaiba started to get the hang of it. Then Abdu showed them each to their own tent and Kaiba was grateful for the air mattress. He slept fast.

The next morning, Nassira and he went out to the dunes in the early morning to experiment more with the PICs. She opened up throughout the day while they fried the sand and destroyed junker vehicles together. A few soldiers tagged along and Kaiba enjoyed blasting the targets they threw into the air. To his surprise, Nassira wanted to have a competition to see who could hit the most targets before they fell to the ground.

Abdu showed up later, suggesting that they practice combat skills with the cannons. The soldiers were more than willing to help, but Abdu made them wear protective gear.

Later, Bennett made Kaiba work on fire, water, earth, lightning, and psychic manipulation. The training drained his body as Bennett forced him to switch between each element. The worst part was that he had to leave the cannon on. Sometimes his fingers would get stuck in the PIC's holes, slowing his reaction time. When he managed to remove his fingers he could manipulate the elements, but his cannon arm weighed down the right side of his body, leaving him open to attacks. When he was totally exhausted, he sat with Abdu and asked about Evan, the pilot who could supposedly control air. Abdu said the man was the second to discover an element, but Kaiba would have to wait to meet him.

The sun grew lower in the sky and everyone came together for another meal; this time chicken, various protein gels and water. Abdu announced that they'd be heading back to Karlen at dawn.

That night Kaiba couldn't sleep. He stared at the waving surface of the tent and decided to go out by the lake. He found Nassira staring at the moon. "Care for some company?"

"Please," she said, not taking her eyes off the sky.

"Thanks." Kaiba plopped down next to her. "Can't sleep?"

"Nightmares keep me up." She smiled sadly and tiny dimples formed in her cheeks. "This is much nicer."

"I know what you mean." The water stood still and the two moons stared back at one another. "I had fun today."

"Me too," she said.

"Are you okay?" Kaiba asked.

"I think so." She looked at him. Her eyes reflected the white moonlight. "Why do you ask?"

"Just wanted to make sure."

She visibly realized he was asking about her family. "I'm past denial about my siblings. Guess I'm kinda just accepting what happened."

Kaiba put his hand on her knee. "Do you need anything?"

She shied away. "No, but thank you."

Kaiba felt stupid. "Er, sorry."

She smiled again. "Don't be."

They stared at each other for a moment and Kaiba wished he could see what she was thinking. A small breeze blew and wisped through Nassira's long hair.

"Why do you stare at me like that?" she asked.

Kaiba blushed and looked out at the water. "What do you mean?"

She giggled. "Why do you stare at me? You look at me like my dad used to look at my mom."

Kaiba wanted to lean forward and kiss her. He wanted to take away her pain and replace it with that beautiful smile. "I guess I can't help myself."

She scooted her body nearer. "You use that line on lots of girls, don't you?"

Kaiba laughed. His heart pumped faster and his palms grew cold. He leaned closer. "It's a good one, huh?" He could feel the heat of her breath and the smell of her salty skin. He was about to kiss her, but something held him back. She was vulnerable and they were at war. Starting something was foolish.

He pulled back and stood up. "I should get back to bed. We have an early start tomorrow."

Nassira looked surprised; her eyes were glazed with hurt. "Yeah. Yeah, me too."

36

A P O L O G Y

Sand Point Air Force Base, California

Emily awoke to the sound of someone pounding on the door.
"Miss Sursten." Then another rap.

For a moment she thought Mo was waking her back in
Australia. She rubbed the flakes from her eyes and the tiny room
came into focus. "I'm up," she said, annoyed.

"Commander Unden is waiting for you in the courtyard."

She stood up and was grateful for sleeping in her clothes. It
meant less time trying to get ready. She stared into the mirror
and tried to untangle her blonde strands of hair. She still didn't
understand how her hair got so messy in the night. After a few
patdowns she stepped from the room. Jordan was already waiting
there, his face neutral and bright as though he'd been awake for
hours.

"Morning."

"Morning."

Breakfast was cold cereal and a tube of protein gel. Emily had
never eaten the yogurt-like substance before. It tasted like metallic

raspberries. Her eyes were locked on Jordan. She was confident in her abilities, but that didn't make her any less nervous. Sure, it would only be sparring, but the fight on the *Archfrost* had to bring back memories for Jordan. That fight, Emily had two elements with her, water and surprise. This time, they each knew what the other was capable of. She wondered if that was why Unden wanted them to watch each other.

After breakfast they were led to the courtyard. Emily tried to contain her nervousness, but her hands were shaking.

They found Unden sitting on a rock near the new pool of water. He was busy looking at a kind of tablet Emily hadn't seen before. Its surface projected 3D images and a voice gave updates from the war. Unden looked up as they approached. The bags under his eyes hinted that he hadn't slept much. "On time. Rare for your generation."

"Not all of us are the same," Jordan offered.

Unden muted the tablet and held it behind his back. "An understatement to be sure. Get yourselves stretched out."

They did as he said and Emily grabbed one arm and pulled it across her body. She repeated the motion with her other arm then leaned to touch her toes. Jordan was flat on the ground twisting his legs into various positions. They were given five minutes and Emily made mental notes of the field's dimensions, realizing Jordan would have the advantage from the start. Although the long edges had water pits, the short sides didn't. Worse was how wide the court was. If Jordan moved her away from either of the water pits she would be helpless. The time ended and Unden ordered that they approach him in the center of the courtyard.

"Sparring is the perfect opportunity to release anger and tensions. Outside of this ring you are allies, but while you stand within it you are enemies. You must keep the mentality that you will kill your opponent. Is that understood?"

"Yes," Emily and Jordan said, their voices echoing.

"Good. Now shake hands."

Jordan's grip was strong, but Emily wouldn't be intimidated. She squeezed even tighter and when he winced she felt confident. This was just another boy.

"Any questions?" Unden inquired.

"How do I win?" Emily asked.

"Simple," Unden said. "Make the other person give up."

Emily smiled doing her best not to seem intimidated. "You can give up now. You'll just save us time."

Jordan stretched out his long limbs. "We'll see. How do we know our abilities aren't still gone?"

"Affinity and recharge time are one and the same. You manipulated for an hour and it takes equal time to recharge," Unden said. "Now, when I say stop, you do so without hesitation. I am the referee here. Now walk to the edge and begin on the gunshot."

Emily walked back slowly as the jittering started in her stomach. She took a deep breath and turned when she'd reached the end of the rock tile. She was careful to position herself slightly closer to the right pool so she could reach it faster. To her surprise Jordan looked confident, maybe even arrogant. He stood lazily upright while Emily was bent low in a sprinter's stance. She knew that if she couldn't reach the water the fight would be over.

Unden raised his gun into the air. His finger stroked the trigger.

Emily felt her heart beating and the wind brushing through her hair. She bounced on the balls of her feet, ready to leap into action.

Bang!

She took off and jumped straight at the pool. As she was about to reach it a wall of rock shot up. She kicked off the barrier and whirled around as Jordan earth surfed for her. Dust trailed him as he moved faster. She sprinted past the wall, but more sprang up. She stood in place, unarmed and exposed. Jordan barreled forward and that was just what she wanted. He leapt off his rock and skidded against the ground.

Emily braced herself against the wall as clumps of rock shot up around Jordan's body.

"This is what happens when you can't access your element." He punched, and each of the stones flew forward.

Just as they were about to pummel Emily, she leapt out of the way. The rocks exploded against the wall, toppling it over just as she'd planned.

She popped up and jumped off the ruins. Before she hit the water she froze the surface and landed with a soft thud. She turned to Jordan, who threw more stones, these ones larger than before. She ducked under one clump, sidestepped another, but before she could evade, a third stone collided with her stomach. She let out a scream and fell from the ice. She plunged into the water, sinking beside the rock that struck her. She clutched her burning gut and lay on the bottom of the pool. Her body jolted in a spasm as she started to breathe underwater. Soon the pain subsided and she smiled; she hadn't revealed everything she was capable of.

She waited at the bottom until Jordan's shadow appeared. Then she pushed off the ground gathering all the water around her. She launched into the air taking in the horrified look on Jordan's face. She slapped her arms together and the waves curled around her. For a moment she was reminded of surfing, only instead of controlling the surfboard she controlled the surf itself.

Jordan was knocked off his feet and carried back with the water. As the wave carried Jordan she forced it into a bubble so that Jordan was trapped within. She spun the water and he kicked against the whirling current. She held him there, walking calmly forward as the droplets dripped from her body. Unden's facial expression was neutral and so she kept on trying to drown Jordan in the sphere of water.

But, in the second that she looked away Jordan had launched a crevasse toward her. She tried to evade it, but the crack tipped her off balance. She fell, causing the mass of liquid to fall away, with

Jordan at its center. The water rushed in all directions as if a plastic pool had exploded. Jordan coughed and snarled as Emily regained her balance. She noticed that the crack had filled with water.

Jordan fired stone projectiles. Emily stood gathering liquid from the crack and it circled around her arms. As the stones flew she engulfed them in water and then froze it. The first ice ball hit the ground and shattered. She danced back and forth repeating her tactic as Jordan got closer. She was forced to the edge of the arena, where she realized that Jordan was still soaked. She ducked under another stone and froze the water in his clothes. A thin sheet of ice coated his body, but he didn't slow. He sprinted and tackled Emily. They hit and Emily's ribs exploded with fire. Her head started to spin as they rolled along the tiles. She tried to fight, but he was too strong. She was pinned. Two spikes of earth shot up on either side of her head.

Jordan was on his knees with his hands raised. "Give up?"

"Never!" she spat, squirming and kicking.

Emily heard the cracking as the spikes neared her temples.

"Stop!" Unden yelled.

Jordan stayed where he was, panting heavily. He looked like a scorpion's tail, primed and ready to strike. His eyes didn't move from Emily. "It's done, then?"

Emily panted also, but she was already readying herself for an escape. She saw the pool of water on her right and she drew some to her. Unden's heavy boot splashed in the moving water. "You've lost, Emily."

Jordan balled his hands as if squeezing an object. The rock spikes crumbled and fell. "Thought you had me there for a second." He extended a hand, looking pleased with himself.

Emily rolled onto her side and dusted herself off. "If Unden hadn't interfered I would have." She strode back to the hanger.

They were allowed a two hour break after the fight. She hated losing. It didn't happen often. She took the time to relax, back in her makeshift room. She sat stretching her muscles on the hard bed when Jordan stuck his head through the door frame. "You busy?"

She rolled her eyes and pretended to be focusing on the peeling wallpaper of the ceiling.

He stood near the bed. "I came to apologize."

This was the last thing she'd expected. She sat up. "What for?"

"I just wanted to apologize for trying to frame you on the *Archfrost*. I feared for Kaiba's safety."

"Oh," Emily said, uninterested and suddenly irritated. She'd almost forgotten about Kaiba, but thanks to Jordan it was fresh in her mind.

"Can we talk?"

Emily groaned. "If you feel so inclined."

In spite of her obvious discomfort he sat down. "We got off to the wrong start. These spheres complicate things and acting as you did, I realize I would have done the same thing."

"Well, that's good," Emily said. "But I don't need your approval."

"I know. I just wanted to say sorry. I didn't look at this from your perspective. Not having a dad makes me biased."

Was he seriously trying to be friends? He played the sympathy card and now she felt guilty. He didn't seem like a bad guy and maybe he was trying to mend things. After all they were the only two people in California with these abilities. She didn't want to get closer, but she couldn't just brush off his comment. "What happened to him?"

"The war started. He didn't want to go so he fled, went I don't know where and I haven't seen or heard from him since."

"I didn't know," Emily said. "I'm sorry."

"I'm not. He provided me with an example of how not to do things. Most people would mourn losing their father, but I don't. He was a coward, and I'll never run from my problems like he did."

"That's honorable of you."

Jordan winked. "Just the way I am."

Emily smiled. A moment ago she was convinced she hated Jordan. Now she couldn't blame him for what happened on the *Archfrost*. He was only trying to do what was best for Kaiba. Would she have acted differently if someone were after Devon? "Was your friend Kaiba the same way, not running from his problems?" she asked.

"Yes and no. I've never seen him break down before, but after he shocked your father I saw something in him I never had. Kaiba's the type of guy that wouldn't hurt anybody unless he's forced to. That's why he felt so bad about your father. He was so guilty he talked about giving his sphere up, no matter what the cost. Would he have given up after that? I like to think not, but now I don't even know if he's alive."

"I wonder the same about my father."

Jordan stared directly into her eyes. "I saw your dad stir, Emily, I know he made it."

She gave him half a smile. "If Kaiba's abilities are anything like yours, I'm sure he'll be fine too."

Jordan smiled again and stood from the bed. "I'd say he'd be screwed."

Emily laughed. Her emotions were muddled and part of her felt strangely close to Jordan. He was going through the exact same problems she was and yet, he found a way to stay positive. Jordan reminded her a little bit of Devon in that respect. She hoped that he was doing okay, but she couldn't lie to herself, something about Jordan made her feel almost happy. In a way that scared her, she didn't want to lose the feelings she had for Devon. Then she realized she was staring at Jordan as he stood in the doorway.

He smiled again. "Wanna see if we can't get some food?"

Emily rose to her feet. "I'd like that."

They walked into the hall when Unden appeared. "Break's up early. Come on."

Their moment of peace and normalcy was over. For a minute Emily had felt like a regular person again. Now she'd have to go back to taking orders. They walked to the pool house when they heard someone shouting.

Barnes ran at them. "Commander, a man named Abdu is on the line. His authentication checks out."

Unden reached for the phone. The man on the other line yelled one word, "Eskylious!"

Emily had never seen Unden show any hint at fear. But he dropped his cane and stumbled. Emily didn't know who Eskylious was, but if he intimidated Unden, she was even more frightened.

37

Loss of a Sphere

Weapons Base Camp, New Mexico

The blistering sun hung in the pale blue sky, baking the sands as if in an oven. Kaiba stretched his arms as he walked from his tent. He was just as eager, if not more so, than the others to get out of the desert. They had been there for two days too many. Kaiba looked out across the yellow fields that seemed to shift in the sun's rays like flowers in a meadow. There were six Humvees waiting across from him, each with a turret on its back. In front of the six Humvees was a single Stryker vehicle. The Stryker was painted to match the color of the sands and its eight tires were just about half of Kaiba's height. He had to crane his neck to see just how tall it was.

"Good to see ya up and ready," Bennett said. He took a sip from a cup of black coffee.

"Wanted to be ready to move and get out of this place."

"I can understand that. Civilization's calling."

Kaiba nodded in agreement. "Isn't that the truth."

They helped the other soldiers load the Humvees with gear and helped Abdu stow the PICs safely. When the soldiers had completely packed everything up they headed for the vehicles.

Nassira approached him. "Morning."

"How'd ya sleep?" Kaiba asked.

"Pretty well actually. What vehicle are we riding in?"

"I don't care what Abadaba says, I call riding shotgun in that thing," Bennett said. He walked to the Stryker and climbed up the ladder on its side.

✳ ✳ ✳

In the distance, Ian sat on the top of a sand dune. He was blazingly hot, but he'd been waiting all night for this opportunity and he wouldn't waste it. He closed his left eye and focused in on the man he knew to be Matthew Bennett. He stroked the trigger softly and rested his cheek against the gun barrel. He waited to see if there was a breeze. There wasn't. He held his breath, thinking only of his son, and then pulled the trigger when the crosshairs were over Bennett's head.

✳ ✳ ✳

Kaiba heard a boom in the distance. It was faint, but an unnatural sound for the desert.

It happened so fast.

Bennett toppled from the top of the Stryker and hit the sands. Blood started to pool around him.

Kaiba rushed forward to his side. "*Get a medic!*" he screamed.

Bennett's whole body started to spasm. Kaiba tried to grab him and stabilize his body, but without warning he went limp.

Kaiba fought back the tears as he tried to shake Bennett awake, but he knew he'd truly died when the metal on his shoulder started to rearrange itself. It moved like a flattened Rubik's Cube that was folding itself inward to regain its original shape. Kaiba watched both in sadness and amazement as a sphere the size of a mango rolled from Bennett's body. He picked up the object and stared into it as though it were Bennett's soul.

Kaiba could hear the others around him, but he didn't move. This wasn't supposed to be how it went. They had survived the winter desert and now they were supposed to survive this desert of fire. He looked around helplessly as Nassira rushed to his side. Men stood over Bennett. From out of nowhere a flash of purple exploded in front of Kaiba. The flash created a shockwave that knocked him back. The sphere flew from his hand and a man emerged from the purple light.

Anger gripped him. "*You!*" Kaiba roared, instantly recognizing the man from his dream as Ian Orokov. He looked like the man you'd meet on the black market. He had scars along his face, a brown beard starting to turn grey, and a crooked nose that seemed to have been broken several times. He bent down and picked up the crimson sphere without giving Kaiba or anyone else the slightest bit of attention.

Kaiba stood up as the psychic energy formed around Ian's body. Just before Ian jumped Kaiba grabbed him.

They emerged in a thin mist on top of a frozen pond. The ice was as solid as concrete. Ian shook off Kaiba's grasp and kicked him into the snow.

Kaiba fell and Ian took off for a towering mansion in the distance.

Kaiba's whole body shook in anger. "*Coward!*" A bolt of lightning exploded from his hand.

Orokov turned and teleported out of the way just before the electricity could hit him. "I want nothing to do with you, boy!" he said in a heavy Russian accent.

Kaiba charged. His boots felt the solid ice and he sensed it. He turned the ice at Ian's feet to water.

Ian fell through, but reappeared on top of the pond the very next moment. The only indication he'd fallen was that his clothes were soaking wet.

The instant he reappeared, Kaiba flung a ball of fire from his right hand and a strand of lightning from his left.

Ian jumped out of the way and Kaiba threw his energies again. This time Ian didn't phase away. Kaiba smiled as the fire and lightning hit, but his smile faded when he realized the elements had merely collided with a thin barrier of purple light. The psychic shield faded as soon as it had appeared and Orokov was left completely unscathed.

Enraged, Kaiba continued to blast his fury, but each time he hurled the elements Ian was able to successfully evade or block them using shields of energy. Kaiba grew more furious with each miss until finally he was left panting in the middle of the pond.

"Done now, boy?" Ian asked plainly. He didn't seem the least bit tired.

Thick clouds of mist hung around Kaiba's face. He didn't have the breath to respond.

"I thought so," Orokov said, and he started to walk from the edge of the pond.

Kaiba stared at Orokov's back and he thought of Bennett in the sand. Kaiba's hand started to glow a light purple. He focused on the small shrub just at Orokov's side and then he teleported forward. He landed right next to him and from both hands flew a jet of molten red and orange. The flames engulfed Ian's form for an instant, but then the man disappeared.

Ian materialized three feet away. Parts of his black cloak were smoldering. He patted out the fire and threw the garment down in the snow where it sizzled brightly.

Kaiba smiled as Ian started to sprint forward. Kaiba laced his palms with lightning and leapt to meet the attack. He swung with his fists as soon as Ian was close enough. His punch seemed to connect, but oddly, Ian flickered away, as though Kaiba had merely attacked the air. He was tipped forward, caught off balance.

A second later Orokov reappeared and smashed his elbow into Kaiba's metal chest.

The force of the blow was so strong Kaiba keeled over. Before he could react, Orokov materialized again and landed a blow to Kaiba's back. His eyes watered and his back stiffened. Ian emerged for a third time, smacking Kaiba across the cheek. The punch twisted him around with such force that he crashed into the snow. Kaiba lifted his aching body from the ice and glared in a fury he'd never felt in all his life.

"You may beat me," Kaiba breathed. "But you'll have to make me bleed to do it."

"So be it," Ian said.

Kaiba yelled and jumped. The two of them teleported around the snowy landscape. Kaiba would attack and Ian would fade away. When Ian reappeared he would land a quick strike and then Kaiba would teleport to safety. It was a dance of ghosts in the shadows, and Kaiba fought furiously. But with each missed punch and disconnected blast he knew he would be unable to best Orokov. They jumped in and out of reality until finally Orokov landed a hit Kaiba couldn't get up from. The punch hit him in the back of the neck and it brought Kaiba to his knees. His body was wracked with impacts and Ian looked at him pathetically.

"My quarrel was not with you, boy."

Kaiba wanted to get back up, to fight, and more importantly to win, but he'd little strength left. If he was to win he had to pretend as though he'd already lost.

"You killed him," Kaiba panted. "That made your quarrel with me."

"He was a target, and a necessary one to ensure I could get my old life back. I meant no intentional harm."

"*You murdered him!*" Kaiba screamed.

"Killing him was the only way for me to get the sphere," Ian said. He held the red ball out tauntingly. "If a sniper shot could best your friend then he was too weak to deserve it."

Kaiba continued to breathe heavily. He waited for a moment, then seized his chance. He jumped up, palms sparking, but Ian was too quick and punched him again. He fell.

Ian walked slowly in a circle around Kaiba as if he were hunting him. "You can teleport like I can but you know nothing else of the psychic element. You cannot handle your abilities and I'm beginning to wonder whether or not you deserve your sphere."

Kaiba heard the snow crunching behind Ian.

"And what makes you think you deserve that sphere any more than the boy does?" asked a voice that sounded as if several people were speaking at the same exact moment.

A seven-foot figure in all-black armor walked forward. Kaiba's heart jumped as he looked into the face of Eskylious.

Ian turned to the virtaiyu with determination.

"I deserve to see my son again, Virt."

The creature's lip peeled back to reveal its needle-like teeth. "How do you figure that? Your Fifth Era boss is dead now, by my own hand. I guess that means you work for me."

"He was my only link to my son!" Ian spat.

Eskylious stuck a massive, six-fingered hand out. "Then I guess you'd better hand over the sphere lest you wish to share his fate."

Ian teleported behind the virtaiyu, but was shocked as Eskylious teleported back in front of him. "You think you're the only one able to use the psychic element, hominid?"

Kaiba didn't think a man like Orokov was capable of being intimidated, but in that instant the Russian looked like a helpless child. Terrified, Ian drew a knife and teleported again in an attempt to stab the virtaiyu. As Ian faded into nothing, a light purple aura formed around the alien. From the aura came a flash of light, and Ian was unable to successfully fade out. Instead he was frozen in place.

"You see," the virtaiyu said as the purple faded and Ian fell to the ground. "You humans think yourselves above all things." It walked closer to Ian at a slow pace. "You believe that because you can, you should, and your species manifests that ideal into the tools you use. For instance, that knife."

Ian took a jab with his weapon. Eskylious grabbed Ian's hand and plucked the knife from his fingers, though it didn't let go of Orokov. "You forge and you build, but nothing you do ever comes from your natural selves. Even now as you face me you are using not only one, but two tools to fight; the knife and that sphere, which is not rightfully yours." It forced Orokov to the ground and Kaiba could only stare in bewilderment.

"But where you humans are defined by what you create, we virtaiyu are defined by what we manipulate."

"You'll burn, alien!" Ian said as he was forced into the snow.

Eskylious leaned over. "Your kind rips this planet apart with your wars and your obsessive need to engorge yourselves. You are killing your own home, your own Earth, and by extension yourselves. I will merely speed your process of extinction and return this planet to its former glory. Insects do not deserve their own world." Eskylious stepped forward and pounded a heavy black boot onto Ian's legs. The bones snapped and Orokov howled in agonizing pain. The virtaiyu thrust the knife into Orokov's broken right leg and twisted it back and forth. "I shall take back the spheres that were stolen from me!"

Kaiba couldn't have imagined how painful it was. He shivered, staring at Ian's agonized face. Part of him wanted to leave Ian. He wanted to watch him suffer for what he'd done to Bennett, but that wasn't logical. Ian was the only person who knew how to form the psychic energies into shields. Kaiba didn't have the skill Ian did. He would need a teacher and now the enemy of his enemy had to become his friend. Kaiba looked at the snow and ice just at Eskylious's feet. He thrust his hands to the sky and a column of blue shot up from the ground. Water engulfed the creature, encasing its body in ice.

Kaiba ran and jumped on Ian. "Teleport us back!"

He heard the virtaiyu breaking through the ice. "Ah, the boy Elemental is alive!" Eskylious exclaimed. "You think running will save you? You delay the inevitable!"

Ian's eyes flickered and he fought the urge to pass out. He wrapped his hands around Kaiba's shirt and the next moment they were back on the sands of New Mexico. Kaiba rolled down the sand dune, kicking up clouds of dirt.

"Kaiba!" Abdu yelled as he ran from the convoy of Humvees.

Kaiba's world spun, and he felt like vomiting. When he finally stopped rolling, he stood up. Ian lay limp, passed out from his injury. Kaiba started to drag him across the sands.

"You saved him?" Abdu asked both with surprise and outrage.

"We need to leave now! Get the trucks out of here!" Kaiba ordered without explanation.

"Where did you go?"

Kaiba released Ian, who plopped to the ground with a dull thud. He grabbed the fire sphere from his pocket and held it out as explanation.

Abdu's eyes widened.

"If you wanna live you'll get those vehicles and get us the hell out of here. We need to protect this."

Nassira rolled up in the turret bed of a Humvee. Her long hair billowed out behind her. "You all right?"

Kaiba didn't answer. Instead he continued to glare at Abdu. "Help me get him into a truck."

Abdu obliged and they carried Ian to the back of the nearest Humvee.

Kaiba trembled, despite his best efforts to keep calm.

Abdu grabbed Kaiba's shoulder.

"Don't touch me," Kaiba growled.

"I know you're angry about Bennett, but that won't bring him back."

Kaiba held his gaze when another flash of lilac drew their attention. At the top of the tallest sand dune stood Eskylious. He had something in his hand and he set it in the sand. A massive column of purple light exploded into the sky.

Kaiba couldn't imagine what was going to happen. "I'm not angry Abdu, I'm afraid."

38

SENDING THE CAVALRY

Sand Point Air Force Base, California

"**R**epeat that, soldier," Unden said furiously.

Emily didn't know who was on the other line, but she could hear the voice.

"I need SOIT Teams on station to Karlen City, as many as you can spare!"

Unden grew red in the face. "SOIT Teams?"

The man's voice on the other line was yelling now. "*I have three spheres with Eskylious in pursuit!*"

Emily thought Unden was about to drop the phone. He pointed to Barnes. "Get me Staff Sergeant Liam now!"

The guard looked alarmed. He sprinted off.

"You're sure?" Unden said in disbelief.

"*Get those teams down here now!*" the man's voice screamed and then the line went dead.

A man in a grey Air Force jumpsuit burst into the room.

Emily assumed he was Liam.

"Yes, Commander?" Liam said breathlessly.

Unden was moving like a storm, gathering up everything in his path. "How many Sub Orbital Insertion Teams do we have airborne?"

"None at the moment sir."

"Are there any in the area?" Unden said. He pointed to Jordan and Emily. "You two with me, now!"

Jordan and Emily exchanged glances and struggled to keep up as they were practically sprinting.

"We have two SOIT teams. Only one bird cleared for combat though."

"I saw two in the hanger bay," Unden said.

"The other finished repairs last night. As I said, it isn't cleared for—"

"I clear it!" Unden yelled. "You and your teams are deploying, tell those drop pods to be ready immediately and alert all other SOIT teams in the area. We need reinforcements to Karlen City."

Liam's mouth was open. "New Mexico? Do you know how much that'll cost us for such a short flight?"

Unden grabbed Liam by the collar. *"Get those soldiers ready now!"* He shoved Liam back.

Liam stumbled, saluted, and sprinted off in the other direction.

"What's going on?" Jordan asked.

"Three spheres surfaced; if we don't act fast the virtaiyu will claim them," Unden said as he turned down a hallway. He whipped out his phone. "Alert Sec Def, we need all available forces deployed to Karlen City, Priority Alpha."

He hung up and Jordan asked, "Do they have Kaiba?"

Unden stopped dead in his tracks. "Why would they have Kaiba?"

Emily noticed that Unden sounded like he knew Kaiba.

"That was my friend who was taken, he must have made it!" Jordan exclaimed.

"My god." His eyes were moving rapidly. He looked at the two soldiers beside him. "Watch them."

"What are you talking about?" Jordan yelled.

Unden was dialing his phone again. "This is no time to throw either of you into the middle of a battle. I won't lose every key we have to the Virts!"

"We can help!" Jordan cried.

"You will stay, that's an order!" He sprinted off in the other direction.

Jordan looked down at the ground. It was concrete. Then he looked up at the soldiers. "Forgive me." He swept his arms forward and two spikes of rock shot up. The stone slammed the men against a wall and they were knocked unconscious.

"What are you *doing*?" Emily screeched.

"Are you with me?"

"What's that supposed to mean?"

"I'm boarding one of the SOIT pods and going to Karlen."

"You heard Unden! We aren't allowed to leave."

"I won't let Kaiba die if I can help him."

Emily positioned herself in the middle of the hallway. "If you try to leave, I'll stop you."

Jordan stood like a boxer, with his hands raised up and balled into fists. "You're out of your element. Just tell them I hit you."

"If you get caught or killed out there, the virtaiyu will have four spheres instead of three!"

"If I don't go I'll spend the rest of my life asking what would have happened if I had been there," Jordan said. "What would you do if you knew your father was in danger?"

"I would fight for him," Emily admitted.

"Then are you with me?"

Emily stood to the side. "I won't fight you."

Jordan leapt forward. "Atta girl. Come on."

"Do you even know where the SOIT teams deploy?" Emily asked, sprinting behind him. As she ran she realized she would be fighting to save the man who attacked her father. Ironic.

Jordan pivoted past a training chamber then rushed up the set of stairs that led to the main entrance. "Didn't you see the hypersonic planes in the hanger when we came in?"

"Hyper what?"

"Just come on! We have to hope they haven't deployed already."

They reached the hanger and spotted Liam near two jet-black planes. She was reminded of the old Spirit bomber model on her father's desk. These planes looked similar, with a W-shaped back that led to a sharp pointed front. These planes were wider and had a round container on their underbelly. Emily remembered the welders she'd seen working on the plane when she'd first arrived. The container appeared to have doors that were down to reveal several seats on the inside. Soldiers were gathering weapons and putting on gear. Several were already being strapped into the pod.

Jordan ran to Liam. "Get us some gear."

"Civilians aren't allowed to travel via pod. Neither of you have the proper training," Liam said as he slung an automatic weapon on his back.

Jordan stamped the ground and a shard of rock rose up. "Unden ordered that you take us. As carriers of the Terraform Keys we are tasked with recovering the others."

Liam looked at Emily, who remained neutral in expression. She hoped her face didn't reveal that she knew Jordan was lying.

"All right then, come on." He pointed to two soldiers that were nearly finished suiting up. "Aims, Indie, you're sitting this one out. Help me gear these two up."

The men nodded and quickly stripped out of their jumpsuits. Neither wore anything underneath and handed them respectively to Emily and then Jordan. Emily looked away, embarrassed.

"These are G-suits," Liam explained. "They've been infused with w-p extract, which is quite possibly the hardest substance we know of. At the same time, they'll help cope with the G-forces you're guaranteed to experience. G-forces can cause you to pass out."

Emily stood holding the suit in her hands. She took off her shoes and started to try to get into it.

"You won't want to wear clothes underneath."

Emily looked down, embarrassed again, but hurriedly slipped on the tight grey G-suit. She was reminded of squeezing herself into a wetsuit. When it was snug she zipped it up and Liam walked up to check her.

"If you grey out, which is when your vision loses its color, or if you experience tunnel vision, don't panic. Your suit will help force blood back into the brain and prevent it from going to your feet. If your vision doesn't return or worsens clench your jaw and shake your head slightly back and forth. It'll help."

Liam grabbed two rifles from the wall and handed them to Emily and Jordan. By that time all the other soldiers had boarded the pods. They sat strapped in their chairs with oxygen masks over their faces.

"Before your pod lands," Liam said as he walked over to the drop pod with two empty seats. "You'll hear a loud popping noise. Those are the reverse thrusters beneath the pod. They'll slow your descent before you crash into the ground."

Emily buckled the straps over her body. "You mean we're going to be fired out of this thing?"

"What did you think Sub Orbital Insertion was?" Liam asked. "Of course the pod is fired out of the plane."

Emily's head burned. Her hands felt clammy.

"Don't worry," Liam said. "It's just like a really really long roller coaster drop."

"I hate roller coasters!" Emily cried.

"Then honey, you are on the wrong ride." He grabbed the oxygen mask and helped slide it over Emily's head.

Liam helped Jordan into his seat next. When they were strapped in he stepped back. "Now, when the pod lands these ramps will go down as they are now."

Emily looked where he pointed. At the base of the pod were boxy-looking metal rectangles. They were arranged like petals around the center of a flower.

"Your masks and restraints are programmed to pop off on impact. Grab your weapons and get out of the pod as fast as you can. Form up on one another, it'll be a war zone and we won't know what we're facing until we get there. If anything goes wrong use whatever the hell abilities you two possess. I'm trusting that Unden knows what he's doing with the two of you. Whatever happens stick together and follow my lead. Got it?"

Even if Emily had wanted to say something she couldn't talk through her mask. She breathed quickly and could no longer feel her toes.

"Good, and oh, I almost forgot." He took out two sets of small silver objects that looked like earplugs. "These will make sure your ear drums don't rupture when you go supersonic. They also act as communication relays. Your suit has a built-in mic positioned by your vocal chords. If you whisper the microphone will pick up the vibrations and we'll be able to hear you crystal clear. They won't work in flight though."

Jordan and Emily fixed them into their ears. They were surprisingly comfortable.

Liam yelled to the pilots as he ran to the other pod, "Let's rip a hole in the sky!"

As he shouted the ramps went up and Emily was submerged into an eerie red glow. In the tightness of the pod she couldn't look left or right. With the earplugs she could hear only her own breathing and the rapid beating of her heart.

She felt the plane as it rolled for what she assumed was the runway. Her seat started to rumble as the plane picked up speed. Then her stomach rose into her chest, but the feeling didn't disappear, it only got worse. She resisted the urge to become sick as her cheeks started to vibrate. Her head was forced all the way back into the cushioned headrest.

She stared at the space in front of her as the red light started to dim and become grey. Emily remembered what Liam had said. She clenched her jaw, but her vision only got worse. The edges of the pod ramp started to go black and she saw as if through a microscope.

She breathed harder, almost panicking. Stars started to fill her vision as the plane accelerated even faster. Her entire body vibrated with such intensity she thought she would explode. But then gradually she stopped jostling as the plane started to slow down again. Emily's view started to return to normal, but she was still terrified. As soon as she could see normally a blue number 10 flashed in front of her eyes.

Then 9, 8. Emily steadied herself as she knew what was coming.

7. She gripped the armrests of her seat, digging her nails in as the numbers ticked down to 4.

3. 2. 1.

A crack split the air and the pod fired. The air was whistling so hard she could no longer hear her own breathing. She screamed as she felt her stomach rise once again. They must have been high in the atmosphere because the freefall lasted so long Emily's voice started to go hoarse.

Then finally she heard the popping of the pod thrusters. She rocked side to side when they crashed. Her seatbelts flew off along with her oxygen mask. She braced herself as the exit ramps slammed into the sand.

Emily stood up, reached for her weapon, and stumbled into bright sunlight.

39

Flight to Karlen City

White Sands, New Mexico, United States

The convoy sped down the faint dirt road as the violet light funneled into the skies. They screeched onto the highway and Kaiba watched as dark shadows began to emerge from the device like spiders from a den.

Abdu yelled into his microphone. "Hailing Karlen City on all frequencies, *do you read*?"

Kaiba heard static in his own earpiece until someone finally responded: "Sandstorm this is Queen Karlen. I read you loud and clear. Picking up energy surges near your location. Can you confirm?"

"Virtaiyu deployed some kind of massive Interligate," Abdu said. "We are in possession of precious cargo. Need assist as we approach the city. Requesting air support."

"Queen Karlen confirms. Predator drones inbound on your location. Linking you to Echo pilots one through five now."

Static filled their ears and Kaiba peered down the scope of the truck turret. He could make out several Manta outlines in the distance. Then he heard the thunder of the predator drones overhead. There were five groups of five bird-like planes, all arranged in the formation of an arrowhead.

"Sandstorm this is Echo One. Above your position and standing by. Bogies in the weeds and closing."

"How many, Echo?"

Static met his question and then booms in the sky drew all of their attentions.

"They're all over us! Bravo through Delta squads, scatter on the eastern skies. Take evasive positions. Tango and Zulu teams head west and attempt flanking maneuvers. All others form up on me! Convoy, you got Mantas closing in on your position fast. We'll draw what we can, but I can't guarantee protection!"

Kaiba saw the ships whistling through the skies. The drones started to scatter and got locked in dog fights. He watched the aerial battles as three objects fell from the sky. They struck the road just behind the convoy, creating a plume of dust. His heart skipped a beat when each object broke into the shape of a V. Just like the smaller Interligates, they glowed purple and from the void came vehicles twice the size of a normal Manta. They hovered several feet off the ground. Narrow rods extended from the sides and they shot lances of sonic energy.

"Nassira! Get on the gun!" Kaiba called into his headset as he squeezed the trigger of the turret. The bullets collided into the first Manta, but they couldn't penetrate its armor.

Her vehicle was just in front of his. She emerged from the hole and turned on the PIC. Fear gripped her as she saw the pursuing vehicles. She aimed the laser sight at the same Virtaiyan Manta. A bolt of lightning cascaded down the ion channel and into the craft. It sparked and crashed in a fiery explosion.

"Nice shot, Nass!" Kaiba called, but his excitement was short lived as three more Mantas appeared.

The convoy staggered itself so that the turrets could get better shots. The guns sprayed a hail of bullets into the pursuing alien vehicles, but it wasn't enough. The five Mantas homed in on one Humvee and all fired at the same time. The truck was ripped in two by the massive amount of energy.

Kaiba ducked back into the truck and Abdu looked at him, worried. "We won't last two minutes out here if we don't split up!"

"Agreed." Abdu swerved and the truck rumbled as a sonic shot rocketed by.

Kaiba tossed the sphere into the front seat. "You keep that safe." He came up guns blazing. He aimed his own PIC at the nearest Manta. It barrel rolled, avoiding his attack, but his next shot was better placed. Lightning engulfed the wing, which dipped and ripped off against the highway. "Two down, five to go!"

Abdu yelled, "Humvees four through six take to the water. Draw what you can to the river and reconvene at Karlen!"

Kaiba noticed the river that ran along the freeway. Nassira's vehicle and two others swerved off the road and headed into the water. Kaiba thought they would crash, but their tires flipped up and they sped off like speedboats. Two Mantas broke off for the river.

Kaiba tapped the EMP generator as the still-pursuing Mantas closed in on him. Sonic projectiles flew by his head, but he stayed calm. He fired the PIC and the blue light collided with the planes. They slowed down as their machinery failed, and hit the hot pavement, exploding on impact.

Kaiba looked out at the river as the Humvee boats swerved in and out. Nassira's lighting exploded into the skies, but the virtaiyu ships spun and dodged. He tried to aim his cannon to help, but they were too far off. The river began to bend away from the highway until Kaiba could no longer see the other trucks. A predator drone swooped just overhead and the Manta behind it descended. It attacked the other truck and Kaiba could do nothing as the Humvee flipped over. Worse, two massive Exo suits appeared about a mile behind and moving just as fast, if not faster than, the Mantas.

"Abdu!" Kaiba yelled.

"I see them. We'll just have to outrun them!" Abdu sped up and headed for the bridge in the distance. The Manta kept on firing and Abdu swerved back and forth. Kaiba aimed as best he could, but with the sharp movements he couldn't get a hit. He knew they were doomed unless he did something desperate. Just when Abdu had reached the edge of the bridge, Kaiba leapt from the top of the turret mount. He fell in slow motion, watching as the truck peeled away. The highway blurred in front of his eyes, but he felt the rock. As he was about to land, he curled the concrete up and around his body. The stone provided a cocoon and he rolled safely on the ground.

Abdu's voice shrilled in his ear, "What are you doing?"

Kaiba broke free from the earth. "Covering you! Get that sphere to the city!"

The pursuing Manta slowed, and dropped a squad of twelve virtaiyu from its underside. Kaiba didn't waste any time. He aimed the ion cannon and hurled lightning bolts into their ranks. They were exposed as they dropped down. They stumbled and several pops exploded in their armor, but they kept coming. Kaiba strode forward to meet them, until he heard a grumbling behind him. He thought Abdu had turned around.

"Jordan?!"

Jordan leapt from a surfboard of stone. He collided with a virtaiyu as spikes of rock shot up around him. The jagged stone impaled three Virts at his side. Jordan tackled another Virt and rolled with it. He skewered the creature like a fish as Kaiba aimed his cannon. The bolt collided with a shorter virtaiyu and threw it over the edge of the bridge. Jordan encased another enemy in stone.

Kaiba swung his cannon arm into the face of an ugly Virt, then ignited his free hand. He charged the final virtaiyu and his burning fist melted straight through the alien armor.

The Manta began to retreat, but Jordan threw up a wall of rock. The ship collided with the barrier in a sizzling plume of crumpled metal.

"You picked up a few new skills," Kaiba said. He kept his gaze on the charging Exo suits. They were each twenty-five feet tall, with wide legs and skinny arms. Their torsos were just thick enough for the virtaiyu pilot to sit in. They had weapons attached to their rounded shoulders, machine hands, and long forearms. The walking tanks were made of metal colored a dark blue-grey to imitate a virtaiyu's skin.

Kaiba slammed the EMP converter strip and fired. A pulse of blue light exploded from the cannon barrel and soared for the Exos. The lead Exo suit was engulfed in the blue light. It stopped mid-stride and fell to its knees.

"Same could be said for you," Jordan exclaimed. "I like the new toy."

The other Exo leapt over its fallen comrade.

Kaiba and Jordan ran to the center of the bridge. "'Member what you taught me in the back yard?" Kaiba asked.

The machine's footsteps shook the ground. Fire flew from the palms of its hands and the weapons on its shoulders aimed at the two of them.

"Try not to hurt your hand this time," Jordan said.

It was six strides away from the edge of the bridge.

Out of the corner of his eye Kaiba saw the other three Humvees jetting across the water. "Nassira, you gotta clear this bridge!"

"What is it?" she screamed into the headset.

"Get past it!" Kaiba yelled. The towering Exo suit cast a shadow over his face. He held as the Humvees reached the water beneath the bridge. *"Now, Jordan!"*

They slammed their palms into the concrete, sending a spider web of cracks through the bridge. The damage fanned out in front of them. Just before the Exo suit could reach them, its massive foot sank. Part of the causeway tumbled away, dragging the monolithic Exo down. It clawed at the breaking concrete, but lost its grip and plummeted to the river. The debris fell with it, narrowly missed the Humvees, and instead fell perfectly on top of one Manta. Kaiba covered his eyes against the bright explosion.

Nassira and the three other Humvees emerged on the other side of the bridge. The last two Mantas were still in pursuit.

Kaiba's own worries were far from over. A swarm of Mantas and Fifth Era trucks were headed their way.

Abdu wheeled the Humvee around.

Kaiba looked at him in disbelief. "I told you to go!"

"Come on!"

Kaiba made the world shift as the buzzing lines of psychic energy appeared. He focused on the back of the truck and teleported into the turret bed. He let electricity spark in his hand and noticed that Jordan hadn't moved. "What are you doing?"

"You cover me," Jordan slammed his foot into the ground and a platform of rock jutted upward. He stepped on and covered his feet with rock, locking him in place. "Let's go!"

Abdu punched it and Jordan burst forward in a cloud of dust. Though the Humvee was speeding at seventy miles per hour, Jordan was able to keep up with his earth surfing. Kaiba was fascinated, but he focused on the enemies behind him. They were still too far out of range and the Predator drones attempted to slow them down with missiles. Some were successful and others were shot down.

Kaiba's ear buzzed with Abdu's voice. "Karlen ahead!" He spared a glance and the wind ripped into his eyes. A massive dome twice the size of a sports arena dominated the skyline. Its surface was made of reflective panels, and turrets popped up on the top of it. Skyscrapers flanked it on either side. In front of the buildings were railguns that lined the horizon like hedges in front of a yard. The highway led them straight to the dome. As they got closer, Kaiba saw two drop pods. The soldiers were setting up defensive equipment. They slowed down and Kaiba looked to the river that fed into the left side of the city. He could barely make out the other Humvees again and this time there were four objects speeding in the water. One of them was a girl.

Emily cut through the river, forcing the waves to carry her. She followed the Humvee with the Brazilian girl in it. The two remaining Mantas fired again. A banshee shriek came with the barrage of sound, but she skated out of the way. The trucks reacted, and the sonic projectile collided with the river. A splash of water funneled into the sky.

She peered over her shoulder at the alien ship and focused on the water beneath it. She threw up a wall of blue. The liquid swallowed the Manta and she froze it. The vehicle split apart from the force of the ice. Machine parts rained down in a wide arc.

Emily sped forward, watching the girl with the cannon as she showered the remaining Manta with lightning. It took several moments, but finally it too crashed.

The Humvees slowed and Emily surfed for the nearest one.

Nassira stuck out her hand. "Thanks for the help."

Emily grabbed it and heaved herself into the turret bed. "Don't mention it. That lightning of yours came in handy, it's a good element to have."

Nassira smiled and the trucks sped to shore. They switched from sea to terrain mode and the tires flipped back down.

The convoy drove over the hill and the city of Karlen came into view. They stopped near the drop pods and Emily spotted Jordan. He was talking to the person who'd attacked her father: Kaiba. She knew the danger of the approaching virtaiyu, but she couldn't help but feel anger when she saw his face.

40

THE ELEMENTALS

Karlen City, New Mexico

Jordan introduced the girl as Emily. She was short, with strawberry blonde hair that ran down past her shoulders and blue eyes like the sky. She had a firm handshake and seemed very confident by the way she walked. Kaiba couldn't have cared less about who she was, as long as she could help. They made their way into the first intersection just in front of the domed building. Soldiers evacuated civilians and set up cover using cars and other bulky objects. Abdu had parked the Humvee off to one side. It was positioned perfectly so that the turret had a clear shot to the highway.

"How are we gonna get the sphere out of here?" Kaiba asked as he approached Abdu.

He was looking over a roll-screen that displayed the city in perfect detail. "I've called air support for retrieval, but I doubt they'll get through all these Virts," Abdu said, pointing to the map. Red Xs marked approaching virtaiyu. "What do you want to do with the prisoner?"

"Who's the prisoner?" Jordan asked.

Kaiba glanced at the truck. "Long story." He could hear the screeching virtaiyu Mantas closing in on the city but the railcannons started to cut them to shreds. Kaiba flinched at the earthquake-like jolts as they went off, but he kept calm. "Is there no detainment facility in the dome?"

Another turret fired, causing a Manta to explode in the sky. As if mentioning the dome was a curse, the plane crashed into the glittering building. Kaiba took cover and threw himself against a car as glass rained down from above. The shards burst like bombs. When the shower of debris ended Kaiba brushed himself off and helped Emily and Jordan to their feet. Nassira stumbled out from behind a pile of rubble.

"I'll see what I can do about Ian," Abdu said. He forced himself to his feet and plucked a piece of glass from his cheek. "For now, help direct citizens deeper into the city. We don't need them on the front lines." Abdu ran for the building entrance, shouting orders to his troops, who were setting up ordnance.

"Come on then," Jordan said.

They raced to the everyday people and helped in any way they could. Mostly that was providing comfort, and directing them down specified streets.

Kaiba helped one mother out from an alley when the railcannons went off again. The ground rumbled as they fired in sync. The star-like bullets destroyed half of the incoming ships. Kaiba actually thought they might win the battle, until another Manta, bigger and faster than the others, closed in. It launched sonic cannon fire at civilians and soldiers alike, and weaved past the defensive batteries with ease.

"On it!" Nassira called. She homed in instinctively and shot at it with lightning. The electricity crackled along the ionized light, but to no avail. The Manta kept its approach, flew in low, and from its underbelly fell a V-shaped Interligate.

"Target that transporter!" Kaiba ordered.

Soldiers drew their rifles and machine guns as civilians screamed, scattering into whatever crevices they could find. Emily stood by a fire hydrant on the street corner. She directed the water from below, and it burst to the surface. Jordan created two rock walls from the ground and Nassira readied her electricity.

The Interligate collided with the middle of the intersection in a spray of concrete and dust. Kaiba focused in on the device with his ion cannon, but stopped when a woman emerged from the purple light.

"Lia?" Nassira cried.

The girl's mouth was duct-taped and a virtaiyu warrior held her at gunpoint.

"You have each fought for an inevitable loss," Eskylious said, stepping from the device next. He inhaled through his nostrils as if enjoying the smells of battle. Behind him came twenty or so other warriors that fanned out around the intersection. "Now this comes to an end."

"Dad?" Emily gasped. Mr. Sursten limped from the Interligate next. He slumped against the virtaiyu that carried him. He somehow looked worse than when Kaiba had seen him on the stretcher in Coronado.

"I never did understand the human necessity for family," Eskylious said, shaking his head. "Makes you weak. Makes you vulnerable."

Jordan choked, unable to bear the sight of his mother being held hostage. His fingers curled into fists. Anger radiated from every inch of his being. The scowl on his face was the most terrifying. He was an awakened beast.

"Are you not all the same species and thus all a part of one family?" Eskylious looked right at Kaiba. "Why should you love one more than any other?"

Kaiba knew who the next person would be, but he couldn't speak or move. This wasn't real. This was a nightmare. Everything from the moment he grabbed that sphere was impossible, and then his mother emerged from the Interligate.

"Let them go!" Kaiba yelled, aiming his ion cannon.

"You so much as flinch and I'll kill them," Eskylious threatened.

Kaiba watched the helmeted virtaiyu push his mother forward. Another person appeared. Kaiba lowered his cannon as the horror stripped him of any confidence and stung at his mind like a poison.

"*NO!*" Kaiba yelled. He dropped to his knees as Cade stumbled out of the Interligate. His younger brother shivered and tears ran down his face. Taniel held him firmly by the shoulders. "Please! Don't hurt them," Kaiba pleaded.

"You drop your weapons," Eskylious ordered.

Kaiba stripped the PIC from his arm as fast as he could. It clanked on the ground. Nassira did the same, as Jordan and Emily raised their hands in the air, letting their elements fall.

Soldiers ignored the order. They crept closer with their weapons drawn.

"You heard him!" Emily shouted at the soldiers. She sounded hysterical.

The men continued to inch forward. Their rifles were pinned on the creatures. One captain yelled, "Let them go, alien!"

Eskylious smiled at the man. "Not a good listener. Let's just kill one of them. How's that sound?" The other virtaiyu grunted in what appeared to be laughter. They lined up the family members and aimed their sonic weapons.

Kaiba stepped forward and thrust a column of concrete into the captain. The man fell back and hit the ground. "Drop your weapons now!" Kaiba shouted. He let fire dance in his palms and aimed at the men. They stared back, bewildered.

Jordan took a step toward the soldiers. "They'll kill them otherwise!"

"Do as he says!" Nassira chimed.

Eskylious laughed with the cackle of a monster. "You can't even get along with your own kind! How amusing."

"Please," Nassira begged. "Let them go."

"You have what I want and I have what you want," Eskylious said.

Emily stepped forward. "The spheres are yours. Just let our families go."

"The spheres were always mine," Eskylious spat. He paced back and forth, savoring every minute. "You stole them from me and now I am kind enough to offer a trade."

Kaiba couldn't take his eyes off of Cade. "We will give you whatever you need."

"What I need?" Eskylious stared at the street, which started to crack as his fists curled. He looked up and his eyes glinted green. "This is not about what I need. Your bodies have defiled something so sacred I have not the words to describe it. I should torture each of you for an eternity for bonding with the Terraform Keys. Instead, you will stand as my soldiers shoot you in the heads, your lives in exchange for those of your kin."

Mrs. Hightower, Mr. Sursten, Lia, and Kaiba's mother struggled and yelled in protest through their bound mouths.

Kaiba had evaded death his whole life. He knew the possibility of dying in war, but he never considered having to choose his time to die. Now that it was upon him he could do nothing other than accept it. He rose to his feet. "Take us then, just don't harm them."

"Smart boy." Eskylious smiled wickedly and shouted something else in virtaiyu. The soldiers let go of the hostages and each strode forward. Kaiba looked at Cade, who cried even harder. He spoke with as much confidence as he could muster. "You're gonna be all right, buddy."

Taniel grabbed Kaiba.

Eskylious yelled again in his native tongue.

The virtaiyu lowered their sonic rifles and Taniel did the same. The barrel felt cold as ice against Kaiba's head. He wouldn't close his eyes; he would go into death with his eyes wide open. He watched his younger brother, then shifted his gaze to his mother and mouthed the words "I love you."

"I told you to pick the winning side," Taniel said.

Kaiba looked Taniel in the eye and said, "You'll get yours."

Taniel's sonic rifle started to hum. "I guess you'll never find out."

Eskylious shouted in what sounded like a countdown. What would death be like? An abyss? Another life? Would he see his brother again? Memories of his childhood flooded in: times spent wrestling with his brother, hunting with his father, swimming with his mother, caring for Cade, and laughing with Jordan. The images flew by like a slideshow. He held his breath as the gun clicked. He tried to fight it, but his entire body trembled.

Kaiba took in one last view of the world, knowing he would never see it again. He watched the dome glitter in the sun, and then he noticed the entrance. Abdu emerged from the structure with soldiers behind him. Both his arms were equipped with PICs and they glowed with iridescent blue light.

Abdu ran forward and yelled, "*Get them!*" The EMPs exploded, engulfing the area.

Taniel and the virtaiyu yanked the triggers, but their weapons no longer worked. Realizing what happened, everyone sprang into motion. Nassira electrocuted the alien in front of her. Emily funneled the hydrant water into a stream that surged with the force of a fire hose. She rolled back as the military soldiers retook their weapons. Kaiba punched Taniel and teleported to Cade's side just as Jordan threw up walls around each of the family members.

Kaiba grabbed Cade and his mother. "Everyone grab me!"

Lia, Mr. Sursten, and Mrs. Hightower gripped a different part of him and in an instant they had reappeared on one of Karlen's many buildings. "Stay here," he said, as he brushed his brother's cheek. "You'll be safe." He wanted to stay and comfort them but the battle wasn't over. Kaiba dived off the building and teleported back to the fight.

The street was chaos. Foot soldiers clashed with virtaiyu infantry. The men had their guns, but they were helpless. It appeared as though every virtaiyu could manipulate an element. Electricity whirled in every direction, fire exploded and street pipes gushed gallons of water. Despite their obvious skill disadvantage, the men still outnumbered the Virts.

Emily dueled with three virtaiyu at once, bending the water around her body and freezing her foes. The moment Kaiba appeared, he threw a column of concrete that crushed the Virts around her. Kaiba ducked under a fire blast and redirected the flames back at his aggressor. Nassira stunned a Virt that attacked Jordan and then they formed up behind Kaiba.

Eskylious fought alone in the center of the intersection. His cape flapped like bat wings. Men foolishly charged him and he cut down every one, scorching them with fire and lightning. When he saw Kaiba, his lip curled and his eyes flared bright crimson.

"TOGETHER!" Kaiba roared.

They charged as one. Jordan hurled the earth, Nassira launched lightning, Emily bent water, and Kaiba blasted a combination of the three. Eskylious threw up purple shields. The elements collided and the group surrounded him, attacking from every angle. Kaiba hurled fire at Eskylious, who dodged and hit him in the knee.

Kaiba cried out as his leg buckled. He threw another blast of heat, but Eskylious disappeared, moving to strike the others.

In a single second Eskylious knocked Nassira to the ground with a hurricane gust of air, punched Jordan across the back, and redirected Emily's water so she collided into a car. Another flash of purple light exploded and Eskylious grabbed Kaiba's arms. His hands glowed lilac and Kaiba's skin burned with more pain than he'd ever felt.

"Scream, human," Eskylious said. His face was madness, devoid of everything good in the world.

Kaiba struggled under the grip as the crunching agony wormed into his arms.

Jordan, Emily, and Nassira moved to attack, but Eskylious knew they were coming. He threw Kaiba to the street and rounded on them. Eskylious inhaled deeply, sucking in as much air as he could. He exhaled, unleashing an atrocious sonic roar. The barrage of the sound waves crashed into Jordan, Emily, and Nassira. Kaiba was helpless to watch as they were thrown backward into the street. They collided into the ground with such force the concrete cracked. The sound seemed to shake the world, filling the air like water. Kaiba drowned in the wail, his ears ringing with torturous sounds.

Eskylious teleported back and grabbed Kaiba by the throat. "Everything you hold dear will die before you."

Kaiba filled his hands with fire and grabbed Eskylious's head.

Eskylious shrieked and grabbed the sides of his face.

Kaiba fell and saw that the skies above were filled with objects. Hundreds of SOIT drop teams rocketed to the ground. They hit, and troops poured from every pod.

Eskylious stared with pure hatred as his forces dwindled around him. He looked at Kaiba, and then at the soldiers. With a flash of bright purple, Eskylious teleported away.

41

PASSING THE TORCH

Karlen City, New Mexico, United States

Kaiba rushed to the middle of the intersection where Jordan and the others lay. Emily and Nassira started to pick themselves up from the pavement. They were shaken, but largely unharmed. Jordan was face down in the rock. Kaiba skidded beside him.

Jordan coughed and sat up. He pulled at his shirt and underneath was the nano-superfluid vest from Coronado. He smiled. "Never took it off."

Kaiba helped him to his feet. "I'm glad for that. You two all right?"

"Perfectly fine," Nassira said.

Emily nodded. "Where's my dad?"

The SOIT team soldiers flooded in.

"Let these guys disperse a bit and I'll grab them." Then Kaiba spotted Taniel crawling to an alley. "Excuse me." He stepped in front of the alley and kicked Taniel in the side.

Taniel laughed crazily. "You'll have to kill me, Cassidy."

"No. You don't deserve death. I'll make sure the world knows you as a traitor."

Taniel laughed again. "You can't detain me. I'll commit suicide first. I won't put my reputation at risk."

Kaiba looked into his eyes, remembering Taniel's threat back in California. He smiled. "Oh, I think you've already done that."

Kaiba put a spark into his hand and grabbed Taniel, who yelped at the electricity. Kaiba handed him to two soldiers and said, "He led the Virts to us."

They dragged Taniel away.

Kaiba grabbed the fire sphere from the truck and secretly pocketed it. Ian was awake, but wouldn't say anything when Kaiba questioned him.

"I'll take care of him," Abdu said.

"Thank you."

"Of course."

"I mean for everything," Kaiba said. "You're the reason I'm still alive."

"You don't need to thank me for doing what anyone would have done." He grabbed Ian and took him away for detainment.

Kaiba walked through the ruins of the street, taking in the horrific damage Eskylious had wreaked. He explained to the SOIT teams what had transpired and eventually they left him alone. When the streets had finally cleared, Kaiba went back to get his family and the others.

Nassira wept at the sight of her sister. She buried her face into Lia's chest, hardly believing she was alive. "You're okay?" Nassira exclaimed rubbing her cheeks.

Lia nodded. "Yes, but Bruno..."

Nassira drew her in close. "Let's not think about it. I thought I'd lost both of you."

Emily held her father's hands.

Mr. Sursten smiled and kissed Emily's forehead. "Are you all right, baby girl?"

Emily laughed and embraced her dad as if she'd never see him again.

Kaiba scooped Cade into his arms. "You all right, buddy?"

Cade nodded. "You beated dem."

Kaiba laughed. "Yes, I think we did." His mother hugged him from behind and they stood rocking in the ruined streets.

Jordan walked up with his mother in hand and asked Kaiba, "You think he'll ever come back?"

"I don't think he'll ever stop until these spheres are his again," Kaiba said.

"We wounded him. That's gotta count for something."

"Shows us he's vulnerable. The Virts might be bigger, but they die just like we do."

"I'm glad about that. You did good out there, Kaiba. Glad we had each other's backs. I'd say our first encounter ended in success."

Kaiba thought of Bennett. "Not for everyone."

✳ ✳ ✳

That night, everyone in the city gathered in the streets. A funeral was held for those killed in action. A pyre of sticks was placed in the street and the men were placed on top. Bennett's body was among the dead. Kaiba stared at the fire as Bennett started to glow in a crimson heat. He held back tears as the lump in his throat grew bigger. The wood crackled and popped and everyone remained, silently paying their individual respects. Abdu shook as though in great pain.

Kaiba stroked the sphere in his pocket. This would be an honor to Bennett, but he waited until the soldiers fired off a single round of ammo. People started to leave.

"Wait," Kaiba said, stepping out of the crowd. He let go of Cade's hand.

All eyes turned to him as he cleared his throat. "Bennett and I became good friends in the short time I knew him. He's part of the reason I stand before you now. He was proud, he was strong, and he was a good man." Kaiba bit his cheek and removed the sphere from his jacket. "As most of you know we lost lives today for this object. I carry one and several others do too, and I have to express how grateful I am for those who defended me. Bennett carried this with him and he did so with honor. It's ironic that he was the first to receive a sphere and also the first to die with one. Abdu?" Kaiba said, walking to the man.

He looked startled. "Yes?"

"Bennett would have wanted someone as brash and brave as he was to carry this. He would have wanted you to have it."

Kaiba put the sphere into Abdu's palm.

"I'm honored," Abdu said.

Kaiba pointed to the fire. Most of Bennett's body had settled to ash. "His power will live in you. Honor him."

Abdu started to stumble and he passed out. Kaiba caught him and laid him gently on the ground.

After the funeral and once his family was asleep, Kaiba walked into the desert that surrounded the city. He sat on the largest sand dune, gazing up at the stars. Nassira walked up from behind.

"Care for some company?" she asked.

He smiled and motioned for her to sit. "Please."

She nestled in beside him and he wrapped his arms around her. They watched the beautiful night sky together and Kaiba couldn't help but feel happy at the beauty still left in the world. He didn't know what tomorrow would bring or how they would stop

Eskylious, if Ian would talk, or what front he might be shipped to, but he had his family, his best friend, and new friends that shared his struggles and his joys. For him, that made all the difference.

 Jared Files is a twenty-one-year-old college student studying the sciences at Washington State University. A longtime fan of science fiction and young-adult fiction, he is fascinated with their ability to give readers a whole new understanding of the world.

After joking about the concept with his friends at the age of fourteen, he was inspired to write a novel about controlling the elements—and the idea of *Elementals: The Seven Spheres* was born.

Files grew up in Sammamish, Washington, with his role-model parents, a loving sister, and friends who he considers his brothers for life.

29145123R00214

Made in the USA
Charleston, SC
03 May 2014